Kitty Kendall is a bucket list achieving, junk jewelry collecting, hopeless romantic who loves great wine and a good adrenaline rush from time to time. She also collect classy shoes and expensive perfume. But her greatest thrill in life is writing romance and the steamier the better.

Bring It On!

She's travelled extensively, some 37 countries and counting and she's addicted to experiences that make her scream… white water rafting, scuba diving with sharks and hang gliding are just a few. Her stories reflect her sense of adventure and her love affair with her very own hero.

Kitty also writes romantic suspense under the pen name of Kendall Talbot. She's won numerous awards including Romantic Book of the Year, Best Romantic Suspense and Best Continuing Series. Several of her books are Amazon bestsellers. Check out www.kendalltalbot.com to find out more.

Read more at www.kittykendall.com

BOOKS IN THIS SERIES

Rise of Memphis Box Sets:

Rise of Memphis Touch Me (January, February, March)
Rise of Memphis Tempt Me (April, May, June)
Rise of Memphis Tease Me (July, August, September)
Rise of Memphis Tame Me (October, November, December)

Rise of Memphis Monthly Chronicles

Rise of Memphis January Chronicles
Rise of Memphis February Chronicles
Rise of Memphis March Chronicles
Rise of Memphis April Chronicles
Rise of Memphis May Chronicles
Rise of Memphis June Chronicles
Rise of Memphis July Chronicles
Rise of Memphis August Chronicles
Rise of Memphis September Chronicles
Rise of Memphis October Chronicles
Rise of Memphis November Chronicles
Rise of Memphis December Chronicles

Rise of Memphis Tame Me

This three book box set contains:

Rise of Memphis October Chronicles
Rise of Memphis November Chronicles
Rise of Memphis December Chronicles

KITTY KENDALL

Copyright
Title: Rise of Memphis Tame Me
Copyright © 2017 by Kitty Kendall

All rights reserves. By payment of the required fees, you have been granted the non-exclusive, non-transferable right to access and read the text of this e-book on-screen. No part of this text may be reproduced, transmitted, down-loaded, decompiled, reverse engineered, or stored in or introduced into any information storage and retrieval system, in any form or by any means, whether electronic or mechanical, now or hereinafter invented, without the express written permission of publisher, Kitty Kendall.

All characters in this book have no existence outside the imagination of the author and have no relation whatsoever to anyone bearing the same name or names. They are not even distantly inspired by any individual known or unknown to the author, and all incidents are pure invention.

www.kittykendall.com
ISBN Print: 9780648027331
ISBN Ebook: 9780648027379
All rights reserved

DEDICATION

This book is dedicated to all the women out there who believe in love.

Kitty Kendall

7TH OCTOBER
MY MAGIC ELIXIR
Room 28 - Hot Horizon Hotel

"I still can't believe you've been holding out on me." The fact that Lolita could even talk, despite running at a frightening pace, was a testament to how fit she was.
I frowned at her. "What?" I spoke between breaths. "No I haven't."
I was pretty certain she was still punishing me for making her eat that cheesecake a couple of weeks ago. Even though it'd only been about five mouthfuls, I'd learned my lesson. Never force-feed Lolita.
"You never told me Corben was that hot."
"Yes I did."
She played with the buttons on her treadmill, and the spinning tread raised to its highest elevation. The crazy woman was running at maximum speed and maximum elevation yet she could still talk as if she were merely taking a stroll on the beach. I loved and hated her right then.
"You said he was hot. That doesn't even begin to describe him. Now that I've met both Billy and Corben, I know you're holding out on me."

"No I'm not."

"Your descriptions fall way short of the mark. I mean, Corben was a total fucking babe. Either you give me all the details"—she waggled her finger at me—"or photos. You choose."

I just shook my head; it was impossible to speak anyway. After a couple more seconds, I decided I'd had enough and jumped off the spinning tread. "I'm done."

"No you're not. Get back on there."

I turned to her and cocked my head. "Nope." That was the first time I'd ever defied Lolita, and she scowled at me.

"No cake for you this morning then."

"Watch me."

She gasped, then burst out laughing. How on earth she could laugh and run at the same time was beyond me. I turned off my treadmill and wiped the sweat off my forehead with a towel. As I sipped my water and waited for Lolita to finish her run, I summarized everything we had to talk about this morning. By the time she jumped off, I decided I'd need a large piece of cake to get through all the topics.

A quick glance in the mirror confirmed my cheeks were as flushed as they felt. Lolita, on the other hand, looked like she could do it all again. We grabbed our things from the lockers and headed to the Blue Haven Café.

Spring was out in all its glory with the sun blazing as a white ball, high over the ocean. The red and yellow lifesaver flags were far apart today, indicating the ocean was behaving itself, and based on the amount of people in the water, I assumed it must be fairly warm, too.

While Lolly sat at our usual table, I went inside to check out the cake selection. My mouth salivated as I glanced from one delectable to the next. In the end it was the chocolate Jaffa cake that spoke to me the loudest.

I returned to the table and sat so I could see both Lolita and the beach.

"How's Needledick been?"

"Weird, as usual. It's like he still doesn't believe what happened but has no choice. I don't care anymore; I'm over him."

"Good. He doesn't deserve your attention anyway."

"True."

Matt arrived, and we placed our orders. The second he left, Lolita tapped her fingernail on the table. "So tell me all about Corben. He's fucking hot."

I giggled. "I know." As we waited for our meals I detailed the unusual date I'd had with Corben. I started with what I wore and moved onto his choice of meal.

"A hotdog stand?"

"I know, weird huh? It was yummy though."

She scrunched up her nose. "Of course you'd enjoy it."

"I had fun. We sat in the middle of the mall, and as we ate our hotdogs we watched the people go by. I didn't mind, and you know what? It suited Corben. I couldn't imagine him doing fine dining."

A frown drilled across her forehead, then she squinted at me. "I think you like Corben. A lot."

Matt arrived with our food, and as he placed our dishes on the table I thought about her comment. There certainly was a lot to like about Mr. Universe. But was he the man for me? I didn't know.

"So do you think he's the one?"

I stabbed my cake with the fork. "He's the one for now."

Lolly burst out laughing. "Ha, you're a riot."

"Thank you." The Jaffa cake was everything I'd hoped for—moist and delicious with hints of fresh orange complementing the rich dark chocolate. Every forkful was a party in my mouth.

"So who else are you really keen on? What about Billy?"

I sighed as I thought about my hunky cowboy. "He's really lovely. They all are. Every one of the men has been amazing in their own way."

"Okay, which ones are at the top of your list?"

"What? Out of all of them?"

"Yeah. Which are your favorites?"

"Okay, well one of the guys at the top of the list is Henry."

She cocked her head. "The old guy?"

"He's not old."

"Whoa, calm down. It's my way of remembering these dudes. Okay, so he's not old. Why do you like him so much?"

"Well . . . he's incredible. His body is amazing. He's smart, funny, suave, and oh my god, does he know how to please me."

"What'd he do this time?"

I cringed at the thought of telling her and instantly regretted it.

"What? Tell me." She reached forward and clutched my arm.

Knowing full well I had no choice but to divulge the details, I closed my eyes and hated myself right at that very moment. "Stuck his finger up my . . ." I cringed, unable to say it.

"Holy shit, babe, you really are stepping out. Did you like it?"

I shrugged. "It was weird."

"But you liked it, didn't you?"

I felt the need to clarify why I liked it. I leaned forward, and with my voice barely a whisper I described in intimate detail exactly what Henry did to me. Lolly barely uttered a sound as I explained how Henry brought my orgasm to a whole new level. When I finished, I leaned back and attacked my cake again.

Lolly fanned herself. "Holy smokes, babe. He sounds fucking amazing."

I grinned at her. "Told you."

She pointed her finger at me. "From now on, that's exactly how you're

3

going to tell me about these romps. No more glossing over the details. I tell you what though—I need to grab Calvin and get me some anal sex going on."

My jaw dropped, and cringing, I scanned the café, hoping like hell nobody had heard her. To my surprise, it seemed she'd gone unnoticed. I turned my gaze to her as she pushed back and stood up. She came to me and wrapped her arms around my shoulders. "You're amazing, babe."

I had no idea why. But adhering to Henry's advice I nodded and said, "Thank you."

She threw her bag over her shoulder. "Calvin better answer his phone or I'll have to get my Venus Probe out."

I had a good idea what the Venus Probe was, and thank god she'd looked away or she would've seen the shock on my face. Lolita jogged off, and as I watched her non-existent ass disappear into the crowd I thought about her choice to own a vibrator.

I'd never used one myself. Maybe, that was because prior to this year, sex hadn't even been close to amazing. Now, though, I understood just how incredible it was. But once I had a man in my life, like Lolita did, I couldn't imagine the need for a vibrator. I chuckled as I hoped that the man who I did fall in love with enjoyed having sex, because he was going to be getting a hell of a lot of it.

As I smiled at that wonderful thought, I put a twenty-dollar note under the salt shaker and stood up to push my chair in.

Back in my room, I showered and crawled into bed. After the workout I'd had, sleep came quickly.

***

The evening shift started slowly and didn't get any better as the night rolled on. Until, that was, just after eleven o'clock, when a handsome stranger strolled through the lobby doors and enchanted me with his beauty. In a flash, my boring shift had become a hell of a lot better.

His skin was creamy white, with a touch of rose to his cheeks. It was obvious that he hadn't been exposed to Australia's harsh sunshine for long. His blond beard was full, covering the lower half of his face, but it was his eyes that drew me in. Fierce, cornflower blue eyes that grabbed me and wouldn't let me go.

He was younger than me I'd say by at least three years, and his strong, confident stride was that of a man who'd figured out the mystery of the universe. He struck me as someone who had an excellent work-life balance. But from the second I glanced into his intense eyes, I was ready to tilt that balance way over to the life side. At least, that was the plan.

"Good evening." I cleared my throat. "Welcome to the Hot Horizon

Hotel."

"Hello, I'm Maxximus Diederik. I've booked for one night." His European accent was strong, sexy.

Dragging my eyes away from his, I stepped to the back counter and after a quick flick through the check-in cards I removed his.

"Here we go, Mr. Diederik. Do you have your identification there?"

As he fished around in a leather satchel over his shoulder, I took the opportunity to explore his body.

He wore a navy T-shirt that showed off the fine tone of his arms, and his hands were exquisite—smooth tanned skin with perfectly trimmed nails. His only jewelry was an interesting silver ring with unusual engravings around the outer edge.

As he handed his passport over, it took all my might not to accidentally-on-purpose touch him. I flipped to his photo and quickly noted his age; this fine young man was indeed younger than me by four years. As I took a photocopy of his passport I decided it was time I explored some younger flesh, and my insides did a dizzying flip at my naughty decision.

I turned back to him, and my breath caught in my throat at his side profile. The discreet down lighting captured the golden tones of his slicked back hair and his beard was thick and bushy, adding length to his already strong chin.

"What brings you to the Gold Coast, Mr. Diederik?"

His smile was extraordinary, and as I blinked at him, I realized Maxximus could be Bradley Cooper's twin. "Please . . . call me Magic."

My eyebrows shot up with a will of their own. "Magic?"

"Yes, Magic Maxx. It's my professional name. I'm here for the Evolution International Yoga conference."

Yoga with Bradley Cooper. Count me in. "Oh wow." I started undressing him with my eyes, peeling off layer after layer to review the body sculpted by the art of yoga.

"Do you do yoga?"

"Oh, ummm no." *But I'm ready when you are.*

"You should try it. You train your mind to see peace, train your body to feel peace."

I'll be feeling a piece of your body later. "Oh." I cleared my throat again and forced my brain into Jane-the-hotel-manager mode. "Sounds wonderful."

"Here, give me your hand." He could've told me to tear my clothes off and I would have. With my hand clasped between his, and our eyes locked, his calm composure enveloped me like a soothing balm.

"Now close your eyes."

I did.

"Can you feel it?"

The only it I felt was my insides twitching and saying *hell yes*. "Uh-huh." I snuck a glance at him. Memphis's next conquest was stunning. With his eyes closed his long lashes looked even longer and his slender nose divided his symmetrical features perfectly. If he wasn't standing right in front of me, I'd think he were Photoshopped.

"You have an inner energy begging to be explored."

You have no idea. "Okay."

"Yoga teaches you how to feel deep inside."

"It does?"

"Learn to tap into that energy and your world will shine."

When he released my hand, I wanted to weep. Magic Maxx curled a thread of hair behind his ear, and it was a simple yet stunning move. I realized he was waiting for me to be a hotel manager again and I cleared my throat, hopeful that my voice would actually work. "Okay, you're staying in room twenty-eight on the fifth floor." I passed his details card across the counter. "Here's your room key. Do you need any help with bags?"

"No I'm good."

"Yes, you are."

Oh shit. Judging by the intrigued look on his face, I'd said that aloud. A blaze of heat raced up my neck as I prayed for him to drag his eyes away from me.

It was an eternity, but he did, finally, and reached down to grab his bag. "Thank you."

"You're welcome. See you soon. I mean tomorrow, probably."

He chuckled and turned, and I watched, mesmerized as he glided to the elevator. He walked on his toes rather than his heels, and it gave the appearance that he ice-skated across the polished lobby tiles.

From the moment he disappeared into the elevator I was obsessed, possessed—taken over by a horny nymph who wanted a man. No, not wanted, needed. It was as if I wouldn't be able to breathe again until he was inside me.

Without another thought, I put the 'back in five minutes' sign on the counter, grabbed my bag from under my seat, and headed after my conquest.

In my room, I stripped off, leaving a trail of clothes in my wake. Naked, in the bathroom, I applied my Memphis makeup, paying extra attention to my eyes, because Magic Maxx had looked right into them. I chose my blue contact lenses and my short blond wig, and with those final touches in place I examined my appearance. With my Retro Red Bobbi Brown lippy jazzing up my look my transformation was complete. Jane was long gone—the woman in the mirror was hot, beautiful, and so ready for a fun, raunchy romp.

Lack of time required me to make snappy decisions. So, using my lippy for inspiration, I quickly decided on my red Marilyn Monroe dress with the halter-neck strap, tucked in waist, and flared skirt. I didn't waste time on a bra and chose a black pair of French knickers.

My shoe choice for tonight was a pair of Saint Laurent black and gold stilettos with gold pencil-thin heels and I matched them with my Chanel black clutch with a gold clip.

I checked my reflection and, happy with the result, I tossed my necessities into my clutch and strode out the door.

Every second in the elevator was a second too long. The ticking clock in my head didn't sway me though—I had a much more important mission on my mind. I knew what I was doing in my work hours was wrong, yet I couldn't help myself and soon every step I made toward seeing him seemed so right.

As I strode along the fifth-floor corridor, my boobs jiggled in time to my steps. It gave me a glorious sense of freedom and had me smiling. At Maxx's door, I didn't feel the sense of trepidation that usually gripped me at this point in my ritual. Instead, I was filled with anticipation.

I knocked, put my shoulders back, curled my wig around my left ear, and reminded myself to disguise my voice.

The door opened a few heartbeats later, and the man who greeted me instantly had my legs quivering. Magic Maxx had increased in sex appeal tenfold in the twenty minutes since I'd last seen him. He wore just a tiny pair of skin-tight blue shorts that left very little to my imagination.

"Hi," I said. "Can you help me?" I ensured my voice was elevated sufficiently.

He blinked. "Are you okay?"

"Oh yes, I'm wonderful. May I come in?"

"Of course." He stepped aside, and I inhaled his manly scent as I glided past him.

I tossed my clutch onto the table and turned to him. "I saw you talking to that lady downstairs. And after you left, once I saw the look on her face, I knew I just had to see more of you."

"Oh, and she told you what room I was in?"

"Ummm, no. I'm a bit naughty." I scrunched up my nose, trying to give him my cute-and-innocent look. "I spied it on your check-in card."

"Hmmm." He skated across the floor toward me and reached for my hand. "So you want a piece of magic, too."

"Uh-huh." Keeping the disguise in my voice was proving very difficult.

He pressed my hand to his chest and rested his palm over mine. Our eyes locked and it seemed as if a seismic shift moved the earth, and I truly did feel the magic. We stood rooted together for some time, and I lowered my eyes to take in the muscular miracle before me. A light sheen covered his smooth flesh, highlighting every contour.

It occurred to me that I'd interrupted an exercise routine or something else just as rigorous. Despite the ticking clock in my head, I wanted to see what this man could do.

I cleared my throat. "Would you mind showing me some of your yoga moves?"

"Hmmm." His eyes twinkled, and I loved the sense of mischief that danced over them. "How about we do this together?"

"Oh." I flicked my palm. "I can't do yoga."

"Everybody can do yoga. Will you try?"

"Okay." No hesitation was required.

"Good. First I'll show you a move, and then we'll do it together."

"Sounds *magic*."

He giggled a beautiful melody. "Seems like I'm at a bit of a loss. You know my name, yet I don't know yours."

"I'm Memphis."

He curled the back of my hand to his lips and kissed. "Pleased to meet you, Memphis."

"Likewise, Magic Maxx." The intensity in his eyes captured me and I had a crazy desire to run away with him. We could live off the land, and spend every day getting to know every inch of each other's bodies . . . and minds.

He strode away, and I gasped at the magnificent tattoo that graced the planes of his back. An elaborate winged eagle, ready to take flight, moved along his glossy flesh with each step he made.

Maxx placed his feet together, then turned to glance at me over his shoulder and with a cheeky grin, he bent over. With my eyes glued to every exquisite muscle, he gave me a truly stunning display of strength as he put his elbows on the floor and gradually raised his feet above his head. The show was spectacular.

Upside-down now, he remained rock-solid. Not a single muscle twitched as he held himself in position.

"Okay," he said. "Your turn."

There was no way I was getting onto my head. I had another idea though. Stepping closer to him, I reached up and undid the knot behind my neck and let the fabric fall. In a flash I was topless, and Maxx's rock-solid pose began to quiver.

He cleared his throat and brought his feet to the floor.

"How did I do?" I suppressed the smile twitching at my lips.

He cleared his throat again and blinked at my boobs. "You, ummm . . . did marvelous."

"Good. What's next?"

His smile lit up his face as he wriggled his eyebrows. Then, standing on one foot, he raised his other foot in the air, clutched the ankle of the raised foot and pulled it so his legs were in a perfect straight line. With his spare hand, he stretched out to point out me. "Your turn." The twinkle in his eyes was undeniable.

One by one, I slipped out of my stilettos, then I padded across the carpet so one of my breasts was an inch from his outstretched fingers. He wriggled his fingers, trying to reach the tantalizing offer, but couldn't. He burst out laughing and dropped his foot to stand up.

"You're a tease."

I lowered my eyes to the bulge in his already-tight lycra shorts. "Are you complaining?"

"Does it look like I'm complaining?" He made a point of lowering his eyes to his groin as if I'd missed it.

"It looks to me like I'm the one creating magic."

His laugh was genuine and hearty, and I laughed along with him. "You, Memphis, are a fascinating woman."

"Why thank you, Magic Maxx." I did a little curtsy. "Now for your next move?" I cocked an eyebrow at him.

Maxx placed his hands on the floor again and raised his feet in the air, but this time he curled his back so his feet hung over his head and the bulge in his shorts faced the ceiling. I stepped forward, placed his feet on my shoulders and, hardly able to believe my magnificent view, I glided my hands down his inner thighs.

He remained in position and each time I travelled my fingers along his legs, I teased closer to his groin. Right before my eyes his cock grew, pushing against the bright blue fabric that restrained it. I truly was a magician.

It was an eternity before Maxx rolled down onto his feet again. His face was red, his smile was broad, and the bulge in his pants was huge. "Okay, what've you got?"

I reached around to my side and undid the zipper holding my dress in place. The fabric blossomed around to my feet, and I stepped out and flung it toward the nearest dining chair.

Maxx's breathing was audible and with each rise and fall of his chest his pecs bulged and contracted. There wasn't an ounce of fat on this fine specimen.

"Your turn." I flashed a cheeky grin.

He ran his hand over his groin as if attempting to tame an unruly beast. Then with a clenched jaw, he hooked his fingers into the elastic of his underwear and whipped the jocks down to his ankles.

I nodded with exaggerated emphasis. "Nice move." His cock was impressive, rod straight, and the swollen pink crown burst from the top as if greeting me. He was clean shaved and I could easily see the two balls in his scrotum dangling below his cock. It was as magnificent as it was confronting.

"Your turn." His voice was slightly higher-pitched than it'd been just seconds earlier.

I did as he requested and slipped my French knickers down and tossed them toward my dress.

His jaw dropped, and he frowned.

It wasn't the reaction I'd expected, and I frowned right back at him. "What?"

"Oh, ummm, you have hair."

In a flash I put my hands over my sex. "Is that bad?"

"No, no. It's not bad, it's just I've never been with a woman with . . . like you. I like it. It's womanly." His comments were loaded with awe. So much so that I lowered my hands, proud to show off my womanly features.

"This is how we do it on the Gold Coast," I lied.

"It's incredible. Like you're concealing a delicious secret."

I tugged my lip into my mouth. I liked that description. I'd shaved myself once, then decided never again. Not only was it itchy and unfeminine, but it took me back to when I was a twelve-year-old girl. I liked being the woman I was meant to be.

As we stood ogling each other, a lightning bolt shot through me as I realized I shouldn't be here. I should be at reception, and as much as I could stare at this fine masterpiece all night, sadly I needed to move this wonderful show along.

But . . . maybe just one more yoga pose. "Can you do one more position for me?"

He wriggled his eyebrows. Then he eased backward and sat on the edge of the bed. He pushed himself back so his hands were between his thighs then, with the muscles in his arms bulging, he pointed his legs straight forward and raised his legs off the bedcovers. His legs were wide, which allowed his cock to point right at me, and his balls dangled below his legs, touching the mattress and just begging me to play with them.

With that idea in mind I stepped forward, placed my knee on the bed, and leaned in to whisper in his ear. "Don't move."

I reached beneath him, and as I took the full weight of his balls into my hand he sucked the air in through his teeth and closed his eyes. Even the most muscular men were delicate creatures. As I gently rolled his testicles in my hand, I glided my tongue up his neck and sucked his earlobe into my mouth.

A slight tremor shuddered over him, and the second I let go of his balls he dropped to the bed. "Come here, you." He grabbed me and before I knew it, he was lying back and I was on top of him, straddling his torso with my legs on either side of his body.

"You make it impossible to concentrate." He grinned as he reached up and cupped my breasts, taking one in each hand.

"I thought you were a master."

"I am." He grinned. "Just not when there's a gorgeous women naked in my room with her hands all over me.

"Hmmm." His cock was a hard rod prodding my butt cheek, and the irresistible urge to push that glorious muscle inside me dominated my thoughts. I squirmed on his belly, rubbing my pussy over his defined torso.

Maxx reached down and thumbed my clit. The sensation shot delicious pulses through me and triggered an urgency that I should've had since the second I stepped into his room.

I held up my finger. "Don't move." Gliding down his body, I took a moment to slide my tongue up his mighty erection. Maxx lashed out and clutched the sheets, tearing them from the bed. With my lips wrapped around the head of his penis, I watched for his reaction as I slowly sucked him into my mouth. And what a reaction it was. He pushed up onto his elbows and with his incredible eyes drilling into mine, his cock swelled in my mouth.

My insides did delicious shudders as I rolled my lips up and down his cock all the while his eyes were on me, watching my every move. He licked his lips and his eyes rolled. Knowing I had him on the edge, I drew my lips to the head of his penis and curled my tongue around his swollen crown as I released.

I pushed up to my feet and trotted to my bag. A heartbeat later I was back, kneeling at his side. "Here, quick, put this on."

He tore the foil packet open with his teeth, spat the top aside, removed the rubber, and rolled it onto his erection. Then he grabbed me again, positioning me so I could glide that monster into me whenever I was ready. And I was oh so ready.

I reached down between my legs and wrapped my hand around his cock. Then, using it for my own pleasure, I glided it up and down my pussy. It was hot, it was hard, and it felt so damn good pressed up against my clit. Over and over I rubbed along my velvet folds, gradually getting faster and faster. My insides begged to be plunged into, and the second my orgasm tore through me I dropped onto his cock, ramming that beast right inside me.

Using my knees, and with my hands on his nipples for support, I rode up and down, drawing out all of that incredible orgasm.

Maxx placed his hands onto my hips, arousing me from my orgasmic stupor. "Lie back."

"Huh? What?" I was still in a haze.

"Lean back." He held his hand out.

"Oh, okay." I was always up for learning something new. With his rock-hard cock still wedged tightly inside me, I obeyed, and holding onto his hands for support, I laid back and nestled my head between his knees.

"Now grab my ankles or feet."

"Oh, like this?" I reached up and wrapped my fingers around his ankles.

He leaned forward, pushing his cock farther into me, and oh my god, did that hit the spot. As I clutched onto his ankles, he raised my lower back slightly off the bed and the penetration intensified. I cried out as the head of his penis touched that thing inside me that loved and hated it at the same time.

Maxx slowly moved out of me, then with an interesting twisting motion he entered me again, pushing all the way until he could go no more. I rolled my head back, closed my eyes, and let my body take over.

He did the move again, slowly, slowly. Each time I savored every inch of him inside me. The intense precision was incredible, and I felt every exquisite aspect of his cock as he glided in and out. With one of his hands digging into the flesh at my hips he used the other to thumb my exposed clit. While he mesmerized me with that fabulous attention, he increased his pace but kept the momentum the same with both penetration and withdrawal.

As I dug my fingers into his ankles and held my body in place, he thrust into me over and over and over. He grew faster, thumping against my insides again and again. I gasped as one pounding thrust took him to the absolute limit. Magic Maxx cried out, and as he squeezed my hips he pounded me until he finally slowed and went limp inside me.

He reached out, floating his fingers gently over my nipples, and when I looked up he offered his hand to pull me onto his lap again.

"Wow," I said as I placed my hands on his pecs.

He nodded. "I agree. This was a wonderful surprise."

I smiled at the genuine inflection in his voice. "It's magic."

"You're magic."

I sighed with contentment, pushed off him, and walked to my collection of clothes. As I started to redress, Maxx went to the bathroom, and I was treated to another moving display of that eagle on his back.

He reappeared moments later with the robe on, and tied the belt around his waist as he walked toward me. "So . . ." He reached for my hand and trailed his finger along my flesh. "Do you do this often, Jane?"

I gasped and jumped back, covering my mouth. Oh god.

"Hands never lie."

Shit. Shit. Shit. "Shit." I tugged my dress on.

"Don't panic. Your secret is safe with me."

"I gotta go. This was a mistake." I tied the knot of my halter straps at the back of my neck.

"Not for me it wasn't. It was incredible."

I couldn't breathe, let alone talk. After tugging my shoes on, I yanked my bag off the table and made a dash for the door.

"Jane, please don't worry. Tomorrow I fly home to Sweden, and you shall never see me again. Other than in your dreams I hope."

I tried to smile at him, but it was probably more like a terrified grimace. Yanking the door open, I made a dash for the elevator. My heart was in my throat as I waited for the stupid elevator, and by the time it arrived I was close to passing out.

As I rode the elevator to my floor, I yanked off my wig and tugged the pins from my hair. It was an eternity before I finally made it to my apartment. I nearly died when I saw the clock on my microwave. It was one-fifteen, which meant I'd been gone from reception for an hour and a half. I dashed to the bathroom, and as I scrubbed off my makeup I tried to ignore the fear in my eyes.

I showered quickly and redressed into the clothes I'd had on earlier. Then, after brushing my teeth and swallowing two large glasses of water, I grabbed my diary, shoved it into my bag, and made the trip down to the lobby. With each passing second my heart thumped louder in my ears.

The doors pinged open, and with one last deep breath I stepped out of the elevator. Everything was quiet. The lobby was empty, the bar was closed, and other than my pounding heart, everything was normal.

Able to breathe again, I crawled to the reception desk, flopped onto my chair, and plonked my head down onto my hands. It was an eternity before I grabbed my diary from my bag, pulled a pen from the top drawer, and turned to the 7th of October.

The elevators pinged, and I watched in horror as Magic Maxx strolled toward me with his arms open and a pleading look on his face. "Jane, I couldn't leave you like that."

I was dumbstruck, my heart set to explode as he came around the counter and reached for my hands. He pressed my palms to his chest and covered his hands over mine. "What happened upstairs was true magic."

I gulped so loud I was certain he heard it.

"I don't want our wonderful experience ruined by how it ended. I will remember you forever, but I want you to remember me, too."

Realizing he wanted me to respond, I swallowed. "Oh, don't worry. I won't forget you."

He tilted his head, sincerity drilled into his eyes. "I promise you, nobody will ever learn of what we did here tonight. I will let this be our beautiful secret."

The way he said it had me believing every word. "Thank you."

He released my hands. "Can I have a hug?"

I chuckled. "Of course."

We wrapped our arms around each other, and it was like a wonderful calming aura floated over me. Maxx had a gift, and once we finished our embrace I felt truly relaxed.

Maxx lifted my hand to his lips. "Goodbye, Memphis. You will live forever in my dreams."

"Goodbye, Magic, as will you in mine."

He did his elegant skate across the lobby tiles, and when he pressed for the elevator the doors opened immediately. With one last fleeting glance at me, he stepped over the threshold and disappeared.

Once again I'd dodged a bullet, yet for some inexplicable reason, I felt like it was meant to happen. Was meeting Magic Maxx written in my destiny?

Wow, that was deep. I really was going crazy.

I sat down, and upon seeing my diary open on the counter, I began to chuckle. Another bullet dodged there, too. It would've been rather awkward if he'd seen it.

Reaching for my pen, at the top of the page I wrote *Magic Maxx Room 28*, and as I thought about how wonderful both my body and mind felt right now I wrote *My Magic Elixir* beneath his name. As the small hours of the morning ticked by, I detailed at great length everything about my encounter with the yoga master.

Hours later, as the morning sunshine lit up the horizon, I made a cup of green tea and headed out to my favorite spot in the hotel. I sipped my drink, watched the sun lighten the morning sky, breathed in the crisp air and welcomed a new day into my life.

12ᵀᴴ OCTOBER
MAXIMUM EXPOSURE
Room 15 - Hot Horizon Hotel

Today was shaping up to be a brilliant day. First up was hours of quality shopping time with Lolita and after that, as if the day couldn't get any better, I had a date with Billy. I'd nearly fallen off my chair when he'd phoned reception yesterday. The sound of his voice had set my heart aflutter and I'm sure I've been grinning like a crazy woman since he invited me to dinner.
Nine o'clock couldn't come quickly enough, and when Lolly pulled her Grand Jeep Cherokee into the drop-off zone I buzzed with anticipation. The second I opened the car door she squealed, confirming her excitement matched mine. "Ready to shop till we drop?"
"Absolutely." I slipped into the passenger seat and leaned over to give her a hug.
"Let's go then." She put the car into gear and pulled onto the quiet street.
"What time do you have to be back?"
"Well . . ."
It must have been the way I said it, because she spun to me with wide eyes.
"Well, what?"
"Billy rang yesterday."
"Oh yay, and?"

"I'm meeting him in his room at seven tonight."
She put her foot on the accelerator, shooting us through a yellow light. "Goody! So I've got you for the whole day before you shag your brains out."
I giggled. "Correct."
Because we arrived at the shops right on opening time, there were plenty of parking spaces. Lolly drove up a brand new car park ramp and pulled into a spot next to the entrance doorway. I hadn't been to Pacific Fair since they'd finished the multi-million-dollar renovation, so I was already disorientated.
We jumped out of the car, and Lolly hooked her arm into mine as we wandered toward the entrance and stepped onto a set of escalators leading down to the center.
"So, give me a rundown of your plans in Mildura."
"Okay. I fly in on Friday and land at about lunchtime. Nothing planned that night. I'm having morning tea with Aunty Ann on Saturday and dad's party is Saturday night. I fly home Sunday lunchtime. That's it."
"Right." She held out her thumb. "So we need an outfit for the plane."
"I'll just wear my jeans."
"Like hell you will." She hit me with her long-suffering fashion tragic look.
I chuckled. "Okay, no jeans."
"No. I'm thinking a stylish jumpsuit and heels to match. Then Friday night you need a couple of choices of clothing, just in case you go clubbing or something."
I burst out laughing. "Lolly, it's Mildura, not Melbourne."
"A girl can never be too prepared."
At the bottom of the escalator she led me straight to the first shop on the left, and we entered without pause. The furniture was sparse, the decor bland, and the shopkeeper looked annoyed that we'd come in. I would've walked right back out if Lolita hadn't strode straight to the nearest rack and started tugging clothes aside. I stood back, ready to witness the shopping master at work.
"Hold that." Without looking at me, Lolita passed me a hanger holding a long flowing dress.
"And this." She repeated the move with another.
Once I had five items of clothing, she turned with a grin. "Okay, let's try them on."
Obediently, I followed her toward the changing room. We passed the mirrored counter and the shop assistant looked up as if she'd only just noticed us. "Would you like some help?"
Lolly showed her a palm. "No. We've got this."
God I love her.
The assistant gasped, and I tried not to giggle as we strode past.
Lolly inspected both change rooms before she chose one, pulled aside a

curtain and stood back. "In you go."

I hung the clothes on the large brass hooks, pulled the curtain across and set about undressing. The first outfit I tried on was a pomegranate-colored jumpsuit. It was simple yet stylish and featured spaghetti halter-neck straps with an open back. It had a thin elastic waist and straight legs that fell to the floor.

I grinned at my reflection, then turned, checked out my ass, and grinned some more. I would never have lifted this off the clothing rack. Luckily for me, Lolita had. I pulled the curtain aside to show Lolly.

"Shit yeah, babe. That rocks."

"I know." I turned to look in the mirror again.

"Totally for the plane. When you land in Mildura you'll have all the cowboys turning their heads so fast they'll fall off their horses."

I chuckled and resisted telling her there were very few cowboys in Mildura. "I really like this."

"Like? You look fucking hot."

I stepped back into the cubicle and tried on the remaining four outfits, but none of them were suitable. We left the store, and I couldn't believe that in the space of twenty minutes I'd spent $140 and already purchased my first outfit for the weekend.

Things went a little downhill from there, though, with the next six dress shops proving unfruitful. "Time for coffee?" I said, all hopeful.

Lolita wagged her head, frowning. "Okay, but remember it's cutting into quality shopping time."

"I'll drink quickly."

The first coffee shop we came across offered both a delightful coffee bean aroma and a table for two out the front. Lolita nabbed a chair like the queen of the plaza she was, and I went in search of the cake counter.

I ignored the baked cheesecake for fear it may make Lolita gag and decided on the healthier option, a blueberry pecan muffin. My timing was perfect as Lolly was placing her order with the waitress as I returned to our table. I ordered my choice of treat and tried but failed to ignore Lolly shaking her head. She should know by now that she'd never get between me and a decent sugar fix.

"So what's the plan after this?" I diverted her attention away from my poor calorie choice.

"We'll head up to the Myer end. There's a few new dress shops up that way I haven't explored yet."

"Okay."

As we drank our drinks and I ate my muffin, our conversation flitted from Calvin and her kids, to my weekend ahead, to the fashion sense of the random strangers who walked past. I drank my coffee as quickly as I could and the second I forked the last piece of my cake into my mouth, Lolita stood up and waggled her minute ass to the counter to pay. I dabbed my napkin to my lips, stood and pushed my chair in, ready to start hustling the second she returned.

Five shops and a dozen or so outfits later, I tried on a dress that was simply stunning. It was black, had delicate lace cutouts that showed off the right amount of cleavage, fitted my curves like a second skin, and the hemline fell just above my knee. I couldn't stop staring at my reflection. I felt like a model. No . . . not a model—I felt like a woman who was at the top of her game and wasn't afraid to show it. The dress was absolutely perfect, but not perfect for a backyard party in Mildura.

"You dressed yet?" Lolita was an impatient woman.

I pulled back the curtain and tugged my lip between my teeth, awaiting her appraisal.

Her jaw dropped. She tilted her head, and a tear sprung to her eyes. "Wow. You are stunning."

I ran my fingers over the smooth fabric, turned, and admired my reflection from the back. "It's beautiful."

"That's the one. That's the party dress."

I shook my head and sighed. "I'll be overdressed."

She waggled her finger at me. "There's no such thing. You're going to own that dress, and you're going to own that party, too. People will want to know who you are, and they'll say that's Jane Nichols, the woman Alexander fucked around on."

I burst out laughing. "You're crazy."

"You only just figured that out? Listen, the best revenge is showing that you've moved on. Make him see that the time you had with him was insignificant."

Insignificant. I dwelled on her word. In comparison to this year and the wonderful men I'd met, it was true. My time with Alexander, on the other hand barely even registered on my radar anymore. It was like he was just a bad storm, a storm that had now been replaced with many wonderful rainbows. "You know what? You're right. This is the dress."

"You bet it is, babe. You look smoking hot. Men will be on their knees begging you to walk all over them."

"Oh my God. Stop it, you crazy woman."

"No, I won't stop. You've waited over three years to get your revenge on that bastard and in this dress, you're going to get it a thousand times over. Oh, I wish I could be there to see his face. Turn around."

Grinning, I did a slow spin. I felt a million dollars.

"I think we should bring out the animal in you and match this with leopard-print shoes and a clutch."

"Oh, I've got my Givenchy zebra-print stilettos and the matching clutch."

"Black and white . . . perfect. And what about long, dangly gold earrings and a chunky gold bracelet?"

I nodded and turned to my reflection again. As I admired every inch of the dress on my body, a layer of anticipation rumbled through me. For the first time in years, I was actually looking forward to seeing my cheating bastard ex-fiancé.

I felt no pain handing over three hundred dollars for the outfit. It was going to be worth every cent.

The remainder of the afternoon was spent in more dress shops, and after trying on about a hundred styles we succeeded in finding seven outfits, including two possibilities for Friday night, and new workout gear just in case, according to Lolly, I felt the need to run off some of the calories I'd no doubt consume over the weekend. We also found a treasure trove of accessories to go with each outfit and two new pairs of shoes. In one day, I'd spent a little more than two weeks' wages. But I didn't care—I was worth it. Besides, I was well and truly overdue for a wardrobe overhaul.

By the time she drove me home, it was half past four and I was exhausted. We said our goodbyes and with my abundant shopping bags hanging off my arm, I made my way to my apartment, placed my bags on the floor, and flopped onto the bed. As the muscles in my back unraveled my mind turned to Billy. My sexy cowboy was waiting for me just two apartments away.

I rolled off the bed and strolled to the bathroom. At the bath, I turned the taps onto full and poured in a good slosh of Marjorie's bubble bath. With the water running, I returned to my shopping purchases and one by one, I unwrapped them, cut off the tags, and hung them in my closet. I added my shoes to my collection and put the jewelry away.

By the time I'd finished sorting my shopping, the bath was ready. I turned off the taps and just before I hopped in, I poured myself a glass of wine. With my hair pulled up on top of my head and my glass of Shaw & Smith Sauv Blanc resting on the edge of the tub, I stripped off and slipped into the warm water. I felt as if I'd run a marathon and the warm water was the ideal therapy for my aching body.

One touch of the bristles on my legs was enough to know I needed to sort that little issue out and I reached for my razor. As I shaved my legs I played through my mind all the people I was likely to see when I returned to Mildura.

There were Mom and Dad of course, and it'd be great to see Tyler again. I hadn't spoken to my brother since he'd called me for my birthday. It'd be wonderful to see Aunty Ann. Of all the people I'd left behind, she was the only one I truly missed. My thoughts drifted to Alexander, and I wondered how much he'd changed. When we'd first started going out, I'd thought he was the most handsome man in the world. He had rugged good looks and could sport a usual man's three-day growth in the space of twelve hours.

His eyes were dark, framed by equally dark eyelashes. By the end of our relationship, however, after I'd learned of the evil he'd done, he'd become the devil. He was as ugly as sin, and his eyes had darkened to menacing.

The tragedy of our breakup, and the thing that infuriated me the most, was that I'd learned to hate. Hate was a soul-crushing emotion that ate me alive. Every second I was awake, the hatred had consumed me, creeping into my personality at every opportunity. It'd taken me a long time to eradicate that hatred. Too long.

Chelsea-Lea was as much of a driver of that hatred as Alexander had been, and from what I'd heard about the demise of her life and body, my revenge was already sweet.

I sat up in the bath and clutched my hands around my knees as one more name came tumbling through my brain. George Whiteman. The very first man to meet Memphis. I grabbed my wineglass and with a huge gulp, I realized I was looking forward to seeing him. He'd literally changed my life. Hopefully our paths crossed again.

As my thoughts drifted from George to the many other men I'd met this year and onto Cowboy Billy who was waiting for me barely forty feet away, I realized that all the hatred I'd been through was worth it. Because if that hell had never happened, then this year would never have happened either.

I smiled as I sipped my wine and turned my attention to the future rather than my past. My immediate future involved a smoking-hot cowboy, reminding me yet again of just how good life was. The lovely affirmation was like a balm to my soul and I eased back, pushed my shoulders beneath the water and closed my eyes.

The water was barely lukewarm when I finally hopped out and dried myself. I released my hair and fiddled around with it for a while, trying a new style Lolita had suggested I wear next Saturday night. Separating out my fringe, I then pulled a portion of hair back and plumped it up, creating some height at the back of my head, and pinned it in place. Then, using my curling wand, I put loose curls into the length that fell down and around my shoulders. My arms were aching by the time I'd finished, but it was worth it. The new hairstyle was fancy. Perfect for a night out with Billy and perfect for one of my new outfits.

After applying a touch of makeup, I decided I'd wear the new dress that Lolly had insisted I buy for my Friday night in Mildura. I pulled the dress out of the closet and placed it onto the bed. It was a wrap dress, a style I'd learned suited me very well. The color was red, not as bright as fire engine red and not as deep as blood red—it was somewhere in between and was patterned with white spots. The neckline was fairly low, showing off ample cleavage, which was something I would never have done before this year.

I chose a white lace G-string and for a little cheekiness, decided not to wear a bra. I curled the dress behind my back, wrapped the belt around and tied it off in the center, at my waist. For accessories I chose my long string of fake pearls and wrapped them around my neck three times, twice close to my neck and once long enough that it fell between my breasts. I chose matching earrings and a bracelet, and a pair of white six-inch-high stilettos.

When I stood before the mirror, I was fascinated by my appearance. It was still so hard to comprehend it was my reflection. I spun around, allowing the skirt to flare. I looked beautiful, but it was more than that—I felt beautiful, too. The smile on my face was genuine and impossible to remove. So with those wonderful feelings coursing through me, I grabbed a white clutch, tossed my bits and pieces in it, and strode out my door.

Billy was in room fifteen, just two doors up from me. I knocked once, and barely two heartbeats later, he opened the door.

His jaw dropped and he blinked. His reaction was the pinnacle to my already wonderful feelings. He leaned in to kiss my cheek, and I inhaled his sexy, familiar scent. With his hand on the small of my back, he led me into the room and the door closed behind us.

Two champagne glasses were nestled next to an ice bucket on the kitchen counter, and assuming they were for us, I strode that way, placed my clutch onto the counter and slipped into the bar stool. The split in my skirt fell aside, revealing more of my legs than I'd usually show, yet I resisted the urge to cover myself. I was pleased I didn't when I saw Billy glance at my legs.

His Adam's apple bobbed up and down. "You look beautiful."

"Thank you. You look handsome yourself." For the first time, Billy wasn't wearing jeans. Instead, he wore dark blue slacks and a crisp white button-up shirt which he'd tucked into his pants. His belt buckle was a large silver oval decorated with a bucking bronco and a rider.

He reached for the champagne. "I took the liberty of ordering us a drink. Would you like one?"

"I'd love one, thank you."

Despite Billy's cotton shirt covering his upper body, it was impossible to miss his toned muscles as he worked the cork from the bottle. It released with a loud pop, slamming into the ceiling, and bubbles spewed from the bottle.

"Oh shit." Billy raced to the sink, and we both giggled as we worked together to clean up the mess. The incident was a nice relaxant, and after that the conversation flowed freely. We sipped our drinks out on the balcony and talked about all sorts of trivial things. The champagne warmed up my insides and loosened my curiosity, and soon I was doing Lolita's trick and asking Billy heaps of questions.

It was lovely just chatting, and I could've stayed there all night if my stomach hadn't started grumbling. I tried to ignore the pains but it was impossible. "So where are we going for dinner?"

"Oh." The startled look on Billy's face indicated he'd forgotten all about food. "I found a nice-looking steak restaurant around the corner."
"Steakside?"
"Yes, that's the one. Is it okay?"
"It's lovely." My stomach made little mewling noises in approval.
"Shall we take a walk then?" He stood and offered his hand, helping me rise me to my feet. I drew up to his chest, placed my hands over his defined pecs, and gazed into his gorgeous molten-honey eyes.
Billy didn't miss a beat and barely a breath later, I closed my eyes and our lips met. I melted into his embrace and curled one hand up around to the back of his neck, urging him for more. Our moans united, as did our tongues. His fingers caressed my cheek, and as he reached around my back with his other hand I drew up on my tippy-toes, positioning our hips together.
The kiss was gentle and sweet, but it said so much more—*I want. I need.* It was a kiss that said our relationship had slipped right on past casual, and as I pushed my tongue into his mouth, probing to taste more of him, I was delightfully happy that it had. The bulge growing in his groin was unmistakable, and I reached around to rub my hand over my creation.
"Jane." Billy pulled back. "You drive me crazy."
I curled my tongue across my lip. "Is that a good thing?"
He cupped my cheek and leaned in for a delicate kiss. "It's an incredible thing, but if we don't go now, we may not eat tonight."
I was torn between the options.
He reached for my hand, and brought it up to kiss my palm. "We can take this up again when we come back."
"Okay." My stomach seemed to be happy with that decision, too.
We gathered our things and headed out to the elevator. It was weird walking right on past my apartment door.
The second we stepped into the mirrored cube, I grabbed him and pushed him back against the wall. Our mouths met in a crazy, heated kiss. Tongues probed. Our hips grinded. Our breathing was erratic and in the confined space, our moans were loud.
I pulled back at the little jig the elevator did to announce its arrival, and when it dinged I started giggling. We crossed the lobby and Bailey, the casual night manager, barely glanced in our direction as we strode past laughing.
The second we stepped out the glass doors, Billy reached for my hand and spun me to him. His grin was magnificent. "You're incredible."
I scrunched my nose up. "Thanks. Come on, I'm hungry." After a brief pause I added, "And horny. We need to solve one or the other quickly or I'll implode."
"Eat first."

"Okay."

We held hands as we strolled toward Steakside, and it felt so comfortable I was fooled into believing Billy and I had known each other for years and not just hours. Ironically, we were offered exactly the same table I'd sat at a couple of weeks ago, only this time I wasn't secretly spying on a man at another restaurant, I was openly admiring the man opposite me.

I didn't need to look at the menu as I planned to order exactly what I'd had last time, but I used the distraction of doing so to try to put my wild emotions in check. The way I was feeling right now, if Billy dropped down on one knee and proposed, I'd probably say yes. Maybe the champagne was driving my crazy thoughts; we'd both had two glasses before we left the hotel. *I should have a glass of water.*

"Would you like me to order a bottle of wine?"

"Okay." *Oh dear, I was in trouble.* But as I watched Billy scour the wine list with intense concentration, I was happy to tumble into as much trouble as I could get.

"Sauv Blanc, right? Do you have a preference?"

"Yes, that's right, and no, you choose."

The waitress arrived again and Billy ordered a bottle of Oyster Bay Sauvignon Blanc, which was just fine with me. We placed our meal orders, and the second the waitress left we picked up our conversation where we'd left off.

Everything was perfect, from the setting, to the wine, to my steak, to my smoking-hot date. We laughed, we talked serious stuff, like the upcoming American presidential election, and we talked about families. I told him about my parents, and it must've been something I said or the way I'd said it because he cocked his head and frowned. "You're not close to them, are you?"

I sighed, unsure whether I wanted to divulge the truth, but his sincerity and the way he looked at me cracked through my defense shield. With my fingers gliding up the stem of my glass, I wondered just how far back I should go.

He reached over and placed his hand over mine. "You don't have to talk about them if you don't want to."

Billy was a true gentleman. It was a pity that couldn't be said for the first man I'd offered my heart to. "Many years ago, I was engaged to a man named Alexander." I looked into Billy's eyes, searching for the disgust I thought would be there, but it wasn't. In fact, it was the opposite. Billy looked as much interested as he was concerned. "We were engaged for three years before I found out he'd cheated on me."

"Ohhh." He shook his head. "Bastard."

That was the first swear word I'd ever heard from Billy, and it was the perfect one to describe Alexander.

"Yep. But it wasn't just with one woman—it was dozens of women, and even worse, one of them was my best friend."

"Best friends don't do things like that."

"True. I learned it the hard way though."

His frown deepened. "What does this have to do with your parents?"

"Right. So when I broke off my engagement, I couldn't stand living in Mildura anymore—every woman I saw had me wondering if they'd slept with him. So when I was offered this position at the hotel, I jumped at the chance to move one thousand miles away from my hometown. But my parents didn't stop seeing Alexander. My dad actually goes fishing with him, even after everything he did."

The horror on Billy's face perfectly suited the story. "I can't believe that."

I shrugged. "It's true, and next Friday I fly home for Dad's sixtieth birthday and Alexander will be there."

"Where? At the party?"

I nodded.

"Oh. That's awkward."

"Not anymore. I've made peace with it. But I hope he's damn uncomfortable."

"Good for you." He held up his glass. "Here's to moving on."

"I'll drink to that." We chinked our glasses together and as we sipped, I melted into his gorgeous honey eyes. I'd never seen eyes like his before, and it had me wondering what the rest of his family looked like. I placed my glass down. "Tell me about your parents."

"You'll love them. Dad's a real salt-of-the-earth type of guy—he's always helping me out with the land. They lost everything they owned a decade or so ago after Dad made a few poor decisions with his finances." Billy shrugged off the confronting story as if he were talking about a losing bingo ticket. "So because I built that house for them on my land, he feels like he owes me. But of course he doesn't."

"And your mom?" I sipped my wine.

A quaint smile formed on his lips. "She too thinks she owes me and despite my constant objections, she's always doing my cleaning and washing. It's nothing for me to come home after twelve hours on the land to find dinner in the oven. I don't know what I'd do without her. But don't tell her that." He laughed, and although I laughed too, the scenario he'd described was one I couldn't comprehend. Breaking free from my parents was one of the best decisions I'd made. I simply couldn't imagine living within walking distance of them.

As Billy carried on talking about his parents, two things became clear—firstly, his devotion to them was unequivocal, and secondly, I was going to need another bottle of wine.

I waved at the waitress and pointed at the bottle. She nodded, and I smiled back at Billy who was still talking. As the hours rolled on and I sipped my wine, Billy told stories of life on the land. It was obvious he loved every second of it. He too was a salt-of-the-earth kind of guy.

The staff were clearing the tables around us when we decided it was time to pay the bill. After a brief discussion, in which I was unyielding, Billy conceded to splitting the bill between us.

As we headed toward the hotel, he draped his arm around my shoulder, which was a good thing because the wine I'd gulped had gone straight to my head the second I'd stood up.

Billy said something funny and a serious case of the giggles struck me. Soon I was both giggling and snorting at the same time. So unsexy. But I couldn't stop. He laughed with me, although I was pretty sure we weren't laughing at the same thing.

We made it to the elevator without incident, and the second the doors closed I was on him. I pushed him back against the wall and as his hands found my breasts, I pushed my tongue into his mouth. The sexual desires that'd gripped me hours earlier were back.

Our lips were still locked together when the doors opened. He curled his arm around my waist and led me out of the elevator. Thank God he was guiding me, or I would've led him straight to my apartment without even thinking. He opened his door, and the second the door closed, he had me against the wall. Our lips locked together, our tongues probed, and our hands explored each other's bodies.

I only realized he'd undone the belt at my waist when my dress fell aside and his hand cupped my breast. My nipple hardened under his touch, begging him to squeeze it. He must've heard my silent pleas as his fingers tweaked my sensitive bud, gently at first, but as our kiss grew heated he pinched harder.

I fumbled with his belt buckle, desperate to release the bulge I knew was there, but the buckle was a labyrinth, foiling my attempts. I grumbled and with my hands on his pecs pushed him back. "How do you get into this thing?"

He chuckled, and with the flick of his wrist had the buckle undone. I seized the moment and pulled on the belt, drawing it out of the loops until it hung between us. His eyes met mine, and the heady excitement shimmering in them was an incredible aphrodisiac.

I flung the belt aside and it fell with a loud thud to the floor. Stepping back toward him, I tugged his shirt from his pants, and as I undid his buttons he played with my breasts, cupping them in his hands as if assessing their weight.

Every time Billy's glorious body was revealed, my breath escaped me. He truly was a masterpiece. Each muscle was formed with detailed precision. His hairless flesh was the perfect shade of bronze, and his nipples were hard pebbles pointing right at me. I leaned in and licked them, first one, then the other, and as I trailed my tongue around the hardened flesh, I undid his pants button and unzipped him.

He stepped back and bent over to pull off his shoes and socks, and his pants fell to the floor. As he kicked them aside, I took a moment to witness my sexy cowboy. Men's physiques did not get much hotter than that. His cock was a thick rod in his red jockey underpants that pointed up to his navel, and the head of his penis teased me as it bulged from the top of the elastic.

It was deliciously enticing.

I went to him and as I ran my hand up his swollen cock, Billy reached for my shoulders and sucked the air in through his teeth.

He wove his hands into my dress and eased it off my shoulders. The heavy fabric fell to my feet, and I kicked it and my stilettos aside. We now stood facing each other wearing only our underpants. His eyes cruised up my body, and my flesh tingled beneath his gaze. My already hard nipples hardened even further, and my purring insides confirmed I liked his attention.

Billy stepped forward and placed his hands on my waist. Our lips came together and from that second on, the control we'd been showing evaporated. I closed my eyes and pushed my tongue into his mouth, wanting to taste more of him. He curled one hand around my neck, drawing us closer, and his other hand squeezed my breast and twirled my nipple between his fingers. Shudders of pleasure ripped through me as we moaned in unison.

Our bodies moved together in a lust-fueled dance, and my hands had a mind of their own. I sought the bulge in his pants, and curled my fingers into the elastic of his underwear and pulled it down, releasing the mighty beast from its constraints. Billy bent his knees as I cupped his balls and marveled at the weight of them.

His testicles filled my hand, and I alternated my attention from them to his rock-hard shaft. As I curled my fingers around his cock and glided up and down, he fed his hand into my pants. I parted my legs, allowing him entrance, and his finger slipped into my pulsing hole sending glorious shivers through me.

"Oh Billy." His name was whispered off my tongue and felt so right.

"Jane." He moaned after saying my name, and I bent my legs, opening myself up, giving him more. As he probed my pussy, pushing his finger in and out, I played with his cock, gliding my hand up and down his full length. We worked together, pleasing each other, and it was if we'd been performing this act for years. He knew exactly where to touch me and based on his moans and body movement, I, in turn, was pleasing him.

Billy stepped back and whipped his underpants off. Following his lead, I did the same.

He reached up and cupped my cheeks. "Can I make love to you?"

The way he said it had both my heart and body melting. "Oh, yes please."

He grabbed my hand and led me to the bed. "I'll be back in a sec." The muscles in Billy's bottom bulged and flexed with each step he took toward the bathroom.

I wriggled up the bed and as I lay back, I savored the delightful pulses throbbing through me. Billy returned in a flash with a condom now fitted to his erection. He crawled onto the bed and positioned his knees between my parted legs. His pupils were dark discs, wide and excited, and as he trailed his hands down my thighs I raised my bottom off the sheets, showing him everything I had.

Billy's tongue lashed out and crossed his lips, and he drove a finger into my throbbing pussy. The intensity on his face was exquisite, as were the sensations drilling through me. He added a second finger and pushed them both in with a twisting repetitive motion. His eyes devoured me with their intensity as every plunge of his fingers sent rockets shooting through my body. I screamed as an orgasm ripped through me. It was fast, explosive. Incredible. I gasped for air as he plunged over and over, drawing out every last drop.

As my chest rose and fell, catching my breath, he wriggled forward, aiming his cock at my opening. I propped up on my elbows, wanting to see his penis glide into me, and our eyes met. The unspoken vibes that crossed between us were incredible, giving depth to the already wonderful sensations running through me.

He guided his hips forward, and I lowered my eyes to watch him enter my vagina. Watching his cock as well as feeling it push into me, sent firecrackers through me. My whole body came alive as my pussy swallowed his full length, taking him until he had no more to give. It was extraordinary to witness, and once again I was reminded of how much I liked being a voyeur.

With his hands on my knees, he pulled out, and the two of us witnessed the most thrilling display of our carnal bliss. At the very tip he pushed in again, and each time he repeated the move his eyes rolled back and his breathing grew deeper.

His cock was slick with my juices as it plunged in and out. The glorious spectacle had an orgasm building inside me that reached greedy heights. I flopped back, fisted the sheets, and yanked them off the bed as my climax ripped through me. Billy continued to thrust, drawing out every last ounce of my orgasm. The sensations were raw and true, taking my body to another glorious world where I knew nothing but the wonderful sensations running through me.

Billy leaned forward, pulling my knees up with him, and he placed his hands beside my shoulders. His already amazing biceps bulged with his weight. He leaned in to kiss me, and as our tongues danced he continued to thrust in and out. I curled my hips in time, matching his movements as if we'd been practicing this for years.

Soon our mouths drifted apart as our breaths grew rapid. He rocked back and forward. Plunged in and out. Every muscle in his body tensed, and a fine sheen covered his already delicious flesh.

A deep rumble erupted from Billy's throat. His plunging became harder, faster. He clenched his jaw, and I knew he'd arrived at the point of no return. Just knowing that tilted me over the edge, and I reached around, dug my fingers into his ass, and gasped as a third orgasm shuddered through me.

Billy groaned, deep and primal as he plunged into me with several pounding thrusts. He slowed down, and soon I felt him soften inside me. He opened his eyes and it seemed to take a little while before he was able to focus.

Our eyes met, and for a moment I thought he was going to say something. Instead, he leaned forward to kiss me. Then he rolled over to my side, and I curled into the nook of his shoulder and rested my hand on his chest. His heart galloped and as I lay there, listening to the steady beat, I relaxed into our after-sex embrace. It was perfect. Billy was perfect. Everything was perfect.

I propped up onto my elbow to look at him, and he smiled at me. "Thank you for a wonderful evening."

"Yes. Thank you."

I kissed him. Just a simple kiss before I crawled back off the bed.

"Would you like to stay the night?"

Billy's question caught me off guard, and I spun to him wide-eyed. "Oh, ummm—"

"It's okay." He must've seen my shock. "Maybe next time."

"Yes, maybe next time." I set about redressing, and when Billy went to the bathroom, I tried to analyze why his question had startled me. As I searched my brain for a plausible reason I realized there really wasn't one.

He returned from the bathroom in a pair of shorts, and a stunning contented smile on his face. "Thank you for a great night. Would you like me to walk you to your room?"

"No thank you. That's not necessary." I gathered my clutch from the table. "Good night, Billy." I stepped over and kissed his cheek before I made my way to the door.

"Good night, Jane. See you again soon."

I strode the short distance to my room and went straight to the bathroom, turned on the shower, and undressed. My body pulsed out lovely throbbing sensations as I stood under the warm cascade. Afterwards, I dressed in my cotton pajamas, sat on the edge of my bed and reached for the diary. I turned to the 12th of October, and wrote *Cowboy Billy Room 15* at the top. I wrote about our wonderful evening together, the incredible sex, and how thrilling it was to watch his enormous erection plunging into me. With that thought, I wrote *Maximum Exposure* beneath his name at the top.

I put the diary aside, and as I curled under the covers and rolled onto my side I imagined falling asleep in Billy's magnificent arms. It was a wonderful way to let sleep take me to another world.

Kitty Kendall

22ᴺᴰ OCTOBER
MY RAUNCHY RESCUE
Room 17 - Hot Horizon Hotel

I'd been so caught up with my dreaded trip back home to Mildura that I'd failed to foresee my other dilemma. It was Thursday night, and my last shift before I took three nights off work. Come nine a.m. tomorrow morning I'd be on a plane, and I wasn't scheduled to return home until Sunday afternoon. That meant, unless I found a man during tonight's shift, I wouldn't be able to complete my sexual challenge this week.

My brain flitted to the possibility of taking up my challenge in Mildura, but the very thought of it launched bile to my throat and I quickly smacked that silly idea away.

I walked to my kitchen in search of something to eat but after staring into my fridge for a while, I closed the door, uninspired. And that was when I saw Hunter's phone number. It was written on the napkin from the Blue Haven Café still secured to my fridge by the surfboard magnet.

I lifted the magnet, and as I stared at the number my fingers trembled. This could be my savior. He could be my savior. My heart galloped at the prospect of calling him. Holding the napkin like it were a sheet of gold leaf, I placed it onto my tiny dining table and plucked my phone from my bag. Before I changed my mind, I dialed his number.

"Hunter McCall here."

"Hi Hunter, it's Memphis. Do you remember me? We met on the Gold—"
"Memphis!" It was both a question and a statement. "Of course I remember. How are you?"
"I'm good, how are you?"
"I'm bloody marvelous, now that I'm talking to you."
My heart fluttered. "Have you been busy?"
"Crazy busy. But that's not unusual. How about you? How's the card sharks?"
I frowned, but then recalled lying to him about working at the casino as a croupier. I cringed at all my terrible lies. "Well, that's why I'm calling. I'm on the Gold Coast again on Sunday night and, well . . ."
"Are you asking me on a date?"
"I, ummm . . ."
"It sounds like you are." His voice elevated a notch as if loaded with anticipation.
"I guess I am."
"In that case, I'd love to."
"You can come? This Sunday?"
"I need to change a few things around, but yes, sounds great."
A smile curled on my lips. "Oh, that's . . . that's perfect."
"Where shall I meet you?"
His question caught me off guard. "Oh, ummm . . ." I hadn't thought that far ahead.
"How about the bar at the Hot Horizon Hotel? Where we had drinks last time? Say seven o'clock?" He saved me.
"Okay, sounds great." His timing was perfect to avoid Needledick's prying eyes.
"Excellent. I'll see you then."
We said our goodbyes, and I grinned so hard my cheeks quivered by the time I'd ended the call. Hunter had just saved me. It was a delightful thought. From the very first moment I'd met him, he'd struck me as the type of guy who would come rescue me should I be lost in the jungle or something. I may not have been lost in the jungle, but my premonition had already come true.
A sense of calm embraced me as I headed downstairs to start work. Fortunately, my nightshift was busy and the hours flew by. Before I knew it, the rising sun signified the end of my shift and I was back in my room, painting my toenails, doing my hair, finalizing my packing and preparing to return to the place that'd been the setting for the first twenty-five years of my life.
Boarding the plane filled me with dread, and with every mile I travelled toward Mildura, anxiety ate at me like a hungry piranha. When I'd left my hometown nearly four years ago, I'd been filled with a torrent of emotions:

hope, trepidation, and fear of the unknown, and now, as I headed back there, all those emotions came flooding right back.

The flight was over before I'd settled my tormented reflections, and after we landed, I walked off the plane into the terminal and sought out my luggage. Once I tugged my case off the one and only carousel, I headed out the exit gate and spied Dad instantly. He hadn't changed—his full mop of silver hair stood out like a beacon, contrasting dramatically with his sunburned face.

"Hey Dad." I stepped into his embrace and smelt his familiar Aramis cologne.

"How's my favorite daughter?" Dad was known for his corny sayings.

"I'm great, Dad. How are you?"

"I'm really good." He stepped back, holding our arms apart to look me up and down. "You look amazing."

"Thank you. Where's Mom?"

He waved a hand as if swatting flies. "Oh, she's busy preparing for the party. Sorry she couldn't be here."

"That's okay."

He led the way and we crossed the tiny terminal and headed out to his parked car. "Is Tyler here?"

"No. His flight doesn't come in until tomorrow morning."

"Oh, okay." I had hoped my brother would be here when I'd arrived. It was always easier to be around my parents when he was there too. Mainly because when he was here, the focus was off me—Mom and Dad were much more interested in their football-star son.

About thirty minutes later, we turned into our driveway, and I'd only just stepped from the car when Mom came rushing out. A sliver of anxiety had me biting the inside of my lip as I adjusted my ponytail and ran my hands down my pantsuit to iron out the creases near my lap.

"Jane." She greeted me with open arms. "Wow, you look incredible."

The anxiety melted away as we embraced. "Thanks, Mom, you too."

She stepped back and touched her hair. "Do you like it?"

"Yes, looks great."

Mom had been going to the same hairdresser for decades. Martha was both the main instigator of town gossip, and the reason why nearly every middle-aged woman in Mildura had short curly hair.

"Roger, bring Jane's luggage," Mom barked her order at Dad, then grabbed my hand and led me up the path as if I had no idea where I was going.

We pushed through the front door, and she dragged me down the picture-lined hallway. "Everything's just as you left it." She entered my old bedroom first and swept her hand before her with great fanfare.

She was right; everything was exactly as I remembered. I'd just stepped into a surreal time warp, and it wasn't pleasant. It crossed my mind that my distaste stemmed from having to move back into this room after I broke up with Alexander. At that time, my broken heart had sucked me into a black hole that'd dragged everything down with it.

"Take a few moments to freshen up." Mom backed up to the door with a smile. "I'll pop the kettle on. I've made a nice apple teacake for us."

"Thanks, Mom. Sounds lovely." *Although I'd much prefer wine right now.*

I sat on the bed and played my eyes around the bits and pieces cluttering the room. Time had stood still here, and it gave me an eerie sinking feeling. Horrid memories flooded back of me crying on this bed until I could barely breathe. I couldn't believe how much time I'd wasted grieving over what Alexander had done.

With a sigh, I stood and strolled to the duchess decorated with dozens of tiny trinkets. Each one had a memory. Gifts from friends. Gifts from family. Items I'd bought at the show that rolled through town once a year. None of them were precious to me. When I'd originally packed to leave Mildura, I'd taken everything of importance. My worldly belongings had filled just two suitcases. All these remaining items could be tossed into a bin and I wouldn't be upset.

I unpacked my suitcase, hung up my clothes, and headed into the kitchen where Mom stood, grinning over her teacake. She wore an apron decorated with pink frills and looked the picture of homely bliss.

"Here you go, darling. Take a seat. How was your flight?"

"It was good thanks, Mom."

"You must be exhausted."

"No, not really."

She poured tea into a fine china cup decorated with tiny purple and pink flowers. "Would you like a slice?"

"Yes please, and cream." Mom's cakes were pretty special. One day I'd learn to cook like that. I'd asked Mom to show me how to bake many times, but her teaching skills lacked patience and she usually ended up taking over.

Maybe Hunter can teach me. That thought tumbled from nowhere and it was a timely reminder of just how much my life had changed.

Mom cut a slice for each of us and then sat down opposite me.

I pushed my fork into the cake and dipped it into the cream. "So tell me what's been happening."

"Oh, you know . . ." She waved her hand. "Not much changes around here."

That was an understatement. The trip from the airport to the home I grew up in was enough to know everything was the same as it had been when I'd left. Even the kitchen I sat in was a blast from the past.

Silence consumed us as we sipped our tea. Except for the clock in the background—I'd forgotten all about the incessant ticking of that grandfather clock.

"Has Chelsea-Lea had her baby?" I couldn't resist asking.

"Oh yes, she had a baby boy. Riley. He's adorable."

"Oh . . . you've seen her?"

"Well, yes." Mom looked about as uncomfortable as someone who'd sat on a cactus. "I saw her at the Milk Bar Café. She still goes there every Friday afternoon."

"Oh, really?" If Aunty Ann's description of the demise in Chelsea's looks were even half true, then I wanted to see for myself. I glanced at the clock. "Would she be there now?"

Mom's eyes lit up. "Yes she probably would."

"Maybe I should go see her?" My brain skipped to fast-forward as I tried to envisage meeting that bitch again.

Mom put her hands together. "That's a lovely idea. It's about time you two were friends again."

I resisted poking Mom's eyeballs out. She was still oblivious to how much Chelsea-Lea had hurt me. Either that or Mom was a complete fool.

"How about I drive you up there? I've got a bit of shopping to do."

"Sounds perfect. Thanks, Mom." She had no idea of the opportunity she'd just opened up for me.

Returning to my room, I changed into the red dress with the white spots that I'd worn for Billy last week. Except this time, I put on a bra. I wore all the same accessories too and as soon as I glanced in the mirror, I knew that an outfit like this was guaranteed to turn heads in the main street of Mildura. Which was exactly the reaction I was hoping for.

Mom talked nonstop during the drive uptown, mostly complaining about how much she still had to do for the party. One of Mom's biggest faults had always been keeping up appearances. Which, I conceded, was probably why she'd maintained friendships with Alexander and Chelsea-Lea. She'd rather do that than cause a scene.

"I'm off to Foodmart, but I'll be back in about an hour or so. Does that suit?"

"Yes, that'll be great."

"You have fun, darling."

"Oh I will." She had no idea.

The door to the Milk Bar Café jingled as I stepped through and crossed the wooden floor toward the red-and-white tiled bar. The décor would be trendy and retro if it wasn't the original 1970s fit-out that the bar had opened with.

A high-pitched cackle at the back of the room confirmed Chelsea-Lea was indeed here. I'd never forget that laugh. She'd mastered the ability to produce that fake cackle whenever it was required. Resisting the urge to glance her way and see who else was there, I did something I'd never done before. I strode to the bar, slipped onto a barstool, and ordered an espresso martini. A caffeine shot was exactly what I needed.

The man behind the bar was young, and based on his English accent, I decided he was probably a backpacker, in town for the fruit-picking season. I was just glad he was someone I didn't know.

I angled my chair, and through the mirror that ran the length of the back wall behind the bar I saw the group of ladies seated in the red lounges in the far corner.

Five women were grouped there, and I recognized all of them. We'd all gone to school together. Vikki sat regal, like a lady at high tea. Her long blond hair cascaded over her shoulders in a style that hadn't changed in the twenty years I'd known her.

Nicole now had short dark hair but her full bright red lips hadn't changed. She'd discovered the retro fashion style decades ago and had been embracing it ever since.

Alice had a young child on her knee and as she hadn't been pregnant when I left, I assumed the child must have been about three years old. Tiffany also had her daughter with her, who I knew would be at least seven.

And then there was Chelsea-Lea. Aunty Ann had definitely played down the demise in Chelsea-Lea's looks. Her hair, once smooth and golden, was now wild and frizzy, reminiscent of a bad 1980s perm, and the dark skunk-stripe through the middle part highlighted just how far she'd let herself go. Her skin was pale, and even from this distance I spied red blotches on her face.

My martini arrived and I sipped the liquid courage, slowly waiting for the perfect moment to approach my old friends.

It came barely two sips later when the group of girls burst out laughing. I turned and made a show of looking at who was having so much fun in the corner. When Vikki caught my eye I waved, stood up, grabbed my martini, and headed in their direction. As a whisper broke out between them, I stuck my chest out, sucked my tummy in, and strode across the wooden floor as if it were a Paris Fashion runway.

"Hello ladies." A couple of them had confused looks on their faces, maybe pretending to not know who I was, so I flicked my hair back as if doing a big reveal. "It's me. Jane Nichols."

Five sets of eyes flicked over my body. This moment had been nearly four years in the making, and every second was pure gold.

"Jane, how lovely to see you again." Nicole was the first to stand. She stepped toward me, and we kissed each other's cheeks.

Three of the other four women followed Nicole's lead. Chelsea-Lea, however, continued to rock her baby in her arms, declining to stand. The child was dressed head to toe in shades of blue and had dark curly hair and chubby red cheeks. Her little boy looked nothing like her.

When the women sat again, I lowered my eyes to Chelsea-Lea. "You and

Alexander must be so happy." *Straight for the jugular.*
The other four women all dropped their jaws to resemble clowns at a cheesy sideshow game.
Chelsea-Lea cleared her throat. "Xander and I broke up months ago."
"Oh, I hadn't heard. That's a shame." I loaded my words with sarcasm.
I bent over getting a better look at the baby. "Wow, he looks so much like Alexander," I said, even though the baby bore no resemblance to him at all.
Chelsea-Lea squirmed and clenched then unclenched her jaw, and the other four women were a combination of bulging eyes and gaping mouths.
Enjoying Chelsea-Lea's obvious discomfort, I sipped my martini and then smiled a cute unassuming smile at the other ladies as I awaited her response.
"Xander isn't the father." Chelsea-Lea finally broke the silence.
"Oh, really? Who is?"
The rash on her neck multiplied before my eyes. "That's none of your business."
"You're right!" I cocked my head. "Just like Alexander was none of your business when we were engaged."
Chelsea-Lea shot me a death stare, then she handed her baby over to Nicole and launched to her feet. With her hands on her abundant hips, she squared off at me. I casually sipped my cocktail, however, my insides curled as tight as a metal spring.
"Alexander never loved you." She scrunched her face, making her even more unattractive.
I tilted my head, making a show of running my eyes over her plump body. "I know." I said with the lack of indifference it deserved. "He never loved you either!"
She stepped toward me, and I held my palm in her face. "Before you think of doing anything stupid, I must warn you I'm a green belt in karate, and I'm not afraid to use it."
The four ladies in the peanut gallery gasped. Chelsea-Lea, however, took a tentative step forward, her jaw clenched. "You don't belong here anymore."
I nodded. "At least you and I agree on one thing." I glanced around her. "Nice to see you again, ladies."
With one final sip of my martini, I placed the glass down, then I calmly eyeballed Chelsea-Lea. "Love what you've done to yourself."
She lashed out, her clenched fist aimed straight for my nose, but I was quicker. I gripped her hand in mine and bent it back until she fell to her knees, screaming.
Vikki and Nicole stood up, hands over their mouths.
As I held Chelsea-Lea at my feet, I bent over and looked right into the red spider veins in her eyes. "Slut." The other girls gasped, and I flung Chelsea-Lea's hand aside. I stood back, flicked my ponytail back over my shoulder, and with a broad smile, I nodded at my old friends. "Goodbye."

I turned and my high heels tracked my departure across the wooden floor as their high-pitched chatter filled the room. I wiped my sweating palms down my thighs, and my heart pounded as I strode out of the Milk Bar Café. But once I was outside, I smiled the beautiful, broad smile that came with sweet revenge.

"Jane!" A high-pitched voice sounded behind me, and I turned to watch Vikki scurrying my way.

"What do you want Vikki?"

"I . . . I just wanted to say I'm sorry."

I put my fists on my hips. "Oh? What for? Fucking Alexander?" I didn't normally say that word aloud, but once I watched her reaction I was glad I had.

Her eyes darted about, and a flush of red blazed her cheeks. Finally, she shook her head. "Yes. I shouldn't have done that. I'm so sorry."

"Thank you for your apology. But don't expect me to forgive you—what you did was despicable."

"I know." She lowered her eyes to the road. "I know."

Capitalizing on her discomfort, I asked the burning question. "So, who is the father of the baby?"

Her eyes darted to mine. Small-town gossip was her specialty. "We don't know. Even Chelsea-Lea doesn't know. They have to do paternity tests to find out who'll pay child support."

I scrunched up my nose, showing my disgust. "How many men?"

"Three. Two of them were married."

I shook my head. "She doesn't deserve to have friends."

Vikki shrugged. "She's better to have as my friend than my enemy."

Maybe that was true, but it wasn't something I could ever do. "That poor baby."

Vikki sighed, and I took that as my cue to walk away.

"Jane," she called from behind me, and I turned back to her. "You look amazing."

"Thank you." I spun on my heel, and the sweet revenge smile was back on my face and remained there all the way up the main street.

Mom was loading the car with groceries as I arrived. "Oh, did you have a lovely time with Chelsea-Lea.?

I nodded. "It was interesting."

As we drove home, Mom continued her monologue about what needed to be done for the party. We arrived, unpacked the groceries and Mom, Dad and I spent the evening working through Mom's abundant list of trivial things she wanted done. By the time I retired to my bedroom I was exhausted.

Alone at last, I replayed in my mind the joy I'd felt over bringing Chelsea-Lea to her knees. I'd never intended for our confrontation to end like that, but in hindsight, not only was it almost to be expected, given her hot-headedness, it was also perfect.

I crawled under my covers and, deeply satisfied with my encounter with my ex-best friend, sleep came quickly.

* * *

I woke early the next day because of the clattering of pots and pans in the kitchen. After I showered and dressed, I made my way to the noisy din. Mom was ridiculously flustered, and the morning was a blur of preparation, cooking, and complaints about Dad not helping prepare for his party. I was relieved when ten o'clock rolled around. I promised Mom I'd be back in three hours, walked out the front door, and headed toward my favorite relative's home.

Aunty Ann hadn't changed one bit. Her welcome hug was homey, her giant boobs were still the majority of her body and her smile was quick and genuine. She led me out to her back porch where she'd set up the table like an English garden tea party. A lace tablecloth crossed over a highly patterned floral one, and she'd set out her fine china with the gold trimmings.

While I pulled out a chair and sat, she poured tea and placed the cup in front of me. My mouth salivated just looking at the delicious cake positioned between us. It was decorated with perfectly spaced caramelized pineapple slices on top and looked as good as any award-winning treat.

She picked up a long knife. "Would you like some cake?"

"Of course, with extra cream please."

She chuckled. "You always did like your sweets."

"Still do."

She cut a huge piece of cake and dolloped two spoonful's of cream. "Tell me about the Gold Coast," she said as she held the cake forward.

As we ate the delicious treat, our conversation flowed freely, and for the umpteenth time I wished Aunty Ann had been my mother.

"So . . ." She winked. "Do you have a boyfriend?"

"I already told you, I have a few men chasing me."

"Excellent." She rubbed her hands together. "Tell me all about them."

"You'd love Henry; he's a bit older than me. He's suave, gentle and fun."

"Oh, he sounds lovely."

"Then there's Corben. He was a Mr. Universe finalist. His arms are like this." I imitated Corben's bulging biceps.

"Oh, yummy."

I chuckled as I forked tea cake into my mouth. It was light and fluffy, with just the right amount of sweetness. "This's yummy."

"I'm glad you like it; it's a new recipe. Now tell me, do these men look after you?"

The concern in her eyes was touching, and I reached over to hold her hand. "They do, Aunty Ann. All of them are really sweet."

"All? There are more men?" Her eyes lit up.

"Yes, there's Billy—he's a cowboy and a true gentleman. And Hunter—he's a chocolatier, and he's really handsome. You'd love every one of them."

"How do you keep up with them all?"

I chuckled. "They have trouble keeping up with me."

She burst out laughing and followed it up with her usual cough. It sounded even more confronting in person and had me wondering just how healthy Aunty Ann was. When she finished, she wiped tears from her eyes with an embroidered handkerchief.

"Are you okay?"

She fanned her hand at me. "Oh yes, just this silly cough. Can't seem to shake it."

She'd had the cough for as long as I could remember.

Over the next couple of hours on the porch, I told my favorite relative all about my life on the Gold Coast. My job. My best friend and her family. My karate. We spent more time talking about the men in my life, and when I told her all about last night's encounter with Chelsea-Lea she laughed until she crumbled into another bout of coughing.

When she regained her breath and we sipped our tea for a bit, I asked her a question that I'd wanted to ask her for most of my life.

"Aunty Ann, have you ever been in love?"

Her eyes flittered down to her teacup, and I sensed she was reluctant to answer. She licked her lips and adjusted her bra strap, and as I waited, I knew I'd touched on a difficult subject.

I reached forward and put my hand over hers. "You don't have to tell me if you don't want to."

She sighed. "It's not that. We've always been honest with each other. But I'd hoped you'd never ask me this."

I frowned and unsure what I should say, I remained silent and just squeezed her hand.

"I was in love once. Deep, deeply in love." She placed her hand over her heart. "The kind of love that makes it impossible to breathe when he's near you, yet it's equally impossible to breathe when he's not."

I was yet to find a relationship like that, but by the wistful look on her face and the love in her eyes, I knew this man had truly touched her heart. "What happened?"

She turned her pale blue eyes to me and sighed. "He fell in love with my sister."

I blinked as I tried to process her words. The implication hit me like a lightning bolt. "Dad? You loved Dad? But how? What—"

"He never knew—neither of them did. I never had the courage to tell him how I felt, and when Margaret told me she was sweet on Roger, what could I do?"

"Oh, Aunty Ann." I couldn't even begin to image what it would've been like to see the man you loved with another woman, especially your own sister.

She sighed long and deep. "I've gone over it a million times. If I'd just told him how I felt, maybe my life would've been so different."

"You never met anyone else?"

She flicked her hand. "In a small town like this, you only get one shot and I blew it."

I knew exactly what she meant. "It's not too late, you know."

This had her laughing until tears rolled down her cheeks. "I wouldn't know what to do with a man now, and I'd have a heart attack if he tried to kiss me."

She started giggling, and I laughed along with her.

Aunty Ann was lovely to talk to and the hours drifted away too quickly. My heart grew heavy when I realized it was time to leave, but I'd promised Mom and Dad that I'd be back to help decorate.

We kissed and hugged goodbye, and Aunty Ann came out onto her front porch to watch me walk home.

Mom was beside herself with stress over the party. According to her, nothing was going right, although I couldn't see anything that'd gone wrong. When I'd been living at home, my parents had rarely entertained. If on the rare occasion people came to visit it would be with weeks of planning to accommodate a simple backyard barbeque. If something spontaneous happened, Mom would have a quasi heart attack.

I sighed at her fussing about in the kitchen. "What do you want me to do?"

"Oh, there's so much."

"Mom, calm down. Just tell me one thing."

"Don't tell me to calm down. This stupid party was your father's idea, and now he and Tyler have decided to play golf before they even come home from the airport."

"It's Dad's birthday. You should be pleased he's spending time with his son."

She huffed. "The whole backyard needs to be decorated."

"Okay, leave that to me."

Grateful to be away from her, I stepped out onto the back porch, and with giant six and zero balloons dancing in the slight breeze beside me, I unpacked grocery bags full of cheesy party decorations. Determined to get through this without getting gray hairs, I sat on a chair and set about pumping up all the other balloons with the helium tank that came with them.

Within two hours I had the backyard transformed into a typical party setting fitting for small-town Mildura. Purple and white streamers hung between the trees and the porch posts. Balloons were secured to every possible anchor point, and I'd positioned plastic cups alongside every available cooler Mom and Dad had been able to borrow from the neighbors.

Tyler came bounding into the backyard with the energy of the professional football player that he was and wrapped his arms around me. "How's my little sis?"

"I'm great."

He stepped back to examine me. "You look amazing."

I did a little curtsy. "Thank you."

"No. I mean, wow. That Gold Coast life is really good for you."

I smiled at his enthusiasm. "Thank you. I love it there."

He leaned in to whisper, "Lucky we escaped, huh?"

"You're not kidding." I chuckled. "I would've ended up like Chelsea-Lea."

He frowned. "Have you seen her?"

"Made a point of meeting her last night."

"And?"

I told him all about it, right down to dropping Chelsea-Lea to her knees, and he burst out laughing. "Oh God, I wish I'd been there. You know that's going to be all over town by now."

I cocked my head. "Good."

"Have you told Mom?"

"Nope. She thinks Chelsea-Lea and I should still be friends. Hey, did you know Dad and Alexander are fishing buddies?"

"No! What?"

I shook my head. How was it that everyone understood why this relationship between my parents and my ex-fiancé was so wrong except for them?

"How's my beautiful daughter?" Dad stepped onto the back porch and removed his faded old cap.

"Happy birthday, Dad." We wrapped our arms around each other, and he planted a sloppy, wet kiss on my cheek.

"It's so good to have both my children home." He pulled us in for a group hug, as he'd been doing since we were little kids.

"Roger!" Mom's voice boomed from the kitchen. Dad kissed my forehead and silently slinked off in that direction. It was a move I'd seen him do dozens of times over.

The final pieces of the party setup came together as the sun began to set and an hour before guests were due to arrive, I excused myself to freshen up and change.

I took particular care with my hair, styling it the way Lolita had suggested with some tucked up to the back and the rest coaxed into soft waves. My makeup also took a fair bit of my time, but I wanted to get it perfect.

The black lace dress felt every bit as amazing as it had the first time I'd put it on, and as I stood before the mirror I tried to tame my tumbling emotions. I was equally as apprehensive as I was excited about seeing Alexander again.

At the sound of the first guests arriving, I pulled my shoes on and buckled them at the sides of my ankles, dabbed on my trusty Bobbi Brown Retro Red lippy, planted a huge smile on my face, and stepped out of my old bedroom.

"Wow, look at you." My dad's comment had everybody turning and my heart skipping in delighted beats. I stepped forward to greet the neighbors who'd been living next door for more than forty years.

"Hello Janice, Don, how are you?"

As the elderly couple hugged me to their chests I was surprised at how much they'd aged in the four years since I'd seen them.

"We're good, luvvy. You look amazing."

"Thank you." I turned to Mom, who was staring at me like she couldn't work out who I was. "Mom, would you like me to take Janice and Donald out the back?"

"Yes. Yes, of course."

"Come on then." As I led the way I made idle chit-chat, asking them about their children and grandchildren.

People came in a steady flow for the next twenty or so minutes, and with each new arrival I braced to see the man I'd once loved. As the minutes ticked by, I began to wonder if he'd chickened out.

My dress had the desired effect, and every person who greeted me said a similar version of, "Wow, you look amazing."

The party had been going for nearly an hour when a weird hush came over the crowd. A prickle rolled up my spine, and I didn't need to turn around to know Alexander had arrived. Despite the pounding in my chest, I carried on flitting from one guest to another, pretending to be unaware of him.

I did, however, feel his eyes on me. The hairs on my neck bristled at the intrusion.

About twenty minutes later, Mom approached my side. "I've put some things in the oven—can you watch them for me? I need to chat with Molly about something."

"Sure, Mom."

She pranced off through the crowd, making a point of saying hello to everyone she passed. I excused myself from Mom and Dad's long-time friends Robert and Mary and made my way into the kitchen. A group of people erupted into laughter and as I looked through the kitchen window I saw Tyler in amongst them, doing a weird dance. It looked like his joy at being the centre of attention hadn't changed.

I turned, and as I bent over to peer in through the oven door, I felt a presence in the room that had my skin crawling. Without even looking, I knew it was him.

Here we go. The moment four years in the making had arrived.

I stood up, flicked my hair over my shoulder, and turned to him. The counter between us was a blessing. "Hello Alexander."

Just looking at him repulsed me. I found it hard to believe I'd once found him attractive. His eyebrows were too bushy, his jaw too large, and his complexion insipid.

"Hi Jane. You look incredible." He'd put on at least twenty pounds since I'd last seen him, and there was more than just a little salt and pepper in his dark hair.

His compliment was worthless to me, but following Henry's rule, I acknowledged it with a nod. "Thanks."

"It's great to have you home." He said it like I was here to stay.

"This isn't my home anymore." My heart thundered in my chest as I stared at the man who'd once captured it and then systematically shattered it into millions of pieces. His eyes were a fraction wider than I remembered, showing whites that had a tinge of yellow.

He cleared his throat. "I heard what you did to Chelsea-Lea."

"She deserved it."

He swallowed loudly enough for me to hear. "I guess so." His lip twitched.

"You two didn't last long."

He squeezed his eyes shut as if searching for the perfect response.

"Was she worth it?"

His eyes shot open, looked into mine for a second, and then, to my disgust they fluttered to my cleavage. I wanted to vomit as the silence fell upon us like a concrete blanket.

"I can't believe how amazing you look." He came around the counter, closing the space between us, and with each inch he drew closer, bile inched up my throat. His presence was a hideous dark shadow, and I fought the urge to run. "I'm sorry, Jane."

I flicked a wisp of hair out of my eyes. "For what exactly? Fucking dozens of women while we were engaged, or breaking my heart?"

He reached with his right hand and I braced for his touch, but he placed his palm on the counter at my side, splaying his fingers as if he needed it for support. "I'm sorry for everything. I've missed you."

"Your words mean nothing to me." My stomach twisted into angry knots, churning the acid that'd lain dormant for a very long time.

His hand crept closer, seeking mine, his dark eyes pleading.

I clenched my fist, clamped my jaw, and rammed my knee into his groin as hard as I could. He buckled over howling and fell to the kitchen floor in a fetal position.

"You worthless bastard. I hope you rot in hell." I stepped around him and ignored the dinging oven as I walked from the kitchen and out the back door. It seemed like every single person in the backyard stared at me, and with each stride I made toward the wine glass I'd left on the table, I felt more in command of my own mind and, more importantly, my soul.

Dad glanced my way before he raced inside, however Mom came up to me, her lips pulled into a straight line. "What'd you do?" Her voice was vehement, loaded with shock and anger.

"Something I should've done years ago."

Mom's eyes grew wide. She clutched her chest and a red flush raced up her neck.

A clap started at the back of the crowd and I turned to see Aunty Ann beaming as she brought her hands together over and over. My brother joined her, then raised his fingers to his mouth to release an ear-piercing whistle. Another couple of people joined in, and soon everybody seemed to be clapping and cheering. Except, of course my mother.

Out the corner of my eye, I saw Alexander rise to his feet, and I turned to watch that piece of shit be escorted from the house by both mom and dad. Tyler bounded onto the porch next to me. "Let's get this party going." He bent over, dialed up the volume on the music, then picked me up and twirled me around. "So proud of you, Sis."

Tears of relief stung my eyes as everything spun past in a kaleidoscope of color and movement.

The rest of the evening went by in a blur, and not all of it was pleasant. I felt dreadful for creating a scene at my father's party. Dad, however, was not as upset as my mother seemed to be. Hours later, after everybody had left, we set about cleaning up, but Mom claimed she had a headache and vanished to her bedroom.

By the time I crawled into bed I was emotionally and physically drained.

* * *

The next morning, I could've cut the air with a spoon. Mom fussed about in the kitchen as if nothing unusual had happened, and Tyler, Dad and I pretended the same with her.

Mid-morning, Dad offered to drive me to the airport and I said goodbye to Tyler, and we made promises to call each other soon. I hugged Mom and kissed her goodbye in the kitchen; she didn't bother to walk me out to the car.

As we drove away, I had a distinct feeling this would be the last time I'd ever return to the home I grew up in. It surprised me that I was at peace with that notion.

"Dad, I'm sorry about what I did last night."
He placed his hand on my leg. "You don't need to be sorry. I do. We do. We should never have invited Xander. In fact, I'm terribly sorry that I even spoke to him at all after what he did to you."
I sighed a huge sigh. "Thank you, Dad. That means so much to me. But Mom—"
"Oh, pfft, don't worry about her." He flicked his hand. "She'll get over it."
"Are you sure?"
"Of course. She just doesn't like to cause a scene." He started to chuckle. "You'll be the talk of the town for weeks. Maybe months. "
We laughed together for a while, and it was really nice. Then I turned to him slightly. "He deserved it, Dad."
"Yes I know."
I blinked at him. His response was perfect, and the knots in my stomach gently unraveled.
We pulled over at the ten-minute drop-off zone at the Mildura airport, and Dad hopped out of the car with me. He lifted my suitcase from the trunk, and when he opened his arms, I stepped into his embrace.
"I'm so proud of you, sweetheart." The sincerity in his voice made my heart swell.
"Thank you, Dad. That means so much to me."
We kissed goodbye, and I made my way into the airport terminal.
During the flight home, a jumble of mixed emotions rolled through me, but the overwhelming one was relief. However, as the miles drifted away, I acknowledged that I didn't feel as much satisfaction over my public humiliation of Alexander as I'd thought I would.
The hurt and sadness he'd brought into my life had dissipated long, long ago.
A couple in the seat ahead of me snuggled into each other and I smiled at how in love they seemed. That was when it hit me—I'd never been in love with Alexander. It had been an illusion. A pathetic, insecure, desperate illusion, and if we'd married I would've been destined for a miserable life.
Now, though, I was the happiest I'd been in years. Maybe ever.
Dropping Alexander to his knees last night had nothing to do with that. I'd created my happiness. I was the driver behind my destiny and as we touched down at Coolangatta airport on the Gold Coast, I turned my focus to my immediate destiny, Mr. Hunter McCall, who I had the pleasure of meeting in about two hours.
By the time I'd unpacked, showered, and done my makeup, I was so ready for a session of red-hot sex with my handsome chocolatier that my weekend in Mildura already seemed like a distant memory.
With my blond wig in place, I went to my closet and decided to wear the second dress I'd bought for my Friday night in Mildura. This outfit was the

one Lolita had decided would be perfect for clubbing. The idea of that happening in my hometown had been laughable, but I was still glad Lolita had insisted I buy it.

The dress was a cute coral color, short in length, revealing at the bust, and perfect for both Memphis and Mr. McCall. I slipped it on, and added a chunky gold necklace, a bracelet, and long, dangly earrings the lovely sales assistant at the shop had talked me into buying. For my shoes, I tugged a pair of colorful Mollini stilettos from the back of the closet. I'd bought these shoes with the very first pay-check I'd earned at the Hot Horizon Hotel.

The shoes had a little peep-toe at the front, and I was grateful I'd taken the time to paint my toenails before I went to Mildura. I did up the strap around my ankle, stood up, and glanced at my reflection in the mirror. It was perfect in so many ways. This dress was so lovely on me that I decided even Jane would wear it.

I grabbed my Michael Kors black bag and tossed in my essentials. With a quick glance at the clock, I noted that I was still a little early, but decided to head downstairs anyway. The elevator took forever to arrive and when it pinged open, there he was. *My hero.*

"Just Memphis!" His lovely blue eyes lit up, and he wiggled his brows. Once again I hadn't thought to give Memphis a surname, and I was already kicking myself.

"Oh, hi Hunter." I tugged my lip between my teeth. Simultaneously, we both took a step forward, placed our hands on each other's waist, and leaned in to kiss a cheek. He smelt divine, a masculine mix of soap and spice.

"You look lovely."

"Thank you. So do you." I was struck once again at how gorgeous he was. The two-day growth he'd had last time was gone; this time he was clean-shaven, showing off the sexy dimple in his chin.

We turned to face the mirrored doors, and I tried not to stare. Hunter was about four inches taller than me, his shoulders were broad, and his bone structure was strong and symmetrical. His tanned flesh finished off his already striking Adonis look.

"Did you have a nice weekend?"

I huffed as I rolled my eyes and instantly regretted it. The last thing I wanted to do was talk about Alexander.

"Ooooh, maybe not, huh?" The softness in his gaze had my heart melting and in the time it took the elevator to reach the lobby, I swear the tiny mirrored cube heated up several notches.

The elevator doors pinged open, providing the perfect distraction from his question, and as we walked side by side to the Triple H Bar, I resisted looking over at reception.

As if we'd planned it, we both headed toward the bar stools we'd sat in last time. He pulled one out for me to sit and placed his hand on my shoulder. "Would you like a wine? Shaw & Smith, isn't it?"

He remembered! "Yes please."

Hunter turned away, and it was impossible not to ogle his bottom as his cheeks bulged and flexed beneath his khaki chinos.

He leaned on the counter to place his order with Tania, and despite his checkered button-up shirt, the toning in his arms was unmissable. He smiled, and once again I was reminded that Hunter McCall could be the lead actor in one of those survival shows.

Carrying an ice bucket with a bottle of wine in it and two wine glasses crossed over at the top, he returned, placed it onto the bar in front of us, and slipped onto the stool at my side. Our knees touched, and my heart fluttered at the familiarity of this simple move.

He filled our glasses, handed one to me, and held up his own glass. "Cheers."

We chinked them together. "Cheers."

As I sipped my wine, I studied Hunter's hand around the stem of the glass. His fingers were strong, manly, and his nails neatly trimmed. I couldn't wait to get those hands on me, in me. I nearly giggled at my naughty thought.

"What are you smiling at?"

"Oh ummm . . . nothing."

"It didn't look like nothing." He raised one eyebrow, and I had a feeling he could wait out my answer all night.

I decided on the truth and hoped like hell I didn't look like a fool. "I was just thinking how glad I was that I called you."

When he smiled, his whole face lit up and his eyes twinkled in the discreet bar lighting. "I didn't think you were ever going to call." He reached his hand forward and placed it on my knee just below the hem of my dress.

His warm touch had my heart doing a little flip. Hunter had a hint of a warrior in him, a man who'd do anything to save a loved one, yet he combined that with a visible softness.

"Did you want to tell me about your weekend?" His eyes were vivid blue and the red lighting had their edges fading to an interesting violet color. But most of all, his eyes showed his genuine interest in my answer, and after a quick debate through my head, I realized I wanted to tell him. I wanted him to know everything about me. But that was impossible. Hunter knew me as Memphis. The irony of the situation nearly had me in tears.

"I had to go home for my dad's sixtieth."

His strong arched eyebrows drew together. "You don't get on with your parents?"

"They're okay, but they invited my ex to the party."

"Oh." He clicked his fingers. "The cheating bastard ex-fiancé."

I burst out laughing. "Wow, you have a good memory."

"Yes, so I've been told. What happened?"

As we sipped glass after glass of wine, I relayed everything that had happened, from the heated encounter with Chelsea-Lea to dropping Alexander to the kitchen floor. Hunter was a great listener, and it felt so right telling him about my whole weekend. But at the end of my story, I sipped my wine and wondered if the brutality of my two encounters over the weekend had me sounding like a psycho nutter.

"If you asked me, I'd say you had a great weekend."

I blinked at him. "Really?"

"Sure. I've always wondered what I'd say to my cheating ex if I ever ran into her again. Especially now that I've had a few years to think about it. You must feel immense relief."

I nodded. His insight was a blessing. "Actually, I do."

He put his glass down and slipped forward on his stool, positioning his legs on either side of mine. "You know, sex is also the perfect cure."

I giggled. "Cure for what?"

The blue and violet medley in his eyes captured me in so many ways. "Just about everything."

"Is that right?"

"Uh-huh. And chocolate. Chocolate fixes everything, too."

I laughed now, a deep, hearty laugh, and after the weekend I'd had it felt so good. "In that case, I think you should take me to your room and rescue me."

He leaned over and I closed my eyes, silently begging him to kiss me. Barely a breath later, my wish was granted and I melted into his caress. His hands curled up my thighs, and as our breaths mingled every slice of angst from my weekend fluttered away.

He pulled back and ran his tongue over his lips. "Would you like to come to my room?"

I nodded, certain my voice wouldn't work. With our fingers knotted together, we strode from the bar to the elevator. The doors opened at the press of the button and we stepped in, turned, and faced the mirrored doors. He nudged his shoulder to mine, grinning, and I smiled, too.

Hunter turned to me, curled his fingers around my neck, and brought his lips down to mine. Butterflies danced across my stomach at his touch, and I pressed my hands to his chest. The muscles I found there were chiseled to perfection. I reached up on my tippy-toes, and as his thumb glided across my cheek our tongues explored. Just like everything about Hunter, his kiss was perfection.

My heart wept when the doors pinged open and our lips parted. With my hand in his, he led me to his room which was four apartments up from mine. He opened the door and stepped aside for me to walk ahead of him.

As the door clicked closed, I placed my bag over the back of the chair and turned to him. Hunter took my breath away.

He ran his hand through his blond waves. "Would you like to try my chocolate again?"

Sensing that he had some kind of plan, I nodded. "I'd love to."

"Okay, take a seat." He pulled out a dining chair, and as he strolled to the kitchen, I ran my tongue over my lips, tasting him again.

Hunter fussed about behind the counter for a minute or so before he returned with a glossy black chocolate box and a bottle of wine. He placed them on the table and fetched two wine glasses from the cupboard over the microwave.

"I want to introduce you to my European range."

"Oh, okay. Sounds like fun."

"I did a three-week tour around the Italian Riviera in August and discovered some fascinating new techniques. You're one of the first to try them."

His eyes were electric with anticipation, and I felt incredible pressure to please him. He lifted the box, and I enjoyed both a beautiful presentation of carefully crafted chocolates and delightful aromas. "Which one would you like?"

"Hmmm. How do I pick? They all look incredible."

"You chose the one that appeals to you the most."

I surveyed the delectable selection, and after much deliberation, I pointed at a miniature dark chocolate corrugated cup that was topped with a chocolate lid that looked like it'd been painted in red wine by a master artist.

"Taste it." His tongue flicked over his lip, and my heart fluttered at the sexiness of it.

I plucked the chocolate from the box and under his watchful gaze, I bit into it. To my surprise it had a liquid center, and I just managed to catch it before it dribbled all over me. It was a flavor explosion of chocolate and lemon, sweet and tart and utterly delicious.

"You missed some." He leaned forward and ran his tongue over my lower lip. It was a highly erotic move that had my heart thumping. It took all my might not to jump into his lap, wrap my arms around him, and kiss him until we both gasped for breath.

"Did you like it?" The pleading in his eyes confirmed how important my response was to him.

"It really was delicious. The flavor was interesting, complex."

"That was my lemon meringue. Limoncello and a touch of coconut meringue in a dark chocolate cup."

"Wow, yes." I ran my tongue around my mouth, savoring it all. "That's exactly what I can taste."

He handed me a glass of wine, and the deep red color of the liquid caught in the downlights.

"Tell me about Italy," I said.

His eyes lit up, and as I sipped the liquid heaven he mesmerized me with tales about all the wonderful people he'd met and how complete strangers had welcomed him into their kitchens to share their family recipes. He spoke with passion and with his hands. His stories were interesting and fun, and I could've stayed there and listened to him all night long. We drank the wine, we savored the chocolates, and the more stories he told me, the more I wanted to hear. Hunter was living my dream, and every new place he mentioned convinced me of what I already knew: I needed to travel.

Hunter's pale, perfectly kissable lips could be ignored no longer, and I leaned forward on my chair, placed my hands above his knees, and kissed him. It wasn't an innocent kiss, like shy Jane would do—this was a Memphis kiss, filled with fiery passion that would leave him with no doubt that I wanted more. Our tongues danced in a delicious tango and when he moaned, I slipped off my chair and went to him. I hoisted up my dress and as I straddled his hips, I wrapped my arms around his neck and he opened his mouth, allowing my tongue to explore him more.

He ran his hands up and down my back, and our passion became more heated by the second. Before I knew it, we were both naked, and he was rolling a condom onto his enormous erection. I led him to the bed and pushed him backward. He chuckled as he fell onto the sheets, his cock bouncing up and down with the momentum.

I crawled up the bed and straddled him. As he squeezed my breasts and his cock prodded my butt cheek, I kissed him, driving my tongue into his mouth, determined to taste more of him. Hunter was an incredible kisser, and I'd be happy to do this all night long, but my throbbing pussy wanted more, demanded more. Obliging that urge, I reached down between my legs, wrapped my hand around his cock, and used that hard muscle to pleasure my clit. As I sat up on my knees, I rubbed his penis along the length of my pussy. His cock was hot and hard and teased my clit in all the right ways, and in a flash, I screamed out as I climaxed.

Our eyes met, and the inferno of desire blazing in his enlarged pupils was mind-blowing.

Curling my back to get the angle right, I aimed his cock at my pulsing vagina and sat down onto him, impaling myself with his length. He filled me right to the hilt, and it felt so fucking good. With my hands on his chiseled torso, I locked my eyes with his as I eased up and down. I pushed back as I did it so his length was hard against the inside front of my vagina, and it was a delicious move that I repeated over and over.

Within seconds another orgasm hit me as his cock slammed into something truly exquisite deep inside me.

Hunter reached up, clutched my shoulders, and pulled me sideways onto the bed. He remained inside me and with my left side on the bed, he stayed on his knees and positioned us so I had my left leg between his legs and my right knee folded up to my chest. I reached up and played with his nipples, squeezing, flicking, and rolling the hard buds between my fingers.

In this position, I was able to rock my hips in time to his penetration, and his cock played with something new inside me that begged for more. He reached down to thumb my clit, and I gasped as the sensation overload nearly shot me right off the covers. With each thrust he flicked my clit, timing it with intense precision. The orgasm building inside me was enormous, mammoth even, and I raised my leg, pointing my toes to the ceiling, giving him more to play with.

His thrusting hit fever pitch, and he rammed me fast and hard. I screamed out, and he released a guttural growl as he drove his cock deep, deep into me. After a few more thrusts with his jaw clenched and his fingers vise-like on my ass, he screamed out as he came inside me.

We were both gasping for breath as he began to slow, and I was truly sad when he pulled his cock out of me for the last time. He crawled up beside me so we lay facing each other. Now I had a close-up view of my hero, and I loved what I saw. He reached up to cup my cheek. "I'm so glad you called."

I chuckled. "Me too."

He curled his arm under my neck, and I nestled into his chest. This simple move had my heart fluttering, and a wonderful sense of contentment enveloped me. I rested my hand on his chiseled abs, closed my eyes and listened to the steady beat of his heart. I'd officially fallen into heaven.

I started to nod off to sleep, and it required a great effort to drag myself up from his side.

"Can't you stay?" His request melted my heart, and I was seconds away from accepting when I remembered I was Memphis. The risk of getting through the night without revealing my horrible lie was too high.

Hunter wanted Memphis to stay, not Plain Jane, and the quicker I got out of there, the better. "I'm sorry. I can't." My heart broke into a million little pieces at the situation I'd put myself in.

I rolled off the bed and dressed as quickly as I could. With my shoes now on, I turned to him. He was lying on his side, the sheet draped over his legs, his head propped up on his hand. "Thank you for a perfect evening."

"I hope you don't wait so long to call me next time." His words were a beautiful melody and an utter catastrophe at the same time.

I blew him a kiss, and with one last glance at my sexy chocolatier, I grabbed my bag and walked out his door before I blurted out my dirty little secret.

It wasn't until I was in my room that my racing heart began to settle. I undressed, had a quick shower, slipped into my pajamas, and brushed my teeth.

At my bed, I reached for my diary. I turned to the 22nd of October, and at the top of the page I wrote *Mr. Hunter McCall Room 17*. I detailed our wonderful date, taking immense care to describe our incredible sex. I wrote about how much I'd enjoyed his company and in particular listening to his delightful stories about travel and food. Hunter had not only made my heart skip a beat, but he'd captured my mind too. He'd saved me from dwelling on the tumultuous weekend in Mildura, and with that thought I wrote *My Raunchy Rescue*.

I truly enjoyed being with Hunter, but the problem was he only knew me as Memphis. How, after three times with him, did I tell him that the woman he'd been sleeping with was a lying imposter? I'd need an ocean of ink to detail the crazy thoughts shooting through my brain. My tumbling emotions were insurmountable, and I simply couldn't put them into the right words on the page. After an eternity of scribbling, I gave up.

I flipped my diary shut, crawled under the covers, and as I closed my eyes, I pictured Hunter and every inch of his amazing body lying beside me.

A tear tumbled down my cheek as I wondered if he would ever get to know the real Jane Nichols.

Kitty Kendall

29ᵀᴴ OCTOBER
BEER AND BOOBS
Room 35 - Hot Horizon Hotel

The weekend ahead promised to be an amazing sensory overload. For the first time since I'd started working at the Hot Horizon Hotel, we were hosting the Total Fitness Expo. Eye candy had never been hotter, and it was impossible not to drool at the bodies that'd been traipsing through my lobby since my shift started an hour ago.
So far I'd been unlucky in my quest to find a man for this week's sexual challenge. Not one available contender had walked through the sliding glass doors of the Hot Horizon Hotel and with only eight weeks remaining of the year, I had every intention of fulfilling my mission. I was excited about what and in particular who was on my agenda before New Year's Eve arrived.
Now, with a hundred or so hot bodies to choose from, I was quietly confident this week's challenge would be fulfilled before Sunday night rolled around.
Tonight was set-up night for the Total Fitness Expo and from tomorrow morning through the next two days, thirty-two stall holders would be showing off a variety of items that could and should improve one's fitness. That ranged from equipment, to clothes, to supplements, and a variety of other products I'd never seen before.

They were a happy bunch, and after listening to their excited chatter for an hour or so, I set the 'back in five minutes' sign on the counter and headed into the conference room to see the enthusiasm for myself.

It was impossible to know where to look, and as my eyes flitted from one hunk to the next I wondered if I'd died and gone to heaven. A man standing on what looked like an oval skateboard caught my eye, and I strolled toward him.

"Hello, I'm Jane Nichols, the night manager here. How's everything going?"

"Hi Jane, I'm Xavier. We're nearly set up. Had a few issues with the power cords, but it's all good now."

"Excellent. So what've you got here?"

His eyes lit up. "Here, jump on." Xavier was the epitome of what a fitness instructor should look like, from his perfectly toned bulging muscles to his tanned flesh to his pearly white teeth.

"Oh, okay." Grateful that I'd worn my flat shoes today, I stepped onto the machine and had to clench my stomach muscles and center my balance to stay upright.

"Hang onto my shoulder."

If you insist. I did as he instructed and felt the corded muscle beneath his flesh as I clutched his shoulder.

"Did you notice that you needed to engage your core muscles?" He glided his hand over his tight-fitting T-shirt and nestled it over his non-existent belly.

"Yes, I did."

He grinned as he pressed a button on a remote control he'd removed from his pocket. In a flash, the skateboard vibrated and I giggled at the new sensation and clutched his shoulder tighter.

"Now try to let go." His smile was extraordinary, worthy of any toothbrush commercial.

I raised my hands and needed to engage my core muscles to keep upright.

"See how it works?"

"Yes, it's great." I giggled at the vibrations rattling through me, teasing all the nerves in my body.

"Ready for more?" He wriggled his neat eyebrows.

"Sure."

He dialed it up. The vibrations hit a new tempo, and I squealed and held onto his shoulder again.

"Let go, you cheater."

Giggling, I let go and grabbed him again. Over and over I tried it, each time letting go for just that little bit longer until soon I was able to stand upright unassisted.

"See? You're a natural." He seemed as proud of me as I was.

I laughed at his encouragement. "Okay, I've had enough now."

Xavier jabbed the remote. The machine stilled, however my body continued to sizzle. "You're still feeling it, aren't you?"

"Uh-huh."

"That's the beauty of it. Ten minutes on this machine and you'll feel it working for another ten minutes after you step off. It's brilliant." His smile positively dazzled, and if I wasn't careful I'd be handing over my credit card. With the way I was feeling, in addition to the way he was looking at me, I had no doubt Xavier was in for a very successful weekend. I had to escape, and quick, before I'd need to find room in my apartment to fit this wonderful device.

I took a brochure, to which he'd stapled his card, and I thanked him for his excellent demonstration. He exaggerated a sad face as I said goodbye, and I giggled as I carried on strolling through the stalls.

At the supplement stand, a woman with boobs perky enough to rival Lolita's encouraged me to sample the protein shake and power bars. They were so good, I promised to come back and buy some tomorrow, and I meant it.

At one of the clothing stalls, I eyed off a lime green Lycra top and matching shorts set that was just to die for. I asked the young man with the tribal tattoo adorning his bulging bicep to put it aside for me. He obliged with a smile, and I carried on. At this rate, I was going to spend my night's pay before the conference had even started.

Laughter at the back of the hall caught my attention, and I headed in that direction. An elaborate stand had somehow been created to replicate an old-fashioned curved caravan. Out the front were picnic chairs and tables nestled on fake grass, and everyone around the caravan held a clear plastic cup with amber liquid inside. I couldn't help but smile as I made my way through the crowd to see what the fuss was about.

The man behind the counter was unlike any other man in the room. He was a tad scruffy, with honey-colored hair that met his shoulders and blended in with his full beard.

"Hi, I'm Jane Nichols, the night manager of the hotel. How's everything going?"

"Well hello, Jane. Let me guess—you're a wine drinker, right?"

I chuckled. "Yes, you got me."

"Well, we need to fix that. Let me introduce you to my low-carb, low-calorie, high-nutrient brew." He handed a plastic cup to me. "I'm Frankie, by the way."

"Hi Frankie. Do you make this yourself?"

"Sure do. Wild Horses is my brewery up in the Adelaide Hills. It used to be a horse stud, hence the name, but we make more money out of the beer than we do the horses. I've been perfecting my beer since before I was legal to drink."

I felt the pressure to like his drink and took a tentative sip, but the taste grabbed my tongue, and before I knew it, I scrunched up my face.

"Okay, so that was Bucking Bronco. By the look on your face, I'd say you're a sweets kind of girl. Let me guess—chocolate mud cakes are your thing. Am I right?"

I was pleased he wasn't upset with my reaction and nodded in response as he took the plastic cup from me and tossed it into a waste bin.

He turned, poured a decent quantity into another plastic cup, and handed it to me. "This's Curious Colt. It's at the other end of the spectrum. It's sweet, laced with hints of honey and pear."

Again I sipped, bracing for the affront to my taste buds, but I needn't have worried. This one was much more pleasant.

"And . . .?" I was taken by Frankie's green eyes as he watched me. They were a fascinating shade, like freshly podded peas, and there wasn't even a hint of any other color in them—no gold flecks, no shades of blue. It was as if his eyes were absolutely pure.

I took another sip, just to be sure, then I nodded. "This is much more to my liking."

"Hmmm, but could you drink it all night long?"

I frowned and sipped some more. "No, probably not."

"Right." He took my cup, tossed it into the bin and spun toward the back of his stand where he had six large silver barrels lined up. He paused, with a cup in his hand, and turned back to me. "Corn chips or white chocolate?"

"Pardon."

"Which one, quick?"

"Corn chips." I laughed as he held the cup beneath a barrel and turned the tap.

He handed the cup to me. "This, Jane Nichols, is the brew for you."

I was fascinated by both his powers of deduction and his conviction that I'd love this drink. With his fabulous green eyes on me, I sipped. It was fresh, crisp—more like a complex wine than a beer. A few sips later I nodded, and Frankie slapped his hands together.

"Boom! I've got you, Jane. You, my lovely, are a Frisky Filly woman."

I laughed at his enthusiasm and the interesting name for his drink. "I guess I am."

Frankie enraptured me. His jovial manner, his fascinating eyes, his enthusiasm—all of it had me wishing I could stay with him all night long. It took a mammoth effort to drag myself away from the bubbly hunk with the honey-colored hair and his vibrant energy, but I'd already been away from reception for too long. I returned to my desk, pleased that there wasn't a line-up of people waiting for me.

The next couple of hours were a beautiful blur as some of the hottest bodies on the Gold Coast cruised through the lobby. They drifted from the conference room to the Triple H bar to outside, and then ultimately, up to their rooms.

Frankie was one of the last to leave. He came out of the conference room, laughing with a couple of buff men. None of them looked my way as they headed toward the elevator. Whilst the two muscular gods at his side walked with a stiff gait, like every muscle were made of steel, Frankie had a manly smoothness to his stride as if he were walking through a grassy meadow. As they waited for their ride, he turned to me and our eyes caught.

"Oh hey Jane."

I blinked at him, stunned that he'd remembered my name. "Hi Frankie."

"What time do you finish?"

"Not until six-thirty tomorrow morning."

He whistled, and the sound echoed about the marble expanse. "You poor woman. I feel for you. Come by and see me tomorrow."

My heart fluttered at his invitation. "Okay, I will."

I was sad when the elevator doors opened and my fun-loving, beer-brewing, green-eyed hunk disappeared from view. Frankie from Wild Horses had declared himself Memphis's next adventure. I just had to figure out how to do it.

* * *

Before I even stepped onto Lolita's driveway, I was affronted by thumping music and raucous voices. It sounded like there were a hundred people in her house, and I already knew I was likely to be deaf by the time I left this afternoon.

I didn't bother knocking and pushed the front door open and made my way to the kitchen. Cal was at the counter, separating sausages, dressed in khaki shorts, a white T-shirt, and an apron that made him look like he was wearing a Scottish kilt.

"Jane." He wrapped his arms around me and kissed my cheek. "How are you?"

"I'm great. Where's that crazy wife of yours?"

He chuckled. "She's out by the pool, supervising the scavenger hunt."

"Right."

The second I passed through the glass door to backyard, the noise levels hit a whole new crescendo. I spied Lolita instantly. She was impossible to miss in a bright orange strapless dress that hugged her torso but flared out into a full skirt that must've had layers and layers of lace beneath. She was stunning and could've easily passed as a human Barbie doll.

"Jane." She waved me over and we hugged.

"Hey Lolly."

"Thank God you're here. You need to save me from all this testosterone. Nine-year-old boys are psycho."

I laughed because despite what she'd said, her grin was enough to know she was loving every minute of it.

"Here, give me a hand will you?"

For the next three hours, we herded the twenty or so energetic kids from one game to the next, and fed them an abundance of food. Lolita had outdone herself with Maddox's birthday cake. It was a pirate ship, complete with four masts with sails that looked to be catching a breeze, and even a gang plank that she'd made out of chocolate. Blue jelly surrounded the cake to look like water, which had seemed like a great idea until nearly all the kids in the room had blue fingers and blue lips that no amount of soap would remove. We laughed at that later, and once all the kids left, Cal, Lolita and I set about cleaning up. Lolita and I headed out to the backyard to pick up all the scraps, and I told her about the Total Fitness Expo conference at my hotel.

Her eyes lit up. "Oooh, that sounds great. I want to see. When does it finish?"

"It's on all weekend. Closes at nine tonight and five tomorrow night."

"Oh goody. I should be able to come later tonight. How about if I got there at seven—then you can have a look with me?"

"Okay, sounds like a plan."

At two o'clock, I said goodbye and headed home. Within fifteen minutes of walking in my door, I was curled up in my bed and more than ready for sleep.

* * *

My alarm sounded at six thirty, dragging me from a deep sleep. I stretched, yawned, and hauled myself into the bathroom. Even after my shower, the creases down my cheek failed to disappear. I devoured a peanut butter sandwich and was brushing my teeth when there was a knock on my door.

I peered through the peephole to see Lolita's giant grin and the second I opened it, Lolita bounded in with her usual abundant energy. She hugged me, pushing her boobs into mine. "This's going to be so much fun."

I returned to the bathroom and spat my toothpaste into the sink. "I know. How was the rest of your afternoon?"

"Not too bad. I took the kids for a bike ride, trying to work off some of that sugar."

Of course she had. Every other human in the world would've conked out on the lounge after a kid's party like that but not Lolita. She was a machine. I grabbed my bag off the kitchen counter. "Ready?"

"Yep, let's do this."

We returned to the elevator, and it opened straight away. The second we stepped in, Lolly examined her reflection in the mirror. She checked her teeth, presumably making sure nothing was there. She adjusted her hair with her fingers, and she reached into her bag and pulled out a lipstick. I didn't know why she was fussing—the woman was perfect.

The doors pinged open, and from the second we stepped onto the lobby tiles we were caught up in the energetic buzz. People were everywhere—women, men, young, old, fit, and not so fit. But the one thing they all seemed to have in common were the smiles on their faces—they all looked super happy.

Maybe they'd all been drinking Frankie's beer. Thinking of him had me smiling, and I was truly looking forward to chatting with him again.

Lolly led the way, practically diving onto Xavier's vibrating skateboard as soon as it was available. If I didn't know Lolita was happily married, I'd swear she was flirting with Xavier. The two of them struck up a banter full of innuendo that had me laughing along with them. When Lolly declined to hand over her credit card, Xavier's sad face had her giving him a hug that had him smiling again.

She strolled to the next stall and sampled the protein powders and power bars. Between the two of us, we handed over ninety dollars. At one of the equipment stalls Lolly purchased a pair of weights that she could strap to her ankles. So now not only would she be running at maximum speed and have the treadmill elevated to its maximum level, she was also planning on wearing an extra kilo on each ankle. I didn't know whether she was amazing or just plain stupid.

At the clothing stand, I tried on the lime green exercise gear the tattooed salesman had put aside for me and it was perfect. I quickly paid him my money before I was tempted to look at any more styles.

"What do you think of this one, babe?" Lolly held up a fluorescent yellow crop top with matching Lycra pants that had a yellow sunburst pattern exploding up from the bottom.

"I love it. Suits you."

"Yep. I agree."

She loaded up her arms with several outfits and headed into the change room. As I waited for her, I turned my attention to Frankie's stand. I could barely see the caravan because of the amount of people hovering around. The noise in the hall was loud, but a good majority of it was coming from the back corner. Even though I barely knew the man, I was happy for Frankie. He was obviously very passionate about his beer. I just hoped he was ready to get passionate with me a little later, though I still had no idea when later would be.

Lolly stepped out of the change room and handed a pile of clothes to the tattooed man.

"Happy?" I sidled up beside her.

"They're awesome. Did you buy any more?"

"No, just the green one."

She scowled at me but I ignored her.

With our bags hanging off our arms, we carried on strolling down the first row, and each time she stopped I strained to see or hear Frankie. It seemed like an eternity before we actually arrived at his cute little caravan.

"Let's try this." I hooked my arm into hers and led her through the crowd.

"What is it? Beer?"

"Yes, but you have to try it."

"You know I don't like beer."

"Just try it." We arrived at the caravan, and I placed my hands on the servery before Frankie.

"Hi Jane." His smile shone through his ginger beard like a beacon.

Yay. He remembers me. "Hi Frankie. Looks like you're having success."

"It's been a hit so far. And who do we have here?"

"This's my friend, Lolita. She doesn't like beer."

His eyes bulged. "Right. Well, we need to fix that. You drink wine, right?"

"Yep." Lolita nodded, all serious.

"White or red?"

"Both, but mostly white."

Frankie held up his finger, turned his back to us, and moments later returned with a plastic cup for each of us. "Here's yours, Jane. The Frisky Filly, right?"

I loved that he remembered and couldn't help smiling. "That's correct." I took the drink he'd handed me and sipped. Once again, I was pleasantly delighted with the crisp, fresh taste.

Lolita accepted the cup offered by Frankie, but by the look on her face she was reluctant to even taste it.

"Try it," Frankie and I said at exactly the same time, and we laughed together.

Lolly alternated her gaze from me to Frankie, and when a mischievous twinkle sparkled in her eyes I stopped laughing for fear of what she was about to say or do. She winked at me, and I knew I was in for trouble.

Lolita raised the plastic cup and sniffed it as if it were an expensive wine. I found myself bracing as she took a sip. She screwed up her face, and I laughed because I was pretty sure that was similar to my reaction yesterday.

"Ewww. Okay, see? Beer's not my thing."

"Wait." Frankie showed her his palm. "We haven't finished yet. That's my benchmark beer; from here I'll be able to work out which way to go."

Lolly put the cup down and pushed it toward him. "I've tried plenty of beers, but I don't like it."

"You haven't tried mine." His tongue lashed out over his lips, and the simple move mesmerized me more than it should have. "So answer me, quick—fish or beef?"

"Fish."

"Olives or grapes?"

"Olives." She grinned at me, and as I smiled back at her, I found myself intrigued by her answers.

"Lemon or honey?"

"Hmmm . . ."

"Quick," Frankie urged.

"Okay, lemon."

He turned away again and returned with another plastic cup filled with a liquid that was paler than the first.

She smiled as she sipped this time, and I tried to take in both her reaction and Frankie's. His fabulous green eyes were intense as if willing her to like his beer. He grabbed his beard and tugged on it. His hands were tanned, his fingers thick and manly, and he wore no rings. *Yay me*. Without a doubt, I'd be seeing Frankie later.

"Mmmm." Lolly licked her lips. "That's not bad."

Frankie's shoulder slumped. "Not bad isn't good enough." He turned again. "I'll get you to try this one."

He handed over another sample, and Lolly seemed eager to taste this one.

"This's called Wild Stampede." Frankie splayed his fingers on the counter and leaned forward as if determined not to miss a word Lolly said. His lovely green eyes flicked to me, and when he blinked I noticed how long his eyelashes were. My heart fluttered at the sight. Frankie may have been scruffy, and nowhere near as buff as all the other men in the room, but I could barely take my eyes off him. Maybe it was his passion for his work. Maybe it was his fascinating green eyes. Maybe it was the genuineness about him. Frankie didn't seem to be trying to be anyone but Frankie.

"Ohhh, I love this." Lolly sipped some more.

Frankie slapped the bench. "Fantastic. You, Lolita, are a Wild Stampede woman."

She laughed, and when I laughed along with her, she turned her intense blue eyes to me and stared.

I frowned. "What?"

"Oh, nothing."

But I knew it wasn't nothing. We moved aside to finish our drinks, and Frankie turned his attention to his next clients.

"You look like a love-struck teenager."

"What?" I scrunched my face up and shook my head.

She nodded, all confident and knowing. "I saw it in your eyes. You were practically drooling over him."
I chuckled. "Was not."
"Frankie's your guy, isn't he?"
I rolled my eyes and flicked my hand as if waving her away, trying to act like I had no idea what she was talking about. But my act was pointless. Lolita could read me like a twenty-foot billboard. Soon, I grinned like a schoolgirl. She slapped my shoulder. "I knew it. So, how are we gonna make this happen?"
I frowned. "Make what happen?"
She pointed at Frankie who was smiling his extraordinary smile at a man muscular enough to compete against my Corben. "Make you and Beer Boy get together."
"Beer Boy? That's not nice."
She wiggled her head. "I'm not being mean or anything. It's just you have a room full of hotties and you chose the hairy dude who looks like he doesn't know what a gym is."
Although it was true that Frankie was easily the least muscular man in the room, I felt an unfounded desire to defend him. "He has the most amazing eyes. His hands are strong, manly, and you know what appeals the most? He seems truly genuine. I think Frankie will be exactly who he appears to be."
"Whoa, hold your horses, babe."
"Ha ha, funny." I cocked my head.
"Looks to me like wild horses wouldn't stop you."
"Oh my God." I rolled my eyes and drank the last of my beer.
"You'll be riding that bucking bronco before—"
"Will you stop?"
"This's fun." She looked to the ceiling as if searching for another corny cliché. Next second, her eyes snapped to me, bulging with excitement, and I braced for her next comment. She clutched my arm. "I have a fucking brilliant idea."
"Oh God." I sighed.
"What? Have I let you down before? Did my act with Corben and Needledick fail?"
"No."
"Exactly. I'm a genius, so hear me out." She leaned in toward me, mischief gleaming in her eyes. "I'm going to cover for you at reception while you take that stallion up to his room and ride him till the cows come home."
"What! Have you lost your mind?"
"Nope. It's brilliant. I can do your job while you do him. What's your job involve, anyway? Just sit there and look pretty?"
I rumbled a breath through my lips. "I have a very important job actually."

"Yeah, yeah, I know that . . . but really, what do you do?"
"I run the hotel, take calls, check in guests."
She flicked her hand, waving away my tasks like they were minor inconveniences. "I can handle all of that. Let's see, this finishes at nine o'clock, right?"
I blinked at her. Somehow, the crazy bitch had declared our discussion closed. Dumbstruck, I just shook my head.
"And you start at nine-thirty. So here's what we're going to do."

* * *

It was five past nine when I returned to my room for a quick refresh before my shift. I devoured a protein bar, washed it down with a glass of water, and then brushed my teeth. I hopped back in the elevator and walked across the lobby to my post at reception with just two minutes to spare.
"Hi Marj, how are you?"
"Hey. I'm great now that you're here. These hunks have kept me busy all day." We laughed together, and we hugged before she grabbed her bag and said goodbye.
The second she left, I scanned the lobby for Lolita but couldn't find her. A steady stream of people poured out of the exit door in the conference hall and even though the crowd was noisy, and the abundant voices echoed off the marble expanse, it wasn't long before I heard Lolita. She was still in the hall somewhere, and I had no doubt she'd be on her way out soon.
It was nearly ten o'clock before she emerged, and I just about died when I saw who she'd hooked her arm into. Frankie's face showed how happy he was to have one of the most gorgeous women on the Gold Coast hanging off him. My breath caught in my throat as I feared she would walk him over to me. They shared a joke that had both of them laughing, and I was able to breathe again when they veered away from me and headed toward the elevator.
As they waited for the elevator, my mind flipped over and over with questions about what Lolita was doing. When the doors pinged open, Lolly gave Frankie a smack on his bottom, and he stepped into the elevator. She blew him a kiss as the doors closed, then she turned to me and bounded across the foyer.
"Okay, you're all set." She flicked her high ponytail over her shoulder and grinned at me.
"Set for what?"
"Frankie knows you're coming up to him. He wants to give you your own private tasting."
I picked my jaw up off the counter and blinked. "Have you lost your mind?"

"What?"

"What'd you tell him?"

"That I had a sexy girlfriend who loves beer, but she missed the expo because she was working. He's expecting you in room thirty-five. Off you go."

I shook my head. "This's crazy."

"No it's not. It's called Girlfriend Code. I'm covering for you while you saddle up with Beer Boy."

"I don't—"

"I do. What's your problem? You were dribbling all over him an hour ago."

"Pfft. Was not!"

"Were too and besides, if you don't do this you'll fail your challenge." She aimed her long fingernail toward me.

She did have a point there.

Her eyes twinkled, and I wanted to slap the dazzle out of them. "What if someone wants to check in?"

"Is anyone due to check in?"

My shoulders slumped. "No."

"Well, that solves that. What other hurdles have you got?"

I cocked my head knowing that not only would she have all the answers, but I was destined to hear horsy puns for weeks.

She came around the counter and clutched my shoulders. "We are doing this. Take your phone, and if anything happens while you're horsing around with Beer Boy I'll call you."

I chewed on my bottom lip in response.

"Go on. Frankie's ready to give Memphis a private tasting. And not just of his beer."

The cheeky look on her face had me laughing. "You're crazy."

"Ha, I'm crazy? Look at you, sister."

I pulled a sad face.

"Oh, stop it. You love it."

With her hands on my shoulders, I allowed her to direct me around the reception counter. "Go ride that stud."

I rolled my eyes, and her giggles echoed about the lobby as I walked toward the elevator.

I pressed the button, and as I waited for the elevator I turned to her. She stood behind the reception desk with a look on her face that portrayed pure professionalism. That woman had missed her calling; she should've been an actress.

The doors pinged open.

"Giddy-up," Lolly yelled across to me, and laughing, I stepped into the elevator.

The angel and devil in my brain gave me a hard time from the second I entered my room.
I shouldn't have left reception.
But I only have eight more weeks on my challenge.
What if Lolly gets caught down there?
Frankie had my insides purring while he was fully dressed. Imagine him naked.
That last thought had me centering my focus on the man waiting for me. My disguise would need to be thorough tonight as I'd spent some time chatting with Frankie over the last two days. I decided on green contacts, to match his gorgeous eyes, and my fiery red wig.
Happy with my makeup, I moved to my closet. My decision came quickly. I chose my Bohemian skirt that fell to the floor, and matched it with my white linen top with the elastic neckline that I pulled down over my shoulders. The top required a strapless bra, but I hated those things, so I went without instead. To add to the Bohemian style, I draped chunky wooden beads around my neck and put on dangly orange earrings.
For my shoes, I chose my caramel-colored ankle boots. When I looked in the mirror, I decided my look was perfect for my down-to-earth beer boy.
With that cheeky thought, I dabbed on a touch of pink lippy, grabbed my caramel tote, checked that I had my essentials, and headed out the door.
I wasn't nervous. In fact, all the worry I'd experienced earlier had evaporated, and now I was keen for whatever my green-eyed hunk had to offer.
As I made my way up to the sixth floor, I tugged my sleeves lower down my arms, showing off more shoulder. On his floor, I rubbed my lips together as I strode to his room. It was weird knowing that Frankie was waiting for me. After his chat with Lolita, I just hoped he wasn't disappointed in Memphis.
I knocked on his door, and after a couple of heartbeats it was opened by my stunning beer brewer. In the space of the thirty minutes since I'd seen him, he'd become a hell of a lot hotter. His beard was now neatly trimmed, showing off a squared-out chin, and his damp hair hung in a messy, wavy style that suited him perfectly.
"Hi, you must be Memphis. I'm Frankie." He offered his hand, and from the second our fingers touched I was grateful to Lolly for allowing this to happen.
"I am. Lolita told me all about your wonderful beer."
He stepped aside, and as I walked past him into his room I inhaled lovely scents of soap and cologne. Frankie had put music on, and the catchy beat was exactly what I imagined he'd listen to. As the door clicked closed, I hung my bag over the back of a dining chair and turned to him.
Frankie wore a plain gray T-shirt, and I spied a black leather strap that hung around his neck and disappeared down his collar. Before the night was out,

I was determined to find out what dangled on the end of that necklace. His jeans were stylish, devoid of any holes or tears, and he wore no shoes. Frankie was a man who didn't need any fancy clothing to make him a man.
"So," he said rubbing his hands together. "You had to work tonight. What do you do?"
"Oh, um." *Shit, I should've thought of that.* "I'm a croupier at the casino." This lie had worked for me before—hopefully it'd work this time.
"Sounds interesting. Well, take a seat, and I'll get this tasting going."
I chewed on my lip before I said something silly *like let me taste you first.*
He went to the kitchen and pulled a couple of bottles from the fridge, then carried them and two glasses to the table.
"What beer do you normally drink?"
Oh faaarrrk. Why didn't I think this through? "Well, I'm embarrassed to say I don't really have a favorite."
"Then I'm about to introduce you to one."
His eyes were incredible. I'd never seen anything like them. I could stare into his pools for hours.
With the bottles on the table, he pulled out a chair, sat at my side, and indicated to an amber-colored glass bottle. "This's Bucking Bronco."
Oh crap. That was the one I'd had downstairs that'd tasted horrible.
He removed the top, poured a good quantity into a glass tumbler and handed it to me.
It occurred to me that his tasting process might reveal the real me. I needed to change this up before he figured out who I was. While his eyes were on me, I sipped the beer, but despite all my efforts, I was unable to stop screwing up my face at the bitter taste.
My thoughts went to Hunter and the chocolate guessing game we'd played.
"How about we play a game?" I blurted out before I changed my mind.
Frankie blinked at me, then raised his eyebrows. "What type of game?"
I put my elbows on the table and twirled my fingers together, stalling for an answer. "All your beers are named after horsy things, right?"
"Correct."
"Okay, so how about I try to guess the names of your beers? If I'm right, you take off a piece of clothing. If I'm wrong, I take something off."
Frankie's grin was stunning as he leaned back in his chair and ran his gaze from my eyes to my lips. "But I'm only wearing two pieces of clothing."
Two? Hmmm, yummy. "Then it could be a very short game."
He laughed and clapped his hands. "You, Memphis, are a very fascinating women."
A blaze of heat coursed through my body, and I smiled as I made a show of examining him. "So, is that a yes to the game?"
"Sure. Sounds like fun."

"Okay, you already told me this one was Bucking Bronco. I bet you've named one Back in the Saddle."
His face lit up. "No, sorry."
"You don't look sorry."
"Actually, you're correct. I'm not sorry at all."
Giggling, I removed my beaded necklace.
"Hey, that's cheating. We could be here all night."
I cocked my head at him. "Are you complaining?"
"No, I'm not complaining." He chuckled. "So, what's your next guess?"
"Let me see. How about Wild Ride?"
"Geez, that's a good one. But no, we don't have that name either."
I did an exaggerated sad face, although I wasn't unhappy at all. I bent down and peeled off my boots.
"You're killing me, Memphis."
I tugged my lip into my mouth as I smiled. Frankie was fun, and if I'd had the time, I'd have been happy to have him gaze at me all night long. "My next guess is Sexy Stallion."
"Nope."
"No! Are you sure?" I exaggerated a frown, highlighting my surprise.
"I'm sure."
I took off my socks. "Well whoever names your beers needs to be shot."
"That'd be me."
I laughed at that. "Oh dear. Now that I know it's you, I'm making my next guess Frisky Filly."
It was his turn to look shocked. "I can't believe you guessed that one."
"Aha! Shirt off."
He whipped his shirt off in a flash and oh my God, Frankie had just got a whole lot hotter. He may not have been as buff as Corben or as sculpted as Billy, but Frankie was all man and so perfect in many ways. A silver cross hanging on the leather strap around his neck fell between his nipples. Up the side of his torso was a tattoo written in another language.
I pointed at it. "What does that say?"
He ran his hand over it, almost as if he were caressing his skin, but his eyes remained on me. "I will not allow my wounds to transform me into someone I'm not."
The sadness in his eyes had me falling in love. I stood up, tore my shirt up over my head, pulled my skirt to my ankles and straddled his lap. Our lips came together in a heated, fiery kiss that perfectly matched the sexual tension that'd been sizzling through me since I'd first laid eyes on him.
I forced my tongue into his mouth, demanding to explore more. His warm hands glided up and down my back, and I drove my fingers through his long hair. Our tongues dueled, our breaths mingled and united, and our moans were deep and primal.

This mild, unassuming man with the fabulous green eyes and passion for beer was an exceptional kisser. It wasn't just his tongue, or his lips, or the smell of him, or his hands on my bare back. My senses were being seduced by everything about him all at once.

As I glided my hips back and forward on his lap, his cock rose to attention, giving me a whole lot more to enjoy. His hands found my breasts, squeezing and fondling them as if they were delicate treasures. My greedy clit wanted more, and as I rolled my hips back and forward, each movement drove delicious shudders through me.

Frankie wrapped his arms around me and lifted me up with him. I curled my legs around his hips, and we continued our kiss as he strode to the bed. He placed me down, and the intensity in his green irises captured me even more. I spied his trembling fingers as he fumbled with his jeans button and zipper. As his chest rose and fell, highlighting his excitement, a delicious tremor rumbled through me.

Naked now, Frankie stood before me at the end of the bed. His erection was thick and long and aiming toward his sexy navel. I glided my hands down my legs and parted my knees, silently telling him I wanted all there was of his mighty cock.

Frankie crossed the distance between us, put his fingers into my panties, and dragged them down my legs in a flash. He stepped back as if examining a masterpiece. A fine sheen of sweat glistened across his torso, showing off that already fascinating tattoo. His eyes were on me, devouring me with their intensity, his green irises grew darker. When I parted my legs farther, his tongue lashed out over his lips, confirming he was enjoying my show.

My insides clenched, begging for that cock to plunge into me. I raised my hips off the bed and glided my finger over my clit. The very first touch had skyrockets shooting me to the stars. Frankie had my body on fire, and he'd barely touched me yet.

A pearl of semen glistened like a dazzling diamond at the head of his penis. My breath caught at the sight of it and my insides fluttered, adding depth to my growing orgasm. "Do you have a condom?"

His eyes snapped to focus, and before he even spoke I knew his answer.

"Grab my bag." I pointed at my tote hanging over the chair.

As he strode away, I admired the bulge and flex of the lovely round muscles of his ass. When he turned, his penis pointed right at me, erect and proud. He handed my bag over, and I rummaged through it to produce a condom from the side zipper. The second I handed it to him, he tore it open and glided the rubber over his erection.

I wriggled up the bed, giving him room to join me. Veins coursed along his biceps as he crawled my way and paused above me. I wrapped my legs around him, positioning the swollen head of his penis at my opening.

His eyes were slightly glazed, as if lost to another world as he pushed his hips forward and drove his cock into me. I clawed his back as he filled me with his thick, hot muscle. As Frankie thrust in and out, I curled my ass up off the bed in time to his movements. We worked as one, drawing out each other's pleasure in the most primal way possible.

His thrusts grew faster, deeper. I pulled on my knees, raising my bottom higher and allowing him to plunge deeper still. His mouth was ajar, drawing rapid breaths. His eyes rolled, no longer seeing. And his thrusts were a perfect combination of speed and depth.

The sensations running through me, from deep inside my pussy to every inch of my body, were amazing. My orgasm clawed to fever pitch, begging to explode, and when Frankie stopped, clenched his jaw, and released a low growl that tumbled from deep in his throat, I braced for the finale.

With a gasp, Frankie's eyes shot open, and his hips plunged and withdrew as his cock drove into me over and over. My orgasm released, scattering thousands of delicious pulses through my body and drawing out the exquisite climax. Together we rode a beautiful, wild, primal moment that had both of us gasping for air.

It was an eternity before Frankie's gorgeous green eyes found mine again, and when they did I was once again lost in the purity of them. He smiled as he slumped to my side, and I rolled toward him.

He reached up and curled a lock of my hair behind my ear. It was such a sweet gesture that I was nearly brought to tears. "Well, that was a lovely surprise." His voice was a macho baritone.

"I agree."

"Can you thank your friend for me? What was her name?"

For some reason, the fact that he didn't remember Lolita's name pleased me. She was a pretty memorable woman. "Lolita."

He nodded. "That's right." When he raised his arm to run his hand through his hair, my eyes fell onto his tattoo.

"Did someone break your heart?" I snapped my hand over my mouth. "I'm sorry—you don't need to answer that. It's none of my business."

"It's okay." He placed his hand on my cheek and sighed. He lowered his eyes as if searching deep into his soul for the best way to answer. I sensed that whatever he was about to tell me had hurt him very, very much, and I put my therapy hat on, hoping I'd react appropriately to his response. When our eyes met, my heart squeezed at the sadness I saw.

"My sister committed suicide a couple of years ago after a nasty breakup with her boyfriend."

"Oh God, Frankie. I'm so sorry."

He shrugged. "There's nothing to be sorry about. I have this tattoo so people I'm close to ask me about it. The wounds after she left cut very deep. I like talking about it. These things should be talked about, not hidden beneath a façade."

I rolled into his shoulder and wrapped my arms around this complete stranger. His story resonated so deeply with me.

For what seemed like an eternity, we remained in each other's arms, and it was only when I thought of Lolita that I forced myself to get moving again. Pulling away from him tugged at my heart, but I was also eternally grateful to have spent time with this wonderful man. I crawled off the bed and turned to him. "It was a pleasure to meet you, Frankie from Wild Horses."

"It was a pleasure to meet you too, Memphis, my amorous filly."

I burst out laughing. His retort was the perfect way to end our encounter. I redressed and grabbed my bag. When I turned to him, he was still on the bed, on his side with the sheet draped around his hips and the silver cross around his neck nestled next to his right nipple.

I blew him a kiss. "Good night."

He tipped an imaginary hat. "Sweet dreams."

Smiling at that, I strode to the door, walked out, and floated to the elevator as if I was walking on air. When I arrived at my room, I was shocked to note that I'd only been gone for forty minutes; it'd seemed like so much more. I undressed, removed my wig and makeup, and showered. Then I redressed in my work clothes. Before I went downstairs, I grabbed my diary, turned to the 27th of October, and wrote *Frankie from Wild Horses Room 35* at the top. As I replayed in my mind how passionate he was about everything from his brewery business to his sister's tragic story to our casual encounter, I wrote *Unbridled Passion* below his name.

I filled the pages with intimate details of our wonderful sex. I included the horrific story about his sister and the tattoo he'd chosen so he could share her tragedy with those closest to him. My evening with Frankie proved yet again that a man who appeared to be Mr. Average could turn out to be anything but.

With that wonderful thought, I closed my diary, grabbed my bag, and headed downstairs.

The elevator opened at the lobby to absolute silence, and for a horrible second I wondered if Lolita had abandoned her post. But as I cruised across the floor, she popped her head up from behind the computer.

"There you are." She flicked her ponytail over her shoulder. "So . . . was he hung like a horse?"

I burst out laughing and knew that Lolita wouldn't go home until I told her every last detail. It would be the perfect way to end my fabulous night.

1ˢᵀ NOVEMBER
ORGASMIC MERCY
Room 49 - Hot Horizon Hotel

My life was ruined, and it was all my own fault. Ever since I'd received that call yesterday my brain had been a crazy scramble of fear and horrible possibilities. Why the executive board of the hotel wanted to speak to me was a mystery they'd refused to reveal. All I knew was I'd been summoned to the boardroom one hour after my shift.
When Needledick arrived at reception to take over my shift, his creepy sneer looked triumphant and made the acid in my stomach churn. Even his stance was cocky and confident. Whatever was going on, I suspected he'd instigated it. And that wasn't good.
"Morning, Jane."
I wanted to slap the cockiness right out of him. Instead, I reached down to grab my handbag and mumbled, "Hi."
Determined not to look at him again, I decided not to do the shift handover, and threw my bag over my shoulder and strode to the elevator.
I spent nearly an hour in my apartment pacing back and forward as I stewed over difficult, unanswerable questions. By the time I got back in the elevator, I could barely breathe. Even swallowing was a near impossible feat.

My career was over. Never again would I be able to work in the hotel industry. For the rest of my life, my name would be bandied around as the lying, deceitful fraud I was.

Each step I made toward the boardroom was like swimming in concrete. My tongue was barren of moisture, making it impossible to swallow. My body was a furnace from the hot flush blazing through my insides, and my thighs rubbed together so much that it was a wonder they didn't squeak.

The boardroom door was ajar and I heard muffled banter inside. I paused outside, wiped my sweating palms down my pencil skirt, sucked in a few deep breaths and counted to ten. When I couldn't delay a moment longer I knocked and the door creaked open.

"Come in."

The banter stopped as I entered, replaced instead with stony silence, and for a couple of horrible seconds I thought I'd throw up.

Five people sat around the table. Two women with blond hair, wearing power suits and high-class jewelry, had stern looks that indicated they'd clawed their way to the top. Two men were of Asian descent. They too looked at me with enough contempt to confirm I was in trouble.

The final man stood upon my entrance and walked toward me with his hand forward. "Good morning, Jane. Thank you for meeting with us. I'm Richard Thompson, and I'm head of Australian operations."

"Hello, Mr. Thompson, it's lovely to meet you." I was surprised any words came out.

"Please call me Richard."

As I rolled his name around my head half a dozen times, determined to memorize it, he indicated toward a chair. I sat quickly before my wobbling knees had me face-planting on the carpet.

Richard sat to my right and picked up a silver pen that he flicked between his finger and thumb. Each of the others had a blank notepad and pen before them and a glass of water that looked untouched. I wanted a water so badly, but was certain my trembling hands would have me spilling it everywhere. I was already in enough trouble.

Richard held his hand toward the first woman. "This is Romana Everson. She's in charge of quality control and hospitality services Australia."

He directed my attention to the woman at her side. "This's Brandi Frost; she's head of human services Australia."

He nodded at the Asian man on the opposite side of the table. "This is Mr. Hinro Nomataki, General Manager Asia Pacific region."

I resisted the urge to throw up as he pointed to the second Asian man in the bright yellow tie. "This is Mr. Akio Chuanli, responsible for strategic planning and control Asia Pacific."

Richard opened his hands. "Jane, for the benefit of us all, can you please give us a summary of your history?"

I swallowed the lump in my throat, and my already frenzied brain hit a whole new level as I wondered why they'd want this information when it would already be on my file. "Well, I grew up in Mildura, which is a small country town in north-west Victoria. My first job was working in my father's stationery store." My voice quivered so much I was certain I was indecipherable, but I carried on regardless. "I was there for seven years before I accepted the position as night manager here."

"So you'd never worked in hotel management before?" Romana's American accent surprised me.

"No. I hadn't."

Both women and the Asian man in the yellow tie scribbled on their notepads.

They continued to fire their questions at me, one after other.

"Tell us what you think of the Hot Horizon Hotel."

"Do you like working here?"

"Have you had any major issues?"

"Where do you see yourself in five years?"

"Give us your opinion of John."

That request had my heart exploding again. "Mr. Karwatsky . . .?" I cleared my throat and raised my eyebrows.

"Yes. Tell us what you think of him," Richard said.

"I don't actually have much to do with him."

"How so?"

"Well, I work the night shift, so we basically have a five-minute changeover each day, and that's all I see of him."

"Is the handover structured?" Brandi's articulate voice quipped off her tongue like a judge's sentence.

"Pfft, no." I said that way too quickly, and the two Asians scribbled something on their notepads.

"What do you know about this Memphis woman?"

My heart leapt to my throat at Romana's question. I swallowed. Hard. "I, ahhh . . ."

"Jane." Brandi looked at me in a motherly way, and the change was startling. "You need to be honest with us about her."

"Memphis?"

"Yes. John told us all about her and we want your opinion."

I cleared my throat and stared at my hands. "Memphis is not a prostitute." The truth was easy; the rest was not going to be though.

"John disagrees with you. Why is that, do you think?" Richard asked.

I shifted in my seat, stalling for an answer. "Mr. Karwatsky is basing his opinion on Memphis's appearance. She's a confident woman who wears provocative clothing, classy shoes, and stands up for herself."

I couldn't be sure, but I think both the women nodded.

"John claims *you* are Memphis," Brandi said matter-of-factly.

My pounding heart was set to explode as I flitted my gaze from one board member to the next. "I have no idea what to say to that."

"Why would he think that?" Brandi said.

"You'll have to ask him."

"We did." Mr. Nomataki spoke his first words of the meeting.

Oh God. The excruciating silence could be cut with a chainsaw as I scrambled over how to respond. But just when I thought I'd pass out, I realized they had actually answered the question for me and I cleared my throat. "Then you already have Mr. Karwatsky's response."

As the seconds dragged on, five sets of eyes tore away my lies and laid bare all my guilty layers. I was exposed. I, Plain Jane, was a conniving, deceitful fraud who deserved whatever punishment was about to be meted out. I was guilty—slap my handcuffs on now and toss me in a padded cell.

"He was convinced enough to bring Memphis to our attention," Brandi said.

Bastard. That was the catalyst I needed. I worked really hard here. Needledick, by contrast, had no commitment to his job, and it was time these people knew exactly who they'd put in charge of their hotel. "Did Mr. Karwatsky tell you about his confrontation with Memphis and her partner?"

A murmur rippled around the room which was exactly the response I'd hoped for.

"No he didn't." Richard spoke for them. "Would you care to elaborate?"

"I was returning from a jog along the beach a few weeks ago and when I entered the lobby, a man and a woman were at reception confronting Mr. Karwatsky about how he'd treated the woman. Her name was Memphis. Apparently Mr. Karwatsky had actually grabbed her wrist."

One of the ladies did the tiniest of gasps, and the two of them turned their attention from me to glance at each other. The Asian man with the yellow tie, and Brandi made notes on their pads.

Richard opened his hands. "It seems John omitted to mention that. Why, then, do you think he would implicate you?"

I leaned forward, clasping my hands together. "Several months ago, I confronted Mr. Karwatsky about always being late for his shift."

Brandi raised her eyebrows. "Always late?"

"Nearly every single day. And not just by a couple of minutes—most days he's late by half an hour or so. I know he has an ill mother, so I understand why. But . . ." I realized I was rambling and stopped before I said something nasty. "Anyway, I don't think he liked me standing up to him."

"Hmmm." Richard pushed back on his chair and steepled his fingers together. "I think we've heard enough." He stood. "Thank you for your time, Jane; you must be exhausted after your long night."

"Oh." I couldn't believe the meeting was over. What about the handcuffs and the padded room? What about the public humiliation for the rest of my life? A cloud of confusion stole my focus as I was given a harried goodbye. Richard escorted me from the room and shut the door behind me.

As I crossed the fifty or so paces from the boardroom to the lobby, I began to wonder what the hell had just happened. By the time I spied Needledick behind the counter I began to wonder if I'd just dodged a silver bullet. I turned my head to him and gave my boss dagger eyes. When he, in turn, gave me a truly triumphant sneer, I realized Needledick thought he'd won some kind of battle.

But with every step I made toward the elevator, I became more convinced that he hadn't. In fact, whatever he'd planned had just backfired. I replayed the meeting over and over, and each time I came to the same conclusion—whatever outcome Needledick had intended to achieve by calling the board about Memphis had totally failed. Until now, it'd never occurred to me how lucky it was that I'd been hired by the human resources department of this hotel chain all those years ago. Clearly it meant Needledick had no authority to fire me.

By the time I entered my apartment, my mind was both exhausted and wired at the same time, and despite my need for a good sleep, resting would be impossible. Instead, I ran the bath and poured in a good slosh of Marjorie's bubble bath. I left the taps to run and went to the kitchen in search of food. My phone rang, and as I contemplated if my morning was about to get better or worse I fished the iPhone from my bag.

My heart sunk when I saw the number. With a big sigh, I sat on the edge of my bed and pressed the green button. "Hi Mom."

"Hi Jane. Now before you say anything, I have something I want to say."

Here we go. "Okay then."

"I want to say I'm sorry. We're sorry, your father and I."

I replayed her words in my head, hardly able to believe I'd heard them right. Certain that I had, I remained silent, hoping she'd elaborate on what exactly she was sorry for.

"Our decision to continue to see Xander after what he did to you was callous. We should never have done that. We especially shouldn't have put you in a position where you had to confront him in public."

Wow. "Thank you, Mom. This means so much to me."

She sniffled, and my chin dimpled as I realized she was crying. "Mom?"

"I feel like it's my fault you had that fight with Xander. Can you ever forgive me? Us?"

"Oh Mom, it wasn't your fault; it was his fault. But you're right—he shouldn't have been there. So thank you, your apology fixes everything. " A tear trickled down my cheek, and I wiped it away. "I want to say sorry too, Mom; I shouldn't have caused a scene like that at Dad's party."

"Don't worry about it. It is the talk of the town, though. Well, you are, actually. What you did to Chelsea-Lea and Xander—everyone knows. And they're all saying how amazing you look. You do look amazing. I'm so proud of you."

"Awww, thanks, Mom."

"I mean it. Whatever you're doing over there on the coast is working wonders on you."

"I'm looking after myself—that's all." I remembered the running water and strode to the bathroom to turn the taps off. I caught it just before I'd need to mop up a disaster.

"What's that noise?"

"It was just the bath. I was about to have one before I went to sleep." I returned to the bed and sat again.

"Are you getting enough sleep? You must be so tired all the time."

"I'm fine. I get plenty of sleep." She always worried about the simplest things.

There was a long pause, and she cleared her throat. "Okay, well have a nice bath and a good sleep. I'm so glad we had this chat."

"Me too, Mom. Thank you for calling. I love you."

"I love you too. Bye."

I stared at the phone for a long time after she'd hung up, trying to recall another occasion when I'd heard Mom say she was sorry, but I couldn't think of one. I went to the bathroom, stripped off, and slipped into the hot water. As the warm water worked its magic on my tension-laced muscles, I mentally replayed the conversation with my mother. Mom's apology was as much a surprise as it was appeasing. I truly believed that she'd never intended to cause me grief. It was her fear of small-town gossip that'd made her do what she'd done.

The water was close to cold when I finally climbed out and dried myself. Naked, I walked from the bathroom and stopped still at a note that'd been slipped under my door.

Covering my breasts for some stupid reason, I went to the sheet of folded paper and opened it.

I couldn't help but smile as I read the handwritten note.

> *'Hey gorgeous. Fancy another lesson?*
> *I'll be in penthouse number 49, any time from five o'clock.*
> *XXXOOO your suave tutor.'*

I folded the note back over, held it to my chest, and skipped to my bed, giggling. Could this day get any better? Hell yes it could—come five o'clock, I was set for another fabulous evening. I tugged my PJ's out from under my pillow and put them on. Turning onto my side, I re-read Henry's note twice. Smiling, I placed it onto my spare pillow, and with an abundance of images of my suave tutor flicking across my brain, I drifted off to sleep.

* * *

My alarm sounded, and yawning, I rolled over and shut off the voice of Adele from the radio. I curled off the bed and pulled my blinds aside to see what the weather was doing. It was another beautiful evening in paradise. I opened my glass door, stepped onto the balcony, and inhaled the crisp ocean air.

Hundreds of people were on the beach, taking in the last of the spring sunshine. The lifesaver flags were still out, and at least fifty people were enjoying the tumbling waves. I placed my hands on the railing, closed my eyes, and breathed in nice and deep. A wonderful sense of calm enveloped me with each breath and the crashing waves were a beautiful melody that enhanced my feeling of peacefulness.

After five or so minutes I went inside, and as I showered, I turned my attention to Henry and his promise of another lesson. By the time I stood naked at my closet, my insides purred at the prospect of spending more time with my suave tutor.

I already knew what I'd wear and tugged the long red dress from the rack. When I'd tried on this dress while shopping with Lolita, all I'd been able to think of was Henry. This dress was for him. It was impossible to wear a bra with it, and so, for something a little cheeky, I decided not to wear panties either. I couldn't wait to see his reaction to that.

I slipped the dress over my head and the heavy fabric draped down my body and fell at my feet. The dress had thin spaghetti straps that met with a section of fabric that covered my breasts and remained open all the way down to the encased elastic at the waist. It was backless with the straps over my shoulder meeting at the waistline. A long split came up from my ankle and stopped high on my thigh, ensuring each step was a game of peek-a-boo with my right leg.

For my shoes, I chose my new pair of gold Lesina evening stilettos. They had a devilishly high heel and a series of gold straps that curled from beside my big toe and splayed perfectly up my foot. These shoes were the epitome of sexy, and when I'd tried them on I'd had no idea that one of the sexiest men on the planet would be the first to see them. He was certainly the man who'd appreciate shoes like these.

Using the gold for inspiration, I added long, dangly gold earrings and a chunky gold bracelet. By the time I inspected my outfit in the mirror, I not only looked sexy but I felt sexy too. I, Jane Nichols, was at the top of my game, and it was so empowering to finally acknowledge that.

With a genuine smile on my face, I grabbed my bag and headed up to see one of the men in my life who was also at the top of his game. I stepped from the elevator, and my boobs wobbled as I strode along the ninth-floor corridor. Once upon a time this would've distressed me. Not now, though—it just added to the sexy vibes coursing through my body.

I knocked on Henry's door and only had to wait a couple of heartbeats before he opened it. His eyes bulged and his jaw dropped. "Wow. You look amazing."

"Thank you, Henry."

He leaned over and our lips met for the briefest of kisses. But it was a kiss that said so much more—I trust, I want, I need, and maybe, just maybe . . . I love. He smelt divine, and every bit the masculine, sexy man he was.

He curled his hand around my back and guided me into the room. "I took the liberty of opening a bottle of champagne."

"That sounds wonderful."

He led me to the spiral staircase, and as I lifted the hem of my skirt to walk up it, I wondered if he would grab my bottom like he had last time. Halfway up, he did. "Hey." I giggled and glanced down at him.

"What?" He acted as if he'd done nothing.

I liked this cheeky ritual we'd started.

At the top of the stairs, we stepped into the glassed in area, and he crossed the room and opened the door to the rooftop terrace. He'd positioned two deckchairs to take in the view, and nestled between them was a cheese platter and a couple of candles that had flames dancing in the slight breeze. Henry was the master of romantic settings.

I sat in one of the deckchairs and shared my gaze between the magnificent view and the magnificent specimen of a man pouring my drink. Henry wore a black-and-white checkered button-up shirt, and over the top of that he had on a black vest. He was stylish and debonair, and not for the first time, I thought Henry would be perfectly comfortable sitting right alongside George Clooney.

He had an interesting expression on his face, like he was on the verge of smiling but was trying desperately to hold it back. The more I watched him, the more I realized he was withholding something. It had me wondering what lesson I was about to learn, and in particular, was tonight the night I'd finally have sex with my suave tutor? The very thought of going all the way with Henry had my insides purring.

He handed me a glass full of lovely bubbles that drifted elegantly to the surface. We chinked our glasses together. "Cheers," we said in unison.

"Would you like something to eat?"

I eyed off his assortment of cheeses, nuts, crackers, and dried fruit. "Of course."

"That's what I love about you, Jane."

"My enormous appetite?" I raised an eyebrow.
"Your zest for life."
"Oh." Henry was a huge contributor to my zest for life, and before I jumped onto his lap and ruined the lust-fueled-anticipation thing he was so good at, I turned my attention to the food. "What type of cheese is this?"
"So I learned this rhyme a long time ago for making up a cheese board. Something old, something new, something goat, and something blue. By doing that, I cover most people's taste. So that one is my something old; it's Gouda. Try it with either the pear or the quince paste."
As instructed, I cut a slice of the cheese, topped it with a sliver of pear, and popped it in my mouth. It was a delicious combination of savory and sweet. I covered my mouth as I chewed. "Oh yum. That's good."
He leaned over and sliced into another cheese, and when his knife came away, I noted blue veins running thought the creamy white center of the cheese.
"What's that one?"
"It's a blue Castello. Here, try it." He topped it with a sliver of fig, placed it on a cracker, and held it toward me.
I opened my mouth, and he popped it onto my tongue. With his lovely pale blue eyes watching me I savored the delicious bite. "Oh yum. That's really good."
"So many people don't eat blue cheese, but it's worth experimenting with."
"Just like sex." I gave him a cheeky smile, and he in turn smiled at me.
"Yes." He raised his eyebrows. "Just like sex."
The dazzle in his eyes was spectacular, and it was all the invitation I needed. I gulped my drink, set my glass down, stood up, and went to him.
"What are you doing, madam?" He chuckled as I raised my skirt to straddle him.
"Seducing you." I brought my lips to his, cutting off his wonderful laughter. Our kiss was heated, passionate, and had my hips squirming over his. I opened my mouth, inviting him to explore, and his tongue pushed past my teeth to dance a delightful duo with mine. His warm hands cruised up and down my back, and I moaned at the touch of his fingers on my bare flesh.
I curled my hand around his neck, drawing him closer. Henry glided his finger beneath the straps at my shoulders, and I sat up as he peeled them down my arms. It was an extraordinary feeling being topless before a gorgeous man like Henry. I curled my arms out of the straps, and Henry reached forward to cup my breasts. His hands were warm, soft, and eager as they curled under and over my mounds.
A delightful shudder rolled through me, culminating in my nipples peaking. They grew into hard, throbbing pebbles in a matter of seconds. Henry pinched my nipples between his thumbs and fingers, rolling them with just the right amount of pleasure to send flutters through my body. I raised my

hips off him a fraction so I could grind my vagina over the bulge growing in his groin.

I leaned forward, placing my hands on the back of his chair to dangle my boobs before his face. He didn't miss a beat, and his hot tongue lavished me from my left breast to my right. His hand curled down my waist and fed into the split in my skirt, and my insides set to explode as I waited for the moment when he realized I was wearing no underpants.

He took his time, sucking my right nipple, caressing my left boob, and gliding his hand up and down my thigh. Each time his hand came closer and closer to my pussy I groaned. The anticipation was a thrilling aphrodisiac.

He touched my exposed vagina, and when he gasped I sat back, grinning.

His smile was extraordinary, and as I licked my lips I wriggled my eyebrows.

"You're a bit cheeky, madam."

"I know." I grinned and curled my hips again, letting him know I felt his hard-on.

"Are you ready for your lesson?"

"Of course."

"Then you'll have to get off me."

I did as he asked, and as I raised my leg over him to stand, I made sure he had a view of my nakedness. A raw lust shimmered in his eyes. The pale blue pools were an intriguing cocktail of all things pure and wicked, and confirmed he had indeed sneaked a peek.

He stood up and shortened the distance between us, bathing me in his body heat.

I reached forward to undo the buttons on his vest. "I must say, you look very dashing tonight."

"I had a hot date."

"Hot indeed."

He allowed me to undress him. First his vest, then his shirt. I took my time, enjoying both the big reveal and the desire in his eyes. Henry had mastered the art of body language, and if I was reading him right, he was just as eager as I was for us to be naked together.

I peeled his shirt and vest off his shoulders and tossed them onto the deckchair at our side. We were both topless now, and he stepped closer, pressing my breasts to his chest and curling his hands around my back, drawing our hips together. He was a fraction taller than me, even with my high heels on, and I tilted my face up to him, parted my lips, and silently begged him to kiss me.

I closed my eyes, and barely a breath later, our lips met. As I glided my hands around his back, exploring his flesh, our tongues danced. His hands curled up and down my back, and as he pulled me closer we united together in a wild passion that begged us to explore each other's flesh.

His hands fell to my hips, and I felt him tug the fabric of my skirt upwards. Our kiss released. "May I?"

"Yes." My voice was barely a whisper.

I raised my hands and he lifted my dress up over my head, and soon I wore nothing but my high heels.

His chest rose and fell as he ran his eyes over me. "I'm the luckiest man in the world."

I tugged my bottom lip into my mouth at the conviction in his voice. The bulge at his groin was enormous, begging to be released, and I stepped forward, pushed my fingers into the waistband of his pants, and looked up at him. "May I?"

"Yes."

His willingness to let me undress him was delightfully different, and before he changed his mind, I fumbled with his belt and had his pants around his ankles in a flash. I showed none of the finesse he had and continued my mission by pulling his underpants down, too.

He stiff cock bounced forward, begging me to touch it, so I went to him and wrapped my hand around that glorious muscle, and as Henry drove his fingers around my neck he pulled my lips to his. Our tongues explored, our hands groped, our moans elevated to fever-pitch, and his hard cock grew thicker and longer in my hand.

His fingers curved down my waist, over my hips, and I bent my knees as he inched between my thighs. He turned me sideways so I had one foot between his parted legs, and his finger slipped into my throbbing pussy. He started with one finger, then joined it with another, and as I bent my knees, opening myself up, he drove his fingers in and out in a way that grinded over my pulsing clit, too.

It was impossible to keep my eyes open and as I closed them, I let my body take over. Electric pulses flashed through me as I clawed his back. Our kiss intensified, and as our tongues fought to please each other, our hands did the same. I pumped his cock faster, drawing my hand along his length in a wild frenzy its magnificence deserved.

Suddenly, he stepped back, his jaw clenched, his eyes closed. His breath hissed through his teeth and I knew he was fighting his climax. Knowing I'd brought him to that delicious point was thrilling, yet I waited for his next move.

He trembled all over, and it was a few heartbeats before he opened his eyes and his focus found me. A breath tumbled from his throat. "You drive me wild."

I curled my bottom lip into my mouth and slowly released it. "Yay."

He rolled his eyes as he smiled. "May I ask you to lie down please?" He indicated to the deck chair, and I obeyed his wishes. He stepped around behind my head, and I was unable to see him. As I wondered what he was up to, a lovely shudder rolled through me, drawing goose pimples over my body and hardening my nipples even further.

When he came back into view, he had a length of fabric that he trailed across his fingers. He sat at my side and I wiggled over, giving him room.

He cupped my breast, leaned forward, and ran his hot tongue over my nipple. "Have you ever been tied up before?"

His question and the way he asked it caught me off guard. "Ummm, no."

"Would you allow me?"

"Yes." There was no need to hesitate. After what Henry had shown me last time, and every other sexual experience we'd had for that matter, I was his willing pupil.

He leaned forward for a brief kiss. "You're adorable."

What he said was incredible but it was the way he said it, with enraptured eyes and a voice loaded with sexual potency that had a blaze of heat pulsing through me. He trailed his hand from my elbow to my wrist and brought my palm to his lips. As he kissed my flesh, he draped the colorful fabric over my fingers, lowered it to my wrist, and then pulled it tight with a knot that I hadn't noticed.

"Okay?" The concern in his eyes had me trusting him even more.

"Yes." I nodded.

He curled both my arms up so my hands were over my head, then he stood, and working behind me, he wrapped the fabric around my other wrist and again pulled the fabric tight. My arms were now secured up alongside my cheeks, unable to move.

"Is that okay?"

"Yes."

He lowered the deckchair so I laid flat. Above me, the sky was a potpourri of purple and pink clouds as the setting sun captured their fluffy edges. Henry came back into view, and I didn't know whether to look at his face or his enormous erection.

He made that decision for me when he straddled my chest, and using his hand, rolled the head of his cock around my nipples. It was voyeur's heaven watching that swollen crown roll around and around my hard pebbles. A pearl of liquid bubbled at the slit in his penis, and I watched, hypnotized as it slipped slowly down his veined shaft.

I glanced up at him. His eyes flickered beneath his closed lids. His jaw was clamped shut, and yet he continued to roll his masterpiece around my nipples. It was exquisite torture not being able to touch him, and the more I squirmed beneath his body the more wonderful it became.

He opened his eyes and our gaze locked together as he wriggled down my body and slipped off the end of the chair. Against the colorful evening sky, his body had a celestial glow, and I wondered if I'd died and gone to heaven. Henry parted my legs and without any fanfare he knelt on the end of deckchair, placed his hands beneath my knees, and raised my bottom. His head lowered to between my thighs, and when his hot tongue glided up my pussy, the fabric ties were the only things stopping me from launching right off the rooftop.

I fought against my restraints as he pushed his tongue and a finger inside me. The heat of his tongue, the drive of his finger, my lack of freedom—it was sensory overload, and an explosive orgasm ripped through me. I cried out as my hot juices squirted from my body over and over. I dug my heels into the chair and raised my hips, and he continued to lick and plunge, coaxing the release of every last drop of my orgasm.

I was panting for air when he finally stopped and raised his face with a smile. There was enough light to see my slick juices over his face, and I didn't know whether I liked that or not. But when Henry licked his lips, oh my God—if that wasn't one of the sexiest moves ever . . .

"Make love to me, Henry."

His eyes met mine, and an unbridled command of desire crossed between us. He stood again and disappeared around behind me, and his footsteps retreated. For a horrible moment I thought I'd scared him, or worse, I'd misread the desire in his eyes.

But seconds later, he released my hands, and when he came into view I spied the condom on his penis. The joy rolling through me was indescribable, and I tried to comprehend that I'd wished for this moment for a very long time.

He walked to the end of the deck chair and when I parted my legs, Henry crawled up toward me. His cock nudged my throbbing vagina, and as he hovered above me, his bulging biceps holding him in place, I flitted my gaze from his eyes to his mouth and back again. I studied his face, taking in every exquisite detail and knew I was looking at one of the most handsome men in the world.

As his thick length filled me, a dark vein pulsed at his temple. His lips parted and his tongue lashed out to wet them. Slowly, slowly he pushed his cock all the way in, penetrating me until it touched that wonderful part inside me that begged to be pounded. It felt so right, so complete, like it was a piece of me I'd been missing for a very long time. His eyes flickered open and the raw passion in his light blue pools made me feel like a sexual goddess.

"Oh, Jane."

The way he said my name was a potent mix of love and lust. "Yes?"

"You feel incredible."

"So do you." I reached up, and as I thumbed his nipples, he sucked air in through his teeth and his eyes glazed over. He withdrew his penis, pulling it out until just his crown remained inside me. He paused there, teasing me with his swollen head. I clawed my nails up his back and curled my vagina toward him, silently insisting he put his cock right back inside me. He plunged again, a bit faster this time, and I reached down, hooked my hands beneath my knees and raised my ass higher off the chair, giving him another angle to explore.

Henry repeated his moves, each time pulling out just to the crown of his penis. His thrusts grew faster, gradually building my climax to monumental heights. A light sheen glossed his flesh, his deep primal groans grew deeper, yet he clenched his jaw, squeezed his eyes shut and continued to thrust.

We worked together as one, drawing out each other's pleasure like only lovers could do. Although we'd never done this before, every move felt as if we'd been doing it forever. He knew how to please me, and by the intense focus on his face, I believed I pleased him.

Every nerve ending in my body tingled, begging for the delicious sensations to last a lifetime. My second orgasm grew quickly, gearing up for the promise of explosive things to come. I clenched my insides around his cock, desperate to feel every inch of him, and he gasped.

His thrusts grew faster, deeper. I clawed my nails up his back and the groan that tumbled from his throat was music to my ears. Unable to hold back a moment longer, I cried out as my juices flowed for a second time. I saw stars, I saw rockets—I saw every feature on his beautiful face. My insides hit party mode and I clenched around him like a vise. Henry gasped as his thrusting reached fever-pitch. I pulled on my knees. He thrust in and out.

"Oh God," he screamed as he buried his cock into me with several final thrusts. His eyes flickered open, but I could tell he wasn't seeing. He flopped onto my chest, his breathing desperate and ragged as I trailed my fingers up and down his back.

As we lay there, still united as one, wallowing in our after-sex contentment, a star shot across the sky and disappeared into the blackness. I closed my eyes and made a wish. My wish came easily—all I wanted was to find soul-embracing love. As Henry's breathing returned to normal, I wondered if I already had.

It seemed like an eternity before he pushed up onto his hands and his arms trembled as he held himself above me. "You, Jane Nichols, are an angel."

I cupped his cheek and smiled. "Thank you."

He grinned as he rolled to the side, and when his penis slipped out of me it was like tearing open my heart. The deckchair was too small for the both of us though so we sat side by side, our shoulders touching, our hands entwined. It was really sweet and comfortable, and it didn't feel at all strange that we were both naked.

I squeezed my palm to his. "Thank you for yet another wonderful evening."

"You too." He nudged his shoulder to mine.

"When are you back again?"

He sighed. "Unfortunately, not for a couple of weeks. We're heading into the crazy season, and between work and Christmas commitments, I really don't know when."

I groaned. My heart was already weeping.

He stood and pulled me to my feet. "Come on. You need to get to work."

"Oh, why'd you have to ruin a perfectly wonderful evening?"

"Sorry."

We redressed, and he took my hand to lead me back inside. I kissed him goodbye, and as I made my way to my room, a dark cloud smothered my feelings as I wondered how long it would be before I saw him again.

Back in my room, I showered and then dressed for work. With a frozen dinner in the microwave, I grabbed my diary and sat at my dining table. I opened it to the 1st of November, and at the top I wrote *Mr. Henry Addison Room 49*. I detailed my new experience of being tied up during sex and wrote about how I'd desperately wanted to run my hands over his flesh, yet not being able to had driven me crazy. I'd been at his orgasmic mercy and it had been undeniably wonderful. With that thought, I giggled as I wrote *Orgasmic Mercy* below his name. As I detailed the sex and how incredible it'd been, I wondered if it were because I'd practically begged for it to happen.

Henry had masterfully crafted our sexual liaisons. He'd deliberately held back from going all the way until I was at the point where I would've got down on my knees and pleaded with him to make love to me. I paused with the pen above the page and blinked at that sentence.

Was that what we were doing? Making love? Or was it just mind-blowing sex?

As the microwave dinged and I removed my steaming Thai chicken curry, I wondered how many more time's I'd see Henry before I knew the answer to those questions.

Kitty Kendall

12ᵀᴴ NOVEMBER
LOSING MY SOUL
Room 43 - Hot Horizon Hotel

Monday morning rolled around without any fanfare. The sun announced its arrival with a blast of golden light just before five a.m. and I poured myself a cup of green tea and headed outside for a short break. A scattering of clouds dotted the horizon giving the sun plenty of targets to aim its morning rays at. The darkness was an impossible match against the golden beams, and gradually the clouds morphed into shades of orange and yellow. The dark sea revealed itself more and more by the second, and soon the sun cast a white stripe that divided the ocean in half.
It wasn't long before people began to emerge. Joggers sprinted past, wired into their iPods as they made the most of the cool morning air. Surfers dotted the water, eager to start the day with a morning wave. Young families and old couples strolled past like they had all the time in the world.
I loved this part of the day. Not only because it usually signified the end of my shift, but also because it showed that no matter what disasters life threw at me, every day could be the dawn of a new beginning.
Once I finished my tea I went back inside, washed my teacup, and did a quick tidy of the staffroom as I awaited Needledick's arrival. The start of his six-thirty shift came and went, as did seven a.m.

The phone rang, and I forced sunshine into my voice to answer it. "Welcome to the Hot Horizon Hotel, this is Jane speaking."

"Hello Jane, it's Richard Thompson here. Is John available?"

Richard? From the executive board? "Oh hello, Mr. Thompson. I'm sorry but he hasn't come in yet."

"Really? Do you know why he's late?"

The idea of covering for him flashed into my mind, but just as quickly evaporated. "No sir, he hasn't called in late."

"Hmmm. Well when he comes—"

The glass door slid open and Needledick strolled through like he was walking into a funeral. "Oh hang on a minute, here he is." His hair was a mess and his shirt wasn't ironed. He looked as if he'd had a particularly bad night, and I suddenly felt sorry for him.

As he neared the counter, I held the phone toward him. "Mr. Thompson wants to talk to you."

His already pale face paled further. He sighed as he reached for the phone. "Hello Mr. Thompson. I'm sorry I'm late, my mother—"

He must've been cut off because he stopped talking, closed his eyes, and ran his hand over his forehead. Averting my gaze, I bent down and collected my bag from the floor. There was no need for me to hang around, and I certainly didn't want to be here when he ended the call. So I tapped his shoulder and when his eyes popped open, I waved at him and mouthed *goodbye*.

I strode to the elevator and hoped it opened immediately. It did, and I stepped in and jabbed the button for my floor.

"I'm sorry Mr. Thompson." John's sorrowful words were cut off as the elevator doors closed.

I really did feel for him. It'd be extremely difficult juggling a full-time job with a sick family member. My stomach churned as I worried over what kind of trouble he'd be in. But my worry was short-lived as my churning stomach turned to hunger pains, and I focused my attention on breakfast. I entered my apartment and went straight to the fridge, but once I opened it I sighed at its sorry state of bareness. Annoying as it was, I couldn't put off grocery shopping any longer.

Without any other choice, I grabbed my bag again and with thoughts of savory mince on toast and strong coffee, crossing my mind, I headed out for breakfast. As I rode the elevator I hoped like hell that John was still on the phone. My wish wasn't granted, and as I stepped from the elevator onto the marble tiles I felt his dagger eyes immediately.

"You fucking bitch."

I gasped, stopped in my tracks, and turned to him, wide-eyed and open mouthed.

"You trying to get me fired?"

I palmed my chest. "What? No."

"You didn't have to tell him I was late."

I put my fists on my hips. "I wouldn't have to tell him if you weren't."

"That's not the point."

"It's exactly the point. You're late nearly every single day."

"Oh and I suppose you told him that too." His voice boomed about the marble expanse.

I stepped toward him and pointed my finger. "As a matter of fact I did. Right after you told them I was a prostitute named Memphis."

His eyes bulged. His lips drew to a thin line. "I never—"

"Don't lie." The anger in my voice surprised me, but the irony was I'd lied about Memphis too. I clenched my jaw and before either of us said another word, I spun on my heel, strode toward the sliding glass doors and stepped outside.

The morning sun was no longer lovely. Its intensity burned my flesh, matching the inferno of anger blazing through my insides. I strode to Blue Haven Café, a woman on a mission. When I'd initially decided to come here for breakfast I'd had visions of devouring a plate of savory mince on toast, but after that encounter I needed a sweet fix instead.

I went to the cake counter and scanned every possibility before I made my decision. The New York baked cheesecake would both fill me up and satisfy my sugar craving. I ordered a double-shot skinny cappuccino to go with it, and then went to my favorite table out the front.

As I watched the world go by, I recalled the conversation with Needledick through my head and no matter which way I played it, I knew there was no recovering from it now. Both of us had implicated each other to the executive board. Who they believed was impossible to interpret. Although . . . this morning's situation had supported my accusations.

My cake arrived, and I wasted no time in forking it into my mouth. It was thick, creamy and sweet. Exactly what I needed.

My phone rang, and as I attempted to swallow the enormous mouthful I'd shoveled in, I fished it from my handbag. I frowned at the screen; the number was not one I recognized. My heart leapt to my throat as a horrifying thought flashed through my mind. *Is this Richard from the executive board . . about to fire me?*

My heart galloped as the phone rang over and over. I sucked in a deep breath, attempting to calm my racing nerves, and jabbed the green button. "Hello?"

"Oh hi Memphis. It's Hunter."

I just about wept at the sound of his voice. "Hunter, oh my god. It's so good to hear from you."

"Really? Um okay."

Oh jeez, I must sound like a total desperado. "Sorry, I thought it was going to be my boss."

"Oh is everything okay?" His concern was as soothing as a hug.

"Yeah, yeah, it's nothing."

"That's good then. How have you been?"

"Much better now that I'm talking to you." It was true; Hunter had me smiling again.

"Excellent. Well I'm heading up to the Gold Coast this weekend and I was just wondering if you'd be there too?"

"Are you asking me on a date?" I reiterated his question from a couple of weeks ago.

"Touché." He laughed, and I laughed along with him. "Yes, that's exactly what I'm doing."

"In that case I'd love to."

"Perfect. I'm competing in an open-water swim at Mermaid Beach."

"Wow, that's exciting."

"I hope so. I plan to win this one." The conviction in his voice was unmistakable.

"What time's your race? Maybe I'll come watch."

"You would?"

"Sure, I'd love to."

"I'd like that. Kickoff is at ten o'clock."

He was so easy to talk to, and it was another twenty or so minutes before we said goodbye. I was glowing both inside and out by the time I hung up. I finished my treat, paid for my order and strolled back to my hotel, determined not to ruin these wonderful feelings by engaging with Needledick again.

Fortunately, he was busy with a family with three young kids, and I made it to the elevator unscathed. I was exhausted by the time I rolled into bed. Visions of my sexy chocolatier filled my mind. I pictured him running up the beach in tiny swim trunks and glistening with sweat. His wet blond curls dancing about his face as if having a party. And his smile . . . *hmmm*. It was a wonderful way to drift off to sleep.

* * *

The rest of the week was a game of cat and mouse as I made every attempt not to run into Needledick again. With each passing day it became more and more awkward, and I was soon entertaining the notion that come next year, I'd have to look for a new job. The worst part about leaving was that I'd need to find a new apartment too. But I didn't want to leave. I loved where I lived. My thoughts spun on a never-ending roundabout of reasons to stay and go.

By the time Saturday morning came around I was looking forward to the distraction Hunter promised to give. After my shift, I escaped Needledick's death stares as quickly as possible and raced to my room. An hour later I dressed in a Memphis disguise that was suitable for a morning on the beach and headed downstairs, ready for Lolly to pick me up at quarter to nine. I dodged the Needledick bullet as he was busy with guests and stepped out into the blazing sunshine.

She drove into the Hot Horizon Hotel pick-up area with a squeal of tires and a just as loud squeal from her when I opened the passenger side door.

"Holy shit, babe, you look fucking hot. That blond wig suits you."

"Thanks." I climbed in, shoved my bag to my feet, put my hat on my lap, and buckled up.

"This's going to be so much fun." She put the car into gear, and I was thrown back into my seat as she planted her foot on the accelerator.

"I hope we don't miss the start."

"We won't." Lolly accelerated through a yellow light, and I gripped onto the seat as the car bounced over the raised intersection.

Hunter's race didn't start until ten o'clock, however we needed time to park, and on the Gold Coast that was always an issue. Then we had to find him, and from what I'd seen during my Google search of open-water swimming races, there were likely to be thousands of people there.

We raced through the morning traffic with Lolita constantly changing lanes to dodge the slow cars, and found a parking spot with forty minutes to spare. I pulled on my big floppy hat and sunglasses and stepped from the car. We grabbed our bags and dodged numerous cars to cross the road toward the beach.

As I'd suspected, there were thousands of people here. Marquees were lined up along the beach offering all sorts of treats and paraphernalia, and a fun festival atmosphere emanated from the crowd and the billowing flags.

The weather was perfect, blazing sunshine, late spring temperatures in the mid-twenties, and a light breeze drifting off the ocean. Together, Lolly and I pranced across the hot sand toward a large temporary gateway that we assumed was the start and finish line.

"Do you see him?" Lolita looked stunning. Her perky boobs filled out an intense sky blue bikini with the white string straps. She covered it with a tiny white sarong wrapped around her hips and wore white Havaianas with a couple of diamante studs on her feet. Lolita was a beach babe pin-up girl, and the heads that turned her way confirmed it. She had her hair up in a high ponytail, and it swished from side to side as she took in all the action around her.

"No, not yet." As I glanced from one hot body to the next, I wondered if I'd even be able to see him. The contestants stood out because they all wore bright yellow bathing caps with numbers on them that matched the numbers painted on their arms and legs, but this only made finding Hunter more difficult. Each competitor was practically a clone of the next, with toned, fit bodies and matching headwear.

We arrived near the starting line and looked for a place to sit. At Lolita's insistence, I left her to set up and went in search of Hunter. There were thousands of people and as the minutes ticked by, I feared I'd missed the opportunity to wish him luck before his race.

I hovered around the starting banner, flitting my glances from one fitness fanatic to the next, and finally I saw him. His body was similar to every other male athlete's—toned, tanned and terrific. But it was his smile that set him apart. Hunter had an award-winning smile that captured me in so many ways.

I waved as I walked toward him. His already stunning smile became spectacular and when he waved back, delightful butterflies dancing across my stomach.

"You came." He picked me up and I clutched my bag to my side and giggled as he twirled me around.

"Of course I did."

He lowered me to my feet and as he leaned toward me, I smelt suntan lotion and saltwater. Our lips met for a brief kiss. It was too brief and I already wanted more.

He entwined his fingers with mine and pointed out toward the ocean. "Have you been to one of these before?"

"No, never."

"Okay. See those yellow buoys out there?" He leaned in so our cheeks touched and I followed his outstretched finger.

"Yes."

"We start here, run into the water and swim out to that one, go around it, swim to that one, go around it, then swim back to shore. The first one to run under this banner wins."

"Oooh, I hope it's you."

"Me too." He cupped my cheeks and kissed me again. "Me too. Maybe you'll be my lucky charm." The dazzle in his eyes reflected the excitement on his face.

I tugged my lip into my mouth as I gazed up at my hunky chocolatier. There were so many facets to Hunter, and I was truly looking forward to discovering every one of them.

"Okay, I've gotta go. Wish me luck."

I reached up onto my tippy-toes and kissed his cheek. "Good luck."

The anticipation had my stomach doing little flips as he jogged toward the start line. With ten more minutes until the beginning of the race, I returned to Lolita. She had both our towels laid out and was busy rubbing suntan lotion over her legs when I arrived.

"Find him?"

"Yes. He's so pumped."

"Oh good. Let's go over and watch the start."

I was so glad she'd said that. We left our towels, but grabbed our bags, and together we raced back to the starting line. At least forty men were lined up, and they were a united bunch, fidgeting as they jiggled from one foot to the next and shook out their arms.

We lined up along the edge of the race track, muscling in between a couple of young guys.

"Which one is he?" Lolly asked.

I pointed him out. "He's in the red swimming trunks, about . . ." I counted the men, "twenty-fifth from the left."

"The one between the guy in the blue and the guy in the black swimmers?"

"Yes, that's him."

Lolly cupped her hands around her lips. "Go Hunter," she screamed.

Hunter looked our way, and both Lolly and I waved madly at him. He gave us the thumbs up.

"He saw us," I squealed, and I jiggled up and down on the sand.

"On your marks," a voice boomed over a loud speaker, and I jumped when the starter gun exploded.

"Go Hunter!" we yelled in unison as smoking-hot bodies ran past us.

The entire group hit the water in a large splash and continued running until it was too deep. Once they started swimming it was impossible to see Hunter anymore yet I couldn't stop looking for him.

Lolly and I stayed in position as the pack of swimmers glided past one buoy after the next. My stomach was a tangle of knots as they skirted around the last marker. Four men were neck and neck at the front of the pack. It was impossible to see if Hunter was amongst them. I danced from foot to foot; I held my breath; I clapped my hands. The tension was excruciating.

Lolly let out the loudest wolf whistle I'd ever heard, and several men around us turned toward her, and by their expressions I'd say they admired her talent.

The contestants hit the beach together running. My eyes nearly burst from their sockets as I saw one of them had red swimmers on. "Go Hunter," I screamed, although I still couldn't be sure it was him. He had his head down as he dug his toes into the sand and pumped his arms and legs like crazy.

The four of them were so close. Side by side.

"Go Hunter," Lolly screamed.

Finally, he looked up, and it was him.

"Go. Go. Go." My heart was set to explode as he and another guy hit the lead. A blaze of arms and legs as they raced up the sand.

"Go!" I screamed. Lolly screamed; the whole crowd screamed.

Hunter's clenched jaw and steely gaze proved his determination. His stride was as fierce as the look on his face. The two of them raced past us, but it was impossible to tell who was winning.

"Go Hunter," Lolly and I screamed together.

And suddenly, the race was over. We had no idea who'd won. Lolly grabbed my arm and the two of us ran up to the front. "Did he win?" I yelled over the crowd noise.

"I don't know."

We raced to his side. He was bent over, heaving in ragged breaths, and we wrapped our arms around him. "Did you win?"

He looked up at us and smiled. "Don't know. Photo finish," he said between breaths.

"I'm sure you did," I said with confidence.

As more and more runners crossed the finish line, the spot where we stood grew crowded.

The officials waited until all the racers had returned before they brought the first three contestants to cross under the finish line up to a stage area.

Hunter was the tallest out of the three competitors, but that wasn't the only thing that set him apart from the other two. He was the only one smiling. After what he'd just done I'd have trouble standing, let alone looking like that.

A short man stepped up onto stage, stood beside the contestants and raised a microphone to his mouth. "I'm sorry about this delay, folks, but for the first time in the history of this race we had a photo finish."

My heart pounded in my ears as I prayed he announced Hunter as the winner.

"Okay, we have a decision. Congratulations, men—that was a magnificent race. I'm proud to announce the winner of the one-mile open-water race is Andrew Winstanley."

The wind punched out of me, and my body deflated. I was completely gutted. My mouth fell open, and I covered it as I glanced at Lolly who matched my disappointment with her bulging eyes. I turned back to Hunter to watch him shake hands and clap the winner on the back.

"That means second place goes to Hunter McCall."

Lolly released another one of her ear-piercing wolf whistles as I cheered.

"And third place goes to Todd Williamson."

Hunter and the other two finalists posed for photos, and I was impressed with how he handled coming second. He seemed genuinely pleased for the man who'd beat him.

It was an eternity before they stepped down from the stage, and when he glanced about the crowd I waved my hand over my head in the hope it was me he was looking for.

He waved back, and the three of us walked toward each other. "I thought

you'd won," I said as soon as we reached him. "I'm so sorry."
"No need to be sorry. Andrew was better than me."
"It was so close."
Lolly nudged me with her elbow. She was an impatient woman.
"Hunter, this is my friend Lolita."
"Hi. Nice to meet you."
"You were incredible." She smiled up at him.
Being this close to Hunter made it impossible to know where to look, and my eyes flitted from his chiseled torso, to his dazzling eyes that were still wired with excitement, to his plum-colored perfectly kissable lips. A trickle of water glided from his shoulder and headed towards his nipple. I couldn't tear my gaze away as the droplet crawled down Hunter's tanned, slick skin. It stopped at the tiny little lumps around the dark part of his nipple, and it took all my might not to lean over and lick it away.
"Memphis." Lolly playfully slapped my arm, snapping me from my fantasizing.
"Sorry, what did you say?"
She rolled her eyes. "Hunter was just asking what our plans were."
"Oh. We thought we'd be here for a while, so we've set up our gear over there." I pointed off to the left of the finish line.
"Okay. I'll have a swim and I'll meet you back there."
"You just had a swim." I giggled.
"Nah . . . that was a race. It's not the same." He touched my shoulder. "I'll be back soon."
He jogged down the beach and with his stunning physique centred amongst the equally stunning backdrop, it was like being on a movie set as he wove in and around the dozens of buff, nearly naked men on his journey to the ocean.
Lolly burst out laughing. "Holy shit, woman, you're drooling."
"No I'm not." But I wiped my chin just to be sure.
"It's okay, 'cause I agree with you—he's fucking gorgeous."
I chewed my bottom lip. "You think so?"
"I know so. I think you like him."
"Yeah, I do."
Once we'd lost him in the crowd, we headed toward our towels. The sand was hot under my feet and the sun was equally intense on my flesh.
We sat down, and Lolly reached for a water bottle from her bag. "So are you going to fuck him later?"
My god, she was loud. I cringed as I gazed at the dozens of people around us and wondered just how many had heard her. "Shhh."
"What? No one's listening; just answer the question."

I glanced around and incredibly, it didn't appear that anyone had heard. "Maybe."

"I would. He's yummy. I bet he tastes yummy with all that chocolate he's eating." She wriggled her eyebrows, and I scrunched up my face cringing not only at how loud she was but at her question.

"Oh, you don't like the taste?"

Holy shit. I turned to the ocean and prayed for Hunter to save me right now.

"Pineapple," she said.

I turned back to her. "What?"

"Yeah, feed him pineapple. It'll make his semen taste better."

I leaned in closer in the hope that she'd dial down her voice. "Really?"

"Sure. Why do you think I cook Hawaiian pizza and sweet and sour chicken every week?"

I burst out laughing. "Are you serious?"

"Cross my heart. And whatever you do, don't give him asparagus."

The sincerity on her face had me laughing until tears flowed down my cheeks. "Oh my god, Lolly, you're a hoot."

"Just imparting my vast wisdom on my young protégé."

I rolled my eyes. "Not so young."

"Oh yeah, you're really old now."

"Gee thanks."

We were silent long enough for me to feel the penetration of the sun despite my enormous broad-brimmed hat. A trickle of sweat rolled from under my boob and down my belly. Worst of all, the damn wig made my brain feel like it was frying. I needed to cool down before I passed out.

I stood up, plucked my bikini bottom out of my butt, unwrapped my sarong and placed it over my bag. "I'm going to watch Hunter. Want to come?"

"Sure." Lolly launched to her feet and as we strolled toward the water, I swear every man on the beach turned to watch her. Lolly could stop a nation in that sexy bikini.

It seemed like hundreds of people were crammed into the safe zone between the red and yellow life-saver flags. We waded into the cool water, up to our knees in the tumbling waves, and tried to find Hunter in amongst the crowd.

The waves were random in size; one would barely touch our ankles and the next would crash halfway up our thighs. Crazy kids on body boards dodged around us as the water pummeled them into shore. Even smaller children played in the shallows with protective parents watching their every move. I was close to giving up on searching for Hunter when a man waved at us from barely ten feet away.

"Oh, there he is." I pointed at him and waved, and his smile lit up his face. He turned, took a few high-knee steps over the water and then dived through a wave. He made it look elegant as he waded back out to deeper water.

It was difficult to keep my eyes on him as he went under and over waves and continued farther and farther out. But soon he seemed to just float on top, rolling up and over the swell before they became a barrel of white water.

He started swimming and next second he was on top of a wave, his right arm pointed forward and his body rigid as he impersonated a surfboard. Hunter rode the wave like an expert, dodging people who got in his way, and let it carry him all the way into the beach. He only stopped when the water was so shallow that when he stood up it was barely knee-deep.

I clapped at the spectacle. Hunter had made it look so easy even though I was sure it wasn't. He waded toward us, water glistening off his chiseled abs, the sun shining on his golden hair as he flicked it out of his eyes, his tiny briefs barely containing what I knew was concealed beneath. I could hardly breathe as I watched the scene unfold before me as if it were in slow motion.

"That was fun." His sexy baritone had my knees buckling.

A little piece of me fell in love with him right then. And it wasn't just his voice. He looked relaxed, fit, and oh-so contented. Some of the men I'd met this year had been desperate, needy, eager to be accepted, but Hunter seemed truly comfortable with who he was.

"Do you get to the beach often?" Lolly smiled up at him.

He cocked his head. "As often as I can. I live down at Byron, so I try to surf at least twice a week. Do either of you surf?"

"I used to," Lolly said.

I wasn't surprised. She'd done absolutely every sport imaginable.

I shook my head. "I don't."

"Maybe I could teach you." He touched my shoulder again, and I was certain the earth moved this time.

As much as I loved the idea of him teaching me anything, the thought of being in the tumbling ocean terrified me. "Maybe." I didn't feel the need to elaborate on my fear right then.

"Would you like an ice cream? My treat."

"Oh, I'd love one."

Lolly shook her head. "I'll meet you back at the towels."

"I'll just grab my bag." Hunter and I strolled toward the race marshalling tent and it was heavenly being at his side. Our conversation flowed so easily I was fooled into thinking we'd known each other for years. The truth, however, was that he didn't know me at all. He only knew Memphis.

My heart squeezed at the terrible web of lies I'd created.

He ducked into the tent and moments later emerged with a backpack slung over his shoulder and again fell in at my side. At the ice cream tent, we selected our flavors, rum and raisin for him and macadamia caramel swirl for me, and headed back toward Lolita.

I spied our spot easily as Lolly had three men standing around her as she applied sunscreen to her toned belly. The woman was a hunk magnet.

The men took off as we arrived and we remained standing side by side to lick our ice creams before they melted down our arms.

"I'm going to head off. Leave you two lovebirds to it." Lolly swung her legs to the side, kneeled, and stood up.

I tried to catch my melting ice cream with my tongue. "Oh no, don't go," I said.

"It's okay, you can stay," Hunter said at the same time as me.

"No. No." She flicked her hand. "Three's a crowd. Memphis and I've already talked about threesomes."

I gasped, and Hunter turned to me with a cheeky grin.

"Ask her about it sometime." Lolly burst out laughing.

Oh god. I wanted to dive into the sand and be buried beneath a giant castle.

Hunter laughed along with Lolly though, and it was such a wonderful, genuine sound that I joined in too. "You'll have to excuse her. She has no scruples."

"What?" She faked hurt by clutching her chest. "Want me to leave both towels with you?"

Hunter looked to me for an answer, and I shrugged. "Sure."

"Okay babe." She leaned in to hug me. "Remember what I said about pineapple."

I gasped again and bulged my eyes at her.

"What's this about pineapple?" Hunter grinned at me.

"Oh, nothing." I licked my ice cream, hopeful that it would provide a distraction.

"She'll tell you later." Lolly smacked Hunter on the bottom, grabbed her bag and strolled up the beach with the eyes of every man she passed turning to her.

He turned to me, smiling. "She's a card."

"You don't know the half of it."

Hunter sat onto Lolita's towel and I sat on mine beside him. We both faced the ocean with our legs splayed out before us but my focus was on my ice cream as I raced against gravity to lick the dribbles before I wore them.

"Are you going to tell me about the pineapple thing?"

"Oh god." I shook my head. "No."

He crinkled his nose at me. "I predict you'll tell me before the night's out."

"No I won't."

"Ah, so that wasn't a no to spending the night with me then."

I couldn't help but smile. "Are you asking me on a date?" I liked this little repertoire we'd instigated months ago.

"I do believe I am." He ran his tongue up the length of his ice cream cone. I'd fallen into a dream. A perfect, highly erotic daydream. "Unfortunately, I start work at nine-thirty tonight."

"Oh, bugger." He blinked at me. "Can I see you before work then?"

I smiled, pleased that he'd asked. "I'd love to."

As much as I wanted to spend the entire day here on the beach with him, I couldn't stand the heat any more, and not only did I risk my abundant makeup melting off but the wig was seriously frying my brain. "Well, I need to have a sleep before work."

I crawled forward in an awkward attempt to avoid getting sand on my towel and stood up. He stood too and stepped toward me. The warmth of his body, the smell of his skin, the depth of his smile—all of them were magnets drawing me closer. He placed his hand on my waist, and I melted beneath his touch. I copied his move and rested my hand on his side, resisting the urge to glide my hand over all the gloriously toned muscles.

He leaned down to kiss me and the second our mouths met, the entire world around me evaporated into obscurity. His touch, his smell, his taste captured me in so many ways. It was over in a flash and I ran my tongue over my lips, desperate to taste more of him.

He reached down to gather his towel from the sand and with a horrible realization, I admitted our brief intimate moment was over.

As we packed up our things, we agreed to meet at his room in the Hot Horizon Hotel at seven o'clock. To avoid his offer to catch a taxi together I made up a story that I had to go grocery shopping. It was true, but the thought of doing it with my brain cooking in the wig was extra motivation for the little white lie.

When my turn for a taxi arrived, Hunter kissed me again and before I knew it I was whisked away with an aching heart.

The second I hopped out of the taxi I scurried inside, fearful Hunter would be in a taxi right behind me. I picked up my pace even more as I crossed the lobby, determined not to let Needledick ruin the wonderful morning I'd had so far.

At my room, I tore off my wig, unclipped my sweat-soaked hair and climbed into a cold shower. It was an eternity before my body cooled down enough for me to step out. By the time I crawled into bed, I was well and truly ready for sleep.

* * *

My alarm startled me awake, and with a groan I rolled over to turn off the blaring music. But I didn't stay there long as I had just forty-five minutes before my hot date with Hunter. The very thought of him had butterflies dancing across my stomach.

As much as I didn't want to, I reapplied the abundant makeup necessary to hide Jane and create the cat-eyed Memphis look Hunter knew me as. My hair was still damp from my shower before I slept, which made it easier to plait and pin up for the blond bob wig again.

My choice of outfit for today was my navy and cream shift dress that showed off today's tanning on my legs. The dress was fresh and summery and suited the day I'd already had with Hunter perfectly. For something a little sexy, I decided on lace lingerie that consisted of a fitted bodice and matching G-string. I'd bought this cute matching set months ago, yet this would be the first time I'd worn it.

I tugged the bodice into place, plumping my lopsided boobs into position, and pulled on the G-string. The dress fell loosely over the top and had no zips or clips, perfect for easy removal. To match the navy, I wore a pair of navy suede lace-up shoes.

Once I was dressed, I glanced in the mirror. The sun I'd had today gave my skin a lovely healthy glow, which was made even more lovely against the cream of the dress. Happy with my Memphis look, I grabbed my bag and headed up to my sexy chocolatier.

Hunter opened the door after I knocked just once, and I was greeted by a dozen kinds of delightful. His smile. His scent. His eyes. I could stand there and admire him all night long. He wore a rust colored T-shirt with a scattering of words that I couldn't work out and dark denim jeans that suited him perfectly. It was casual attire but on Hunter it screamed sexy and devilishly dangerous. He leaned in to kiss me, and this morning's scents of suntan lotion and sea salt were replaced with hints of floral and spice.

"Did you have a good sleep?" He shut the door and led me into the room.

"Yes, thank you." *It would've been much better with you in my bed beside me.* That thought tumbled from nowhere and my insides purred at how delightful it sounded.

"Would you like a drink? I bought wine."

"Oh I shouldn't really. Not before work." The smile on his face fell away, and I felt like I'd ruined some master plan he'd set up. "Okay, I will, but just one glass."

His smile was back, and I hoped I wouldn't regret that decision come midnight tonight when I was bored at the reception desk downstairs.

He poured the wine into our glasses, and I was grateful it was white wine and not red. I'd definitely be in trouble with red. He led us out to the balcony, and we sat side by side on the chairs. Hunter had arranged a plate of food and the second I laid eyes on it, I realized I'd forgotten to eat before I came up. That wasn't like me. Food usually dominated most of my thoughts.

"What have you got here?" I couldn't resist asking and scoured the plate, examining the tantalizing nibbles.

"When I told Mom I was coming up to see you, she insisted on making something."

"You told your mom?" My jaw dropped.

My horror must've shown on my face because he blinked at me and reached over to touch my arm. "Oh, don't worry. It's not like that. I have to drip-feed Mom information or she won't stop asking questions. But I was at their place yesterday, and she grilled me over why I was coming up to the Gold Coast again. She's good at that. Anyway . . ." He shrugged. "I couldn't help but talk about you. I find you fascinating."

Fascinating! Okay, he's forgiven. My heart fluttered at the intense desire in his eyes. I was two seconds away from jumping his bones when he glanced away from me and down at the food.

"Anyway . . ." He pointed at tiny pastry cups that looked to be filled with a white custard. "These are Mom's famous cheese puffs. You top them with the quince jelly. It's heaven in your mouth. Trust me."

Oh hello. It was impossible to resist after that introduction. I plucked one, topped it with quince jelly just like he'd suggested, and popped it into my mouth. He copied my move, and we watched each other eat.

The taste was sensational. Creamy complex cheese, buttery pastry, sweet quince—I was in culinary heaven.

"Oh my god. Yum." I reached for another.

"I told you. People line up for these whenever Mom entertains. The trick is the cheese; Mom has our local deli specially import it for her from France. You can't get it here otherwise."

"Wow."

While Hunter chatted more about the cheese and the lovely region in the French Riviera where it came from, I devoured another two pastries and became enraptured with his voice. We sipped our wine, ate some more, laughed a lot, and as the night rolled on, we touched each other more. Fleeting touches at first—his hand on my arm, mine on his. He wiped a crumb from my lip, and I fed a nibble into his mouth.

I wanted to stay all night long.

No, it was more than that—I wanted to stay with Hunter forever. It was a wonderful realization. He made me feel incredible. My heart swelled just looking at him, but when we shared a conversation my heart leapt for joy. I'd never used the term soul mate before. I'd never thought they were real, but now, after spending more wonderful hours with my handsome chocolatier, I wondered if I may have found mine.

Hunter reached over and wove our fingers together. I turned to him and our eyes met, and the silent communication that sizzled between us had my heart soaring. Pushing off my chair, I went to him, straddled his legs, put my arms around his neck, and planted my lips on his.

Our kiss wasn't constrained. It was wild, heated, and full of passion. Our tongues explored, our hands groped, and my body heat elevated. We moaned together, and I drove my fingers through his hair and grabbed a handful, holding him to me.

He pushed forward on his chair, curled his arms around me and lifted me up. I wrapped my legs around him, and our mouths remained locked together as he carried me inside. He put me on the kitchen counter and together we raised my dress up over my head, and his eyes widened when they lowered to my sexy lingerie. He ran his hand from my neck to between my breasts, and I planted my hands behind me on the counter and arched my back as his hands travelled down my body.

My flesh sizzled. I was an inferno about to self-combust, and I wriggled my hips in reaction to the party raging in my pussy. I parted my legs farther as his hand reached my G-string. He ran his thumb over my vagina, and the pressure he applied and the friction of the lacy fabric was fantastic.

He hooked his fingers into my underpants and peeled them off. I parted my legs and his hands glided up my thighs. He wasted no time pushing a finger inside me. I gasped, and he sucked the air in through his teeth as he drilled his digit into me with a fascinating twisting motion. I laid back on the counter, gasping at the coolness on my skin, and next second, his tongue was on me. In me.

He licked my pussy and sucked my clit into his mouth. When he added a finger to his already magical repertoire I clawed at the counter. I raised my hips. I gasped for air. Every nerve ending was set to explode as he continued to build my orgasm.

I screamed out as I tipped over the magical edge, and my juices squirted from my body.

Hunter left the counter and through my sex-fueled haze I watched him strip off and roll a condom on. He returned to me, his eyes glazed, his jaw ajar, and his penis thick and long. I reached up and planted my hands on his shoulders, ready to watch the show.

And oh, what a show it was. Hunter guided his penis to my vagina, pushed the head into my folds, spreading me apart. His fingers dug into my hips as he guided himself into me, driving right to the very hilt. He filled me so completely, like the last piece of a puzzle slotting into place.

Our eyes met. Our souls met. The two of us, united as one, was the most incredible thing in the world.

He lowered his eyes to watch our union, and I joined him in observing the spectacle. His cock withdrew, slick with my juices, and he came all the way out, showing off his swollen crown. He entered again, driving that beast all the way into me with slow precision. As I felt every inch of him, I was certain he too explored every inch of me.

Over and over he drove into me, each time slightly faster than the last. Our breathing grew rapid. His fingers dug into my flesh. My pussy pulsed, begging to be thrust into again. I clenched my muscles around him, trapping him in my core.

He cried out.

I cried out.

His thrusts hit fever pitch, and I grabbed hold of his shoulders, arched my back, and screamed as my orgasm tore through me. Hunter released a deep primal moan and slammed his cock into me over and over until finally he slowed.

His fingers gradually released their grip on my hips as his cock softened inside me. He pulled me to him, and as we wrapped our arms around each other I heard the comforting sound of his beating heart.

"Where have you been all my life, Memphis?"

His words broke my heart twice over. I squeezed him tighter and clamped my jaw, determined not to cry. He pulled away too soon, and I swallowed back the lump in my throat.

I reached up to cup his cheek. "I wish I didn't have to go to work."

"Me too." He helped me off the counter.

"May I use the bathroom?"

"Of course."

I picked my G-string off the floor, stepped around him, went to the bathroom and shut the door. I sat on the toilet, put my elbows on my knees and covered my face. The lump in my throat made it impossible to breathe. How the hell did I get myself into this mess? I knew only too well the answer to that. But what I didn't know was how to get out of it. I really, really liked Hunter, but after my continual deceit why would he forgive me? The thought of losing him strangled my heart.

I wiped my eyes, then used the toilet paper to clean myself up. I pulled on my G-string and flushed, and at the sink I checked that I hadn't ruined my makeup.

Memphis was still there, staring right back at me with her fearful eyes.

Stupid girl. "Stupid. Stupid. Stupid." I shook my head, and it was several minutes before I convinced myself to get moving again. I pulled open the door, and wearing nothing but my undies I crossed the room to Hunter, who'd collected my dress from the floor and was holding it for me.

"Thank you." I pulled the dress over my head and wriggled it into place.

He stepped to me and placed his hands on my waist. "When can I see you again?"

"Soon I hope." The urge to blurt out my horrible truth was excruciating, and I fought it with all my might.

His beautiful eyes softened and he leaned in to kiss me. Our lips met, and the lump burning in my throat ruined a perfect moment.

We parted, and I grabbed my bag. "Good night. See you soon."

"Yes you will." He blew me a kiss, and I turned and strode to the door.

I walked to the elevator and instead of my usual walking on air, today I was swimming through concrete. Every step away from Hunter hurt. My deceit and lies threatened to shatter my sanity a thousand times over.

Somehow I arrived at my room and if I didn't have to go to work, I would've crawled under my bed covers and cried myself to sleep. I sucked back the sobs as I showered and my tears mingled with the warm cascade. It was an eternity before I stepped out.

I dried myself off, and with the towel around my feet, I gripped the sink and stared at my reflection. My bloodshot eyes were a terrible shade of pink but it was the fear in them that scared me most. With my bathrobe on, I went to the kitchen, made myself a peanut butter sandwich, and then grabbed my diary and sat at the table.

Writing down my tumbling thoughts had become a form of therapy but even as I turned to the 12th of November, I wasn't sure if any amount of therapy could save me from the mess I'd put myself in.

At the top of the page I wrote *Mr. Hunter McCall Room 43*. After a big sigh, I lined the page with every wonderful aspect of my day with him. Everything from my tumbling nerves as I watched him race up the beach, to the pleasure of sharing his mother's divine cheese treats, to listening to his travel stories, to our incredible sex.

Finally, I detailed my horrible situation. I wanted to learn everything about my sexy chocolatier. But most of all, I wanted him to know me—the real me. To do that, however, I had to reveal my disgusting lies. No matter which way I analyzed how that scenario would play out, the ending was always the same.

I was destined to lose him. The idea of that ate away at my soul. As a tear trickled down my cheek, I wrote *Losing my Soul* at the top of the page.

Snapping the diary shut, I sighed and as my appetite had evaporated, I pushed my sandwich away. My mind flitted to my silly notion earlier today when I'd proclaimed that every new day was the dawn of a new beginning. It suddenly seemed foolish, and I was fairly certain I wouldn't feel any better come daylight tomorrow.

With just five weeks left, I wasn't sure if I wanted to finish my challenge.

15TH NOVEMBER
BREAKING ALL THE RULES
Room 32 - Hot Horizon Hotel

Exercise was usually the perfect way to clear my mind. Not today though. Running on the treadmill was nothing but a chore. I tried to empty my brain of the swirling thoughts and focus solely on pumping my arms in perfect coordination with my feet, but it was impossible. It'd been four days since I'd seen Hunter, and nearly every second since then I'd been analyzing my relationship with him and the stupid mess I'd put myself in.

Lolly jumped her feet to either side of her spinning treadmill and turned to me. "What's up, babe?"

I stepped to the sides of my treadmill too. "Nothing." I sighed. "Everything."

She reached over and touched my arm. "Shall we go to the coffee shop?"

Asking Lolly to cut her exercise routine short would be like asking her to cut off her left arm. Obviously, not an option. "No. I'll be okay."

"You don't look okay."

"Gee thanks." I wiped sweat from my brow.

"You know what I mean. How about we finish this workout then you can pump yourself full of sugar and tell me what's troubling you?"

"Sounds good." I jumped back on the treadmill and ran to keep up with my spinning mat.

"Thata girl."

Lolly hit the treadmill at full speed, running at a frightening pace. Her high ponytail swung from side to side and her arms thrust back and forward, yet she breathed like someone who was out for a stroll on the beach.

Forty minutes later, after an intense core body session with weights where she nearly broke me, it was finally over. We grabbed our towels and bags from the lockers and headed to the Blue Haven Café. Our usual table was vacant as if begging for our presence. Matt served us with his constant sneer, and I ordered a white chocolate and macadamia muffin warmed up, with cream on the side, and a cappuccino.

Lolly placed her standard order of green tea and the second Matt ambled away, she leaned forward and placed her hand over my wrist. "Tell me what's going on."

"It's Hunter."

"The chocolate guy? Did he do something to you?"

"No. No. Nothing like that. It's just . . . I really like him. I mean a lot. But he doesn't even know the real me. He doesn't even know my name."

"Oh babe. It'll work itself out."

I shook my head. "No, it won't. How could he forgive me after all my lies?"

"Whoa! You like him *that* much?"

I nodded. "Yes, but how do I tell him the truth after all this time?" I searched her eyes, anticipating her solution to my problems. But as the seconds ticked on, I conceded the worst . . . she didn't have one. Even Lolita, who had an answer for everything, couldn't help me. My chin dimpled, and I tugged my lip into my mouth, determined not to cry.

She squeezed my arm. "Oh babe. Don't cry."

That, of course, opened the floodgates. Tears spilled down my cheeks and I flicked them away, angry with myself. Our food and drinks arrived, and I utilized the distraction to temper my emotions. Lolita's intense blue pools examined me and I felt like she was peeling open my skull to read my brain. The second Matt left, she leaned forward. "Tell me what you're thinking."

"That I'm such an idiot."

"No you're not."

"I am." I clenched my jaw and swallowed the lump in my throat. "I've been lying to all—"

"Hello ladies. I'd hoped I'd find you here."

"Billy!" A gasp caught in my throat. My heart slammed into my chest and tears stung my eyes as I tried to take in my sexy cowboy through my blurred vision. As usual, his attire was out of place at this beach setting—a plaid shirt, tucked into jeans and hemmed in with a belt adorned by an oval buckle that caught in the sunshine. Yet rather than look ridiculous, he looked amazing. Like he belonged. He probably looked like that no matter where he was.

I wiped my eyes, hopeful he wouldn't see my tears, but when the smile fell from his face and his eyes softened, I knew I was too late. He placed his hand on my shoulder. "Hey, are you okay?"

The kindness in his voice was unbearable, and my lip quivered as I fought my sorrow. "Yes, I'm fine. Sorry." I flicked at a wayward tear.

"You don't have to be sorry. As long as you're okay."

"Would you like a seat?" Lolly probably thought she was saving me from his inquisitiveness, but the idea of him joining us was a disaster.

"I'd love to, but I can't, I'm afraid. I just wanted to invite you to come to my show today." He held a ticket toward me, and I chewed on my lip as I reached for it. "I'm sorry, Lolita; I didn't think to buy you one, too."

She fanned her hand. "It's okay; I'm busy anyway. But Jane's free, aren't you, babe?"

I tried to kick her under the table but she was out of reach. Billy's eyes drilled into me, as if silently pleading for my acceptance. As much as I'd prefer to crawl into bed, I couldn't resist him. How could I? It was amazing he even talked to me after my terrible deceit. But he hadn't just forgiven me . . . he'd come back. Many times over. I looked up at him and studied his handsome features. He was an honest man, and I was so lucky to have received his forgiveness.

"I'd love to come." I attempted to grin, though it probably looked more creepy than anything.

His smile dazzled. "Excellent. The show starts at midday—shall we meet in the hotel lobby at say eleven?"

The idea of waiting around under the ugly gaze of Needledick had me cringing. "Can we meet at the sun lounge out the front?"

"Of course." He leaned forward and when he kissed my cheek, I inhaled his sexy cologne. "I'll see you then."

He kissed Lolita's cheek too and as he walked away, I admired his butt in the tight, fitted jeans.

"Now that's a stud."

I grinned at her. "I know."

"So you get to see the cowboy in action. Giddy up."

"It does sound like fun."

"Are you kidding? Man and beast working together? That's what I call a show."

I laughed at her enthusiasm.

"You know . . ." She tapped her pink fingernail on the table. "He's proof that it's not all doom and gloom with Hunter."

I cocked my head, eager to hear her thoughts.

"If Billy can forgive you, and Henry, and that sexy hunk Corben, for that matter, then of course it's not unfeasible that Hunter could too."

I took a huge bite of my muffin, and as I chewed I considered her answer.

Was that possible? Could I hope to continue seeing Hunter after he learned of my dishonesty? I ran my spoon around my mug as I tried to envisage how that conversation with him would go. "I hope you're right."

"I'm always right. You know that."

I waggled my head at her acting like she was being silly, but of course it was true.

It was eight-thirty by the time I returned to my room and showered. I had two hours to kill before I needed to get ready for Billy, which wasn't enough time for a decent sleep. Instead, I decided to watch a movie. I rummaged through my dusty collection of DVDs and fifteen minutes later, settled on *Letters to Juliet*. After setting up the DVD, I grabbed a packet of corn chips and curled up in bed to watch it. Fearful that I may fall asleep, I set my alarm just in case.

The hours flew by and at the sound of my alarm, I went to the kitchen and made myself a strong coffee. Between sips, I splashed water on my face, applied a touch of makeup, fixed my hair and then went to my closet to decide on what to wear.

Jeans seemed the most appropriate for the Outback Spectacular, so I slipped into my underwear and tugged on the denim. I tucked the jeans into my long, tan knee-high boots, and put on a plain red button-up shirt. By the time I was dressed, thoughts of watching my sexy cowboy in action had my insides doing a little happy dance.

With my bag over my arm, I walked out the door and headed for the elevator. As I rode the elevator down to the lobby, I silently prayed John was busy.

The doors opened, and I sighed with relief at the sound of voices. As Needledick attended to two guests I dashed across the marble tiles, stepped out into the sunshine, and pulled on my sunglasses.

I was only there a minute or so before a black Holden Rodeo pulled into the drop-off zone. The window glided down, and I spied Billy behind the steering wheel. "Going my way?" he said.

I laughed, and by the time I'd stepped down the stairs to him he'd hopped out of his seat and walked around to greet me. He was a showstopper in his country-styled attire. Fitted jeans showed off the toning in his legs, and his chambray shirt, embroidered in intricate patterns across the lapels, finished off his western style.

"Wow, look at you."

His broad smile made his look all that more special. "Thanks."

We kissed each other's cheeks, and I inhaled his now familiar manly scent.

He opened the passenger door and as I slipped into the seat I was grateful Lolly had been there when Billy had asked me to go with him today. The way I'd been feeling all morning, I would probably have said no, just so I could blob in bed all day long.

"Did you have a nice morning?" He climbed behind the wheel again.
"Yes thanks. I watched a movie, *Letters to Juliet*."
"Oh, I like that movie."
"Me too." We smiled at each other, and I sensed our relationship had just crept another inch closer.

I could've gazed into his molten honey eyes for another hour or two but it was not to be. He turned his attention to the windshield, put the truck into gear, and drove onto the street.

Our conversation flowed nicely and we talked about our weeks since we'd last met. While he'd fixed fences, bought and sold a few cattle, helped a cow give birth, and fixed a broken feed trough, I'd practically done nothing. At least nothing that didn't involve the other men in my life. The only excitement I'd had was meeting the executive board. I told him what had happened.

"That manager of yours needs a reprimand."

I shot a glance at Billy. If I hadn't heard those words myself, I'd struggle to believe he'd say anything nasty about anyone. "Oh."

"He's never very friendly when I check out. It's like I'm an inconvenience. That's what I wrote on my survey, anyway."

"You did the survey?"

"A few times. I like letting places know when the service is good or bad. If they ask, I tell them."

"Oh." I didn't think anybody did those things. "Have you mentioned me in your comments?"

The dazzle in his eyes matched his brilliant smile. "Of course. I mention you to anyone who'll listen."

I returned his smile as a lovely warmth flooded my body.

The twenty-minute drive was over in a flash. Billy cruised off the highway along the service road, drove past the enormous car park designed for guests at the Outback Spectacular, and headed toward the back of the complex. We passed a staff parking sign and drove to the rear of several enormous buildings. Corrugated iron and heavy timbers gave the location an iconic Australian theme, along with the well-thought-out placement of the native plants.

We parked, and Billy raced around to open my door for me. After he shut the door, our fingers slotted together as if this were something we always did, and he led me to a door marked for staff only.

We entered without needing a key. The rustic, earthy smell of horses and hay filled the complex. Billy led me through a series of passages and then opened a door to a fancy horse stable. It was made to look rural with timber fencing and giant feature ropes draped from post to post, yet I was certain it'd have all the modern commodities.

Billy squeezed my hand. "I thought you'd like to meet Gypsy."

He led me past several stalls, and I had a quick peek into each one to spy the beautiful horses housed inside. Stopping at the fourth stall, Billy opened the gate, and we stepped into the straw-covered bay. The horse neighed at our arrival and walked over to nudge Billy with her pink nose. Other than her nose, the horse was pure white. Her mane was long and thick and obviously well maintained. Her tail, too, was just as well-groomed, and the long, flowing hairs nearly touched the ground. Billy lovingly ran his hand down the horse's nose and Gypsy, in return, nodded her head.

"This's my girl." He rubbed her behind the ears, and she pushed against him.

"She's beautiful." I stepped forward and held my hand out. Gypsy wriggled her lips over my palm as if I had something to offer.

"Gypsy, this's Jane, the girl I told you about."

Gypsy nodded as if she understood every word he'd said. Then she turned away from us and swished her tail as she plodded to the back of the stall. She reached up with her nose and when she turned back to us, she had a rose in her mouth. I gasped as Gypsy walked up to me and stopped. Her black inch-long lashes blinked as she placed the rose in my hand.

I giggled. "Oh my god. How'd you get her to do that?"

Billy smiled, triumphant. "She's a clever girl."

"I'd say her master is just as clever." If I'd thought Billy couldn't get any more handsome before, I'd been so wrong. He'd just become the poster model for cowboys everywhere.

I sniffed the rose as Billy and Gypsy nuzzled into each other. "Can she do other tricks?"

The dazzle in Billy's eyes convinced me I'd asked the right question. "She can but sometimes Gypsy is lazy." Gypsy threw her head up as if in protest, then she swished her tail, moved her hind legs forward, and sat her rump on the ground.

I laughed and clapped my hands. "That's so clever."

"She can dance too." He over-exaggerated a bow and Gypsy stood up again. Billy placed his arm up the side of Gypsy's face and put his right hand on her flank and as he stepped back and forward and side to side the horse followed his every move. They spun around and side-stepped across the stall, then finished with Billy wrapping his arms around her neck as he pulled her in for a hug. Their incredible bond was delightful to witness.

Billy turned to me, wove his fingers into mine, and led me from the stall.

"That was amazing."

"Thanks. She really is a clever horse." Billy downplayed his skill, and I imagined he always did that. My mind snapped to Henry and his lessons about accepting compliments, and I was two seconds off saying something when I stopped. I wanted to slap myself for comparing these two incredible men.

"Are you okay here for a minute?" Billy dragged me from my tumbling thoughts. "I'll just grab her a treat."

"Of course." I nodded.

"Back in a sec." He squeezed my hand and then turned and walked in the opposite direction to which we'd come. I leaned on the railing, and Gypsy walked up to me. She raised her nose and nudged my hand so I had no choice but to pat her. I'd been around horses before but had never felt as safe as I did with Gypsy.

"Who're you?"

I jumped at the sharp voice and turned to a woman in jeans and tight-fitting T-shirt, walking toward me with a bucket in each of her hands.

"I'm Jane. Billy's friend."

She huffed. "So *you're* his girlfriend."

The snide remark caught me off-guard. "Well, we're just friends at the moment."

"Is that right?" She squinted as she made a show of looking me up and down.

I stepped back, uncomfortable under her leer. After a couple of awkward seconds, I wondered if she was jealous of Billy and suddenly wished I hadn't corrected her statement.

She put the buckets down, and I stepped back farther as she put her hands on the gate. "Hey girl." Gypsy nuzzled her as she'd done with Billy, and I had a feeling this young lady had done this many times before.

"Oh hi, Sam." Billy's voice was welcome relief.

The woman turned to him and the scowl that she'd shown me converted to a smile, morphing her into a beautiful young woman.

"Hi Billy." It was painfully obvious that Sam was very interested in my cowboy.

Billy reached the stable and leaned over the gate to offer Gypsy a carrot. As the horse chomped at the treat, Billy held onto the end of it, fighting against the horse's strength with each bite. Sam giggled as she watched the struggle between man and beast. While Billy glanced in my direction, Sam, on the other hand, didn't take her eyes off him. He was completely oblivious to her attention.

Gypsy devoured the carrot in a few seconds, and Billy rubbed her nose again. "Okay, Gypsy. I've gotta take Jane up to her seat. I'll be back for you soon."

The horse whinnied as if protesting, and he pulled Gypsy's nose up to his lips and kissed her. "You're still my girl."

The horse nodded, and I was certain she'd understood every word he'd said.

"See you soon, Sam."

"It was nice to meet you," I said, although it hadn't been nice at all.

"You too." Sam's sneer proved she didn't mean it either.

Billy led me away from the stables, and with each person we encountered along the way to the arena he introduced me. It seemed like not only did he know everyone, but based on their weird ogling, I imagined that Billy had told every one of them about me.

Crowds of people poured into the stadium, seeking out their spots as Billy led me to mine. I had a front row seat in the middle of the arena. At his indication, I sat with my rose on my lap, and he leaned in to kiss my cheek.

"Are you okay here?"

"Of course."

"Okay. I'll see you soon."

No sooner had he left than a waiter arrived to take my meal order. My grumbling tummy was happy with the meal choices, and within twenty minutes, my steak and salad, squishy bread roll, and a glass of wine arrived and was positioned on the narrow table before me. People filled the seats quickly, and just after I finished my meal, a layer of smoke billowed across the sand-covered arena floor. The lights dimmed, and a hush fell over the crowd as if everybody held a collective breath. Loud music echoed about the enclosed space and spectacular lighting announced the start of the show.

And then Billy arrived.

He was at full gallop on his beautiful white horse. His cowboy hat was white too, matching Gypsy perfectly. He was a white knight. My white knight. I smiled so broadly at that wonderful thought my lips quivered. The crowd cheered with me as Billy launched up from the saddle to stand on Gypsy's back as she galloped around the outer edge of the arena. The two of them were a magnificent spectacle, and I was as star-struck as a lovesick teenager when Billy tipped his hat at me as he galloped past.

Two other horses came out to join Billy. Their riders were scantily clad women and I sat forward in my seat, desperate to see if Sam was one of them. Their tricks were timed to choreographed perfection as the horses galloped around the stadium. It wasn't until the horses had been around twice that I confirmed that yes, Sam was indeed one of the riders. Knots of jealousy prickled my stomach, and I fought to smack that silly emotion aside.

For the next hour, Billy did one clever horse trick after another. Each one was more daring than the last, and I cheered and clapped them all. Dogs, too, were in the show, enthralling the crowd with their funny yet highly skilled antics. Billy's tricks were a cut above all the other riders', and I had a silly notion he did them all just for me. Considering he'd always presented himself as shy when he was in my company, he was anything but in this environment.

After the show, the lights came on, and people stood to make a hasty exit from the stadium. I remained seated, certain Billy would find me as soon as he could.

I didn't have to wait long. My sexy cowboy was at my side within five minutes of the closing act. He still wore his white hat and looked as stunning as ever with his broad smile dominating his face.

"What'd you think?" He sat at my side, and I kissed his cheek.

"It was magnificent. You're so talented."

"I'm glad you liked it." He stood up and reached for my hand and with my rose in my fingers, led me from the stadium, back out to the stables. We returned to Gypsy's stall, and after I'd fed her a carrot, Billy showed me how to brush her down. I caught Billy's molten honey eyes glancing at me over Gypsy's flank, and each time I met his gaze, his smile warmed my insides. The horse shared her attention between the two of us, nudging us when we stopped rubbing.

"She likes you." Billy looked as proud as a father with a newborn.

"I think she likes the attention."

"Not necessarily. She's pretty feisty with some people."

"Really?"

"Oh yeah. Horses are clever. They have an instinct for someone not being quite right."

I tried to stifle a yawn, but felt awful when he noticed. "Sorry."

"It's okay, you must be exhausted. Let's get you home for some sleep."

"I'm fine."

He touched my arm, and our eyes met. This strong, amazing hunk of a man had a lovely soft side to him, and my body turned to mush as he curled his hand on my cheek and I leaned into him. "It's okay. I understand." He took the horse brush from my hand and hooked it up on the wall with his brush. After another lengthy goodbye with Gypsy, he led me out the back again and to his truck.

During the ride home, I fiddled with the stem of the rose as we talked about the show. I tried not to voice my lousy opinion of Sam every time he mentioned her name, which was often.

The conversation turned to his other horses back home, and it was impossible not to notice the pride he had for his animals. I imagined he'd spend loads of time out in his vast paddocks tending to his animals, and as the miles cruised past, I wondered how or even if I'd fit into that picture.

We turned off the highway, and he reached over to touch my knee. "I know you're tired but . . . ummm, would you like to come up to my room?"

"I'd love to." No hesitation was required. It didn't matter how tired I was; I had all the time in the world for Billy.

His magnificent grin dazzled me, and I smiled back at him. The two of us were like giddy teenagers and soon we broke out into fits of laughter. As I wiped my laughter tears away and his melodic chuckle filled the car, I reminded myself once again of just how lucky I was.

He drove the truck down to the hotel parking garage, and as he pulled into his designated parking space, I recalled the time Henry had brought me down here and how I didn't want Needledick to see me with a man. This time, however, I didn't care what he thought. I wanted to walk right alongside Billy, and be proud of the man at my side. My chest swelled at that decision and as we hopped out of the truck and met at the hood, our hands wove together like they were meant to be.

In comfortable silence, we walked up the ramp and onto the steps. At the top of the stairs the glass doors slipped open, and I made a show of sniffing my rose we strolled hand in hand across the lobby. For the first time in . . . probably ever, I wanted Needledick to see me, but he wasn't there. The lobby was empty and eerily silent. I had no idea where he was, and I didn't care either.

The elevator dinged open, and we stepped in and with Billy at my side, I pressed the button for my floor. When the doors shut, I leaned across the gap between us and closed my eyes, and a heartbeat later our lips met. I had intended for it to be a brief kiss, but the second we touched and I inhaled his sexy scent it was like I was possessed. I moaned and parted my lips, allowing his tongue entry. His breathing increased, and as our kiss deepened a lovely tremor purred through my insides. Billy knew how to ignite all my senses.

Our kiss ended and I reluctantly pulled back, but the lust in Billy's eyes confirmed he'd felt the same fireworks I had. I cleared my throat and twirled the rose in my fingers. "So . . . I'll see you in about twenty minutes."

"Come up whenever you're ready. I'm in room thirty-two."

"Okay, I won't be long." At my apartment, I filled a glass with water for my rose and positioned it in the center of my table. This was the first time a man had ever given me a flower, and I now understood why such a thing was considered so special. I smiled and stood back to admire the rose's beauty. The way Billy had presented it would probably make it the most special flower I'd ever receive.

I went to the bathroom, brushed my teeth, and stood out on the balcony for a couple of minutes, giving Billy time to get to his room. Lovely butterflies danced in my stomach at the prospect of going up to my hunky cowboy. I yawned again and decided I needed to keep moving before sleep took hold completely. I just hoped I didn't yawn once I was in his company.

Twenty minutes after I arrived in my apartment, I grabbed my bag and left again. Billy answered the door at my first knock. The towel in his hand confirmed he'd just stepped from the shower. My timing was perfect. His slicked-back hair had him looking just like Chris Hemsworth, and my

breath caught in my throat at the spectacle. "Am I too early?"
"Not at all." He stepped aside, and I entered the room.
I crossed the carpet, tossed my bag on the table and turned to him. Billy wore jeans and a white T-shirt, and as hard as it was to believe, the casual style had him looking a hell of a lot hotter than he had earlier. I stepped up to him, placed my hands over the pecs bulging through the T-shirt, and smiled. "You look incredible."
The dazzle in his eyes had him looking at me as if I were a goddess. My whole body glowed under his gaze. He tossed the towel aside, glided one arm around my shoulders, drove another through my hair, and pulled me in for a kiss. It wasn't a slow tentative kiss—this one was driven by passion. Passion and a whole lot more—desire, lust, longing . . . All of it tumbled into one, driving my mind and body crazy. I wanted this hot cowboy on me, and in me. Now.
Fumbling with the button and zipper on his jeans, I was grateful he didn't have his fancy belt buckle on this time. I peeled the denim open, glided my fingers across the taut muscles between his hips, and fed my hands into his T-shirt. The warmth of his flesh was heavenly as I curled my hands up his torso and helped him out of his shirt.
I latched my lips around his nipple to suck and gently nibble at the hardened flesh. Billy hissed and clawed his hand through my hair. As I repeated the move, I wove my fingers into the elastic of his underpants, curled them under his cock, and released that glorious muscle from its constraint.
I stepped back to admire his beast, and my eyes were witness to the greatest masterpiece on earth. Billy was exquisite in every way. Highly toned muscles in all the right places, narrow hips that fed into designer jeans, and a cock that protruded from the zipper, large and proud and with a slight curve to the left, begging me to touch it.
With Billy's molten eyes on me, I stepped back and my fingers trembled as I stripped out of my clothes as quickly as I could. Naked now, I stepped forward again, fell to my knees, peeled his jeans to his ankles, and with one hand around his cock, I glided my tongue around his swollen crown.
Billy dug his fingers into my shoulders, and I inhaled glorious scents of both soap and hot-blooded man as I sucked him into my mouth. His cock pulsed along my tongue, growing and swelling by the second. The power I had over him had my insides pulsing out a heady beat. Warmth blazed through me, down my spine, between my legs, and deep inside my body. I curled my tongue across his shaft as I slipped my lips down, drawing him into my throat. I reached around to dig my fingers into the muscular flesh of his derriere, squeezing the perfect mound in my hand.
I drew back, gliding my lips up his shaft, and as I rolled my tongue around his crown I looked up at him. His eyes were glazed; his dark pupils almost

swallowed his gorgeous honey-colored irises, but when he clenched his jaw and sucked air in through his teeth I knew he could see me.

A pearl of semen bubbled at the slit in his crown, and I groaned at the gloriousness of it. I made a show of curling my tongue around his swollen head, gradually getting closer to the tempting treat. It was hard to know what to watch . . . what I was about to lick or his eyes watching me lick it. I couldn't hold back a moment longer, and I glided my tongue over the semen and then probed the hole, seeking more.

It was salty and sweet, not entirely delicious, but not nasty either. As Billy dug his fingers into the flesh at my shoulders, I continued to have my way with him, sucking him into my mouth, rolling my tongue around his shaft, and lapping up tasty droplets as soon as they appeared. Billy was putty in my hands, and the sizzling sensations coursing through me confirmed I loved every moment of it, too.

Soon my greedy pussy demanded attention, and the second I pulled back and went to stand up, Billy hooked his hands under my arms and launched me to my feet. He pulled me in, wrapped his arms around me and glided kisses down my neck. His lips and tongue teased my flesh, drawing out tantalizing goose bumps.

His hand on my boob squeezed my flesh and pinched my nipple, no longer that of the sweet gentleman I'd known before. This was different—as if he'd been gripped with a passion that'd sapped all his control. The wild rawness of our desires drove me crazy, and I grabbed his hand and fed it between my parted legs. He took my invitation and from the moment his finger slipped inside me, I launched into another glorious, sensation-filled world.

My body took over. Shudders of pleasure rolled through me, starting deep inside my pussy and pulsing to every one of my nerve endings. I gasped for air and bent my knees as he drove two fingers into me with perfect repetition. The build-up was magnificent, taking me to that exquisite edge of gloriousness. My insides clenched around his fingers. My tongue lashed out, seeking any part of his flesh I could taste. My hand wrapped around his rock-hard cock and pumped with a wild abandonment to match his probing fingers.

An orgasm ripped through me, and I threw my head back, gripped onto his torso, and gasped at the waves of pleasure pulsing from my vagina. Over and over my juices spilled across his hand, down my legs, and trickled onto the carpet. I panted for breath, and my knees trembled as Billy placed his hands on my hips and guided me toward his bed. He lay me down, ever the gentleman, and as I enjoyed the post-orgasm pulses throbbing through my body I watched him tear open a condom packet and slide the rubber onto his magnificent erection.

I wriggled up the bed, centering myself on the covers and giving Billy room. As I parted my legs, he crawled up toward me. He leaned forward, placed one hand beside my breast for support and with his other hand, he guided his cock to my opening. He paused there, his eyes glazed, lost to another world, then as he sucked in a breath, he pushed his penis into me.

He filled me so completely, like he was meant to be there, then he stopped. Billy reached for my ankles and pulled my feet up so they rested on his shoulders, bending me at a ninety-degree angle. It was a little uncomfortable, but a lot of incredible. When he leaned forward, raising my bottom higher off the sheets, he placed his other hand on the bed and hovered above me like a muscular warrior who'd captured his conquest. He could capture me like this any day.

His cock was now deep, deep inside me, and I tried to keep my eyes open, eager to watch the magic happen. His muscles rippled with each movement, bulging and flexing in time to his thrusts. His tongue lashed out over his lips and his breathing grew faster. His penetration increased, ramming me over and over, building my next orgasm with expert timing.

I clawed my nails up his back and squeezed my eyes shut as his jackhammer slammed into me. Billy was out of control, thrusting into me with a ferocious intensity that I hadn't seen from him before. It was fast and hard, and out-of-this-world incredible.

I screamed as my orgasm shot through me, spilling my hot come around his plunging cock. Billy released a primal growl and slammed his hips forward again and again and again.

Soon his tempo slowed, and his penis softened inside me. The hardness in his face relaxed, and after a while, he opened his eyes. "You okay?"

I smiled and reached up to place my hand on his cheek. "Of course."

He curled his right arm around my leg, unhooking my ankle from his neck and allowing me to lower my foot to the bed. He repeated the move with his other arm and rolled onto his side. I wriggled into his embrace and trailed my fingers over his abs, tracing out the chiseled muscles. His breathing gradually returned to normal, as did his heartbeat, and it was a blissful dream finishing this way.

"Jane, I want to ask a question, but you don't need to answer straight away."

I stiffened, and for some inexplicable reason I feared he were about to propose. My mind went crazy, and I sucked in a shaky breath and I forced myself to calm down. "Okay," I finally managed to say.

"I'd like to take you out to my farm to see where I live. To see my home, my horses, and my folks. Please think about it, and you can tell me when I'm here next time. I'm due back in a couple of weeks."

Both relief and worry strangled my emotions with equal intensity. I was grateful he'd offered me time to think about his request.

"Okay. I'll think about it." As I breathed in deep I realized this was the most logical next step in our relationship. *Oh god, are we in a relationship?* That thought shattered all the wonderful feelings that'd been coursing through me just moments ago. Not because I didn't want to be in a relationship with Billy. Lord no. It was because I was also seeing several other men. I'd officially slipped into two-timing, or in reality, multiple-timing, and the realization threatened to split my heart in two.

With my brain about to crack open with horrid frenzied thoughts, I pushed up onto my elbow, gave Billy a quick kiss on his cheek, and slid off the bed. I put my clothes on as quickly as I could and reached for my bag.

Billy was on his side, a pillow covering his groin, and I blew him a kiss, walked to his door, and exited the room. On autopilot, I made it to my apartment and took a long, hot shower. My brain was a crazy scramble as I weighed the pros and cons of his request.

After my shower I put on my PJs, reached for my diary and turned to the 15th of November. At the top I wrote *Cowboy Billy Room 32*. Beneath his name I listed in great detail all about my wonderful day with him and his glorious horse, Gypsy. My pen couldn't keep up with my brain as I relayed our fiery sex, and finally I outpoured my concern over his question. By the time I'd finished writing I'd filled two pages, and I still didn't have an answer for Billy.

Whilst the idea of seeing the real man behind the Gold Coast version I'd met many times over was exciting, the thought of meeting his family and stepping further into a relationship with him scared me. Not because I didn't want Billy—no, he was still very, very high on my want list. But there were other men I liked too. A lot. With that thought, next to Billy's name at the top I wrote, *Breaking all the Rules*.

"Oh god." I snapped the diary shut and flopped back onto my bed.

As I stared at the ceiling, I found it impossible to comprehend that this time last year the men in my life were as scarce as my diamond rings. Now I had so many to choose from, my head spun with the possibilities.

I stood, pulled back my covers and climbed into bed. As I tugged my sheet up to my chin, pictures of all the wonderful men I'd met this year flashed across my closed eyes like they were on a roulette wheel.

I jumped at the sound of my phone and groaning, I crawled out of bed. I tugged it from my bag and glanced at a number I didn't recognise.

I jabbed the green button. "Hello?"

"Hi Jane, it's Richard Thompson here. Sorry to bother you, but the executive board would like to arrange another time to meet with you."

Oh faaark. My heart exploded so fast, it was a wonder I didn't pass out. "Okay." More words wouldn't formulate.

"Would next Friday suit you, the 25th at say ten-thirty?"

I swallowed. "Okay," I repeated barely able to breathe.

"Perfect. We shall see you then."

I stared at the phone long after he hung up. If I'd thought my world was messed up before, now I was totally screwed.

I put the phone on my bedside table, crawled back into bed, and rolled onto my side. But as I stared wide-eyed at my spare pillow, I knew there was little chance I'd fall asleep.

Kitty Kendall

25ᵀᴴ NOVEMBER
MISSION COMPLETE
Room 11 - Hot Horizon Hotel

I glanced at the clock for the hundredth time and huffed. It was only just past five a.m. Every minute of last night's shift had dragged by and only served to give me more time to think about this morning's second meeting with the executive board. Ever since they'd called me last week, I'd had knots in my stomach as I contemplated if I was about to lose my job.
If it did happen, I was undecided if that was good or bad. On one hand I felt it was time for me to move on and look for a job with more normal hours. But on the other hand, I liked working here.
In addition to this was my challenge. I was five weeks off completing my sexual journey, and I had every intention of succeeding, but the idea of doing it anywhere else was impossible to comprehend.
I went to the staffroom and turned on the kettle. As I waited for the water to boil, I nibbled on a protein bar and tried to weigh up in my head the pros and cons of not working here.
"Is anybody home?" The deep voice coming from reception shattered my introspection and I strolled toward it, wiping my mouth for crumbs.
"Corben!" My morning just got a thousand times better as I ran my eyes over my gorgeous hunk. Like usual, his arms were in full view, showing off the spectacular tattoos adorning his golden flesh.
"Memphis Jane, how you doing?"

"I'm okay."
"Oh wow. You don't sound okay."
I rolled my eyes. "Well no, not really, but I'll be fine."
"What's happening?"
I waved my hand. "It's a long story."
"Right. Well how about we go for a run and talk about it?"
The idea of getting a little sweaty with Mr. Universe was tantalizing, but not possible. "I wish I could, but I've got a meeting this morning."
"What time?"
"Oh ummm, ten-thirty."
"Excellent. That gives us time for a run and a fuck."
"Corben!" My jaw dropped as I scanned the lobby, even though I knew it was empty.
"What? Nobody heard."
It was true, but still . . . "I don't know."
"Yes you do. Don't you want to run with me?" He folded his arms across the counter, and his stunning rose tattoo bulged on his equally impressive bicep.
"Yes, but—"
"It's the sex then."
"What? No it's—" I shook my head.
"Well that settles it." He slapped his palm on the counter. "I'll meet you out the front at seven."
He turned, and I ogled his incredible bottom retreating from me as he jogged across the lobby and vanished through the sliding glass doors. Giggling, I returned to the staffroom and poured boiling water onto my green teabag. Corben sure was a bossy boots, but I couldn't imagine him being any other way.
The more I contemplated the idea of going for a run and having steamy sex before my meeting, the more I realized it was perfect. Not only would it take my mind off the executive board, but also, if I did lose my job, then it promised to end with a bang. A hot and steamy bang.
I laughed as I crossed the lobby with my tea, and the sound echoed about the marble expanse like a lovely melody. The sun had bounced up from the ocean about half an hour ago and its golden rays were already loaded with a dose of heat. Not even a whisper of breeze rustled the Pandanus palms and the rainbow lorikeets, who normally welcomed in the day with hyperactivity and raucous screeching, were absent today. I sipped my tea and breathed in the fresh ocean air. As the minutes ticked by and I inhaled my marvelous vista, I realized that what I'd truly miss the most if I lost my job was my apartment. I loved living here. Well not necessarily here, but by the ocean.
I finished my tea and strolled back inside. My final hour whizzed by as four couples with early checkouts occupied my time. The end of my shift arrived

without any sign of Needledick, and as the minutes ticked by, I wondered if he was meeting the executive team this morning too. If he was worried about losing his job he sure had a funny way of showing it.

It was ten minutes to seven when he finally lobbed through the doors. The dark shadow across his lower face confirmed he was unshaved. His hair was scrambled in all directions, and the crinkles in his shirt made it look as if he'd slept in it. But it was the nasty scowl on his face that showed he didn't want to be here. If anything, it should've been me scowling at him.

"You *do* know you start at six-thirty, right?" I gave him my best sneer.

"Shut up, bitch."

I gasped. *Holy hell.* I hadn't expected that. Stunned beyond responding, I grabbed my bag from under the counter and strode to the elevator. His eyes were poisonous darts in my back and I clenched my jaw, determined not to turn his way again.

The second the elevator arrived I jumped in, jabbed the button a million times, and once the doors closed, I stared at my wide eyes as it rode up to my floor.

My life had been pretty cruisy in the confrontation stakes, but in the last month I'd experienced it three times, first with Chelsea-Lea, then Alexander, and now my boss. Was this my doing? Was I changing? The answer to those questions were a resounding yes. Previously, people had walked all over me. They'd told me what to do and I'd done it.

Not anymore though.

Except Corben—he could tell me to strip off and bend over the kitchen counter and I'd do that. I smiled, liked what I saw in the mirror, and smiled again. If this was going to be my last day at the Hot Horizon Hotel, then I might as well make it a good one.

The second the elevator opened I raced to my apartment. At lightning speed, I undressed and redressed in my new lime green jogging gear and runners, slapped on some sunscreen, grabbed my hat, sunglasses and room key, and raced back out of the room.

This time when the doors opened to the lobby, I hoped Needledick wasn't busy—I was ready to give him a piece of my mind. But it wasn't to be. Not only did he have customers but they were having a heated discussion. It was impossible to know what was wrong, but whatever it was had the man thumping his fist on the counter and raising his voice. I couldn't help but laugh, and when Needledick glanced my way, I raised my middle finger in his direction.

I'd never done that before, but damn it felt good.

I bounded out the door and spied Corben immediately. He was impossible to miss as he stood like a muscle mountain silhouetted against the sun. Carrying on my cheeky streak, I slapped his butt. "Come on."

Giggling, I launched down the stairs, sprinted across the grass and onto the sand as if there were a devil behind me. I glanced over my shoulder and it wasn't the devil—it was my muscular hunk and his fabulous grin that showed he was up for the challenge. I squealed as I ran harder. My feet dug into the soft sand and soon my calf muscles burned. I was laughing so hard my coordination was all over the place.

His feet thumped in the sand behind me and my heart exploded with the anticipation of him grabbing me. I darted to the left, then right, desperate to get away, yet at the same time begging for him to wrap his arms around me. I didn't have to wait long. After two close escapes where his grunts matched my giggles, his hands trapped my waist, and he wrapped his arms around me like a giant bear. "Gotcha."

"Yes, you do." It was almost impossible to talk. "What're you going to do with me now?"

He laughed a deep, hearty laugh. "Well, aren't you the cheeky one this morning?"

"Yep."

He unwrapped me, and as we caught our breath we fell into stride together and continued to walk away from the hotel. Everything about this moment was perfect—the sun on my face, the rolling waves crashing into the shore at my feet, and the sexy man at my side. Life truly didn't get much better than this.

A soccer ball tumbled down the sand toward us with a young boy chasing it. Corben picked up the ball and when the boy arrived, he tussled the child's hair and handed the ball to him. "There you go, kid."

The boy looked up at Corben with his mouth wide open. I imagined the poor kid thinking he'd just met Dwayne Johnson. Corben could easily pass for The Rock, with his dark sunglasses, buzz haircut and bulging muscles.

The boy wrapped his arms around the ball. "Thanks." He ran back up the beach toward another couple of kids.

I smiled at Corben.

"What?"

"You like children, huh?"

"No."

"No?" I pushed a wayward hair off my lip. "You looked pretty comfortable with him."

"That was five seconds with a complete stranger. I have no intention of having my own."

My jaw dropped and I blinked at him, wondering if I'd heard right.

He cocked his head. "What?"

"You don't want children?"

"No. Never have. That'd mean settling down."

I didn't know what to say. I'd never met anyone who didn't want kids or to settle down.

He put his arm around my shoulder and pulled me to him. "What's the matter, Memphis Jane? Have I shocked you?"

I wrapped my arm around his waist and enjoyed the muscles moving beneath my hand as we continued walking arm in arm. "As a matter of fact, yes. You never know what the future holds."

He shrugged. "Maybe, but I know it doesn't hold children. That family-life stuff just isn't for me."

I stopped, and when we broke apart he turned to look down at me. The sun glistened off his sunglasses, and I wished I could see his eyes. My heart hammered in my chest at what I was about to say. "In that case . . . I don't think we should see each other anymore. I really want—"

"Okay then." He shrugged as if what I'd said was an everyday occurrence.

I gasped. "Okay then? You're not upset?"

He shook his head. "Oh Memphis Jane . . . it was never like that."

"What was it like then? Just sex?" It flashed through my mind that I was being hypocritical, but I couldn't help it.

"Sex, yes, but also fun. We had fun, didn't we?"

"Well yes, but . . ."

"But what? Come on—you don't really want a guy like me. I'm a drifter, I like to party, I've got no assets to speak of, and well, quite frankly, I like women."

His honesty was as shocking as it was refreshing. I could've wasted months with Corben before I'd worked this out. Thoughts ran through my mind at frightening speed, and I had no idea what to say.

"Don't be sad. We had a great time. In fact, we should still have sex now. One last time, for good measure."

"Are you serious?"

"Absolutely. Besides, I can't have your last memory of me being the last time we had sex." He screwed up his nose.

I frowned. "Why? What was wrong with last time?"

"Well . . ." He shifted his feet in the sand. "You were all floppy, like a jellyfish."

I burst out laughing. "What? I was not."

"You were! All arms and legs, dribbling and stuff, and then you passed out."

Giggling, I slapped his arm. "Shut up. I didn't dribble."

"Did too. We should have one final fuck to remember each other by."

I gasped. "You're crazy."

"Is that a yes?"

Hell yes. Sounds like a perfect plan. But I didn't want to be too keen. I sighed as if uninterested. "Maybe."

"Maybe?" A cheeky grin lit up his face, and I knew what was coming. I yelped and dodged his attempt to grab me. Once again we ran up the beach, me giggling and squealing like a teenager as I ran as fast as I could with the sexy hunk of a man right on my tail.

Gasping for breath, I made the terrible mistake of stepping onto the soft sand and just about tumbled. Corben was on me in a flash. Next second he threw me over his shoulder like a sack of potatoes, and I smacked his ass and squealed as he carried me up the beach.

The adrenalin rush quickly petered out, and I struggled to catch my breath. I did enjoy the spectacle that was Mr. Universe's sexy derriere, though, as he trudged across the soft sand.

By the time he put me down on the grass, I was able to breathe again. He was puffing though, and I liked that I'd given him a workout.

"So whadya reckon? One last fuck for good time's sake?" He stood with his hands on his hips, and I couldn't be certain but this could've been the pose that put him into the Mr. Universe finals. God damn he was hot.

I looked to the sky, pretending to assess his question, and after sufficient pause I looked into his mirrored glasses. "Okay then."

He nodded as if he'd expected that answer. It was frightening how well he read me. "Off you go then. Don't want that asshole seeing us together."

I rolled my eyes. "You're right about that."

"I'm in room eleven. See you in twenty minutes."

I turned, and jumped out of the way of Corben trying to pinch my bottom. Giggling, I crossed the grass and the footpath and climbed the steps to the hotel. The glass doors slid open, and it took a little while for my eyes to adjust after the sunshine outside. I avoided looking toward reception as I crossed the marble tiles. The lobby was absent of any customers, and a knot twisted in my stomach as I expected Needledick to yell at me at any second. But he was nowhere to be seen. This was the second time I'd experienced this. Frowning, I shoved the idea of satisfying my curiosity of where he could be out of my mind and strode to the elevator.

The doors dinged open immediately, and I stepped in and admired the healthy glow to my cheeks. Exercise and sunshine did that. As did Corben. And the idea of sex. Wild, crazy sex. I pictured our playfulness on the beach. His stunning physique was permanently etched into my brain, and I'd be quite happy to keep it there forever.

At my apartment, I stripped off and had a quick shower, and after stepping out, I dried off and toweled my hair. Without time to do anything else, I left the wet bangs to tumble around my shoulders and dry naturally. However, in an attempt to stop it going frizzy, I rubbed in some Argan oil and scrunched it into loose waves. It was the best I could do . . . I didn't want to keep Corben waiting. Blinking at my reflection, I wanted to slap myself at that pathetic thought. Corben could wait as long as I made him wait. "Yeah." I nodded at my reflection. *That's better.*

At my closet, I decided on my Bohemian floor-length skirt with the ruched elastic waist and matched it with a plain white T-shirt. I put on leather flat sandals and accessorized with dangly orange earrings.

I glanced in the mirror and scrutinized my reflection. Without my hair done and with no makeup or fancy clothing I was back to Jane, plain Jane. My instant thought was to return to the bathroom and fix my hair and makeup, but quickly decided against it. This was me. The authentic me. Not Memphis.

It only seemed fitting that I should go to Corben as the real Jane Nichols.

My phone rang, and I plucked it from the side pocket of my bag. Smiling, I punched the green button. "Hey Lolly."

"Hey sista, I've been thinking about you. Ready for your big meeting?"

"Oh yeah. I suppose."

"Don't admit to anything. Make out that Needledick is psycho."

"Ha, that won't be hard." I told her about his outburst this morning.

"Holy shit, he's losing his marbles."

"Maybe."

"Go for a run, babe. That'll take your mind off it."

I chuckled. "I already did that."

"You did?" The surprise in her voice was justified.

"Uh-huh, with Corben."

"Oh fuck yeah. How's my sexy hunk?"

"Well . . ." I sighed. "I broke it off with him."

"Oh . . . why's that?"

"He told me he wasn't ready to settle down and that he never wants kids. And well, once he said that I guess . . . I guess I just didn't feel like I should see him anymore."

"Oh well."

"Oh well? You're not surprised?"

"No. He was a good fuck buddy, but he wasn't the one."

I flopped back onto my bed. "Oh god. That's nearly exactly what he said. Hey, did you two plan this?"

"What? Of course not. I just knew he wasn't the one. It was fun while it lasted."

"Oh my god, you sound just like him."

"Ha ha, that's funny. Pity. I bet he was an incredible root."

I rolled my eyes at her blatant comment. "I'll let you know in a few hours." I bit my lip, trying not to laugh.

"What? He's there?"

"I'm going up to his room now. He called it one last time for memory's sake." I didn't tell her about the jellyfish thing.

She burst out laughing. "That's gold. Well go fuck his brains out and give him something he'll remember forever."

I laughed with her, and as I thought about her comment I decided that that was exactly what I was going to do. "You're right. I'm going to show him what he'll be missing."
"Yay! Take photos for me."
"Not going to happen."
"Well, I want all the juicy details on Tuesday, and I mean everything."
"Of course. I always do."
We said our goodbyes, and before I ruined everything by glancing in the stupid mirror again, I grabbed my bag and room key and headed out my door. *I'm going to give Corben the best sex of his life.*
By the time I knocked on his door, my heart was galloping. But it skipped a few beats when he opened it. As usual, Corben was smoking hot. He wore a tiny pair of sports shorts, and every muscle glistened as if he'd oiled up for me.
"Jellyfish, huh?" I strode into the room and at the sound of the door shutting, I turned to him, dropped my skirt to my ankles, jumped onto his hips and locked my lips on his. His arms hooked under my ass and as he carried me into the room our fiery kiss set the pace. Our tongues probed, our breaths mingled, and my racing heart rose a few more notches.
I clawed my nails over his shoulders and through his hair as I inhaled his sexy scent. Corben put my back against the wall and released one hand to squeeze my breast. To help him out, I reached around and single-handedly unclipped my bra through my T-shirt. The second it released, his probing fingers tweaked my nipples.
Our already heated kiss hit a whole new level when his cock nudged at my bottom. I convinced myself it was my sexy-tiger moves that had produced that rapid reaction. With him holding onto me, I pulled my T-shirt up over my head, and the heat of his body against mine set my flesh on fire.
Our lips parted, and I opened my eyes to examine him. The irises in his fierce dark eyes were huge. Lust was etched into his handsome features, and it was an incredible aphrodisiac that had my hips wriggling and set my pussy on fire. "Put me down."
He did as he was told, and the second my feet touched the ground, I tugged my undies off. Naked now, I turned my attention to Corben. I stepped forward, and in a flash I had his shorts around his ankles. His erection pointed at me, thick and strong, perfectly matching everything about him.
I fell to my knees and sucked that glorious muscle into my throat. He groaned, and I groaned with him. I dug my fingers into his ass, squeezing and massaging every ounce of his firm flesh. He drove his hands through my hair and held my head in position as he glided his cock in and out of my mouth. Rather than me controlling the depth and speed of his plunges, it was him. Realizing I'd put myself at his mercy, I pulled back and stood up.
"My turn." I was in charge, and he'd better know it. But my intentions were

kyboshed when he put his hands on my waist again, hoisted me onto his hips, and strode to the kitchen. I was his plaything, and when he set me on the kitchen counter, guided me back so I lay down, and put his head between my legs, I didn't mind one bit.

His tongue, hot and hard, glided up my pussy. He matched it with a finger as he flicked my clit and probed my throbbing hole. I cried out and clawed at the countertop as he took me to another world.

It was already sensation overload, but when he added a second finger to his first and rammed them into me with a twisting, thrusting motion, my orgasm tore through me. It was fast. Explosive. Fucking fantastic. And I'd happily do it all over again.

I'd barely caught my breath when Corben pulled me up from the counter. My slick juices shone on his lips, and he made a show of licking them clean. He hoisted me onto his hips again, and his cock nudged dangerously close to my opening as he carried me across the room.

At the bed, he unhooked my legs and rolled me onto my hands and knees. He was in charge again, and I was quite happy to leave him there. He stepped to the bedside table and grabbed a condom. Seconds later, he was back at my ass, and he slapped his hand across my bottom.

"Hey." I squealed from the nasty sting, but then giggled as I realized that I didn't mind it.

His fingers dug into the flesh at my hips. His cock flicked up and down my pussy. Then, without warning, he slammed that beast into me. It was fast and hard. It rocked my world.

I screamed, and he pulled out and did it again. It hurt, but at the same time it felt so fucking good. With each thrust my boobs rocked back and forward, slamming into my chin and torso like melons on a pendulum.

Over and over he pummeled me, and soon the pain stopped and pure, exquisite joy took over. I matched his thrusts by rocking back and forward with him, and we worked together as if we'd been perfecting this for years. But after an eternity, his momentum plateaued, same depth, same speed, in and out, over and over, and once again I had a feeling Corben could do this all day long.

My pussy, however, was becoming dry, and I knew I had to get things moving or I was going to be sore. Increasing my rocking, silently telling him I was ready, I reached down between my legs, eager to rub my clit. To my delight, I could also touch his plunging cock at the same time.

It was a glorious sensation to feel that beast pummeling me, and I closed my eyes fingered my clit and succumbed to the glorious stimulation. Several thrusts later, I cried out as another orgasm tore through me. My hot juices spilled around his cock and dribbled over my hand.

I expected him to come with me.

He didn't. Instead, he ran a finger over my anus once, twice and then without pause, pushed it in.

"Hey." I nearly shot right off the bedsheets and attempted to pull away. But with his finger in me, he gripped my hips with his other hand and continued to slam his cock into me over and over. The finger inside my ass remained there, unmoving, and as much as it felt wrong it also felt a little bit right.

I forced my brain to switch off and let my body take over. Soon, the brutal shock dissipated, and new and interesting sensations took over. I pushed back on Corben, silently signaling my acceptance, and he didn't miss a beat. As his cock repeatedly rammed into my pussy, his finger probed my ass too. I fisted the sheet. I closed my eyes. Every nerve in my body demanded attention, and I let it take over.

My third orgasm was explosive. It blew my fucking mind.

Corben cried out, pulled his finger from my ass, dug his hands into my hips, and thrust into me like there was no tomorrow. I held onto the sheets, desperate to ride out the Corben wave.

It was an eternity before he slowed; it was even longer before he finally pulled out of me. I flopped onto the bed face-first, and as I looked to my side, I ogled his incredible body as he strode to the bathroom. Moments later, he flushed and appeared in the doorway.

His body may've been amazing, but right then, it was his smile that captured me. Corben was magnificent.

"So what do ya think? You gonna remember me now?"

I giggled. "You'll be impossible to forget."

He strode toward me, his cock flopping between his legs. Corben sure was confident in his own skin, and with a body like that, he should've been. He sat on the edge of the bed and patted the spot at his side.

Taking his lead, I sidled up next to him. "I told you I didn't do anal."

He huffed. "That wasn't anal."

"Really?" I said with the sarcasm it deserved. "What was it then?"

"That was fun."

I slapped his thigh, feeling the steely muscles beneath. "Fun for you, maybe." I didn't want to admit that I kinda liked it. "How'd you like it if I did that to you?"

He shrugged. "I'd love it."

I gasped, and grinning, he put his arm around me and hugged me to his side. "You'll do okay, Memphis Jane."

His words were absolutely perfect, and I leaned into him. "I know."

"I'm going to miss you."

He surprised me with that. "I'm going to miss you, too."

"I know," he said, matter-of-factly.

I chuckled. "Oh you do, do you?"

"Sure. Sex like that doesn't come around every day."

With that comment, I knew my mission was complete. "Good. Now I know you'll remember me too."

He squeezed me to him, and I sighed with contentment. Before this year, I'd never thought sex for the sake of sex could be so satisfying. But oh boy, was I wrong.

As much as I wanted to stay there all day, I couldn't. I groaned as I pulled back from him. "Thank you for a great morning."

"Thank you for a great year."

I stood up, nodding. "Yes, it has been." As I pulled on my clothes, Corben watched me from the edge of the bed, and I had a feeling he wanted to say something. I waited, hoping he'd voice whatever was on his mind.

Finally, I grabbed my bag and leaned over to kiss his cheek. "Goodbye, Corben. It's been fun."

"Would you like my number? Maybe you could call me sometime?"

I chewed on my bottom lip. The idea of having sex on tap with Corben was so damn appealing, yet I knew at the same time, it would screw with my brain. For once this year, I forced my head to do my thinking, not my pussy. "No thank you."

He nodded, and the sadness in his eyes startled me. "Good for you, Memphis Jane."

"Thank you." Without another glance in his direction, I headed out his door.

Back in my room, I noted I still had ninety minutes before my meeting. I ran the bath, and as the warm bubbles embraced me I revisited my morning with Corben. I was deeply satisfied with how our relationship had ended. It wasn't nasty, and I didn't feel like either of us had been hurt by our actions. Instead, it was as if I'd found treasure at the end of an epic journey.

The bath water was nearly cold by the time I stepped out. I wrapped the towel around myself, grabbed my diary and sat at my kitchen table. I turned to the 25th of November, and at the top I wrote *Corben Willis Room 11*. As I wrote about our break-up, I didn't feel even a twang of regret. What we'd had was special, but it had to end. Corben and I didn't have a future together, and I was glad I'd discovered this now.

I wrote in great detail about our sex. The wild, unadulterated passion where I'd tried but failed to take charge. I wrote about what he did with his finger and how it'd felt weird and uncomfortable, yet at the same time, there'd been something tantalizingly erotic about it too. As I finished off the entry, I thought about my intention to give Corben the best sex he'd ever had and giggling, I wrote at the top of the page, *Mission Complete*.

A glance at the clock confirmed it was time to get ready. As I dressed in conservative work clothes and put my unruly hair into a tidy bun, I felt strangely complacent about the meeting. It was out of my hands now, and I was confident I'd handle whatever was about to happen.

However, my confidence didn't stop the butterflies attacking my stomach, and by the time I rode the elevator down to the lobby, it was difficult to swallow. The doors opened and there was still no sign of Needledick. I strode toward the boardroom, and despite being five minutes early, I knocked on the door.

"Come in."

Richard greeted me with a smile, as did Romana and Brandi. It was a vast contrast to my last meeting with them, especially as neither of the Japanese gentlemen were there.

"How was your shift?" Richard asked as he pushed the door so it remained half open. He indicated for me to sit.

I cleared my throat. "It was a quiet night."

"Is that good or bad?" Romana asked, her smile broader than it'd been moments ago.

"Well, a quiet night means the hotel is running smoothly. So I guess it's a good thing."

"Good answer."

I frowned at Richard's response.

He put his hands together and leaned forward on his elbows. "We've transferred John to another hotel, and—"

"What? When?"

"Effective immediately," Romana said.

"Why?" I frowned on the outside, but inside I did my best dance moves ever.

"We've received several complaints about him." Richard nodded at the other two ladies, and they nodded in return. "And quite frankly, after we spoke to you, we decided he was detrimental to the quality of our hotel."

I swallowed and glanced around at them. "What's going to happen to him?"

"We offered him a . . ." he looked to the ceiling as if searching for the perfect word. "*Different* position in our Tweed Heads hotel, however he declined."

"Oh." I had no idea what to say.

"So, as we've had such glowing reports about you in our guest surveys, we'd like to offer you John's position as hotel manager."

I covered my mouth and blinked at them, hardly able to believe my wish had come true. "Yes! I mean, oh my gosh. That's amazing."

"We thought you'd be pleased."

"But . . ." My heart slammed into my chest at what I was about to say.

"Yes?" Brandi said.

"I'd like to make a request."

"Of course."

I swallowed. "I'd like to have at least one day off on the weekend."
Brandi chuckled, and soon Romana and Richard chuckled too, and I had no idea if I'd blown the one and only promotion opportunity I'd ever had.
Finally, they stopped, and Richard tapped his hand on the table. "As hotel manager, you will be in charge of the roster. So I guess you'll be deciding who has what days off."
I wanted to cry. I wanted to get up on the table and break out my fancy moves. I wanted to scream from the penthouse rooftop. This was the best outcome I could ever have asked for.
Tears of joy stung my eyes, and I forced them back. "It that case, I am truly honored that you've chosen me to look after your beautiful hotel. I accept and know in my heart that I won't let you down."
"We know you won't." Richard leaned forward to shake my hand. "Congratulations. From the surveys we've read, you deserve this one hundred percent."
Brandi stood up, as did Romana, and both the women shook my hand too.
A bell tinkled outside, and Romana held up a finger. "Excuse me for a moment." She strode to the boardroom door and walked out.
"So, let's get down to business, shall we?" Richard said as Brandi sat back down. "What we'd like to do is give you Sunday night off, full pay of course, and ask that you start in your new position on Monday."
Oh my god. Could this day get any better? "Sounds good to me."
"Regarding your pay structure, we'd like to offer you an increase of nine thousand dollars per annum, and once the probation period of six months is over, if we're all satisfied, we'll increase it a further three thousand dollars per annum. Are you happy with that?"
An extra thousand dollars every month? I couldn't believe what I was hearing.
Suddenly, it hit me. As day manager, I'd lose my room. "I'd like to keep my apartment." I blurted that out and instantly wanted to retract it. "I mean, I'm sorry. It's just I've been living here three years and I love it. I'm willing to sacrifice some pay in order to keep it."
Brandi and Richard looked at each other, and as my heart thumped, I wished I had Lolly's skill of reading minds. Finally, Richard turned back to me. "We wondered if you'd ask that."
"And?" I tensed and bit my lip so I didn't blurt anything out.
"We're willing to let you keep your apartment, if you're willing to forego the pay increase. However . . ." He held up his finger, "we will readdress this in twelve months, as we may want to return your apartment back to the letting pool."
"Thank you, that's perfect. I accept." In the back of my mind, I knew I should negotiate. But I didn't want to. Everything they offered was over and above what I'd ever expected.

Romana reentered the room, and once again left the door ajar.
"Wonderful. Brandi will draw up your contract and have it ready for you on Monday." Richard stood, and I stood with him and held out my hand. We shook, and he smiled. "Oh and by the way, don't be late for your shift."
I laughed. "Never."
I shook hands with Romana and Brandi and left them in the boardroom. Knowing I didn't need to watch out for Needledick's dagger eyes had me floating across the lobby to the elevator. My grin dominated my reflection in the elevator mirrors as I rode it up to my floor.
At my apartment, I squealed, ran for the bed, and cheered as I dived face-first onto the covers.
"Yeeha." I screamed. This called for a celebration, and it didn't matter one bit that it was before midday.
I strode to the kitchen, pulled a bottle of wine from the fridge and a packet of corn chips from the cupboard, and took them out to the balcony. Breathing in the glorious sea breeze, I poured my wine to the very top of the glass.
I held the glass up to my spectacular panorama. "Cheers."
The wine was delicious. My view was magnificent. My body still glowed with glorious after-sex vibes.
Life was spectacular.

3ʳᴰ DECEMBER
SEX IS MY DRUG
Room 6 - Hot Horizon Hotel

My first week as manager of the Hot Horizon Hotel had been incredible. Brandi from the executive committee had been teaching me some of the processes, and the two of us got on as if we'd known each other for years. We laughed a lot and her management style was like nothing I'd ever experienced. It was fun yet informative, gentle yet firm.

Bailey, the guy who had been covering my shift on my nights off, was offered my old position of night manager and he'd accepted, so he didn't need much training for the role. For the final piece in the staffing puzzle, the executive committee appointed a lady named Tracy from the Brisbane hotel to replace Bailey's position as our shift relief officer, and so far, she was proving to be perfect.

I was certain the executive committee would think my transition into hotel manager had gone smoothly. And after some further negotiation, I'd sacrificed a drop in pay to work alternating five- and six-day weeks. For the first time in my working life, this week I had two days off, Sunday and Monday.

Life couldn't get any better.

At least that's what I thought until, just after I'd devoured a couple of macadamia cookies for morning tea, Mason Cole, the guitarist from Empire

Angels, walked through the sliding glass doors with four other people. I recognized his brother and Zenon Justice, whose name I'd never forget. But I was pretty sure the two women who'd walked in with the men were different to last time. These two were skinny, too skinny, if you asked me. They both had long, straight platinum hair, loads of makeup, and were scantily clad. Both had tattoos but nowhere near as many as the last two women had had. As they approached the counter, I wondered if they were identical twins.

I had to remind myself that I shouldn't know who they were, because Mason only met Memphis last time. "Welcome to the Hot Horizon Hotel."

"Thanks. We're booked in for tonight. Zenon Justice is my name." They must've made the booking with one of the other staff because I would've recognised his name.

"Thank you, Mr. Justice." As the men handed over their identification I noticed how tired they all looked, and wondered if they'd been up all night. "What brings you to the Gold Coast?"

"We're in a band, Empire Angels. We got a gig tonight." Zenon was their spokesman. One of the girls squished up to his side, cocked her head at me, and chewed on her gum with smacking lips. I had a terrible feeling she was staking her claim, as if I were a threat. I turned to the photocopier, stifling a laugh at the absurdity of the idea. Zenon had absolutely no appeal. Mason, on the other hand, with his stunning eyes the color of deep sea ice and his delicious lips, was the man I had my sights on.

An idea hit me like a bolt of lightning. This was my first free Saturday night in years, and it was time I experienced Saturday nightlife like every other normal human being. I wanted to have fun. I wanted to drink. I wanted to watch Mason play guitar. And if all that went to plan, I wanted sex with Mason Cole again, too.

Ideas flipped across my brain as I went through the motions of checking the group into their three rooms. I handed over their room cards and as Mason ran his tongue over his plum-colored lips I pictured that tongue gliding over my nipples. A blaze of heat flashed up my neck at that horny thought, and I smacked the vision away before I self-combusted.

As they moseyed to the elevator with each of the women owning their man by wrapping their arms around their waist, I fixed my eyes on Mason. He was the obvious outsider and not just because he didn't have a women hanging off him. His clothing was classier, his hair was professionally styled, but most of all, while the others had a cocky, you-can't-touch-me attitude, Mason had a confident professionalism about him that implied he was going places.

The second they vanished into the elevator, I grabbed my phone to send Lolita a text.

'Hey, you got plans for tonight?'

'Just Hawaiian pizza and a DVD with the kids.'
I giggled at that, knowing full well what the implications of the Hawaiian pizza meant. 'Fancy a night out with Memphis?'
'Fuck yeah.' Her reply came in a flash.
'Mason, that guitarist I told you about, is back. They're playing at Surfers. Want to go?'
'Only if I get to dress up like Memphis.'
The idea of the two of us doing the Memphis disguise thing had my head spinning. 'Ha ha, OK. Want to meet here? We can go to dinner first.'
'Luv it. I'll be there at 7.'
'Excellent. C U then.'
I turned my attention to the computer and typed in Empire Angels. The first website to pop up was a group of technology start-ups in New York. I giggled as I wondered what they thought about a rock band sharing their name. The second website was the one I clicked. It was plastered with pictures of the four original band members, and I was disappointed that Mason wasn't featured in any of the photos. The older brother who'd offered to fill in for the original bass guitarist still wasn't getting the attention he deserved.
I felt an uncharacteristic desire to defend him. Maybe tonight I'd get the chance.
One of the first decisions I'd made as manager was to re-jig the staff rostered hours. My main reason was to allow Marjorie to finish earlier so she could spend a bit more time with her kids before they went to bed, so I'd moved everyone's shift forward an hour. This meant that although I started at five-thirty in the morning, I also finished at two o'clock.
Unlike Needledick, Marj always arrived at least fifteen minutes prior to her shift and every day this week, I'd been surprised when Marjorie had come bounding into the lobby; today was no different.
"Hey Marj, how are you?" I hugged her bony shoulders to me.
"Excellent. How's your day?"
"I can't believe my shift is over. The days go so quick."
"That's a good thing." She was the happiest I'd seen her in ages, and I liked to think my decision to tweak the shifts was a contributor to that.
After going over my new handover checklist, during which we spent as much time completing the list as we did chatting about her kids, we said our goodbyes, and two minutes before my shift officially ended, I headed up to my apartment. The last five days had been a struggle with my body clock, and the transition from sleeping during the day to sleeping at night hadn't been as easy as I'd hoped. After ten minutes in my apartment, my eyes grew heavy, and by the time I'd eaten a cheese toasty, I could barely keep them open.

Resisting was pointless and I changed into a T-shirt and undies, set my alarm for six o'clock, and crawled into bed.

* * *

It seemed like only ten minute before my alarm went off, and when I rolled over to glance at the time I couldn't believe I'd slept for nearly four hours. Based on the dried dribble trailing from my bottom lip to my chin, it must've been a deep sleep though.
Groaning, I dragged my body to the kitchen and turned on the coffee machine. I filled the cow mug Henry gave me to the rim with strong black coffee and stirred in two sugars.
Carrying my mug to the bathroom, I then turned on the shower taps. It was ages before the warm water had my brain back in focus. As I was drying myself, I heard a knock on the door. Thinking time had got away from me, I glanced at my clock, but it was only six-twenty. Frowning, I pulled the towel around myself and went to the door.
I peeked through the peephole to see Lolita and pulled the door open. She bounded into the room and dropped a large bag to her feet. "Hey babe." Her boobs squashed against mine as she squeezed me in a hug.
"You're early."
"I know." She plucked a wine bottle from her bag. "I'm thinking a few wines while we get all Memphised up." Her eyes were wide, and with her excitement playing out in her jittery feet, how could I refuse?
"Sounds great."
While she went to the kitchen to get wine glasses, I went to my lingerie drawer and pulled on a black lace G-string. I didn't bother with a bra; Lolly had seen my boobs dozens of times. I returned to the kitchen topless, and she offered me a glass that she'd filled to the rim. We raised them in a toast.
"Cheers," we said in unison.
"This's going to be so much fun. Now what color contacts are you wearing? 'Cause I want to give them a try too. And can I wear one of your wigs?" Lolly spoke at a million miles an hour.
"Of course. Come on." I picked up my wine and headed to the bathroom.
"So I'll have to wear the violet contacts because that's what I wore last time I was with Mason."
"Okay, so maybe I should try the green ones." Why Lolly would want to hide her beautiful blue eyes was beyond me, but I handed her the unopened packet containing the green contacts anyway.
"Show me how you do it?"
"Okay." I opened my container, plucked the purple disk from the solution, pulled down my lower lid, and with the contact balancing on the end of my finger, popped it into my eye.

"Oh shit. You made that look so easy."

"Now it is . . . but it took me a while to get used to it."

Lolly poked her long blue fingernail into the end of the packaging box to open it.

"Look at your nails. Wow."

She wriggled her fingernails for me. "Gillian did them to match the dress I wore at the dance class Christmas breakup party yesterday." She reached for my hand and scrunched her nose at my disastrous fingernails. "You should get your nails done, too."

"Nah."

"Hey, you're hotel manager now. You need to step things up."

"I have stepped things up, thank you."

She unscrewed the lid on the contact container. "It only costs sixty dollars for a full set of gel nails. You should treat yourself for Christmas. Men love a woman with long nails."

I cocked my head at her. "Really?" I said with sarcasm. "I haven't had any complaints yet."

"Pfft, that's because you're distracting them with your pussy."

I burst out laughing, and she chuckled with me. With the green contact now balancing on the end of her finger, she pulled down her bottom eyelid. "Here we go."

I held my breath, bracing for her reaction as she eased the contact to her eyeball. She popped it in and blinked. "Ha. That was easy."

Of course it was. Lolly made everything look easy. She put the second one in just as calmly and stared at her reflection. "Wow, I love it." She turned to me. "What do you think?"

"Amazing, huh?"

"I reckon. Don't forget to put your other one in; you look like a freak."

"Thanks." While I put my contact in and blinked it into place, Lolita walked out to the lounge room. When she returned she had a large plastic wet-pack in her hands.

"Brought the secret weapons." She unzipped it to reveal the most organized and comprehensive makeup kit I'd ever seen.

"Jesus, we could be here all night."

"Ha, funny. This is only a fraction of my makeup. Now what about the wigs? Which one do you want?"

I turned to the wigs that I'd lined up on the towel shelf in my bathroom. "I should wear the black one, because that's what I wore for Mason last time."

"Oooh, look at that red one." She reached up and pulled it from the shelf. I grabbed the black wig again. It was a disaster, but that only made it perfect for my rock-chick look. I showed Lolita how I pinned up my hair and then pulled the wig on.

She chuckled. "Oh yeah." She pointed at me. "I remember picking you up at the park dressed like that. Holy shit that was a hoot. Tonight's gonna be a total crack up."

We chinked our glasses again, and I took a long sip of my drink. The wine was delicious but on an empty stomach, I was already feeling the effects, and that was dangerous. "Where shall we go for dinner?" I'd need something substantial if I was planning a big night drinking. Pasta jumped to mind. "How about that Italian place around the corner? We can share a pizza?"

"I just escaped pizza at my house."

"You can have a salad then, and I'll have risotto." I hoped my eyes reflected my eagerness.

"Okay. Sounds good. What time does the band come on?"

"Not until ten."

She clicked her tongue. "Cool, that'll give us time to have a few wines before we get there. Now help me out with this wig."

By the time we finished in the bathroom, I was transformed with my black wig on and violet contacts in, and I'd recreated my makeup from my last time with Mason with gold eye shadow and very dark eyeliner. Lolita looked stunning in the fiery red wig and green contacts. She'd enhanced her eyes with a dozen or so colors so her eyelids blended from a light pink to a dark purple. On me, that makeup would've looked ridiculous, but on Lolly the bold colors looked incredible.

We raised our glasses at our finished looks and drank the last of our drinks. Back in the kitchen, Lolly filled our glasses again, and we set about dressing in our cheeky Memphis outfits. I pulled on faux leather leggings that Lolly had insisted I buy on our last shopping spree. Since I'd been thinking about what outfit to wear ever since I'd texted Lolita this morning, I dived into my closet and removed a pair of thigh-high purple boots that I'd never worn. In reality, I never thought I'd wear them, but I'd loved them so much when I'd first seen them in the shop that I'd bought them regardless.

"What do you think of these?" I held the boots up.

She turned to me wearing nothing but a G-string, and I was shown once again just how perky her boobs were. "Fuck babe, they're fantastic." She reached for one. "Where'd you get these?"

"I bought them years ago from this obscure boutique down in Broadbeach. I've never worn them though."

"I'll have to borrow them sometime."

"Sure." Her stamp of approval was perfect, and I took the boots to the bed, sat down, put on socks and pulled them on. The boots had a velvet finish, with a fake laces that zig-zagged all the way up the front of the boot. The heel was about eight inches but with the wedged toe at the front they didn't seem that high at all.

I stepped up to the mirror and tried to ignore my lopsided boobs as I checked out my boots. "What do you think?"
She turned to me, wearing a tight-fitting dress in a shimmering rose-gold fabric that hugged her curves perfectly. The dress was very, very short, showing off her shapely tanned legs. With her red wig curled over her shoulder, Lolita looked a knock-out.
"Wow! You look amazing."
"Thanks. I bought this today."
I chuckled. "Did you?"
"Of course. Never miss an opportunity to buy a new dress."
She said it so matter-of-factly that I had to laugh.
"What? I mean it." She pointed her blue nail at me. "You should etch that piece of wisdom into your memory. Now that you've got Saturday nights off there'll be no more excuses from you when I ask you out. And we need to fit in a hell of a lot more shopping time to keep topping up your sexy new wardrobe."
I grinned at her and turned back to the mirror. "Okay. I can handle that."
My purple boots were perfect, and I turned to admire the sexy heel. With the purple as my inspiration, I went to my lingerie drawer and removed a purple bra that was squashed down the back. It was plain satin, with a bit of padding in the lower part of the cup for extra oomph, and had little diamantes on the satin straps. I put it on, and over the top I wore a plain black button-up shirt that I tied in a knot at my waist.
"What do you think?"
She frowned, stepped forward, and undid the buttons on my shirt until it was open all the way to the knot. "Better."
I turned back to the mirror. My shirt was wide enough to reveal my purple bra and a decent amount of my boob bulge. "I look like a tart."
"You look like a rock chick who has the best tits in the world."
God, I love her.
"Selfie time." She plucked her phone from her bag, and we grinned at it until she'd snapped several photos. "I promised Cal I'd send him a pic."
As she tapped away on her phone, I inspected my reflection. It was a new style for me, and damn, if I didn't feel totally sexy in it. I couldn't wait to see Mason's reaction when he saw me again. Grinning, I turned to check out my butt in the leather pants, and Lolita burst out laughing.
"What?" My jaw dropped.
"Oh, just Cal. He reminded me he'd eaten pineapple for dinner and told me to get my sexy ass home."
I chuckled along with her, but really I was just relieved that it wasn't my ass she was laughing at.
"So, are we ready to go?" She raised her perfectly formed eyebrows at me.
"I think we are."

We gulped down the last of our wine, grabbed our bags, and headed to the elevator.

Twenty minutes later we were seated at Valentino's restaurant. As much as I felt totally out of place in my thigh-high boots and exposed bra, Lolita looked like the queen of the restaurant. Each time I tried to do up my buttons Lolita slapped my hand away. *Maybe we should've ordered takeout.*

It was too late, though, as the divine smells of garlic and grilled cheese coming from the kitchen had my stomach barking. The elderly Italian woman who took our order had an accent that indicated she'd just stepped off the plane, and she served us with brutal efficiency. Twenty minutes later, I tucked into creamy risotto packed with seafood, and Lolita nibbled on a bunch of spinach leaves. I succumbed to foodie heaven and refrained from speaking until my stomach was at peace again.

I'd resisted drinking the Prosecco Lolita had ordered until I had a decent amount of rice in my belly, but when I did, I was delighted by how delicious it was. Lolita and I rarely had dinner together with just the two of us, and our conversation focused on the men in my life again.

She paused with her champagne glass at her lips. "So are you upset about Corben?"

I shrugged. "Yes and no. He was fun, and the sex was amazing, but . . ."

"But what?"

I sighed and sipped my wine as I formulated my answer. "I'm glad I called it off. It could've taken me a long time with Corben before I discovered his reluctance to settle down and have kids."

"That means a lot to you, huh?"

I frowned. "What do you mean?"

"Well, you've never really mentioned kids before."

I raised my eyebrows. "Really? Hmmm. Well, of course I want children."

"Okay. If you say so. But just because you're a woman doesn't mean you have to be a mother. It's hard work. It changes your life. They cost a bloody fortune and it's not all wonderful."

"Wow, you know how to make it sound amazing."

"Just giving you a dose of reality."

"Can I buy you ladies a drink?" The young man who arrived at the end of our table had to be at least five years younger than us.

Lolly giggled. "You can, but . . ." She flashed her hand, making a point of showing off the enormous rock on her wedding finger. "She'd love one." She pointed her blue talon at me, and I attempted to kick her under the table.

I smiled up at the blond-haired spunk with the husky voice and dazzling smile. "Thank you, but not today."

His mouth drooped, and he shrugged. "Okay, but if you change your mind, I'll be over there." He pointed at a group of guys who were all looking our way. Lolita waved, and several of them waved back.

The second the young man left we started giggling, and as we sipped our Prosecco and the minutes ticked lazily along I realized just how wonderful it was to have my weekend nights free. A lovely sense of contentment flowed through me, and it wasn't just the alcohol causing it.

When we stood up to go, I curled my bag over my neck to position it diagonally at my hip. We left the restaurant just after nine-thirty, walked to the main road, and five minutes later caught the tram to Surfers Paradise. The tram stopped at the Cavill Avenue mall, and the second the doors opened we were affronted with the buzz in the street. We stepped out with the crowd. People were everywhere. Sights, sounds and smells were all amplified. It was fantastic, and I felt so alive.

Walking up the mall with my tits hanging out was weird though, and I was certain every person got a look down my top. Lolita, however, strutted up the mall like she owned the place, and I tried to ease in behind her slipstream but she hooked her arm into mine, which only opened my top farther.

The entrance to Elsewhere Nightclub was protected by a bouncer who could've given Corben a challenge in the muscle stakes. We paid ten dollars each to the scantily clad brunette behind the counter, Muscle Man stamped our wrists, and we entered through the heavy black curtains.

The nightclub had a trendy, colorful vibe, with concrete pylons and exposed steel beams giving it an industrial feel. The DJ's music was loud and the people were louder. Flashing lights aimed at the large wooden dancefloor were as vibrant as they were erratic.

Lolita worked her magic and found us a bar table to the side of the dancefloor. She instructed me to sit, and then weaved her way through the crowd to the bar. I flipped my bag from my hip to rest it on my lap and turned my attention to the people setting up equipment on stage. My breath caught when I spied Mason. It was like I was destined to see him.

He was in black skinny jeans and a white T-shirt printed with a simple yet striking black and grey picture of a woman with wild flowing hair and parted lips that were contrasted in bright red. Mason's hair was styled to give height at the front, and his dark eyeliner matched all the other band members' who were setting up with him.

When he picked up his guitar and strummed the strings, I was mesmerized by his concentration. The nightclub was a writhing concoction of rowdy people, flashing lights and blaring music, yet he looked like he was the only person in the room.

Lolita returned with martini glasses filled with a red liquid, each decorated with a sliver of orange peel. I recognized the drinks as Cosmopolitans, one of the drinks Corben had introduced me to. We grinned at each other and chinked our glasses, and I sipped the sweet, potent nectar.

I pointed to the stage. "There he is."

"Ooooh, he's hot."

"I know." We had to yell over the noise, yet it was perfect.

The lights dimmed, the music stopped, but the crowd noise didn't. "This is so cool." Lolita's green eyes were wide, showing her enjoyment.

"I know."

"Welcome Surfers Paradise. Are you ready to rock the house?" Zenon's gravelly voice cut through the crowd, commanding attention. People stopped what they were doing and turned. Several people moved forward, edging up to the stage. Lolita grabbed my arm. "Down your drink."

"What?"

"Do it." She drained her glass in one gulp and cocked her head at me.

I did as instructed, and before I'd recovered from the affront to my throat she grabbed my hand, and I clutched my bag at my hip as she dragged me forward. Next second, I was standing to the left of center stage, front row, looking right up at my sexy guitarist.

"Mason." Lolita cupped her mouth as she yelled, and when he looked down at us she waved and then pointed at me.

I could've died, but when he looked down at me and the stern concentration on his face transformed into a glorious smile, my embarrassment gave way to sheer joy. He gripped his guitar and strummed out a hypnotic, soothing beat, and certain he was playing it just for me, I lost myself to the rich, full tones.

A few minutes later, the band kicked into their first song and my body let loose to the music. Lolly and I danced, cheered and attempted to sing the songs as we picked up the catchy lyrics.

Mason didn't just play the guitar; he totally rocked it, caressing it like a lover. The music thumped so hard my bones rattled. Occasionally they played a song where he lovingly thrummed the strings with a delicate touch that had me wishing those fingers were on me.

"We'll be back in half an hour," Zenon announced to the crowd, and in a flash the DJ took his place and Blink 182 blared from the speakers. Lolly and I returned to our table and muscled in on a couple of girls who'd laid claim to it in our absence. I went to the bar this time and jigged along to the beat as I waited my turn.

I just about died when I returned. Mason was talking to Lolita. Her smile lit her face like a beacon. When Mason smiled at me, my heart exploded and my hands trembled as I put the Cosmo cocktails down. "Hi Mason."

He wrapped an arm around me and planted his lips to mine. It was as confronting as it was fucking awesome, but it was over as quickly as it'd started.

"It's so great to see you." He had to lean into my ear to be heard over the crowd, and I inhaled his incredible heady scent of leather mingled with smoking-hot man.
"You too. I love watching you play—you're so talented."
"Thanks. Can I buy you another drink?"
"I just got one thanks, but can I buy you one?"
"Nah, it's okay. We get them for free anyway."
"Oh. You met Lolita?"
"Yes, she was just telling me how you've been following me on the tour."
I scowled at her. It seemed Lolita was as good at lying as I was. "Well . . ." My mind raced for a response. "I'd hoped you'd come back to Surfers."
"We love it here. Anyway, I've gotta go." He leaned into my ear. "Will you come back to my room later?"
His hot breath shot lovely shivers down my spine. "I'd love to."
He planted another quick kiss on my lips, then he turned and wove through the crowd until he disappeared behind a curtain.
"Holy fuck, babe, he's so into you."
I nibbled on my bottom lip. "He's pretty hot, huh?"
"Hot? He's fucking smoking!"
We laughed aloud, and as the music switched to a new song I let the beat take my body to another world. We danced, we laughed, we made fleeting comments about the people around us, and every second was a bundle of fun.
The band came on again, and we moved to prime position in the front. Mason grinned down at us, and we smiled up at him.
The lights dimmed and within seconds the crowd had us hemmed in at the stage. United, the entire audience seemed to dance to the catchy rhythm. I broke out all my best moves and tried but failed to match a few of Lolita's.
One song finished, and when Mason moved to the microphone, I blinked up at him and watched wide-eyed as I prepared to hear him sing.
"This song is for my girl, Memphis." He pointed down at me, and as my bones liquefied the crowd roared. Lolita grinned at me, confirming what he'd said was the most amazing thing in the world.
A puff of smoke plumed from Lolita's mouth, and I spun to her. "What're you doing?" I'd never seen Lolita smoke.
"Smoking a joint."
"What! Where'd you get it?"
"Dunno, someone just gave it to me." She sucked on the stick again and closed her eyes as she inhaled.
"Are you nuts?" My mind was torn between watching Mason sing for me and the crazy bitch at my side.
She blew out the smoke and grinned. "Yep. Here, your turn."

"No way."

She slapped my arm. "Come on. It's not going to hurt."

"But I've never tried it."

"So this is your chance. You may never get another opportunity." She shoved the joint at me. "Memphis would."

I tilted my head. "I'm Memphis."

"Then you know you want to."

I grabbed it and tried to ignore my trembling fingers.

"Go on." Her eyes were alive.

The angel and devil in my brain both screamed at me.

Go on. Don't be such a baby.

Are you crazy? It's illegal.

You'll never get another chance.

You could pass out.

It's your first Saturday night out in years. Make it one to remember.

That last thought blazed through my head like a tomahawk missile, and I raised the joint to my lips and sucked on it before I changed my mind. It tasted weird, like I imagined grass would taste. It wasn't great, but it wasn't disgusting either.

But nothing happened. I didn't know what I'd expected, but I got no effects from the marijuana at all. I glanced at Lolly.

"And?" She bulged her eyes.

"I don't get it."

"Have some more."

I shrugged, raised the joint to my lips and inhaled deeply. Again, nothing, so I sucked the smoke for a third time. Moments later, the room tilted on its axis and my eyes couldn't keep up as my surroundings melted into a crazy mix of light and shapes.

Lolly fished the joint from my fingers, and as I tried to focus on her image it wiggled like I was looking at her through a heat wave. I giggled. I giggled some more. And soon the two of us were laughing like a couple of drunk hyenas. We passed the joint back and forward until it was finished.

The beat of the music had my body moving and in a delicious haze, I let it take over.

I gazed up at Mason like a love-struck teenager, and he in turned gazed at me. We were the only people in the room, and the connection between us was raw and true. He bent over and held his hand toward me. I reached for it, and next second I was on the stage. I didn't know whether to laugh or gasp as the crowd cheered.

The expectation to do something amazing was excruciating. Flashing my tits was an option, but as they were already out, I rode the crazy unpredictable moment by lighting up the stage with my stunning moves. The connection between Mason and his guitar was so real, like the instrument was part of his body. His gaze flitted from the guitar to me, and each time our eyes met I wanted to jump on him and stick my tongue down his throat.

It was an eternity before the song ended. I stopped dancing and just stood there as the crowd eased back from the stage and the DJ hit us with a dose of Kings of Leon. Lolita grinned up at me and I waved to her, but still didn't move. Mason wove his guitar strap over his shoulder and placed the instrument at his side.

He leaned in to kiss my cheek. "I'll come and find you in a minute." He reached for my hand and led me to a set of steps at the side of the stage.

Lolita squeezed me for a hug. "Holy fuck, babe, that was awesome."

"I know. I can't believe he did that."

"You were so sexy up there."

"Really?"

She nodded a little too hard, and I couldn't decide if she was lying or not. Especially now that I knew she was so good at it. Lolly went to the bar and returned with two more Cosmos, and we spoke at a thousand miles an hour as we sipped our drinks.

We'd nearly finished our cocktails when Mason returned to my side, wrapped his arm around me, and planted a kiss on my lips again. He was so good at that.

Lolita put her empty glass on the table. "Well, I guess I'll leave you crazy cats to it."

"Oh no, don't go." I reached for her arm.

"It's okay. Cal had pineapple, remember?" She wriggled her eyebrows, and I burst out laughing.

"Let's walk to the tram together." I didn't make it a question. "Are you okay to go now, Mason?"

"Sure. Let me grab my guitar." He turned and strode to the dark curtain that flanked the back of the stage and disappeared through it. Moments later, he returned with his guitar hanging at his hip. He arrived at my side, curled his arm around my waist, and with Lolly cutting a path through the crowd, we made our way to the exit.

I had no idea what the time was, but there were even more people in the mall than there had been when we'd first got here at ten o'clock. Maybe the marijuana had heightened my senses or something because the crowds seemed much louder, and given that our ears had just been blasted by the music in Elsewhere, it was a wonder I could hear at all.

At the tram stop, Lolly and I wrapped our arms around each other. "I had the best night." I squeezed her tight.

"Me too. We're definitely doing this again."

"I agree."

"I want to hear all about this stud tomorrow, okay?"

I giggled. "Of course." I was already missing our Tuesday morning debriefs about my sex life. That was probably the only downside of my promotion.

Lolita's tram arrived first, and she blew us a kiss before she stepped through the sliding doors. Rather than grab a seat, she hung onto a pole and within seconds a man started talking to her. A flicker of worry crossed my mind, but I knew deep down that she'd be fine. I'd seen Lolly take a man down at karate who was three times her size. She may have looked fragile in that dress and heels, but she was lethal when she needed to be. She gave us one last wave as the doors shut and the tram pulled away.

"Did you have a good night?" Mason commanded my attention with his sexy voice.

"I've had the best night."

He wriggled his eyebrows. "It's not over yet."

"Thank god."

He laughed, and it was such a delightful melody that I laughed along with him. My laughter quickly turned to giggles, and as we boarded the tram and rode the three stops to Florida Gardens station, suddenly everything he did was hilarious, and my jaw ached by the time we walked arm and arm up the street toward the Hot Horizon Hotel.

We crossed the lobby, and when Bailey popped his head up I waved. "Hey Bailey, how's the night going?"

"It's good, thank you."

It was only when he frowned that I realized my mistake.

Mason cocked his head at me. "So you've been to this hotel a few times?"

Oh faaark. I needed to shake this fog from my brain, and fast, or there was every chance I'd blow my secret.

The elevator opened and we stepped in. Mason pressed the button for the first floor, and the second the doors shut I shoved his back to the wall and provided the perfect distraction.

Our lips mashed together, and when his parted I drove my tongue into his mouth, eager to explore. My hands groped his chest, thumbed his nipples, and travelled down to his groin, seeking out their own pleasure.

We moaned together, bent our knees, and moved our bodies in a way that showed we were already in perfect sync with each other. The doors pinged open, and I jumped onto his hips, planted my lips on his, and he carried me to his room. He strode along the passage in a fine display of strength and agility. He was a man on a mission, and that mission was me. Yay.

He paused to open the door and I turned my attention to his ear, sucking the lovely soft lobe into my mouth and pulling back till it snapped from my lips. I'd never done that before but it was fun, and I did it over and over till he pushed through the door and into his room. I curled my bag over my neck, dropped it to the floor, and when he backed me up to the wall, I lowered my legs to the floor to stand.

Our kiss was soft yet heated. Our hips grinded together, and the bulge in his pants grew by the second. I glided my hand between us and pushed it into his jeans, eager to feel that beast for myself. It wasn't easy because his jeans were skin-tight, but I was determined, and soon my hand wrapped around his cock. It was bent over slightly and when I pulled it upright, Mason squeezed my left boob so hard I thought it'd pop.

I tugged my hand from his jeans and fumbled with his button, eager to set him free, but it wouldn't budge. With my hands on Mason's pecs, I pushed him backwards. "Take your jeans off." It was a take-charge command so fitting for Memphis, and Mason didn't hesitate. In a flash, he had his jeans around his ankles and his shirt off. Every muscle in his body seemed tensed. His abs were chiseled and met with those lovely muscles that created a V at his groin. A line of thick, dark hair led from his sexy navel down his belly, drawing my eyes to his enormous erection.

He wrapped his fingers around his cock and pumped it just once as if kick-starting it. Oh my god, did that set my heart on fire. I wanted him inside me . . . now.

I flopped onto the bed. "Take my boots off," I commanded, raising my right foot toward him.

He wrapped his hand around my ankle and pulled. It was a little game of tug-o-war before he had both boots off. My fake leather leggings were as much of a challenge, and as he pulled and I pushed, I made a mental note never to wear them again. Especially when sex was a possibility.

It seemed like an eternity before I was naked, but the freedom was glorious. When his fabulous blue eyes travelled up my body, the sizzling sensations ripping through me hit another level.

I glided my hands over my flesh, pinched my nipples and squeezed my boobs, and with his eyes drilling into me, I parted my legs and ran my finger over my clit. The very first touch had me sucking air through my teeth. My body was so sensitive tonight, and for a fleeting second I wondered if it was the marijuana or my sexy boy-toy that'd caused that.

Mason moved around to between my legs and I continued my explorations, gliding my finger over and around my clit. My hips writhed on the bedding, and my knees flipped open and closed as the wild sensations took over.

I set a pattern in motion around my clit and into my throbbing hole, and Mason stepped forward, placed one knee on the bed and joined in. His fingertips were like flames, licking with heat and intensity, and his musky aroma was as potent as the heady scent of our impending red-hot sex.

My mind was in a groggy haze but my body was wired. All my senses were alive, and I heard every breath he took as he sucked air through his clenched jaw with rapid succession.

Sex was my drug, and Mason was my pharmacist.

Letting him take over, I leaned back and hooked my hands onto the headboard. He crawled up the bed and I popped my head up to watch my young man in action. He leaned over me and licked his tongue from nipple to nipple, drawing out my buds until they were so hard they hurt.

His tongue cruised down my belly, and when he parted my legs I writhed beneath his touch. He trailed little nips up and down my thigh, each time inching toward my pussy. It was exquisite agony, and I was seconds from yelling at him to lick me when he did. His tongue was hot, hard, and glorious as he glided it up my vagina and curled around my clit.

With incredible skill Mason not only had his tongue working its magic on my hypersensitive pussy, but his fingers also played with my boobs, squeezing and tweaking my nipples simultaneously. My body was on fire. Every nerve ending buzzed.

His hands moved back to my pussy, and he thrust a finger inside me. I pushed my heels into the bed, raised my hips, and parted my knees, giving him room to play. A second finger joined the first, and as they twisted in and out of my pulsing hole, his hot tongue glided up and down my velvet folds.

He wrapped his lips around my clit and sucked so hard, I dug my nails into the headboard and clamped my knees shut, trapping him there as a shudder ripped through me. I parted my knees, let go of the bed, clutched a handful of his hair and held him in place. A wild scream burst from my lips, and I bucked beneath him as every sensation in my body erupted in a mind-blowing orgasm. As I rode the glorious wave, my hips writhed, my clit pulsed, and my insides clenched with each lick of Mason's tongue.

He looked up from between my legs with a drunken-like gaze. "Holy wow."

It was wow—every bit wow. But I wanted more; I wanted to feel him inside me. I'd barely caught my breath when I rolled off the bed in one fluid movement and practically ran for my bag. I attacked the zipper and plucked out a condom packet. As I returned to him, I tore the packet open with my teeth. I handed the condom over and as he rolled it on, I crawled onto the bed on my hands and knees and thrust my ass at him, telling him in no uncertain terms that I wanted that cock inside me . . . now.

His fingers dug into the flesh at my hips, and in one swift movement his cock rammed into me. It was fast, it was furious. It blew my mind. As I fisted the sheets and cried out, he thrust into me with brutal repetition. He pounded something deep, deep inside me—it was as much painful as it was magnificent.

"Oh, yes," he yelled, and over and over he drove into me, impaling me with every inch of his solid muscle.

My second orgasm shot through me, surprising me with its swiftness, and I screamed at the gloriousness of it. Mason cried out too, a deep, primal groan that tumbled from his throat and matched his final thrusts. His grip on my thighs petered out as his cock softened inside me. I fell forward and rolled to my side, gasping for breath.

As Mason strode to the bathroom, I admired his youthful body. He wasn't muscle-bound like Corben or nicely tanned like Hunter, yet he had just as many equally appealing qualities that had me praying I'd remember every inch of my young lover.

He emerged from the bathroom naked, and I rolled to sit on the edge of the bed. He sat beside me. Our legs touched.

I put my hand on his bare thigh. "That was amazing."

"It was fucking incredible." He scrunched up his nose, and it was so cute that I started giggling.

"What?" He smiled at me.

"Nothing, it's just . . ."

"What?" He was truly grinning now, and it was such a lovely sight that I prayed I'd remember it forever.

I reached up and kissed his cheek. "You're lovely." I stood and walked toward my leggings that were half inside-out.

"Do you have to go?"

His pleading big blue eyes nearly had me agreeing. But thankfully, the angel in my brain dominated this time. "Yes, I have to go." I pulled my undies on and flipped my leggings the right way around. I sat on the bed and pulled on my pants in a totally unsexy way. Once the battle was over, I tugged on my boots, shoved my bra in my bag, put my black shirt on, and did up the buttons. I hooked my bag over my shoulder and sighed as I turned to Mason. "Thank you for a wonderful night."

"Thank you."

I strode out his doorway and went to my apartment. Aspects of my incredible night bounced around my brain as I removed my disguise, showered, and brushed my teeth. I dressed in my PJs, and at my bedside table I pulled my diary onto my lap.

I turned to the 3rd of December, and at the top of the page I wrote *Mr. Mason Cole Room 6*. Then I filled the page with intimate details of our sex—the urgency, the roughness, the incredible oral sex, and questions on whether or not the marijuana had heightened the intensity. With that thought, I wrote *Sex is my Drug* at the top of the page.

By the time I'd finished, I'd filled two and a half pages with details of my evening with Mason. I flipped the diary closed, crawled under my bedsheet, and rolled onto my side. I tugged my spare pillow to my chest, wrapped my arm around it, and let the lovely post-sex throb ebbing through my body lull me to sleep.

Kitty Kendall

7ᵀᴴ DECEMBER
CAPTURE MY HEART
Room 18 - Hot Horizon Hotel

The second I hopped out of the taxi I was affronted by two things. The first was the bustling crowds, and the second was "Jingle Bells" blaring from the discreet speakers in the newly renovated shopping center walls. Pacific Fair was alive. I had hoped by coming here on a Wednesday afternoon I'd miss most of the crowds. I'd been so wrong.
With my Christmas shopping list in hand, I headed toward the first jewelry store I knew of. Half an hour later, I walked out four hundred dollars poorer and with my first two Christmas gifts hanging off my arm. The heavy silver football cufflinks were perfect for my brother, and with the amount of fancy dinner functions Tyler attended I knew he'd use them. For Aunty Ann, I found the perfect pair of gold drop earrings with the dainty pearl dangling at the bottom. I could easily picture her wearing them.
My next purchases were a bottle of Chanel No. 5 perfume for Mom and Aramis cologne for Dad. I spent too much time choosing Christmas cards for them all and then headed to the post office. Unlike I had the previous three years, I put a bit more effort into my written messages to the people I loved, and it occurred to me that my visit back home had improved my relationships with them all. For the first time since I left home, I actually

felt a twang of loneliness knowing I'd be spending another Christmas without family around me.

I boxed up the gifts and handed them over the counter to be posted.

With that done, I went in search of the remaining gifts on my list. Cal's present would be similar to the one I purchased him each Christmas. A large glass jar filled to the rim with sweets. Lolita never had treats in her house. Each year I helped Calvin out with his sugar cravings and each year Lolita would scowl at me. It'd become a running joke. It took several shops to find a suitable jar, and the one I chose had me giggling. I couldn't wait to see Cal's reaction when he unwrapped it on Christmas day.

The jar was a Big Ass Jar—literally. It was shaped like a woman's bottom with a blue G-string painted on it. Once I filled it with Jelly Beans, it'll be the perfect gift for Cal. After I paid for it, I headed toward Kmart. I purchased a remote-control helicopter for Maddox, and for Savannah I chose a coloring book filled with exotic flora and fauna, and a giant pack of coloring pencils. My gift for Lolita would have to wait. I planned to get her the same purple knee-high boots that I'd worn for Mason Cole the other week. I just hoped the store I'd bought them from still stocked them or could get them in for me.

With my shopping bags weighing down my arms, I headed toward the grocery store. I walked past a nail salon, stopped, and with a recollection of Lolita's comment about me stepping things up a notch, went back to Dawn's Nails and Beauty.

I went in and within a couple of minutes a young woman named Laura who had the most stunning eyelashes I'd ever seen was explaining the differences between gel and acrylic nails. With the decision made, Laura set about applying layer upon layer of gel to my nails.

While she was busy, my mind flitted all over the place. One minute I was contemplating the fact that both my brother and I were unmarried and without children, and the next I was thinking about the other men in my life. In particular the three men who I'd seen many times this year: Billy, Hunter, and Henry. They were all drastically different. It was impossible to understand how I could be attracted to all three.

In my mind, I tried to list what I found appealing about them. All three were incredible in bed. They all had amazing bodies. They were kind, considerate, compassionate, and confident. It occurred to me that maybe they weren't so different after all.

"What color polish would you like?" Laura dragged me from my introspection.

"Oh, what are my choices?"

Laura handed me a booklet containing what seemed like thousands of pictures of nail art. The choice was overwhelming . . . much like my men.

After much deliberation, I chose a pretty Christmas theme which consisted of a beautiful ruby red base with a tiny gold outline of a Christmas tree. It was simple yet stylish and I was impressed when Laura painted the tree on freehand. She topped the nails with yet another clear layer, and forty minutes after I walked into the salon, I walked out with the best-looking nails I'd ever had.

I couldn't stop glancing at them as I made my way toward the grocery store. Pushing the cart, I zipped up and down the aisles tossing necessities in. My mind, however, was back on the three wonderful men in my life and whether or not I should buy Christmas gifts for them. And if I did, what would I get.

As I stewed over this decision, I realized I barely knew them at all. Sure I knew every inch of their bodies, and I knew they were incredible lovers. I even knew what they each did for a living. But I had very little knowledge of what they liked and didn't like. Between the three of them, Hunter was probably the one I knew the most.

I smiled as I thought of him and how wonderful our conversation flowed. Hunter and I could talk for hours and never run out of things to say.

Was that the definition of love?

My mind was still replaying all the fabulous times I'd had with Hunter as I passed through the checkout, paid, and pushed the cart out the store. Right next to the Coles was the liquor store and as I recalled the delicious Limoncello chocolate he'd made, I headed into the shop.

I was surprised to discover a dozen or so choices of Limoncello on the shelf. After much deliberation where it was the look of the bottle rather than the price that dictated my decision, I chose a twin bottle gift set. One bottle was Limoncello and the other was Orangecello made from blood orange. The bottles themselves were a work of art and nestled amongst straw in the custom made wooden box, made the perfect gift.

My heart fluttered at the prospect of presenting him with this Christmas present. Hunter did that to me . . . made my heart flutter and it was such a wonderful acknowledgement.

I couldn't help but grin as I pushed my cart up the shopping center toward the taxi stand. A man walking toward me in a cowboy hat caught my eye, and as my jaw dropped, his face lit up, and I instantly felt terrible about my gift to Hunter sitting right on top of the cart.

"Jane." Billy wrapped his arms around me, and as I sunk into his warm embrace, I inhaled delicious manly scents. His touch was gentle yet strong, and my body glowed inside and out at how wonderful he felt. I caught people looking at us and squeezed him tighter relishing in the public display of affection with my handsome cowboy.

Our embrace ended too soon and when I stepped back, I looked up into his stunning molten eyes. "What're you doing here?"

"I just finished a show," he said, "and I dropped in to do a bit of shopping before I went back to the hotel."

"Did you stay last night?"

"Yes. I checked in after nine, but you weren't there."

"Oh, I've had a promotion. I'm now the hotel manager, so I work during the days."

His expression faltered, and I couldn't decide if he were happy or upset with my news. But the confusion written over his face changed in a flash and a smile quickly ensued. "That's fantastic. We should celebrate. Can I take you out to dinner?"

I couldn't help the grin curling at my lips. "I'd love that."

"Would you like to come to my room first?" His honey eyes dazzled.

"Sounds great."

"I'm in room eighteen. Does six o'clock suit you?"

I checked my watch. That gave me just one hour. "Perfect."

He glanced down at my cart. "Would you like a hand with your shopping?"

"No, I'm fine. Thank you." I reached up to kiss his cheek, but he turned his head and cupped my chin so our lips met. It was just a brief touch but lovely butterflies danced across my stomach at the familiarity of it. The smile on my face must've been enormous. "See you soon."

As I pushed the cart away I glanced at him over my shoulder, and when he waved my heart skipped a beat. I tugged my bottom lip into my mouth, and the lovely glow pulsing through me had me floating on air.

The taxi returned me to the hotel within fifteen minutes, and I lugged my bags from the trunk and up the stairs. A luggage trolley was positioned at reception, and as I strode toward it, I smiled at Marjorie who was on the phone. I loaded my bags onto the trolley and waited for her to finish the call.

"Been shopping?" she said as she hung up the phone.

"Christmas gifts and groceries."

"Good on you, I haven't bought any presents yet. I need to get a move on."

"It's crazy out there already."

"Always is."

"Everything alright here?"

She smiled. "Of course."

"Okay, have a good night."

"You too."

I pushed the trolley to the elevator, and to my delight it pinged open straight away, and I shoved the trolley in. As I rode the elevator up, I thought about what to wear for Billy. It was getting too hot to wear jeans, so my mind flicked to my dresses. I still hadn't made a decision when the doors opened again.

The stubborn trolley wheels fought against the carpet, and as I struggled with them on every step to my kitchen, I made a mental note to get these fixed for the guests asap. One glance at the clock had me moving, and I shoved my groceries away in record time, placed the gifts I'd bought on my dining table, and jumped into the shower. I didn't have time to wash my hair, but I did shave my legs and under my arms.

After I hopped out and dried off, I applied a touch of makeup—just enough to cover my freckles, lengthen my lashes, and add color to my cheeks. At my closet, I flicked the clothes back and forward. Before this year, barely any of my clothes had a memory to go with them. Now, however, I was finding the opposite. Every dress or shirt I held up conjured images of the man I'd been with while wearing it. It'd feel weird to wear a dress for Billy that I'd worn for Hunter or Henry . . . but I was running out of options.

Lack of time had me forced to choose, and in the end I decided on a Bohemian patterned halter-neck shift dress that'd been shoved to the very back of my closet. When I'd bought it years ago, it was perfect to show off my shoulders, but at the same time it had hidden the roll of fat that used to bulge from my underwear. I'd stopped wearing it because it required a strapless bra and just the thought of wiggling my lopsided boobs into that contraption again put me off. So I decided not to wear one. As I pulled on a pale pink G-string, thoughts of Billy cupping my boobs in his hands had little flutters scooting across my belly.

I slipped the dress over the top and did up the tiny button at the back of my neck. The dress was shorter than I remembered, falling halfway up my thigh, and the full fabric draped loosely around my body and had me feeling free and easy. *Yep that's me. Free and easy.* I chuckled. I'd never thought of myself like that, but now that I knew how damn good sex was, I had no desire to play hard to get. Especially with my stunning honey-eyed cowboy.

With two minutes to spare, I glided on a lick of pale pink lipstick, grabbed my bag, and headed out my door.

Billy greeted me after just one knock, and I stepped into his open arms. His embrace was a sensory explosion. I felt the delightfully taut muscles in his back. I inhaled his familiar manly scent. I heard his pounding heart through his chest, and when I looked up into his stunning eyes, I was lost to a glorious lust fueled world.

I dropped my bag to my feet, put my hands around his neck, and drew his lips to mine. My tongue dueled his in a heady dance, eager to taste, eager to explore. His hand glided up and down my back, and united, we emitted a primal groan that said so much. My fingers found the buttons on his shirt, and despite my new fingernails making it difficult, I managed to pluck the buttons free. I drove my hands into the opening and glided my fingers over his warm flesh to explore all the delightful muscles languishing there.

Heat coursed through me, starting deep inside my body and pulsing out a delicious beat across my skin, across my clit. His erection was as swift as it was hard, and the solid muscle pushed against my belly. Reaching down, I rubbed my hand over it, letting him know I knew he was there.

I pulled back, eager to study my handsome cowboy, and I wasn't disappointed. His moistened lips were parted, as if he were about to speak. His pupils were enormous. When his tongue lashed out and glided over his bottom lip, lust took Billy to a whole new glorious level.

Our chests rose and fell as I reached up to undo the tiny button behind my neck. Free now, I raised my hands, and Billy needed no invitation to undress me. The fabric pulled up over my face and fell in a balloon at our side. His eyes explored my body, creating an intense heat that blazed through me.

It was my turn for voyeurism and I tugged at his pants, anxious to release him from his constraints. The heavy denim was around his ankles in a flash and his cock bounced forward, begging me to touch.

I travelled my eyes over his body, examining every inch of his exquisite flesh. His Adam's apple bobbed up and down, and his cock did, too. Knowing I'd created that beast shot a firecracker through my body, and I stepped forward and put my hands on Billy's shoulders. With his hands beneath my bottom, he launched me onto his hips.

His cock prodded my ass, and our mouths locked together as he carried me across the room. He placed me down on the kitchen counter, and our lips parted. His breathing came in short, sharp gasps. I leaned back, placing one palm on the counter for support, and offering my breasts to him. Billy leaned forward, and I crawled my nails through his hair as he sucked my breasts, one after the other, into his mouth. I gasped as he pulled my nipple upward until it snapped from his lips. With my focus diverted, he surprised me when in one swift movement, he pulled my G-string aside and glided a finger into my throbbing hole. I groaned at the erotic intrusion, but eager for it to happen again, I lay back on the counter, hung my head over the other side, raised my feet to the flat surface and pushed my bottom upwards.

Billy put his head between my legs, and with one hand pulling my underwear aside, he glided his tongue up and down my pussy as he drove his fingers into me. My body ached for him. My heart did, too. This glorious man knew how to bring out my arousal, and the orgasm growing inside me swelled and burst at lightning speed. I lashed out, clawing at the counter as my climax rocked through me.

I'd barely caught my breath when Billy pulled my underwear from me and cast it aside. He stepped forward, and the intensity in his eyes told me I'd need to hang on for this one. I was ready, oh so ready to have my sexy cowboy fuck me stupid.

With his hand around his swollen cock, he nudged it toward my vagina. A pearl of semen bubbled at the top, and the glory of the raw spectacle was the jolt I needed. "Billy . . ." My voice was barely a whisper. "You need a condom."

His eyes bounced to me, then he turned and strode to the bedside table. He pulled the drawer so fast the whole thing came out and fell with a thud onto the carpet. He bent over, came up with a foil packet in his fingers, tore the packet open with his teeth, and glided the rubber on as he strode back to me.

He nudged his hips between my thighs again and I reached down, wrapped my hand around his swollen muscle, and glided his cock up and down my throbbing clit. My insides clenched, begging me to push that beast inside me, but I wanted to wait. I wanted this very moment to last a lifetime.

I wanted Billy to last a lifetime.

With that glorious thought, I aimed his swollen crown at my vagina and like a perfect choreographed move, Billy thrust his cock into me. I cried out as his length filled me, right to the hilt, fast and hard, all the way in one driving thrust. His fingers dug into my thighs. His jaw was clamped shut but his eyes were fierce, driven by a passion that fueled my fervent libido.

I put my feet on his shoulders and raised my ass. The change in angle had him pounding something deep inside me. It was pleasure and pain, heaven and hell.

"Oh god." I clawed at the counter.

His thrusts grew faster—in and out, over and over and over. The tendons in his neck were as taut as tensile wire, and his bulging biceps gripped my hips as he continued his thrusting.

Each plunge into me built another layer atop of my already raging climax. I reached forward, clutched his wrists, dug my nails in, and screamed as I came. He cried out too, a wild, primal moan that tumbled from deep in his throat and was sustained for as long as his final thrusts.

Soon his plunging slowed, and his breaths became deep and steady. I let go of his wrists and propped myself up on my elbows so I could witness his awakening from carnal bliss. A fine sheen glistened across his spectacular body. His chest rose up and down with each calming breath. It was an eternity before his eyes opened and focused on me. A smile lit up his face. It was *that* smile, the one that said every single thing in the world was perfect and not a damn thing could take that away.

I dropped my feet from his shoulders, and Billy pulled me to his chest. As I wrapped my arms around him, I listened to his thumping heart. I'd be happy to stay in this very position for ever.

He kissed my cheek and then lifted me off the counter so I could stand. "Excuse me for a sec."

As he strode to the bathroom, I sighed with wonderful contentment. I picked up my G-string, slipped it on and ambled toward my dress. The fabric had fallen in an almost perfect circle. I gathered it up and pulled it over my head. As I fumbled with the tiny button behind my neck, Billy stepped from the bathroom wearing a pair of jeans. My heart melted at the sight. Billy was *the* poster boy for cowboys everywhere.

He turned to the closet, glided the mirrored door aside, and bent over, and when he turned back to me my heart leapt to my throat at what he was holding.

"Merry Christmas, Jane."

I covered my mouth, feeling awkward and horrible and confused. "I didn't get you anything. I'm sorry."

He stepped my way, smiling. "You didn't need to. I wanted to buy you this." The package in his arms was large and beautifully wrapped in gold paper with a red bow centered on top. "Go on. Open it."

He forced me to take the present, and I was surprised at how light it was. My heart struck up a steady beat as I walked to the bed and placed the gift down. With Billy at my side, I undid the bow, then peeled open the gold paper. The box was plain white, giving no indication as to what was inside. Billy was a bundle of energy beside me and as I lifted the lid, I prayed my first reaction was exactly what he'd hoped for.

Inside was a cowboy hat. My heart raced. The hat was lovely and feminine, unlike any I'd seen before. I lifted it from the box.

"Do you like it? It's beaver and hare felt. And see the hat band? I thought you'd like the blue and aqua colors in the beads. Put it on." Billy's energy was contagious, and I couldn't help but be caught up in his excitement. I tucked my hair behind my ears, and the second I put the hat on, he put his hands on my shoulders and led me to the mirror.

His smile reflected at me. "It looks great. What do you think?"

I diverted my eyes from his, but the second I saw my reflection I had an instant flashback to my childhood. I was about twelve years old, thirteen at the most. My brother and I were at my uncle's farm, where we went every school holidays. The memory galloped across my brain. And it wasn't a good one. I remembered standing in a cow paddock, the midday sun burning my flesh as I helped Uncle Terry rewire a fence. The unbearable heat made sweat trickle from under my cowboy hat and down my temples in little rivers that caked the incessant red dust to my skin.

At first, going to the farm had been fun, but as my childhood progressed, each trip had become a taste in slave labor as we helped Uncle Terry with all manner of never-ending jobs. It was only when Dad's brother passed away that the school holiday trips had ended.

As I stared at my reflection, I knew what I'd always known . . . country life was not for me. And as my eyes flicked from Billy's enormous grin to my own look of distress, I came to a brutal decision. I had to tell Billy now, before it was too late.

But as I turned to his beaming face, I knew it already was.

"Billy . . ." It must've been the way I said it, because his shoulders sagged and his smile melted. "I'm so sorry." My chin dimpled as I stared at the sadness in his eyes. "I can't live on a farm."

He reached for my hand. "But how do you know?"

"My uncle had a farm, and my brother and I spent school holidays there when I was a kid."

"This won't be same. You'll love it, I know." His voice had changed; the pitch was higher, pleading.

I sighed. "But it's not just that—it's the isolation. I love living near the ocean and knowing that a coffee shop or restaurant is not far away. I couldn't go back to the country. I'd be miserable, and that would tear us apart."

"I could move here."

I covered my mouth, shocked at his offer. Swallowing the lump in my throat, I shook my head. "Oh, Billy. The farm is your life. I see it in your eyes when you talk about it, about the animals, about your parents. You couldn't live here. It would crush you."

He reached for my hand, and we squeezed our palms together. "We'd make it work. The two of us. We have something special."

I looked to the ceiling, and when I squeezed my eyes shut a tear trickled down my cheek. Billy thumbed it away, and after a deep breath I lowered my gaze to look at him. I swallowed back the enormous lump in my throat. I needed to be strong. This was best for both of us. Our lives were too different, we were headed on different paths, and if we carried on, one of us would end up miserable. This needed to end before it was too late. No . . . it needed to end *today*. My heart tore apart at that decision, but deep down I knew it was the right one.

With our fingers woven together, I led Billy to the bed and sat him down. I took off the hat, placed it on the covers behind him, and sat at his side. "I'm sorry, Billy. This . . . us, it would never work. It's been beautiful, special, the most incredible journey, but it has to end. We were never meant to be together."

"What were we meant to be then, Jane?" The anger in his voice caught me off guard, and when I shifted to look at him and saw tears welling in his eyes, I wrapped my arms around him and sobbed into his shoulder. Great racking sobs tumbled from me. My tears spilled down his back, and I could barely breathe. But Billy didn't move. He didn't put his arms around me—he just sucked air in through his clenched teeth, fighting what I assumed were tears.

Sucking in several shaky breaths, I pulled back, determined to finish what I'd started. *I wanted a relationship that was one hundred percent perfect.*
What Billy and I had was not.
I sat back on the bed and flicked tears from my eyes. "I'm sorry, Billy. I never meant to hurt you. I just wanted it to be fun. But I know we went so much further. Too much further."
"There's never too much when it comes to love."
His words pierced my heart and I closed my eyes, nodding. "I know. I'm sorry."
We sat in silence, the two of us sucking back shaky breaths. It was an eternity before I formulated what I needed to say. I reached for his hand, wove my fingers into his, and squeezed. "I want to thank you."
His jaw squared out as he blinked at me.
"I want to thank you for showing me everything good there is in a man. We shared some truly magical times both in the bedroom and outside. I am stronger because of you, and I feel blessed that we met." His Adam's apple bobbed up and down, but that was his only movement. "But I know we won't be happy together. We may be for a while, but soon the cracks will show. We'll begin to fight a little, then it'll be a lot, and one day we'll wake up hating each other. I don't want that to happen. I want to remember this year and all the magical moments we had together. I want to remember you exactly as you are—incredible. I'm sorry, Billy. I never meant to hurt you. I hope that in your heart you know I'm right and will one day forgive me."
I kissed the back of his hand and stood. My heart pounding in my ears was the only sound as I strode to my bag, which was still on the floor at the front door. I picked it up and with my hand on the door handle, I turned back to Billy. He hadn't moved. His bare back faced me, but in the mirror I saw his slumped shoulders, his downward face, and most of all, I saw the sadness in his eyes. "I will never forget you, Billy."
I pulled open the door and stepped into the corridor. Every step toward the elevator was hell. My heart squeezed so tight I could barely breathe, and tears blurred my vision making it impossible to see.
Somehow, I made it to my room. I strode straight to my bed, flopped down face-first, and bawled my eyes out.
Poor Billy.
I couldn't get that final image of him from my mind. He was a broken man, and it was all my fault.
It was an eternity before I was able to move again, and when I rolled onto my side and saw my bag, I knew what I had to do. I tugged my phone from the inside zipper and dialed Lolita.
It rang a few times, which wasn't like Lolita, but when the phone clicked and the raucous music blared down the line, I was surprised she'd answered the phone at all. "Hey babe."

I didn't even get a word out before I broke down sobbing.

"Hey, are you okay?"

I still couldn't speak.

"Hang on. Let me go outside."

I wiped snot from my nose and rubbed it on my dress. As I inhaled and let it out slowly I hoped I'd be able to speak again soon.

I heard a door shut, and the noise simmered down. "Are you okay?"

"Yes . . . and no."

"Okay babe. Tell me what's happened."

"I broke up with . . . with . . ."

"With who, honey?"

"With Billy." I howled, squeezed my eyes shut, and flopped back onto the bed.

Lolita spoke to me, but her soothing voice only made me cry more. Eventually, I couldn't cry anymore.

"Hey, do you want me to come over?"

"No." I rubbed tears from my lower lashes. "I'll be okay. I'm just being a sook."

"You're not a sook. Do you want to tell me what happened?"

I wiped my nose again and sniffed a few times. Then I told her everything, from the mind-blowing sex on the kitchen counter, to the hat, to what I'd said, and finally, to the shattered man I'd left sitting on the bed.

"Listen to me, babe. What you did shows how strong you are."

"You should've seen the look on his face, Lolly. He was a broken man." I waited for her response and prayed her words of wisdom would lure me back from the swamp I'd fallen into.

"Most women would've carried on with a man like Billy for all the wrong reasons, even when they knew deep down it wasn't right. You, though, are a smart woman; you knew that the two of you weren't made for each other. Sure, the sex was amazing, and his company was special, but love . . . well, that needs a hell of a lot more than that. And if it didn't feel right now, then it wasn't going to feel right when one of you moved thousands of miles to live a completely different lifestyle."

As I rolled her words of wisdom around my brain, I did feel a little better. Deep down I knew my decision was right, but it didn't make me feel any less cruel.

"I feel so mean."

"You're not mean. You were true to your feelings. A guy like Billy will find a woman. Trust me, babe—he was pretty special."

"Yeah, he was."

"You feel better now?"

"Yes, thank you. I'm sorry to interrupt. Where are you anyway?"

"At home."

"Oh, it sounded like you were at a party."

"Nah, kids are at a sleepover. Cal and I cranked up the music, opened a bottle of wine, and were playing naked Twister when you rang. I was winning, of course."

I burst out laughing, and it felt so good. "Oh my god, why did you answer the phone?"

"Cause it's you, of course. Don't worry. Cal will wait."

I smiled, once again feeling the love from my best friend. "Thanks, Lolly. I love you."

"Love you too, babe. Now go and have a hot bath and pour yourself a huge glass of wine. But remember, you did the right thing."

We said goodbye. I clicked off the call and went to the bathroom. My face was a disaster. My eyes were bloodshot, and the tiny bit of mascara I'd worn had turned into black steaks down my face. I put the shower on, and as I waited for the water to warm up I removed my makeup.

The shower was hot and therapeutic, and as I stood under the cascade I replayed my decision over and over. By the time I stepped out, dried off, put on my PJs, and grabbed a bottle of wine and a glass, the decision was still boiling in my brain.

I opened my sliding glass door, stepped onto the balcony, filled my glass to the top and placed both on the table. It was a beautiful night. The cool breeze drifted up from the ocean like a lover's touch. I stepped to the railing, clutched it, closed my eyes, and inhaled the salty air. It was a cleansing potion to my soul. I breathed long and deep, over and over, performing my own form of therapy. When I finally opened my eyes a wonderful sense of calm enveloped me.

I went inside, grabbed my diary and a pen, and returned to the table. After a couple of sips of my wine, I turned to the 7th of December, and at the top I wrote *Cowboy Billy Room 50*. Between sips, I filled the page with details of my night. Everything from the wonderful sex on the kitchen counter where together we soared to extraordinary heights, to his Christmas gift, and finally, to my decision to let Billy go. By setting him free, I in turn had set my heart free. My soul was open, ready to be captured by the right man. With that thought I wrote, *Capture my Heart*, at the top of the page.

I carried on writing, recalling in vivid clarity everything that had happened so I could look back and know I'd made the right decision. I wrote about the childhood memory that'd triggered my reaction, the clarity of which was a brutal reminder of how tough living on the land was. No tears came as I described breaking up with Billy, not even when I wrote about how shattered he'd looked as I'd said my last goodbye.

Love was meant to be easy, but if it involved a complete lifestyle change how easy could that be. It wasn't that I wasn't willing to move. I'd do that in a heartbeat for the right man. But if I were to move, it would need to be somewhere that made me happy. Because I couldn't imagine my love sustaining if I was miserable in my own home.

My decision to break up with Billy was the right one. I knew that. I'd probably known it for a while. My judgment had been clouded by the incredible sex and his wonderful company.

But I want more than that.

I want a man who I want to spend the rest of my life with. I want us to share dreams together and set about making those dreams come true. I want everything about our life to be perfect. I want to fall asleep in his arms every night knowing that each day we'd shared something special, something that I couldn't experience with any other man but him.

Was I asking too much?

I decided the answer was no. I wasn't. I, Jane Nichols, would find the man of my dreams.

I flipped my diary closed and stood with my wine in my hand. As I eased against my railing and listened to the crashing waves I realized that the loss of Billy meant I was down to just two of my regular men—Henry, my suave tutor, who melted both my body and my heart, and Hunter, who captured me in so many ways but didn't even know my real name.

I tried to picture my future with these men and it was Hunter who popped into my mind. I could see a future with him. The two of us living by the ocean and travelling to exotic corners of the world together. My heart swelled and two seconds later deflated at the brutal realization that he didn't know me at all.

Wonderful visions of Hunter danced across my mind as I finished off my wine.

Would he forgive me?

Was there any hope that the two of us could have a life together?

There was no way to answer those questions. But what I did know, was that the very next time I saw him, I'd tell Hunter all about my rotten lies.

My heart squeezed at that horrible but necessary decision.

Kitty Kendall

16ᵀᴴ DECEMBER
HUNTER EXTRAORDINAIRE
Room 48 - Hot Horizon Hotel

It'd been years since I'd put up Christmas decorations, and I was amazed at how long it was taking. Tania, Marjorie and I had been at it since my shift ended two hours ago. Luckily we were only doing the bar area as we still weren't finished. To fit into most of the staff's work and life schedules, the Christmas party was due to start at five o'clock and would go for just three hours. We could've forgone the decorations, but it was the first Christmas party the Hot Horizon Hotel had had in two years and the staff were excited, so I wanted to make it a little special.

Tania had cranked up the music the minute we'd started decorating and even though both Marjorie and Tania were on duty, I allowed her to pour the three of us a drink each to get into the party mood. It was fun, we laughed a lot, and it wasn't long before both ladies started voicing their opinions on John. It seemed Needledick hadn't just picked on me.

"He was always perving at my ass. Gave me the creeps," Tania said as I climbed the ladder to reach the top of the Christmas tree. I tugged the golden angel into position at the top of the tree, and for the hundredth time I scowled over my annoying gel nails.

I climbed down the ladder and frowned at her. "Why didn't you say something?"

She shrugged. "Who was I going to tell? It doesn't matter now anyway. He's gone."

"I'll drink to that." Marjorie held her cocktail up, and the colorful Tequila Sunrise looked spectacular in the red bar lighting. We clinked our glasses and toasted the demise of Needledick.

I glanced around the decorations. Tiny fairy lights flickered along the glass racks above the bar. Alternating gold and red tinsel was draped from the far wall to the bar and the ten foot Christmas tree was decorated top to bottom with ornaments and colorful lights. "Okay, I think we're ready. I'm going to head upstairs to change, and I'll see you back here in half an hour." I pointed a finger at each of them. "Don't refill your drinks. You're both on duty, remember?"

"Yes, boss." Marjorie saluted me, and I shook my head and chuckled as I walked off.

As I rode the elevator up to my room, I smiled at myself in the mirror. It was good to know I'd brought some sunshine to the Hot Horizon Hotel staff. I quickly changed into the red dress Lolly had helped me choose the other day during our post-Billy retail therapy. The dress was fire engine red with a fitted bodice that came in at the waist and flared out into a classic 1950s retro style. I spun in a circle, and the skirt billowed around me. It was fun and sassy and perfect for a staff Christmas party.

While I was in front of my closet, I plucked out the dress I'd wear later for Hunter. When he'd phoned earlier this week, I couldn't believe my luck. He wouldn't be available until about nine o'clock tonight, and if all went to plan and the work Christmas party wrapped up at eight thirty, that'd give me just enough time to get back up to my room to change into my Memphis disguise.

My sadness over Billy had dissipated with Hunter's call, and I hadn't stopped smiling since. I touched up my makeup, styled my hair, brushed my teeth, and grabbed my room key to head back down to the party.

The elevator doors opened to Coldplay blaring out their "Christmas Lights" song from the bar, and I smiled as raucous laughter erupted. I stepped around the corner to see dozens of hotel staff watching Dan from the Horizons gym walk across the room and flicking his non-existent hair as if impersonating someone. They all laughed again, and I joined in as I strolled into the bar. "What's going on?" I asked Tania.

"Dan's pretending to be John."

I chuckled, even though I didn't see the resemblance.

"Knock. Knock."

I turned to the voice and waved the chef over. "Thank you so much," I said as Wyatt, the chef from the Blue Haven Café, carried two trays toward us.

"You're welcome. Any time." He placed the trays down. "I'll just get the other two."

I peeled off the silver foil to reveal an assortment of pastries, tarts, and meatballs. Hopefully Wyatt's savory cooking was as delicious as his sweet treats I enjoyed every week.

"Oh yummy." Peter reached for a meatball and dipped it into the red sauce at the side. It was the first time I'd seen him smile and I liked what a saw. As the hotel cleaner he probably didn't get much joy at work.

"Okay who's up for a Slippery Nipple?" Pete had lined up shot glasses on the bar.

"Hey, who authorized those?" I attempted my best scowl at the bar manager.

Pete wriggled his bushy eyebrows. "It's a party."

Nora nudged her shoulder to me. "Just one?"

Her pleading voice had me giving in. Not that I tried really hard.

"Okay, just one."

As Pete layered the Baileys Irish Cream and butterscotch schnapps into the shot glasses, Wyatt returned with another two trays of food. I thanked him again and after he walked away, I peeled off the silver foil to reveal an assortment of sushi, cheeses and cold meats on one, and the other loaded with sweet treats.

"Make a toast, Jane," Marjorie said.

"Oh, ummm." A shot glass was shoved into my hand. As everyone turned my way, my mind scrambled over something inspirational to say. I sucked in a quick breath and held up my glass. "I know how hard you all work to make our beautiful hotel a success, and I know the last couple of years have been light on with acknowledging your dedication. But I plan to change that. I love working here, and I hope that you all do too."

"We do now," Tania said.

"Yeah, it's already better, now that you're in charge," Nora said.

"Thank you. Merry Christmas, guys, and I look forward to a wonderful new year working with you all. Cheers."

"Cheers," they said in unison, and together we all shot our drinks down our throats. I gulped back the sweet liquid and placed my glass on the table.

During the next couple of hours, as we drank a few more drinks and ate the delicious food, I made a point of talking to each staff member individually. Although we'd essentially worked under the same roof for years, other than Marjorie, I barely knew any of them.

It was something I intended to change.

Several guests checked in during our party, and each time Marjorie made her way to the counter, I prayed she didn't breathe on them. Fortunately, her shift finished soon, and then Bailey would start his shift. I'd been watching him and other than the shooter he'd had earlier, he'd been holding onto the same beer for most of the evening. Unlike Tracy, the new staff member from Brisbane—she'd had more drinks than I could count, yet she barely showed any signs of inebriation. I'd be flat on my back if I'd had as many as she had.

A teenage girl came bounding into the bar and wrapped her arms around Marjorie. "Hey Mom."

"Roxanne. You're here already."

"It's nearly eight o'clock." Marjorie's daughter smiled up at her mother, and I recognized their likeness. Russell, her son, strolled to his mother's side, and by contrast he looked nothing like Marjorie.

"Hey everyone, these are my kids, Roxanne and Russell."

Everybody said hello. Russell had changed dramatically since I'd last seen him. His jaw had squared out, he'd grown about seven inches, and his shoulders had become broader. At just shy of seventeen, Russell was growing into a very handsome man.

"You guys want something to eat?" I pointed at what was left of the food and when they both strolled that way, Marjorie stepped toward me.

"Thanks for the party. It was great."

"My pleasure; I'm glad you enjoyed it. What're you doing now?"

"Helen and I are taking the kids ten-pin bowling. That should be fun after the drinks I've had."

"It might be more fun with the alcohol."

She chuckled. "Yeah, maybe."

"Do you want to take some food home with you?"

"Hell no, those little buggers will eat it all. Save some for me in the staff fridge."

I giggled, agreed to her suggestion, and stepped forward to save some treats for her before Dan devoured them all.

The bell at reception chimed, and I turned to see who'd pressed it. Even with his back to me, I knew it was Hunter, my sexy chocolatier and my date for the evening. My heart skipped a few beats as he turned toward us. I spun my back to him, fearful he may recognize me as Bailey scurried past and headed toward reception. I nudged in behind the Christmas tree and stayed there until Bailey rejoined us a few minutes later.

Marjorie took forever to leave and I felt the pressure of the clock ticking toward my date with Hunter. The rest of the staff looked like they were settling in. I thought by eight o'clock they'd all be leaving.

"Would I be able to take some of these home?" Nora pointed at the food trays.

"Of course, help yourself."

Nora selected a few nibbles, and sealed them up in the foil that'd originally covered the trays.

Dan shoved a few more in his mouth, tossed back the last of his beer, and plonked the bottle on the bar. "Thanks for a great night, Jane."

"You're welcome. Thanks for coming."

"Hey, if the boss's paying, I'm in." He gave me a gentle punch on my bicep, and I chuckled at his comment.

"Are you going home?" Tracy pulled a sad face, and Dan's instant smile could've lit up the Christmas tree.

"Don't have to."

"Cool. Want to show me around Surfers?" She tugged her lip into her mouth, and it became plainly obvious that I'd missed the relationship that was brewing between these two.

Dan put his elbow out. "I'd love too."

"See ya, Jane. Thanks for a great night." Tracy tucked her arm into Dan's, and the two of them giggled as they strolled from the bar.

My jaw was still ajar as I turned to Tania and Pete.

Pete huffed. "That didn't take long." I wasn't sure if I detected jealousy in Pete's comment or not.

"You're not kidding." I glanced at the clock over the bar but didn't really need to. The *tick, tick, tick* in my head was as loud as a jackhammer. Hunter was likely to come strolling into this bar at any second now and I needed to get out of there. "Sorry guys . . . but I have to go."

"That's okay. Thank you for a great party," Tania said.

"You're welcome." I felt terrible leaving before they'd all gone, but the prospect of seeing Hunter quickly changed my focus. As I counted the seconds for my ride to arrive, I prayed for Hunter not to be in there when the doors finally opened. He wasn't and I sighed with relief as I stepped into the empty elevator. By the time I entered my apartment, I was already five minutes late; by the time I was dressed in my Memphis disguise and my cute rust-colored shirt-style dress that buttoned all the way up the front, I was twenty minutes late.

Horrible thoughts of Hunter leaving before I got there whizzed through my brain as I rode the painfully slow elevator back to the lobby. I took the opportunity to check my reflection confirming all traces of Jane were gone. Satisfied, I glided on another layer of lipstick, ensured none of my dark hair escaped from the blond wig, and tried to calm my beating heart.

The doors opened, and I strode toward the Christmas carols still emanating from the bar. My heart slammed in my chest when I saw at least twenty staff members still hanging around. That wasn't good. I needed to get Hunter out of there and quick. I spied him immediately. Hunter was a magnet—a hunky sex magnet drawing me in with his stunning physique and handsome features.

He smiled as I approached and stood to greet me. "Hey, Just Memphis."

I cringed at that name. Not for the first time this year, it felt so, so wrong. I placed my hands on his hips, feeling the corded muscle beneath my fingers, and angled my face up to him. Our lips met for just the briefest of kisses, and I already wanted so much more. "I'm sorry I'm late."

"That's okay. I've ordered us a glass of wine, but after that I thought we could go eat somewhere. I'm starving."

Even though I'd already devoured a mountain of food during the Christmas party, anything to get us out of the bar was a good plan. Tania arrived with our two wine glasses, and I pretended to scratch my forehead as I looked away. When she left I was grateful we were seated at the far end of the bar as it was a fair distance from where Tania, Pete and the rest of the staff hovered.

"Cheers." Hunter held his glass up, and I chinked mine to his.

"Cheers." I sipped the wine and admired Hunter over the glass. Each time we were together my feelings for him grew deeper, more complex, yet also more complete. Everything about him was bewitching, and I'd long ago fallen under his magical spell.

My instincts told me Hunter and I were meant to be together. Yet I still found it difficult to believe that a man like Hunter would be interested in a girl like me. But I had to remind myself that it wasn't me he was interested in . . . it was Memphis.

The very thought just about broke my heart.

My only hope was he'd see past my deceit. I was Memphis. Everything about Memphis came from me. She was me and I was her. Hunter and I had spent so much time together, I prayed he'd understand that.

It was at that moment I decided that tonight I'd tell him the truth. Whatever the consequences of that admission were, I'd just have to suffer them. I couldn't go on deceiving him anymore. I just had to wait for the perfect moment.

Hunter drained his glass. "Shall we go eat?"

"Of course."

He collected a bag from the floor, and I was about to ask him about it when he diverted my attention by flashing his brilliant smile and bending his elbow just like Dan had done with Tracy earlier. I curled my arm in, and together we walked from the bar and across the lobby like a couple of lovers would. Once we reached the steps, Hunter took my hand and we crossed over to the beach side of the grass and walked in the opposite direction to Surfers Paradise.

"What do you feel like for dinner?" he asked.

"I don't mind."

"Well . . . I brought a towel with me." He tapped the bag. "I thought we could grab fish and chips and sit down on the beach."

"Oh, that sounds wonderful." The moon was barely a sliver on the horizon, and I knew from experience that within half an hour it would light up my beach beautifully.

As we strolled to the Happy Snapper our conversation flowed freely. Hunter talked about his business and how well it was going in Queensland,

and I told him all about Aunty Ann and the funny things she was known for.

At the fish and chip shop we ordered our meal. While we waited for it to be cooked, we went a couple of shops down and bought a bottle of wine and two plastic wine glasses. We returned to the Happy Snapper just as they called Hunter's name.

With him carrying our meal and me carrying the paper bag containing the wine, we strolled along the grass and onto the raised wooden platform that would lead us down the beach. I paused where the boardwalk met the sand and stepped out of my stilettos.

"You okay with this?" The concern on Hunter's face was highlighted in the moonlight.

"Of course."

"Put your shoes in here, if you like." He opened the bag and I placed my stilettos on top of the towel.

"Lead the way."

There was enough light from the buildings behind us to illuminate Hunter's sexy bottom, and I watched his cheeks rise and fall with every step he took.

"You're checking out my butt aren't you?"

I giggled. "Maybe."

He stayed high up on the beach in the soft sand, and found a little spot that was fairly flat and almost fully encompassed with beach grass. There were people way down at the waterline, and I could hear people behind us, but amongst this vegetation we were totally secluded. It was our own little hidden oasis.

He held the bag containing the food toward me. "Can you hold this for a sec?"

I curled the bottle of wine beneath my elbow, and as I held the food container horizontally between my hands, Hunter plucked the towel from the bag and laid it out so we'd sit facing the beach. He then began undoing his shirt buttons.

I chuckled. "Hey, we haven't even eaten."

With a cheeky smile on his face he cocked his head at me, then placed his shirt on the sand in front of the towel. "It's for our food."

"Oh." I giggled, feeling a little silly. The moon was now a giant white globe, and with each passing second it rose slightly higher off the horizon, casting warm light over the tumbling waves. With my shirtless man basking in the moonlight, I was absorbing the most spectacular scene ever.

He took the wine and food from me, and I lowered onto the towel. While I wriggled into position, he put the plastic bag on his shirt, reached in and opened the lid on the polystyrene container holding our food. Then he cracked open the wine and poured each of us a drink.

Seconds later, Hunter was at my side. "I'm starving."

He offered me first choice, but it was difficult to focus on the food with my half-naked man sitting beside me. He commanded attention in all the right ways. The heat of his body was more exotic that the full moon rising high off the ocean.

I plucked a prawn cutlet from the tray and as I munched away, I absorbed my glorious setting. "It's beautiful tonight." I reached for my cup and took a sip. "

"You're beautiful."

I tugged my lip into my mouth as I turned to him. "Thank you." I accepted his compliment, however it was Hunter who was beautiful. Everything about him was special—his incredibly handsome looks, his gentle demeanor, his fun nature, his ambition, his sense of adventure. I was pretty sure I could go on listing his endearing attributes all night long.

As he passed the food tray over again and I plucked a piece of crumbed snapper, I wondered what it was about me that he liked. Once again, the brutal reality of my never-ending lies hit me. Hunter didn't even know my name. Or my job. The reality of my stupid situation was brutal agony, and as we shared a meal and the conversation flowed so perfectly, little pieces of my heart drifted away with the gentle breeze.

I had to tell him. As much as I didn't want to ruin our perfect night, I couldn't delay this a moment longer.

"So tell me Just Memphis, when do I get to know your surname?"

My body froze to ice. This was it; he'd opened up the perfect opportunity. My heart pounded, my breath shot in an out, and I clenched my jaw in an attempt to stop my chin dimpling.

I put my glass down and sucked in a long, shaky breath. "Hunter, there's something—"

"Oh look, a shooting star. Quick, make a wish." His excitement was electric, childish even, as he pointed at the blaze of light.

"What? Oh."

"Quick make a wish." He squeezed his eyes shut, and I did the same. It wasn't hard to think of a wish. The only wish that meant anything was that Hunter would forgive me.

He gulped back his drink and placed his glass on his shirt. "Want to know what I wished for?" His eyes dazzled in the moonlight.

I giggled at his enthusiasm. "You can't tell me, or it won't come true."

"It'll *only* come true if I tell you."

"That's not how this game's played." But after his comment, I really did want know.

He wriggled around to rest on his knees, giving me more of his body to look at. "Come on . . . indulge me."

Unable to resist his boyish charm, I smiled. "Okay, Mr. Hunter McCall, what did you wish for?"

"I wished to see your boobies."

I burst out laughing. "Boobies?"

"Yes. I'd like to see your boobies in this fabulous moonlight." He tried to be serious, but soon a mischievous smile lit up his face.

A delightful flutter danced across my stomach from the way he looked at me. It was more than just desire in his eyes—there was passion, too, wild, primal passion that looked on the verge of bursting.

The delicious pulses curling through my body confirmed I was ready to get naked with this sexy man. Even out here in the open. I was feeling sexy, and horny and ready to get a little reckless too. I ran my tongue over my lips, then placed my hands on the towel behind me and pushed my *boobies* forward. "You just need to undo the buttons."

"Okey dokey." He rubbed his hands together and matched the move with a cheeky grin as he inched closer. His gaze flitted from my eyes to my mouth to the buttons he undid, and with each release my nipples hardened. The delicate buds were no longer meek and mild—they were standing to attention, ready to be exposed to the world.

Halfway down my dress, before he peeled the fabric open, he leaned forward on one hand, and I closed my eyes as our lips met. A delicious shudder rolled through me, starting at my clit and weaving its way right up to my peaked nipples. I opened my mouth, allowing Hunter entry. His tongue danced with mine in a delicious tango that had a beautiful tune playing across my heart.

He pulled back and silently carried on with my buttons. His breathing was faster, deeper, and his chest rose and fell. The crashing waves added to the wonderful sounds. Nature's grand show played out around me as the most amazing man on earth played my heart strings.

Again he paused, two buttons from my hem, drawing out the final release. He trailed kisses from my lips to my neck and I turned my head, offering him my flesh. As he kissed from my collarbone to my earlobe, tiny goose bumps blazed across my skin. A flame of heat licked through me, matching the pulsing in my pussy. I clenched my insides, trying to tame my own beast that was eager to launch onto Hunter.

He pulled away and returned to my buttons. With the final one released, he took his time peeling my dress open, doing a gradual reveal. His extraordinary patience drove me wild, and I fisted the towel into the sand. He trailed kisses from the top lace of my G-string up my belly, to between my breasts. My nipples begged to be sucked, and when he pulled back and placed a hand over my breast I braced on one hand and reached behind my back to unclip my bra.

The red lace loosened, releasing my breasts, and Hunter curled his hand beneath my bra and pulled my lingerie upward. I glanced down at my boobs. My nipples were rock-hard pebbles, almost to the point of hurting, and in this moonlight, the tiny nodules around the dark part of my breast stood out too.

Hunter glided his tongue around my hardened bud. The moonlight provided the perfect amount of glow to witness the wonderful spectacle. I curled my pussy back and forward on the towel, riding the glorious pulses that raged through me.

He alternated between his tongue pleasuring my boobs by rolling around and around my nipple, to wrapping his lips around it and sucking my nipple into his mouth. With my focus diverted, I barely noticed his hand feed into my G-string. But the second I did, I parted my legs, eager to have another part of my body ravished.

I groaned as his finger touched my clit, and I gasped when he entered my throbbing hole. With his mouth working wonders on my breasts and his fingers plunging in and out of my pussy, I tipped my head back, closed my eyes, and let my body take over.

It was sensory overload, and the pounding waves faded to obscurity as Hunter took my body to another world. The orgasm building inside me grew swiftly, stacking layer upon layer until I was ready to burst. Hunter may have been able to take his time—not me though. I was on the edge, so, so close.

"Hey, get a move on."

A beam of light blazed up the beach, and I squealed as I grappled for my dress.

Hunter turned toward the light, his upper body silhouetted against the powerful beam. "Sorry, Officer."

"This is a public place. We'll have none of that."

Giggling, I fumbled with my buttons.

"Yes, sir. Sorry."

"You will be. Get a room, you stupid randy teenagers."

I stifled a laugh as Hunter stood up. The bulge in his pants dominated his shape in the blazing light. Shielding me from the police officer's view, Hunter offered a hand and launched me to my feet. As I grappled to do up my buttons with my stupid nails, Hunter picked up our gear. It was only once we started walking that the giant light was turned off, and the police patrol continued in the sand buggy up the beach.

Within a minute, Hunter and I were chuckling; within two, we were laughing so hard I could barely breathe. I hadn't done up my bra and my boobs wobbled freely.

It perfectly matched how I felt . . . *free.*

Alive.

We stepped from the sand and onto the boardwalk that led us up off the beach. We fell in side by side, and Hunter put his arm around my shoulders and tugged me to him. "Well that was a first for me."

I chuckled as I put my arm around his waist. "Me too."

"So, you heard what the nice police officer said. We need to find a room."

I glided my hand up the side of his torso, feeling the steely muscles beneath his shirt. "We do."

"Would you like to come to my room then?"

"I'd be delighted."

We stepped from the boardwalk onto the grass and took a moment to brush the sand off our feet. "Do you want to put your shoes back on?"

"No, I'll be fine."

"Hmmm," he mumbled.

I blinked up at him. "Hmmm, what?"

"What? Nothing?"

I turned to him, placed my hands on his pecs, and looked up into his magical eyes. "It didn't seem like nothing to me."

His face softened, and he curled his hand across my cheek. "It's just . . . I find you fascinating. You dress beautifully, and in a way that I thought you'd die if you got your hands or feet dirty, yet that's not the woman I see. You're a mysterious puzzle, Just Memphis." His long lashes flicked down and up my body as he smiled. "And I look forward to unravelling that mystery."

I was torn between jumping onto his hips and kissing him wildly, and telling him exactly why I was a mystery. He grabbed my hand, saving me from my indecision, and we walked up the Hot Horizon Hotel steps and crossed the lobby in silence. Bailey waved at us from behind reception, and Hunter and I both waved back at him. The elevator door opened immediately and we stepped in, and he pressed the button for the eighth floor.

At his floor, we strolled arm in arm to room forty-eight. Hunter opened the door and stepped aside for me. I walked to the dining table, placed my bag over the back of the chair. When I turned to Hunter I just about melted at how handsome he was. He had an inner beauty about him that shone as brightly as a diamond.

He stepped up to me and placed his hand on my waist, and as he curled his other hand around my neck, his eyes burned into mine. "There's something you should know about me."

I blinked and just about burst at the seriousness in his demeanor. "Okay."

"I always finish what I start." His words oozed sexuality.

"O . . . oh." I could barely breathe, and I stepped into his embrace as he lowered his lips to mine. Our kiss was heated, loaded with lust. But it was more than that—so much more. With his arms around me, I felt safety, peace, at home, and could I dare to believe . . . in love.

The restraint Hunter had shown on the beach was long gone, replaced instead with eager fingers that flipped open my buttons. I, in turn, undressed him at lightning speed, and in a flash we were both naked, our bodies pressed together as our hands explored each other. As our kiss deepened, we each moaned and I drove my fingers through his hair, pulling him down to me.

I sought out his cock and wrapped my hand around the masterpiece. As I glided my fingers up and down his length, it thickened, growing more impressive by the second. His hand nudged between my thighs and I parted my legs, allowing him easy access. His finger drove into me and our united moans filled the room.

Barely a few heartbeats later I was right back on that delicious precipice between a building orgasm and mind-blowing release. Hunter's fingers rubbed my clit with every plunge. I raised my knee, contouring my upper body to his and giving his probing hand a whole new angle.

I was there, oh so close to exquisite release.

Hunter must've sensed it as his finger-fucking grew wild, in and out, over my clit. I screamed into his neck, dug my fingers into his back, and hung on as he guided me through my incredible orgasm.

He edged me across the room, and when my calves touched the bed I sat down and wriggled up the sheets. As much as I could've stayed right where I was and ogled the incredible man before me, with chiseled abs and his erection large and mighty, I wanted that beast inside me.

He strode to the bedside table and removed a condom, and I watched his trembling fingers as he glided it into place. Seconds later, he resumed his position at the end of the bed. I parted my thighs, welcoming him in. He took my invitation by crawling up my body and positioning himself over me with his strong muscular arms. Again, our eyes locked, silently communicating a singular desire—a desire to ravage each other.

As he lowered himself, molding our sweat-slicked skin together, I closed my eyes. I drove my fingers through his hair, fisted a handful, and pulled him onto me. Our kiss was driven by greed, and our tongues lashed together. He tasted divine, he felt incredible, and the heady scent of our passion drove me wild.

Hunter eased my hand out of his hair, and with our palms together, he pinned my left hand above my head. His raised his hips off mine and drove his hand down between us, guiding his cock to my opening. I raised my knees, lifting my bottom and giving him entrance. But he held his cock there, prolonging the anticipation as our kiss intensified.

I curled my ass off the bed, trying to push his cock into me, desperate to have him inside me, but he pulled away. I wanted to reach down and push that beast into me myself. I was wet, and hot, and so fucking ready I thought I'd explode.

I pulled my lips from his. "You're killing me, Hunter."

The glaze in his eyes evaporated. His dilated pupils found me, and the fire I saw in them took my already wild libido to raging. I clawed his back with my right hand and raised my hips to angle his swollen crown at my hot throbbing hole.

His breath hitched, his jaw clamped shut, and as he glided his shaft into me, his eyes shot open and closed in a flash. My insides clenched around his cock, clamping him in my velvet vise. When he couldn't push any more, he stopped there, impaling me with his length. His cock pulsed, swelling inside me, and I squeezed tighter around him, letting him know I felt him.

Hunter let out a long primal groan and pulled his cock out and slammed it right back into me. It was fast, furious, and fucking fabulous. He did it again, quickly out to the very tip and fast and hard right back into my throbbing pussy. Each time he slammed into me it touched that part of me that loved and hated it at the same time. It felt so damn good.

As he drove into me, over and over and over, a tidal wave of pleasure barreled through my body, building a climax of mammoth proportions. But I didn't want it to stop; I wanted Hunter to fuck me all night, every night, for ever and ever.

His pace increased and every muscle in my body stiffened. Gasping, I tried to trap him inside me, clenching him in my core. He cried out, and together we climaxed. His thrusts were deep and hard and complete, and I rode every one of them to their full glory. After one last thrust in which he released a deep, primal groan, he began to slow, and the breath he'd been holding came gushing out.

He glided to my side, and I whimpered when his penis slipped out of me. With our fingers still entwined above my head he rolled me onto my side. My back was now against his torso, and with our hands still locked together, Hunter laid his arm over my waist and beneath my boob.

As our breathing gradually returned to normal, I realized we were spooning. I'd never done this before. This was everything perfect and wonderful in life all rolled into one. It was chocolate syrup, crackling fireplaces, and fabulous wine. It was homey bliss.

He released my hand, cupped my breast, and squeezed, firm but sensual. "Stay right there."

He slid away and I admired his sexy butt as he walked to the bathroom. The toilet flushed, he walked out and moments later, slipped into position behind me again. He returned his hand to cover the back of mine, entwining our fingers. My heart swelled to bursting as I listened to his steady breathing. I'd officially slipped into heaven. If this were my last night on earth, then I'd be happy with the ending.

Our breathing grew long and steady, and as a beautiful warmth flooded me both inside and out, I closed my eyes for just a moment.

* * *

Consciousness trickled from my sleep-filled mind. I didn't want to wake up. I was warm, happy, at peace. But a sense of urgency rattled from deep inside me. My eyes fluttered open, and I squinted against the glare. Distant visions of last night forced their way to the front of my brain, and with a jolt I snapped my eyes open.

I gasped as I realized where I was. In fact, I hadn't moved all night long.

Neither had Hunter. His arm was still draped over my torso, and by the bulge pressing against my bottom, I'd say he was quite happy there.

My heart hit panic mode as I realized the sun was almost up. That meant I'd either missed the start of my shift or it was fucking close.

I peeled Hunter's arm off me, and he groaned as I crawled out from his side.

"Don't go."

Oh god. I knelt on the bed and kissed his forehead. "Sorry, but I have to work. Thank you for a wonderful night."

"Call in sick." He blinked up at me as I pulled on my clothing.

"Can't. Sorry. But I'll call you."

"You better." The stupid nails hampered my rush to do up my buttons.

"I will. I promise."

I tossed my bag on my shoulder and raced over to kiss him again. He tried to pull me onto the bed, and I squealed at both the joy and the disaster of it. I won the tug of war, blew him a kiss, and ran for the door.

My feet couldn't take me fast enough. Neither could the elevator, and when I pulled my phone from my bag and checked the time, I nearly died. I had just twenty minutes before I started work. In my apartment, I yanked off my wig, scrubbed off my Memphis makeup, and dove into the shower. Five minutes later, I was tugging on my sensible work clothes. I spied Hunter's gift on the table and was annoyed I didn't have time to take it up to him. It just meant I'd have to see him again before Christmas. *Yay.*

I grabbed a protein bar and my diary, shoved both into my bag, and with five minutes to spare, I stepped back into the elevator.

Utilizing my time in the mirror, I tucked my shirt into the pencil skirt, pulled my hair up into a high ponytail, and glided nude lipstick over my swollen lips. My heart was still a thundering gallop when the doors opened and I strode across the marble tiles.

"Morning, Bailey. How was your night?" Jane Nichols, hotel manager, was back.

"It was pretty steady. Not too bad for a Friday."

"Excellent. So what do I need to know?"

We went through the shift-change checklist, and ten minutes later, when I was all alone, I flopped into the office chair to catch my breath. Holy shit. With a huge sigh, I went to the kitchen to make myself a strong coffee. With a steaming mug in my hand, I returned to my desk, unwrapped my protein bar, and opened my diary to the 16th of December. At the top of the page I wrote *Mr. Hunter McCall Room 48*. I started with our fun on the beach, listing how special I'd felt as he'd teased me with his tongue and fingers. Giggling, I wrote about the beach police catching us and calling us naughty teenagers.

The elevator dinged, and I shoved the diary aside as a family of four tumbled into the lobby with an abundance of suitcases. I went through the process of checking them out and returned to my diary. I wrote about our incredible sex and how desperate I'd been for him to make love to me. I think I would've imploded if we'd had to stop a second time. Hunter drove me wild. I also wrote about spooning and then falling asleep in his arms and how that was the most magical moment of my life. As I thought about how special he made me feel I wrote *Hunter Extraordinaire* in capital letters at the top of the page.

Hunter really was extraordinary and I was pretty sure I was in love with him. My heart skipped a beat at that wonderful acknowledgement. He was everything I wanted in a man and so much more. My doodling pen created a love heart on the page, and feeling like a giddy teenager I wrote, *I love Hunter* beneath the drawing. Then, for a bit of fun I wrote *Mrs. Jane McCall*.

"Hi, I'm Mrs. Jane McCall." I chuckled. Those words sounded so good. No . . . they sounded absolutely perfect. Giggling I practiced writing the name, pretending it were my new signature.

Again the elevator dinged, and I pushed the diary aside to greet the guests. The universe was against me, and each time I began writing in the diary another distraction interrupted my process. At one point I had four groups of people lined up. It was busy, but I was grateful for the distraction. With how exhausted I felt, I'd be just as likely to fall asleep at my desk if I wasn't careful. I went through the motions of checking people out and as I smiled up at the waiting crowd, and apologized for the delay, the elevator dinged again and there he was . . . Mr. Hunter McCall. I had to remind myself I was Jane Nichols, hotel manager, but as he waited in line, my fluttering heart couldn't decipher the difference.

Finally it was his turn to step up to the counter and I hoped like hell he didn't recognise me.

"Good morning. How can I help you?"

"Checking out of room forty-eight." He passed his room card across the counter top, and when I reached for it, his eyes focused on my fingers. Then he clutched my hand. A wave of confusion distorted his beautiful features. His eyes darkened.

As I tugged my hand free, I realized too late my terrible mistake. My nails. My pretty Christmas nails, had blown my disguise. I covered my mouth. My heart thumped. I could barely breathe. I couldn't think.

"Memphis? Or is it Jane?" My names spat off his tongue as his eyes bounced from my name badge to my face. "What the fuck is this? Some kind of joke?"

"Hunter, please let me explain."

"Explain what? Who are you?"

"I'm Jane, but I . . . I—"

"You what? Fucking liar." He stepped forward, his lips twisted to a nasty scowl.

Tears stung my eyes. My chin dimpled. I shook my head. "I'm so sorry. I tried to tell you."

"When? The first time? The second time? How about the fourth time we were together?" He shook his head, and when he stiffened and leaned forward, my heart exploded. Hunter launched over the counter, and I dived for my diary. But I was too slow. The book was ripped from my fingers.

"Hunter extraordinaire! What the fuck's this? A diary of your conquests?" He flicked through the pages. "Am I just a number to you?"

"No, Hunter, you're not." Tears spilled down my cheeks. "I'm sorry. Please let me explain."

"Why would I believe you? You've been lying to me since the day we met." The hurt in his eyes cut deep. With my diary fisted in his hand, he grabbed the handle on his suitcase and stormed away.

I raced around the counter, my heels clunking on the tiles as I chased after him. "Hunter, please don't go. I want to tell you everything."

"No! You don't get that privilege."

As he strode out the doors, I clutched at his wrist, but he snapped his arm away and turned to me. His eyes were loaded with hurt. "I thought we had something special."

"We did. We do." Great wracking sobs burst from my lips. Tears streaked down my cheeks. "I'm sorry."

"No, Just Memphis," he spat my name. "It's me who's sorry. Sorry I ever met you." A taxi pulled into the drop-off zone, and I couldn't breathe as Hunter stomped down the stairs and tossed his bag and my diary into the trunk of the car.

I tumbled to the steps. The car door slammed and the taxi drove away.

With my hands covering my face, I released a deep howl of pain as a chunk of my heart broke away and crumbled to dust.

23ᴿᴰ DECEMBER
TO NEW BEGINNINGS
Room 11 - Hot Horizon Hotel

Since Hunter had left me sobbing on the steps on my hotel, I'd had six days of hell. Not even an evening shopping with Lolita had cheered me up. When I'd told her about him taking my diary and explained the extent of the intimate details I'd put in there, she'd burst out laughing. I, however, failed to see the funny side, and she'd apologized about a dozen times since. I'd tried ringing Hunter twice a day, every day since last Friday, but of course he didn't take my calls. *Why would he?* What I'd done was despicable, and I didn't deserve anything less. All the crazy messages I'd left probably had me sounding like a complete lunatic too.

Even working the day shift had quickly lost its gloss. It was two days before Christmas, and I'd officially hit rock bottom. When I'd started my year-long challenge, I'd only considered me and my stupid libido. I'd never thought about what my actions would do to the men I'd lured into my trap.

After fifty-two weeks and dozens of men, only one man was left standing . . . *Henry*.

As I stewed over this result, I recalled my discussion with Aunty Ann where she'd lost the love of her life because she'd never voiced her feelings for him. If I'd told Hunter my feelings, would that've changed what had happened? It squeezed my heart to acknowledge that I'll never know.

The phone rang, snapping me from my tumbling thoughts. I forced happy into my voice and picked up the handset. "Welcome to the Hot Horizon Hotel. This's Jane, how can I help you?"

"Jane, it's Henry."

"Henry!" His timing offered my heartbreak a glimmer of reprieve.

"How come you're answering the phone? You normally finish at six thirty."

"I got a promotion—I'm now the day manager."

"Congratulations, that's wonderful news. Does that mean you have tonight off?"

I smiled. "Yes, it does."

"Well, if you're not busy, would you like to spend the evening with me?"

"I'd be delighted." My response was instant.

He chuckled, and it was so lovely that for a brief moment I forgot all about my shattered heart. "In that case, I'm flying in at three. You could come to my room at sunset, if you like?"

"Sounds perfect."

"Do you know which room I'll be in?"

"Hang on, I'll check." I put the phone down, and with a newfound spring in my step I walked to the back counter to grab the check-in cards. Flicking through them, I tugged out Henry's and went back to the phone.

"You're in room eleven." The penthouse must've been already booked.

"Okay, I'll see you soon."

"Oh, I almost forgot why I rang. Is it possible to have a late checkout tomorrow?"

"Hang on, let me see." I scanned the computer for tomorrow's schedule. "The latest we can do is midday. Does that suit?"

"That's great. Thank you, see you soon."

After we said goodbye, I flopped onto the reception chair and plonked my head on the table. Once again, Henry had saved me, and a lovely glow warmed my heart at the prospect of seeing him later. But my heart also had a dark cloud smothering it from my breakup with Hunter and I wondered if it would ever be the same again.

I didn't want to look back on this year with regret. I'd had an incredible twelve months; I'd met amazing men, and as I turned my focus to Hunter and Henry, I could even admit I'd fallen in love.

Was it possible to feel strong emotions for two men?

Before this year I would never have thought so.

The minutes ticked over to lunchtime, and as I nibbled on a protein bar and sipped green tea, my brain flicked between visions of Hunter and Henry.

People came and went across the lobby, all smiling and laughing as they embraced the fabulous summer weather and the holiday festivities that'd gripped the coast.

This time of year was meant to be fun, and I wanted to slap myself over my depressing mental debate.

This year *was* fun.

I sat up in my chair and forced my brain to focus on everything good and fun about this year. First was the sex. Before this year, the minimal sex I'd experienced had been for a man's enjoyment. Not anymore, though. Sex was now about me, for my pleasures, and after what I'd learned, I was going to ensure I experienced that forever.

Second was the men. I'd met many, many incredible men. And not just the guys I'd seen more than once. There were also the one-night stands. Before this year I'd firmly believed casual sex was not for a girl like me. Boy, had I been wrong. If I hadn't challenged that silly notion I wouldn't have met Luke Stone, my one-legged fashion designer, or Maxwell Bradford, my Dreamy Doctor, or Cameron Jax, the wedding planner who'd left my hotel much happier than when he'd arrived. And then there was the guys I'd seen twice. My guitarist Mason Cole and of course Dontrel Lewis, my Jamaican drummer who was hung like a horse.

With a giggle, my mind flashed to Frankie Cunningham, my beer brewer, and the horsey puns he'd brought with him. I also had lovely memories for some notable days in the year. Valentine's Day may never be the same after my nude drawing session with Blade Nichols, and my birthday may be impossible to top after my beach picnic with Clayton followed by my rooftop tango with Sebastien De Marco.

In addition to the sex and the men, this year had also brought about a better work/life balance. My promotion had come out of the blue, and after some deep soul-searching over the prospect that I may've lost my job, I was glad I hadn't. I'd always been a believer in things happening for a reason. My close calls with Needledick in my Memphis disguise may've been stressful, but if he hadn't seen me, the incredible events that led to my promotion may never have occurred.

Because of fate, I'd met Henry, and Hunter, and Billy, Corben, Clayton, and David Lawson, and all the other wonderful men that'd helped transform me into the confident, empowered, and dare I say, sexual diva I was today. I giggled again. *Sexual diva . . . yep, that's me.*

By the time the end of my shift approached, I was feeling a lot better. By the time I began dressing for my suave tutor, I was ready to show him just how much sexual diva I had. Henry brought out the best in me, and I was so ready to have all my best bits teased into a climax that rocked my world.

I wanted this night to be fun and sexy, and although I had no doubt it would be, I wanted to make sure it was memorable for both of us. So, as Henry hadn't seen it yet, I decided on my cheeky nurse uniform. I went all-out with it. Sexy red lace bra and matching G-string, fishnet stockings, and a pair of d'Orsay glossy red court shoes with a killer heel and ankle strap dotted with silver studs.

The shoes had been a purchase made during my post-Billy breakup shopping spree with Lolita. They'd been sixty percent off. I reflected on my earlier thoughts about fate. If I hadn't broken up with Billy and gone shopping with Lolita, I may never have seen these shoes. It was a shallow thought, but as this was the very last chapter in my sexual challenge, I wanted to focus on all the positives. I wanted the best night ever and with Henry as my final man, I had every belief it would be.

But although I was sad my challenge was over. I was glad too. It was time to look to my immediate future. A future without Memphis. A future where I was Jane.

Confident, sexy, empowered Jane.

I scrutinized my reflection and saw the sexual diva I'd become. Reaching into my bra I plumped up my boobs and tugged my zipper down a fraction to show off more cleavage. Now I was a smokin' hot sexual diva. My smile was huge as I glided on my favorite Bobbi Brown Retro Red lippy. I tugged on my trench coat, grabbed my bag, and headed out the door. Not having Needledick to worry about was a blessing, but I did acknowledge that I looked rather strange in my trench coat in the height of summer. I only had to go to the floor below, so hopefully I'd make it to Henry's door unnoticed.

I did. And outside his room I removed my coat, draped it over my arm, pulled back my shoulders, thrust my boobs forward, rolled the zipper down my cleavage even more to show a tease of the red lace bra, and knocked.

My heart pulsed a tidy beat as I waited out the silence, but when my suave tutor opened the door and his jaw dropped, the beat skipped to a funky dance. Henry was in a casual yet stylish plain white button-up shirt that had a couple of buttons undone at the top, and he wore it out over khaki chinos. I was reminded once again, that Henry was a man who was at the top of his game, and it was delightful to be here with him.

"Who do we have here?" His cheeky grin was stunning.

I curtsied "Nurse Jane, at your service." I strode past him, trailing my fingers over his chest, and walked to the table. I folded my coat over the back of a chair, tossed my bag onto the glass tabletop, and when I turned, my breath caught at how magnificent Henry was. My suave tutor was all class. His smile was stunning as he strolled to me, but most of all, it was his eyes that captured my attention as they devoured me with their intensity.

When his hand caressed my hip, I melted beneath his touch. As he reached over to the zipper nestled between my breasts, his tongue glided across his bottom lip, leaving moisture in its wake. He pulled the zipper down an inch, revealing more of my lingerie. His eyes bounced up from my boobs and met mine. His pupils were huge, just about swallowing his light blue irises, and highlighting the intensity that simmered below the surface.

He curled his fingers around my neck, and I tilted my head back slightly, parted my lips, closed my eyes, and silently begged him to kiss me. A heartbeat later, my wish was granted. It wasn't the usual gentle Henry kiss—this one was heated, loaded with passion as our tongues probed each other's. I reached for his chest, founds his pecs, and flicked my thumbs over his nipples.

We eased apart, and I turned my attention to his neck.

"Oh Jane," he whispered as I sucked his earlobe into my mouth.

He tugged my zipper, and I pulled back from his neck, eager to watch his eyes as he gradually revealed my body. The fabric burst apart with each inch he lowered it. He paused at my belly button, leaned in, and as he ran his tongue over the mounds of my beasts, I clawed my nails through his hair and closed my eyes. This very simple move captured me in so many ways. Henry was a master of taking me to another world. My flesh came alive, ignited with passion.

Gliding my hand down his torso, I ran my fingers over the bulge in his pants. Henry reached into my bra and eased my left boob over the lace. It was a little uncomfortable, but totally worth it when he sucked my nipple into his mouth. I glided my palm up his cock, enjoying the feel of it growing and stiffening beneath my touch.

He groaned and stepped back. "Jane."

"Yes." I tugged my lip into my mouth and slowly released it.

"I have a little Christmas present for you."

"Oh." I covered my mouth at the awkwardness. "I didn't buy you anything." Now I felt even worse that Hunter was the only man I'd bought a gift for.

He walked to the kitchen counter. "Oh, don't worry. This one's for both of our pleasures." He returned with a hand-sized gift wrapped in red paper with a white satin bow and placed it in my palm.

I couldn't help but smile at his cheeky grin. "I like the sound of that." The mischievous look on his face had me wondering if this was part of another lesson.

"Open it."

I tugged on the ribbon and let the satin tumble to the floor as I tore open the paper. Inside was a little black box that was held down with a magnetic clip at the front. I pulled on the magnet and raised the lid to reveal what looked like a silver bullet nestled in the red velvet.

I frowned. "Ummm, what is it?"

"It's called a TingleTip. I thought we could have a little fun together."

Grinning, I plucked the silver bullet from the casing. It was about the size of my little finger, a bit fatter though, and shaped like a bullet with a point at one end. At the flat end it had just one tiny button.

"Press it," Henry instructed.

I did and giggled when it vibrated like crazy. Laughing, I pressed it again and it stopped. Open mouthed I turned to Henry, and the dazzle in his eyes showed his delight. Whatever he was about to show me, I was oh so ready.

He stepped up to me and cupped my cheek. "You're such a pleasure to watch."

I leaned into his palm. "I was just thinking the same thing about you."

My heart fluttered as he placed his hands on my cheeks and lowered his lips to mine. I pushed my tongue into his mouth, eager to taste him. As our breaths mingled, a delicious pulse trembled from my clit and rolled up my body. I glided my palm over the length of his cock, the hardness beneath confirming how much he wanted me. I wanted him, too. On me and in me. With my finger on the button, and with him still distracted with our dueling tongues, I pressed the silver bullet against the length of his cock and turned it on.

"Hey." Henry jumped back, grinning. "What do you think you're doing, madam?"

"Just getting a little buzz."

He reached for it, and I willingly gave it to him. If Henry was keen to show me something new, I was ready. It was crazy how much this man had taught me about myself. He could read both my mind and my body like a large-font book.

He slipped TingleTip into his pocket, and I pulled my best sad face.

"Oh, don't worry. It'll come out to play later."

I over-exaggerated a smile. "Okay."

Laughing, he grabbed my hand and led me to the kitchen. With his help, I launched onto the counter and sat with my legs apart. He nestled his hips between my thighs. "Now, where were we?"

"I believe you were undressing me." I wriggled my shoulders, making my boobs jiggle a bit.

"Hmmm, that's right."

He fed his fingers into my bra to release my other boob and sucked my nipple into his mouth. I placed my hands on the counter behind me and thrust my breasts his way, allowing him to do as he pleased.

Henry didn't disappoint, alternating his attention from breast to breast and switching from licking to sucking at random. His hands threaded up and down my inner thighs, each time edging closer to my pussy, and as I closed my eyes my breathing grew deeper. The delightful pulses starting at my clit raced through me and had me wriggling on the counter in no time. My nipples were rock hard, aching. "Undress me."

"Soon, my love."

My love! Oh my god. Firecrackers shot through me at those two glorious words.

The teasing continued, his tongue over my breasts, his lips wrapped around my hardened nipples, and his hot breath whispering off my flesh as his fingers continued to inch closer and closer to their target. My lips parted of their own will, and my breath came in short bursts as I savored the glorious orgasm building inside me.

Bracing myself with one hand, I drove my other through his hair and pulled him down to my boobs. His fingers finally touched my clit through my G-string and I gasped and parted my legs, eager for more. I wanted to tear my clothes off; I wanted his fingers inside me; I wanted *him* inside me.

My flesh was on fire but with each flick of his finger over my clit, the inferno racing through me got hotter. I couldn't stand it a moment more and flopped back onto the counter. I reached down and hooked my hands beneath my knees, pulling them up and giving Henry full access to my pussy.

I was already lost to another world, but when a jolt of vibration hit my clit, I screamed as my orgasm released. My hot juices squirted over my G-string, over my fishnet stockings, and I couldn't help it. I was on fire, and it took me a few moments to realize Henry had used the silver bullet to create that reaction.

Finally, he withdrew the TingleTip and I just lay there, gasping for breath, my mind a world away from the cold counter I lay on. Henry came into the kitchen area behind me, and when he placed his hands on my cheeks, I opened my eyes to look at him upside down.

"Are you okay?" His concern, as usual, nearly brought me to tears.

"I'm not sure," I said, and his eyes darkened. "I think I need to do it again just to be certain."

He burst out laughing and leaned in to kiss me. Just a brief upside down kiss on my lips. When he pulled back, I pushed up from the counter as he returned to his position between my legs.

I held my palm out. "Hand it over, mister."

"What?"

"You know what."

"Oh, are you complaining?"

"No, but it's my turn."

His pupils bounced wider as he placed the bullet into my palm. I slotted the TingleTip between my boobs, and, squashed into the bra like they were, it easily stayed there.

It was time to get us both naked. "Can you take my shoes off please?"

Henry did as instructed and removed the other shoe too, then I put my hands on his shoulders to ease him back and jumped off the counter. I went to him, and as I undid the buttons of his shirt, he thumbed his finger across my hardened nipples.

Anticipation sizzled between us.

I peeled his shirt open and glided my hands over his shoulders to remove it all together.

As the fabric fell to our feet, he glided my zipper down and gave it a tug to release the dress completely. My nurse uniform spread apart and Henry peeled it off the rest of the way, letting it drift to the carpet. We took our time, taking turns to remove each other's clothing, and soon we stood naked. The silver bullet fell to the floor with a hard thud, and we both ignored it as we ran our eyes over each other's bodies. His gaze was like flames licking heat all over me.

I stepped closer, reached down, and cupped his balls in my hand, their size filled my palm. With each gentle caress, Henry sucked air between his teeth and his eyes glazed. When I turned my attention to his solid cock, he clenched his jaw and squeezed his eyes shut.

While he wasn't watching I fell to my knees, and the second I wrapped my lips around his swollen crown he gasped and clutched my shoulders. I slid my lips down his shaft, taking him into my throat. As I glided back up, I rolled my tongue around his cock, and when I reached the crown I clasped my hand around the base of his penis and pushed my tongue into the slit at the head.

Henry gasped, put his hands beneath my armpits, pulled me to my feet, and wrapped his arms around me.

His cock prodded my belly, and he sucked the air in through his teeth as if fighting release. I loved that I'd caused that reaction.

A couple of heartbeats later, he guided me back to the bed. When my calves touched the mattress I sat down, ready for his next instruction. He went to the bedside table, and as he kept his back to me, I assumed he was rolling on a condom. My assumption was confirmed when he turned back. He made a detour to gather the silver bullet from the floor.

He then sat beside me, his cock a rigid flagpole between his legs. "Come here. I want you to sit on me."

"Do you now?" I wrinkled my nose, acting all coy, but I was every bit eager to fulfil his wish. I put my hands on his shoulder and raised my foot over his legs to straddle him.

"No. turn around."

"Oh." I turned with my back to him, and he placed his hands on my hips, guiding me in. I now stood between his knees, the warmth of his chest nestled against my lower back. I reached down, put one hand on his knee, and wrapped my other around his cock, gliding my fingers up and down his shaft. I went slowly at first, but as I increased my speed, I also alternated my attention between his cock and his testicles, taking my time with each. His balls were heavy, full in my hand as I squeezed and caressed them with a lover's touch.

"Oh god, Jane."

My name sounded so perfect whispered off his tongue, so perfect, in fact, that the pulsing across my clit became impossible to ignore any longer. I bent my knees, lowering my pussy to the head of his penis. Just feeling it nudge my opening sent rockets through me. I gripped my hand around his cock and used the head of his penis to rub my clit, flicking it back and forward, over and over. My insides clenched, driving pulses from my sensitive bud to every nerve in my body.
Henry reached around my hip and as I pleasured him, he joined in by thumbing my clit. Next second, the TingleTip came into play.
Vibrations shot through me. Incredible became mind-blowing.
I screamed as I came. Hot come dribbled over my hand, over his groin, yet I continued to flick his cock, and he continued to trigger the vibrations on and off in a random pattern that had me riding wave after wave.
The squatting had my legs in a quivering mess and I was gasping for breath by the time I finally stood up. Henry wrapped his arms around me and trailed kisses across my shoulder blades. His hands glided from the sides of my torso to my waist and cupped my breasts. His touch was feather-light, trailing goose bumps in its wake. His exploration had my nipples stiff, aching. I put my hands over his, riding his explorations as his fingers continued to map my flesh. He knew my body so well.
My breathing grew deeper, as did his. His hand glided down my torso, as did mine. And together our hands cruised over my sex. His finger touched my clit, and the sensation was like a firecracker that nearly shot me forward. He retreated quickly and continued his study of my flesh.
He took his time, continuing his kisses across my back, and I closed my eyes and concentrated on our hands moving together. My body was alive, bristling with lust-fueled energy. My greedy pussy begged for attention too, and soon I bobbed up and down, tapping his swollen crown to my throbbing hole.
His hands roamed, he kissed my neck and sucked my earlobe, and his cock nudged my pussy with every bend of my knees. It was exquisite pleasure and I'd love to continue it forever, but I couldn't put off plunging that cock into me a moment longer. Without pause, I aimed his cock at my opening and drove him into me, ramming his length all the way.
Henry clutched my hips, digging his fingers in as I rose and lowered my hips in a wild, crazy drive to push his cock right up inside me. He went deep, really deep, slamming into something that begged for more.
Henry tensed, his fingers a vise on my hips, but I didn't stop. I couldn't, and when he cried out, I screamed too and rode him like there were no tomorrow. As my boobs slapped together, an orgasm tore through me, great rolling waves of pleasure that felt so fucking good.
Gasping for breath and unable to raise up and down any more, I sat on his lap and leaned back with my head on his shoulder, and with us still united

as one, Henry wrapped his arms around me. As I listened to his breathing gradually slow to normal, I relaxed into his embrace, feeling every bit at home.

The second I stood Henry excused himself and went to the bathroom. I lay on the bed on my side, waiting for him to reappear. The toilet flushed and seconds later, when Henry stepped from the bathroom and his cock swung from side to side as he strode straight to me. He crawled onto the bed and flopped onto his back with a huge sigh.

I wriggled upwards, placed my head on his shoulder, curled my leg up over his hip and put my hand on his chest.

He trailed his finger over the back of my hand. "You're lucky, you know?"

I raised my face and plonked my chin on his chest so I could look at him. "Because I found you?"

He laughed. "No, because you can orgasm."

I smiled. "You make me orgasm."

"No. It's you. Trust me, not every woman can orgasm. They just don't let their minds go so their body can take over."

I frowned. "Well that's a shame."

"It sure is. Watching you let go like that is one of the most amazing shows on earth."

"Thank you." I accepted his compliment just as he'd taught me.

He smiled, and a sense of knowing crossed between us. Henry pushed a lock of hair behind my ear and my heart wept at how sweet and tender it was.

My mind flicked to Aunty Ann, and her sadness over losing the man she loved because she was too afraid to voice it. I looked into Henry's beautiful blue eyes. A smile curled at his lips, and I knew he felt the same. "I love you."

He stiffened and I instantly wanted to retract what I'd said.

A darkness crossed his eyes, and I wanted to die. He squeezed his eyes shut and I knew . . . I knew I'd blown it. "Oh Jane, I'm so sorry. I should never have let it go this far."

I pulled back from him. A lump solidified in my throat as I rolled to the side and went to push off the bed.

He grabbed my arm. "Jane, please let me speak."

I sat rigid, my back to him, my chin dimpling as I fought the tears burning my eyes.

"What we have is beautiful. Special. But you're confusing lust with love."

I swallowed, loudly. So loudly I was certain he would've heard it.

"You don't love me, Jane. You don't know anything about me."

I flicked a wayward tear away. "That's not true. I feel you. I feel us. That's what matters."

"Not at my age it doesn't."

I spun to look at him. "Your age has never been a problem."

"Not for sex. No." He lowered his hand to cover the back of mine and squeezed. "I'm in a different time of my life. I'm about to be a grandfather, for goodness sake. You, Jane, need to be with a man who wants to start a family with you."

"What if I don't want a family?" The words were half-hearted because I knew it wasn't true. I did want children, but even more than that, I wanted a family.

"No. That's not true." Henry read my mind. "You've mentioned your friend's kids enough times that I know how much you love children."

I sucked in a shaky breath. "So you don't love me." My dimpling chin made it nearly impossible to talk.

"Oh, I love you. I love you so much it hurts. Which is why I need to let you go. You need to find a man to spend the rest of your life with. A man who'll give you a family. A man who you can grow old with."

"I want to grow old with you."

"Oh, Jane. You're just beginning your life." His voice had a velvet touch. "And I'm not going to get in the way of that."

A sob released from my throat, and I twisted away from him.

"I never meant to hurt you." He wriggled behind me and wrapped his arms around my shoulders. "I'm sorry . . . but this's what's best for you."

"*You* are what's best for me."

He sighed. "For now maybe. But what about in ten years' time, when you're forty and you haven't had children? You'll look back with regret. I won't do that to you."

It occurred to me that his speech was nearly identical to the one I'd said to Billy. I squeezed my eyes shut, forcing tears to trickle down my cheeks. Henry curled to my side then fell to his knees at my feet. I opened my eyes, and he reached up to thumb a tear from my cheek.

"I've had the most incredible year with you." His words were calm, soothing, and a complete contrast to the torrent raging through my brain. "I was dead inside when we met in January. Now, I'm alive. You've brought out the best in me, and I've loved every minute. But now that your challenge is over, it's time for you to set new challenges for yourself."

"I wish I'd never told you about that."

"I don't." He cupped my cheek. "Please don't be mad. Be happy that we've had this time together. It was special."

I blinked the blur away and looked right into his eyes. "It *is* special."

He eased up on his knees, and when he wrapped his arms around me the dam that I'd been struggling to hold back opened. Tears poured from my eyes down my cheeks and fell onto his bare back. Soon, I wrapped my arms around him too, and as I cried on his shoulder he continued to whisper sensibilities into my ear.

I felt like a fool. A stupid, naïve fool.

He released me, cupped my cheek, and forced me to look into his eyes. "I never meant to hurt you. I'm sorry that I let it go this far."

"I'm not."

He sighed, and his shoulders sagged. "No, you're correct. I'm truly honored to have shared this experience with you. I know you'll find someone. Someone truly special that you want to spend the rest of your life with."

"You—"

He touched his finger to my lips. "I'm not, Jane. You're blinded by our amazing sex. The man you love will give you amazing sex too." He stood up, then leaned over to kiss my forehead. "Thank you for giving me my life back. I hope one day you'll understand why I did this, and you'll forgive me."

It took me a few seconds to realize he wanted me to go. As a prisoner of my new brutal reality, I allowed him to help me stand. I dressed in only my trench coat, tugged the buttons into place, and tied my belt. Henry gathered my other bits and pieces from the floor and put them into my handbag.

He placed my bag over my shoulder, cupped my cheek, and kissed me on my forehead. "I will never forget you."

I blinked up at his eyes, hardly able to believe this was goodbye. Silently, I turned and somehow made it to his door, and when he opened it for me, I refused to look at him as I stepped through and walked away from my suave tutor for the last time.

I was numb, so numb that even tears failed to flow. My heart was a lump of lead in my chest that weighed me down with every step I took toward my apartment.

I went through the motions of having a shower and in a brain fog, I stepped into my PJs and crawled into bed. Normally, I'd spend this time writing in my diary. Pouring out all my crazy thoughts had become my therapy. Instead, all my stupid thoughts were trapped in my brain, whizzing around on a roulette wheel of hell.

My broken heart was a brutal realization that I was about to end this year exactly how I'd started it . . . single. It was impossible to comprehend that after fifty-two weeks, fifty-two sexual experiences with God knew how many men, I was still all alone.

Something changed in me. I knew it—I felt it as if it were a pimple on the end of my nose, but I couldn't decipher what it was. I just hoped I'd be able to deal with it when I figured it out.

I closed my eyes, and as I prayed for the wheel of hell to stop spinning, I succumbed to sleep.

* * *

Christmas Day at Lolita's was always a huge event as their home was a revolving door of friends and family who came and went as they pleased. I arrived at her place just before lunch. It was a miracle I'd made it. With the crap I'd been processing over the last thirty or so hours, it was a wonder I'd even crawled out of bed.

I hadn't told her about Henry for two reasons. The first being it would be impossible to talk about it without getting emotional, and the second was, it was Christmas. Nobody needed to hear my crappy story.

I pushed through the front door, placed my Christmas gifts under the tree, and went in the direction of the laughter coming from the backyard. About a dozen people were on the perfectly manicured grass playing quoits.

"Jane," Lolita squealed and hugged me to her perky boobs. "'Bout time you got here. Us girls are outnumbered by all this testosterone."

I chuckled and made my way around the grass, wishing everyone a merry Christmas. Cal wrapped his muscular arms around me and planted a kiss on my cheek. Both Lolita's and Cal's parents were there, and they welcomed me as if I were their own daughter. Cal's brother wrapped me in a bear hug, and Lolita's two brothers both kissed my cheeks at the same time, which had everybody laughing. A bunch of kids in the pool dive-bombed the water together in an attempt to get me wet.

"Ha, you missed," I yelled to them when seven heads reappeared above the surface. Within five minutes of arriving at Lolita's place, I felt a thousand times better.

The following five hours were a fantastic concoction of fun, food, and alcohol. Neighbors dropped in to say hi, and friends did, too; it seemed that every time we got settled into our seats we'd be up again saying hello or goodbye to someone.

It wasn't until six thirty and the sun was beginning to set that Lolita, Calvin and I were the only adults left in the house.

"Can we do our presents now?" Lolita jiggled from foot to foot like a seven-year-old kid.

"Sure," Cal said, and I nodded too.

While Calvin went to the kitchen to make Lolita and I Mojitos, Lolly and I went in search of Savanah and Maddox. We found them in the playroom, each on a separate television playing different computer games.

"Okay you two, enough of that." Lolly clapped her hands together.

"Oh, but we only just started." Maddox's voice was way too deep for a nine-year-old boy.

"Stop! I don't want to hear it." Lolita strode to Maddox's side. "Jane wants to give you your Christmas present."

Savanah smiled at me. "Okay." She tossed her controller aside, jumped up, and put her hand in mine. A wonderful glow washed through me when her tiny fingers grasped mine. As the seconds ticked by, we watched Lolita wrestle Maddox from the lounge, and I had a fleeting thought that maybe Henry breaking up with me was the right thing after all.

We went out to the Christmas tree, which, like everything else in Lolly's life, was the epitome of perfection. Maddox and Lolita sat cross-legged on the floor while Cal and I sat on the lounge nearby. Savannah came and sat on my lap. My heart swelled at the familiarity of it, and I curled her long hair over her shoulder and squeezed her tiny body to mine.

Lolita plucked one of my gifts from beneath the tree. "This's for Cal, from Jane."

Cal rubbed his hands together and sat forward on his chair. Even though he would've already guessed what I'd bought him, he didn't deny me the delight of seeing his pleasure over my choice. The kids giggled at my Big Ass Jar, and Lolita scowled at the jelly beans inside. The second Cal opened the jar, he, Savannah and Maddox immediately tucked into it.

Lolly opened her present from me next, and I watched the curiosity on her face dissipate when she pulled open the long rectangular box to reveal thigh-high purple boots, exactly like mine. She squealed. "Oh yay! These are awesome."

Despite it being twenty-six degrees Celsius, even with the air conditioner blowing cool air on us, Lolly tugged the boots on and made a show of strutting her stuff around the lounge room.

"Thanks babe, I love them." She hugged me to her chest.

The kids opened their presents, too, and each of them gave me a hug. After twenty minutes playing with them, they both slinked back into the playroom. Lolly handed a gift to me from both her and Cal, and I reflected that the diary she'd given me last year had changed my life. It would be difficult to repeat that.

The gift was about the size of a shoe box, and very light. I unwrapped the Christmas paper, and my guess was right—it was a shoe box. Lolly had great taste in footwear, so I was excited to see what she'd chosen. I glanced at her and didn't miss the edge of excitement simmering in her eyes. I lifted the lid, but it wasn't shoes—it was another box.

Lolly and Cal chuckled as I unwrapped the next box, only to reveal another. I unwrapped six boxes, each one slightly smaller than the last, and with each reveal Lolita edged forward across the floor toward me. I peeled off another layer of paper to reveal yet another box. This one was decorated with a red ribbon, and, hoping I'd reached the end, I yanked it off and opened the lid. Nestled inside was a plane ticket. My jaw dropped as I read it.

"Sydney!"

"Yep. We're gonna have a fucking awesome girly weekend in Sydney."

I slipped off my chair and we hugged and squealed together. Lolita was the best friend in the whole wide world.

After the presents were done, we grabbed a cheese platter, filled up our drinks, and headed out to the spa by the pool. Over the years, we'd come to know the spa as the 'crab pot' because once us ladies got in there, we had trouble getting out. We'd been known to stay in there for hours.

The bubbles danced around us, we sipped our cocktails, and the hours of nibbling yummy food and sipping potent drinks had me feeling contented.

"So, babe, I feel like we haven't had a girly chat in ages. Did you finish your challenge with a bang?" She giggled.

I must've screwed up my face or something, because Lolly stopping laughing and raised her perfectly formed eyebrows. "Oh wow. It looks like you have something juicy to talk about."

I rolled my eyes. "Do you want the good news or the bad?"

With her cocktail glass held above the spa bubbles, she nodded, suddenly all serious. "Let's start with the bad."

I sighed. "Henry broke it off with me." I said it matter of fact and to my surprise it didn't hurt as much as I thought it would.

"What?" Her eyes bulged.

I sipped the entire mojito as I told Lolita everything from the mind-blowing sex with the TingleTip, to Henry's final words to me.

"You know what?"

I put my empty glass on the edge of the spa and lowered my shoulders beneath the water. "What?"

"A little piece of me just fell in love with Henry for doing that."

"Huh?" I cocked an eyebrow at her.

"He truly is a gentleman. His selflessness saved you, babe. Many other men his age would do anything to keep a gorgeous young woman like you hanging off his arm."

I blinked at her.

Cal placed a jug of mojito at the edge of the spa and slipped into the water with us. He had a glass tumbler with a ginger-colored liquid that I assumed was Canadian Club, his favorite spirit.

"Come on, Jane. It's not all bad." Lolita frowned at me.

"I've wasted a whole year."

"Like hell you have. You've had the best fucking year of your life. That's not a waste. That's just the beginning."

Cal held his glass up. "Hear, hear, to that."

Lolly raised her glass to me. "To new beginnings."

"Yeah, new beginnings," Cal said.

"Not you, stupid." Lolly playfully slapped Cal's arm.

"Of course not me," he said. "I'm happy with the same old thing."

"Really?" Lolly jumped onto his shoulders and when she pushed him under the water he managed to save his drink by holding it above the bubbles.

As we refilled our drinks several times and I made the cheese platter my new best friend, the 'crab pot' lived up to its name.

It was nearly two in the morning when Lolita and Cal helped me out of the spa and into their spare room. Lolly shooed Cal out the door, then dressed me in one of Cal's long T-shirts. She pulled back the bed covers, and I fell face-first into the mattress.

Giggling, she rolled me onto my side and tugged the sheet up under my chin. "Good night, babe."

"I love you." My tongue was like a strip of leather.

She kissed my cheek. "I love you, too."

I closed my eyes and was pretty sure the last thing I heard before I drifted off to sleep was my own snoring.

31ST DECEMBER
DAWN OF A NEW BEGINNING
Room 13 - Hot Horizon Hotel

The last sunrise of the year arrived in spectacular fashion, and as I sat out on my balcony I watched the sun cast golden bolts up from the horizon in a perfectly symmetrical fan of light. I sipped hot coffee and inhaled the fresh ocean breeze that drifted up the beach. Even though it wasn't yet five in the morning, council workers were out in force. A tractor was driven in endless loops back and forth, raking the sand for rubbish and debris, and dozens of laborers were busy setting up stages, fencing, and other temporary erections in preparation for tonight's New Year's Eve festivities.
I found it hard to believe that this year was over. It felt like only last week that I'd done the craziest thing in my life and snuck into George Whiteman's room to pleasure myself. I giggled at that. I'd come a long way since then. Full circle, in fact. At the height of my year, I'd had five men who I was seeing on a regular basis. I blinked at that realization. Five men. Five gorgeous, unique, stunning men. Clayton, Henry, Hunter, Billy, and Corben. Five men.
And now I had none.
Tomorrow was a new day. A new year, too. Maybe I could set myself another challenge? But even as that idea whizzed through my head, I smacked it away. Although this year had been amazing, I doubted it could ever be topped.

No . . . next year would be the year when I dated men properly . . . as Jane Nichols.

Despite the tumultuous emotions that'd attacked me during the last two weeks, I was still optimistic about next year. I'd learned many, many things in the last twelve months, and one of them was to look at the world with my eyes wide open.

I now knew it was impossible to judge a person on their appearance. Luke Stone was a testament to that—on appearance, the one-legged fashion designer was a man in control, but scratch the surface a little and he was a man who'd only just survived six years of personal demons.

I finished my coffee, and as I showered, all the wonderful men of this year danced across my brain. Three of them stayed in my vision longer than the others—Henry, Billy, and Hunter. They were the only three who had truly touched my heart. But it was the loss of Hunter that hurt the most. I shook his image free and hopped out of the shower.

Twenty minutes later, I stepped from the elevator and strode toward reception. "Hey Bailey, how was the night?"

"Morning, Jane. It was busy."

"Kept you awake then?"

"Yeah it was good." His grin seemed genuine.

"Alright, what have I got today?"

We went through the changeover and at five thirty, after Bailey stepped into the elevator, I was all alone in the large open marble expanse. I strolled into the kitchen and popped the kettle on, but my isolation was short-lived. I didn't even get to drink my tea as nearly every minute of my shift was occupied with guests checking in, checking out, and asking questions about the New Year's Eve festivities on the beach.

It was crazy busy and before I knew it, Marjorie stood next to me, chatting about her plans for the night. After the changeover, I hugged her goodbye and headed up to my room. Other than Lolita's New Year's Eve party later, I didn't have anything organised for the rest of the day, however that changed the second I walked into my room and noticed how gorgeous the day was. I slipped into my exercise gear and headed out to the sunshine.

Once outside, I walked over the grass and crossed the soft sand on my way toward the water's edge. The beach was always busy, but today it was exceptionally crowded. It was a stunning day, not too hot and not too windy. Beachgoers were out in droves, soaking up the summer sunshine. People were everywhere, and the holiday spirit was in full swing.

I headed away from the hotel in the direction of Mermaid Beach Surf Club. The afternoon sun blazed on my right cheek, and I adjusted my cap on an angle so I didn't get sunburnt. I picked up my pace and set a steady jog on the firm sand. Sucking in the ocean air and absorbing the sun on my skin was the perfect way to spend the last day of the year.

About a half mile past the surf club I stopped, pulled off my shoes and socks, and started my return journey home. As I strolled along the water's edge with the waves splashing against my ankles, it was impossible not to think about Corben. His ideas of fun had me smiling. Corben was an interesting man—a man who knew what he wanted and went after it. Although I was going to miss him, I was glad we'd said goodbye. He wasn't the man for me, and even though it'd been a shocking reality at the time, I knew it was true.

As the waves tumbled to the shore, I tried to focus on nature's therapeutic melody rather than the endless pairs of people who strolled toward me holding hands. It seemed like I was surrounded by couples. Young couples, couples with kids, elderly couples, gay couples. Everyone had a partner but me.

Before I succumbed to the failure vibes that threatened to grip me, I made a beeline for the Blue Haven Café, sat in my favorite spot, and ordered a glass of wine with a serve of lasagna and salad. With all the drinking I was planning on doing tonight, I needed to line my stomach with some serious food.

As I savored the tasty pasta dish and sipped my wine, I forced my brain to focus only on all things good and special in my life. First up was my fabulous relationship with the most amazing best friend in the world. My life wouldn't be as interesting as it was without Lolita in it. And her family, for that matter—they were just as special to me as she was.

There was my awesome shoe collection. I was pretty sure there weren't too many women who could boast about a collection like mine. There was also my family, my job, my apartment, my finances, my health—even my boobies apparently were pretty special. I giggled at that. The list went on and on, and by the time I headed back up to my room to get ready for Lolita's party, I was primed for a fun night.

I showered, applied a good dose of party makeup, but not too much that I slipped from Jane to Memphis, styled my hair the same way I'd done for my dad's sixtieth birthday, and applied a touch of rose lipstick.

I decided to wear the dress I'd bought the day I'd had my stupid fake nails removed. According to Lolita, post-breakup shopping was compulsory. And despite my reluctance, after the nails were gone, I'd wandered Pacific Fair aimlessly, hoping for a shopping miracle. I held up the little black dress that'd been the result of that trip.

It was a cute sleeveless number that alternated horizontally between sheer lace and black fabric that conveniently covered all the important body parts. The flared skirt was short, stopping high on my thigh, and the dress came in to accentuate my waist. I put on matching black lingerie of French knickers and a strapless bra, and pulled the dress on. The zipper in the back was a bitch to do up, but once it was in place I turned to the mirror.

It looked good. Simple, yet stylish.

I added some color with my orange Aquazzura Wild Things suede stilettos that had a funky leather frill at the front and two leather straps that I wrapped around and around my ankle several times and tied off at the tasseled ends. Keeping with the orange theme, I put on dangly orange crystal earrings and a chunky orange bangle.

I glanced in the mirror at the finished result and declared it perfect for a New Year's Eve party.

With my tote over my shoulder, I grabbed my bag containing three bottles of Bollinger, walked out my door, travelled down in the elevator, out the hotel entrance, and along the street toward the tram station.

I didn't have to wait long at the station, and two minutes after my arrival I was sitting on the tram and on my way to Lolita's. Fifteen minutes later, I stepped out at Main Beach station and walked to Lolita's house.

Other than the abundant crowds and the overt party atmosphere, my trip to her place was uneventful. I pushed through her front door without knocking, like I always did, and went straight to the kitchen. Lolita sat on the kitchen counter with her husband locked in her leg embrace as she spooned something into his open mouth.

"Oh sorry, sorry." Aware that I'd interrupted something, I backed away.

"Jane, hey, babe. Don't be sorry. We were just having a moment. But it's okay, moment's over." She giggled at Cal, and he didn't seem to mind one bit.

He walked my way and wrapped his arms around me. "Happy new year. You look amazing."

"Thank you."

He took my drinks bag off me and set it on the kitchen counter.

"Holy smokes, babe, you look hot. New dress?" Lolly circled her hand in the air, and I spun around.

I nodded. "Post-Hunter breakup shopping."

"Niiicce. I told you it'd be worth it."

I chuckled. "So . . . what do you want me to do?"

"You can help me with this cooking. Cal keeps distracting me." Lolly rolled her eyes at him.

"You love it." He clutched his heart, feigning shock.

"You know I do—that's why it's distracting. Now shoo. Go and get ice or something."

Cal pulled a sad face and turned to me. "She's so mean."

Lolly smacked his butt. "I'll make it up to you later."

"Okay." Cal's face lit up, and he practically skipped from the kitchen.

Lolita pulled an oven tray from the dish drainer and set it on the counter. "Want to help me with these?" She pointed at miniature tart cases in several Tupperware dishes, which Lolita no doubt would've made herself.

"Sure." We lined the tray with the tiny tarts, and then filled each one with bocconcini cheese, semi-dried tomatoes, and a scattering of prosciutto. It was a pity we weren't cooking them until later because I could've easily devoured a few now.

As we moved from one canapé preparation to the next, Lolita cranked up the music and we sang, danced, drank champagne, and chatted about all things wonderful and good. Before we knew it, seven o'clock had arrived, along with the first guests.

Lolita and Cal had converted their backyard into Party Central. The grass had been covered in a wooden dance floor with a giant marquee tented over the top, and colorful lights hit the area from every angle. Giant ice buckets were dotted about the place and Cal had put glow sticks in each one, lighting them up in a variety of colors.

Within twenty minutes, about fifty people filled the dance floor. The music was loud and funky, and it was impossible to resist moving to the beat. As I made my way around the room with my champagne, I made a point of saying hello to everyone and introducing myself to those I didn't know—which weren't too many. Every time I finished my champagne, either Lolita or Calvin filled it up. My glass was officially bottomless, and I was sooooooo happy with that.

Abundant alcohol was about the only thing guaranteed to save me from the never-ending questions people asked about my love life. I didn't think I'd ever understand why my single status was so fascinating to everyone but me. The more I drank, the more the bombardment annoyed me. All I wanted to do was stand on one of the bar tables and regale the crowd with all the sordid details about my glorious Memphis romps. I wanted to scream that I, Plain Jane, was getting loads of sex. About fifty times this year in fact, with dozens of hunky men. I was a fucking sexual diva.

Thankfully, as quickly as the stupid idea whizzed around my brain, it whizzed right back out again because I quickly realized just how bad that sounded. Nobody would understand, and I could just picture the partygoers' horrified faces at my announcement.

Instead, I sipped my Bollinger and moved onto the next group of people in the hope the conversation would be much more interesting.

Several hours into the party, I spied Clayton standing at a bar table with a beer in his hand. He looked stunning, and stylish, and totally handsome. Our eyes met as if we were meant to see each other, and next second he stood and walked toward me. I sipped my bubbles and tried to calm my racing pulse. My heart skipped a beat when he strolled right up to me and planted a kiss on my cheek.

"It's lovely to see you, Jane."

I blinked at him, hardly able to believe he meant his comment. "It's lovely to see you too."

As if we'd planned it, we edged to the side of the marquee, where there were less people and the music wasn't as loud. "You still working at the hotel?"

I tucked a slip of hair behind my ear. "Yes. I've been promoted to day manager."

His eyes lit up. "Oh, so you get your nights off now?"

I nodded. "I do." My heart was going crazy. I couldn't believe Clayton was actually talking to me after I broke up with him.

"That must be a nice change. So have you been anywhere exciting with your nights off?"

"A few places. Lolly has been chaperoning me."

He chuckled. "I bet she has. She's up for any party."

"How's Telitha?"

"She's wonderful. Feisty, courageous, fun—everything a little girl should be." His smile grew spectacular as he looked at me, and I felt as if we'd never been apart. I sipped my champagne and allowed lovely thoughts to flow through me.

"There you are." A woman came striding toward us and planted a prolonged kiss on Clayton's lips as if I wasn't there at all. She was a raven-haired, golden-skinned beauty, and I admired her and hated her in an instant.

My jaw dropped, and despite myself, I struggled to pull it back into place.

"Jane, I'd love you to meet my girlfriend, Sunny. Sunny, this's Jane, the friend of Lolita's I told you about."

"Oh right. Lovely to meet you." Sunny held her hand toward me and we shook.

I swallowed. "Lovely to meet you too."

"We've been dating for about two months now." Clayton put his arm around his stunning girlfriend. "Sunny has a daughter the same age as Telitha." He turned to Sunny, and when their eyes met I just about threw up. "We're all so happy together."

"That's wonderful. I'm happy for you." *What the hell's wrong with me?* Two seconds ago, I'd thought we were flirting. *Am I that desperate?* I had to get away before the plain Jane in me said something totally lame.

"Anyway, I'm going to see if Lolita needs help in the kitchen." Sunny and Clayton barely glanced in my direction and with each step I slinked away, I felt like everyone else stared at me with pity in their eyes. I was swimming through a pit of mud, barely able to breathe. I needed to get out of there. I needed to go home.

I went upstairs to Lolita's bedroom first and grabbed my bag from her duchess, then I returned back downstairs and sought her out. She was at the oven checking something cooking inside. She shut the oven door and turned to me with a smile, but before I even spoke, her smile fell away and her eyes bulged. "Hey babe, what's wrong?"

My chin dimpled, and I fought it with all my might. "Clayton has a girlfriend."

"I just found that out too." She frowned. "But why does that upset you?"

I splayed my fingers on the counter. "I don't know."

"Come here." She wrapped her arms around me, but it only made my sorrow ten times worse.

Using my knuckle, I dabbed a tear from my lower eyelid. "I'm going home."

"No." She pulled back. "Don't go. It's only just gone ten o'clock."

"I don't care. I just want this year over with."

She frowned at me, and I could tell she was on the verge of arguing. I beat her to it by leaning forward and kissing her cheek. "I've already called an Uber," I lied. "He'll be here soon."

She tilted her head to the side. "Are you sure?"

I nodded, unable to speak.

"Okay, well . . . I'll call you tomorrow. Maybe we can go to lunch or something."

I nodded again, and pleased with how easily I'd gotten away, I headed out the front door. As I stood in her driveway, the noise drifted from the backyard in a dull cacophony of laughter and music. I used my phone to check if there was an Uber nearby. There were about fifty, and I pressed the button and leaned back on the garage pillar as I waited. The bricks were warm, the result of baking in the western sun, and I tried to use the heat to settle my rattled nerves.

The Uber only took seven minutes to arrive. I climbed into the back, and the lady driver made a few attempts to make conversation before thankfully, she gave up. The crowds and blocked off streets made the drive much longer than I'd hoped, and we arrived at the drop-off zone at the Hot Horizon Hotel just before eleven.

I went straight to my apartment, stripped, scrubbed off my makeup, unpinned my hair, and had a long, hot shower. Afterwards, I pulled on my cotton PJs, and with a bottle of wine in hand, a glass and a packet of corn chips in the other, I headed out to my verandah, ready to watch the fireworks. I filled the glass to the brim, swallowed back a huge gulp, and shoved an entire corn chip into my mouth.

"Now this is living," I spoke to the enormous crowd lining the beach.

As it ticked into the final hour of the year, the noise from the beach grew louder and my thoughts about how I'd feel waking up tomorrow grew more and more confusing.

On one hand, I hadn't found a man. But on the other, I'd found me. And although I'd end this year alone, I no longer felt lonely. This year had taught me how to like myself.

I'd learned to laugh at my little idiosyncrasies that made me . . . well, me. Despite all the breakups, I couldn't deny I was happy. Most of all, I was completely confident that I would find a man. I was no longer the meek and mild wallflower who was sitting back and waiting for the perfect partner to come to me. I was a tiger. A tiger who was ready to get on the prowl. I raised my glass. "Look out world, here I come." I giggled and gulped back a huge sip of my wine.

A knock on my door had me frowning. Thinking it was Lolita, determined to drag me back to her party, I strolled through my apartment and I peeked through the peephole. My frown grew deeper when I spied the top of a fireman's hat. I tugged the door open, and my jaw dropped. It was a fireman. A sexy, shirtless fireman, with red braces that skimmed up his bare sculpted torso. His head was tilted down so I couldn't see his face, but the rest of him looked pretty damn fine.

"Can I help you?"

"I believe it's me who can help you." He looked up, a brilliant smile dazzling his face.

"Hunter!" My heart exploded in my chest.

"I read there's a woman up here who needed rescuing."

I covered my gaping mouth. Tears stung my eyes. "But how did you find me?"

"Thirteen is your lucky number . . . according to your diary."

"You read my diary?"

He cocked his head. "Fascinating reading."

"But why . . . how?" Sentences failed to form.

"I told you I always finished what I started, and I started falling in love with you the moment we met."

"Oh my . . ." Goosebumps rained across my flesh. "I tried to call you."

"I know . . . seventeen times. May I come in?" He stepped across my threshold, and I couldn't hold back a moment longer. I jumped into his arms. His fireman's hat went flying, and as he carried me into my room, the door closed. Our lips met and our kiss was on fire, filled with an unprecedented passion I'd never felt before.

He carried me to the bed and sat me down, and when he kneeled on one knee at my feet, my chin dimpled. The lump in my throat was enormous. I could barely breathe.

I reached for his hand, and strangled his palm to mine. "I can't believe you're here. Especially after reading my diary. Aren't you disgusted in what I did . . . in me?"

"At first I was so angry with you that I wanted to scream. It was only after about your tenth phone message that I picked up your diary. You're a persistent one."

"You deserved an explanation. I wanted to apologise." A tear tumbled down my cheek, and he thumbed it away. "I'm so sorry."

He nodded. "I know. As I read your entries, I learned about a courageous, funny . . . albeit naive woman who wasn't afraid to take control of her destiny."

"But I had sex with all those men."

"Only fifteen this year. Eighteen in your whole life."

"You counted them?"

"I needed to put it into perspective."

I blinked at him, frowning, incapable of working out what perspective that would be.

"The only difference between you and me is that you condensed your sexual relations down to one year. I spread mine out over twenty."

"Oh."

"And that you invented Memphis to do it."

"That was just clothes and makeup. The rest of her was me. But I never meant to hurt you. My lies just . . ." My quivering chin nearly made it impossible to talk.

He caressed my cheek. "I know, and I'm willing to forgive you."

I covered my mouth as a sob released from my throat.

"As long as there's no more lies."

"I promise never to lie to you again."

His eyes pierced mine. "What about Henry?"

My heart stammered. It would be easier to fib, to tell him I broke it off with Henry. But I wouldn't. I'd just made a promise never to lie to Hunter again, and I meant it. So I looked into his beautiful blue eyes, took a deep breath, and let it out slowly. "Henry broke up with me. He said he was too old for me and that I needed to find a man who I could have a family with. A man who I could grow old with."

"Is that what you want?"

I leaned forward, clutched his cheeks, and let my tears flow. "You are what I want. I've dreamed of our future together. I've dreamed of our little house by the beach and lots of babies who grow up being taught by their daddy how to cook and surf. I've dreamed of holidays together, where we explore exotic locations and eat amazing food. I've dreamed of falling asleep in your arms every night, knowing in my heart that I've found my home."

His eyes softened and his Adam's apple bobbed up and down. "You don't know how much I needed to hear you say that."

I drew my lips to his and kissed him. He opened his mouth, and our tongues danced. His hands glided up and down my back. I pushed him backward, and as he fell onto the floor laughing, I pulled my pajama top off and lowered myself down to straddle him.

When he cupped my breast, I was certain Hunter would feel my raging heart. "I can't believe you're—"

He placed a finger over my lips. "Shhh."

I kissed his fingers, and as he squeezed my breasts, I leaned forward, placed one hand beside his head on the carpet, and kissed his lips. The heat of his body beneath mine, was heaven, and I wanted to stay there forever.

It was an eternity before our lips parted, and I eased back, placed my hands over his pecs, and looked into his stunning blue eyes again. Our gazes locked together, and a wonderful sense of completeness embraced me. Hunter was the man of my dreams, and I'd thought I'd lost that dream forever. It was worth the wait. It was worth the agony. "I still can't believe you're here. How'd you know I'd be home?"

"I knocked on your door earlier, but you weren't around, so I went down to the bar and waited."

"Oh." I could only imagine the state he saw me in when I'd whizzed through the lobby earlier.

"You were in a hurry when you went past about twenty minutes ago."

I didn't want to elaborate, but at the same time I wanted Hunter to know everything. He deserved that. "I was at a party at Lolita's place, but . . . but I didn't feel like partying. I just wanted this year to be over."

"It nearly is. Oh that reminds me—I have a gift for you."

I sat back and blinked at him. "You do?"

"Hop up and I'll show you."

I pushed off his chest to stand, and offered my hand to help him up. He strode to the door and collected a bag that I hadn't noticed him bring. Reaching inside, he removed a gift wrapped in Christmas paper. He walked back, and when he handed it to me I could tell it was a book.

"Open it."

My heart was a racing staccato as I peeled off the paper. "A diary."

"Yep." His beaming face was beautiful. "Turn to the first page."

The diary had a hard cover, patterned in pinks and purples. I turned the cover over, and on the very first line where it had *'This is the personal diary of* Hunter had written *'Jane'*.

I tugged my lip into my mouth in an attempt to stop my quivering chin as I looked at him.

He shrugged. "I didn't know your surname. And I assume you're not Just Jane."

I half laughed, half cried, and it came as a snort, so damn unsexy. "Nichols . . . I'm Jane Nichols."

He held his hand toward me, and when I reached over and our palms touched, sparks danced across my mind and body. "Pleased to meet you, Jane Nichols."

Hunter took the diary off me and pulled me in for a hug. When he wrapped his arms around me, I squeezed him to my chest. Our naked flesh molded together as one. His beating heart was a beautiful melody.

Hunter pulled back. "I have another gift."

"What? You do?"

"Stay there."

Once again, he strode to the bag at the door, and this time he brought the whole thing back. The mischievous look on his face was one of the things I loved about him. He wriggled his eyebrows as he handed the bag to me.

When I looked inside I burst out laughing. "A pineapple."

"Uh-huh."

"Oh my god. That's so not fair—you know all my intimate secrets."

"Yes, I do. Are you complaining?"

I rolled my eyes. "God no. Absolutely not. I can't believe you're here after reading all that stuff."

He put his hand in mine and led me back to my bed. *My bed.* He then crawled on, lay on his side, and patted the cover for me to wriggle up and join him. I did. The second our faces were together, our bodies aligned. Our flesh touched in all the right places. We were a perfect match for each other.

He reached up to cup my cheek. "I wouldn't be here if I hadn't read your diary."

"Really?" I screwed up my nose.

"Yes. It explained so much about why you did what you did. I feel like I know Jane Nichols now, and yet I look forward to learning everything else about you, too."

"And I want to tell you everything. I want you to know the real me."

"No more lies, then?"

I shook my head. "I promise. Never, never again will I lie to you." I leaned in to kiss him. Our kiss was gentle at first, our lips barely touching. Our breaths mingled, united as one. I glided my tongue across his bottom lip, tasting him, and he repeated the move with me. It was truly sensual, and I lost myself to his bewitching tenderness.

Our kiss grew heated, more intense by the second. I opened my mouth, allowing his probing tongue to dance with mine. It was a delicious tango that had my insides dancing. As my tongue entered his mouth, I glided my hand up his torso, exploring his divine flesh, committing every inch of his body to my memory.

His braces nudged against his nipple, and I glided my fingers beneath the stretchy fabric and pinched his hardened bud in my fingers. He pulled back from my kiss and I looked into his crystal blue eyes. The seduction dancing in his glossy pools drove me wild. Shivers coursed through me at the intensity of his gaze, and I knew how lucky I was.

I'm the luckiest woman in the world.
"You're so beautiful, Jane." His words made me melt, but when I realized it was me he was talking to, the Jane me, I wanted to cry, too. I wanted to scream his name from the rooftop. I wanted to wake up in the morning with his arms wrapped around me. I wanted this man more than I'd ever wanted anything in my whole life.
He reached over and twirled a lock of my hair around his palm.
"My real hair." I scrunched up my nose.
"I see that. I always felt that something wasn't quite right about your blond hair, and I never could figure it out."
"I'm sorry."
He touched his fingers to my lips. "Shhh. Dark hair suits you much better."
I smiled at his comment, pleased that he liked what he saw. I had no makeup on and for the first time, he was seeing the real me.
His hand glided over my neck, and down to my breast. He curled his palm beneath my boob, caressing the tender skin there. He continued his exploration down my torso, around my navel, and along the elastic of my pajama shorts.
I peeled his elastic brace off his right shoulder and leaned over to kiss his nipple. He fed his fingers into my pajama bottom and tugged it down to expose my right butt cheek. The desire to have Hunter naked gripped me, and I pushed up onto my knees and rolled him onto his back. He chuckled as he let me have my way with him.
His eyes watched my every move as I crawled off the bed to start at his feet. With the urgency of a woman bursting with uncontrollable lust, I yanked at his shoelaces, tugged his boots free, and tossed them aside along with his socks.
I turned my attention to his fluorescent yellow pants, and as I undid the button and the zipper, I didn't miss the bulge growing beneath. I glided my hand over his erection and pulled the zipper down. Knowing I'd caused that wonderful reaction drove me wild. I wanted to see his cock, to watch it grow, to feel it in my hands, and I tugged his fireman trousers off, desperate to set his beast free.
In a flash, he was naked, and oh my god, it was the most magnificent sight ever. I wanted to pinch myself at the realization that the hottest man in the world was naked in my bed. Hunter took my breath away.
"Come here, you." He held his hand toward me.
I crawled up his legs but paused at his groin. He made his cock bounce, and I giggled at the fun of it. He did it again, and I leaned forward and kissed his pink crown. Before my eyes, his cock grew hard and long. It was erotic magic and the best show on earth.
I touched my tongue to his swollen flesh, and he made his crown bounce toward me. My insides clenched at the gloriousness of it. I wrapped my

hand around the base of his shaft, feeling his steely muscle in my palm, and as he ran his fingers through my hair, I glided my tongue around his head.

"Oh, Jane."

To hear Hunter say my name, *my real name,* was the most wonderful sound in the world. My insides purred at the lovely melody.

I turn my attention back to my prize and admired his manhood. His crown was pink, swollen, and totally lickable, and with my hands around the base of his shaft, I looked up. As our eyes met, I rolled my tongue around his crown.

His jaw squared out as he clenched his teeth, and his eyes rolled as if lost in their own world.

I wrapped my lips around his crown and glided down his shaft, drawing his length into my mouth. When I couldn't go any farther, I held him there, trapped in my throat. He squeezed my shoulders and sucked the air in through his teeth. We remained locked together, his body rigid, his fingers like pincers, and when he released his grip on my shoulders, I rolled my tongue around his cock as I glided back up his shaft.

Hunter's fingers pinched my shoulder again, and I looked down in time to see a pearl of semen ooze from the slit in his penis. I made a show of gliding my tongue over it to lap it up and then licked my lips, enjoying the salty tanginess on my tongue.

"Oh Jesus, woman."

His words drove me wild, and as I glided my tongue around and around, ensuring I'd savored all I could, my pussy pulsed a steady beat.

He reached down and dragged me up so again we lay side by side. "Your turn."

"Oh . . . okay." Who was I to argue?

His hand nudged between my thighs and with our eyes locked together, I raised my knee and curled it over his hips, giving him room to play.

And play he did.

Ever so slowly, he glided his finger over my clit in one long, drawn-out motion. I closed my eyes and groaned at the sweet pleasure of his intimate touch. With the tip of his finger, he pressed down and rolled my sensitive bud. My insides curled and pulsed at the exquisite sensation. I sucked air in through my teeth as he continued the teasing. It became a pattern, rolling over my clit, then pressure on my clit, tracing around my clit, and as I rode it, predicting what would come next, an orgasm built inside me. Layer upon layer of lust stacked on top of each other until I was close to bursting. I moaned long and loud, and dug my fingers into his hip.

"Hunter." His name was so perfect as it crossed my lips.

"Yes?"

My eyes snapped open, but when he flicked my clit they closed again.

"What do you want, Jane?"

"Oh, god."

"Yes, Jane, say it . . . what do you want?"

"I want to come. I want you to make me come."

He groaned, and I gasped as his finger plunged into my throbbing hole. It was fast. It was incredible, and I cried out as he rammed his finger into me over and over. He joined his finger with another and pushed them into my pussy with a fabulous twisting motion. Each time he pushed in or pulled out, his finger grinded over my clit. The repetition was erotic perfection.

As I writhed beneath him, balancing on the glorious edge between incredible build-up and exquisite release, he leaned forward and sucked my earlobe into his mouth. "Come for me, Jane."

And I did.

Hearing Hunter whisper my name tipped me over the precipice that'd gripped me. I dug my nails into his flesh as my climax exploded.

My whole body was consumed by this moment, this glorious magical moment with Hunter that just an hour ago, I was certain would never happen.

Hunter pulled me onto him and I straddled his hips, trapping his cock in a way that it nestled along the length of my pussy. His eyes were on fire, as if blazing with sexual tension. His flesh glistened with a light sweat, highlighting every muscle in his incredible torso. I moved my hips back and forward, allowing my clit to glide up and down his length. It was an incredible sensation, one that I'd never felt before.

He ran his tongue over his lips as his hands squeezed and massaged my breasts. He wasn't exactly gentle, but I didn't care—it was like he was driven to feel me as much as I was driven to feel him. With my hands over his pecs, I leaned forward, changing the angle a bit so there was more pressure on my clit as I continued to slide my pussy up and down the length of his cock.

Oh . . . my . . . god . . . it was out-of-this-world mind-blowing.

But my insides were greedy, begging to be plunged into, and I couldn't ignore that needy pulse a moment longer.

I reached down, wrapped my hand around the base of his cock, and aimed his swollen crown at my opening. Gradually, I lowered onto him, trying to memorize every inch of his body inside me. His cock was thick, filling me so completely that it was utterly perfect, a long-lost puzzle piece finally slotted into place. I wanted to keep him there, to savor that special part of his body inside me forever. The glaze in his eyes evaporated, and I knew he was looking at me, really, truly looking at me.

Hunter placed his hands on my hips, and I put my hands on his chest, feeling the steely muscles beneath them as I pulled my hips upward, gliding his rigid cock out of me. The sensation was just as magnificent as it had been going in. I closed my eyes, savoring every inch of the journey in and back out again. I rose and fell in slow measured movements, taking my time, willing this moment to last forever. I opened my eyes again, desperate to watch every moment. This was officially voyeuristic heaven.

Hunter was everything I wanted in a man and so much more.

My rhythm built as my body got greedy, wanting the same pleasures my eyes were receiving. My clit pulsed with every solid drag of his cock inside me. I pulled my knees up and sat on him. I placed my hands on his belly on either side of his sexy navel, and as he massaged my breasts I got ready to ride him like I'd never ridden a man before.

Wild, unbridled passion took over, and I slammed his cock into me again and again. Every nerve in my pussy pulsed at the pounding. I rose up and down, ramming the head of his penis deep inside me, so deep that it hurt. Yet I wanted that pain. I wanted it so badly that it felt so good. It was exquisite agony. It was mind-blowing. It was absolutely perfect.

An explosion shattered the world I'd fallen into, and it took me a moment to realize it was fireworks. As red, blue, and green lit up the sky, I tipped over the glorious edge, and an uncontrollable scream burst from my throat as my orgasm released. My body succumbed to delicious shudders that rolled from deep inside me. Hunter gripped my hips like a vise, his beautiful face distorted in passion, and as he cried out too, I continued to ride him until I couldn't do it a moment more.

Gasping for breath, I fell forward, and Hunter wrapped his arms around me.

As I listened to his thumping heart, I was deliriously happy and content in his arms. A wonderful warmth washed through me, embracing me in a way I'd never felt before. With crystal clarity, I realized this was the dawn of my new beginning. It was beautiful, it was special—it was everything I'd wanted in my whole life and so much more.

Hunter kissed my forehead. "Come on," he said. "Let's watch the fireworks."

"Oh, okay." As much as I didn't want to leave his embrace, I couldn't ignore his boyish exuberance.

My legs were a quivering mess when I stood. As Hunter yanked my cover off the bed, I couldn't help but notice that for the first time ever, my bed had a sprinkling dark patches . . . evidence of our love-making. It wasn't embarrassing or yucky—it was a sign that something truly magnificent had happened here.

It was a proud moment for me.

My brain was still in an after-sex fog and couldn't comprehend what Hunter was doing when he pulled the sheet off my bed too. However, all was revealed when in one swift movement, he billowed it out and wrapped the sheet around the two of us.

Cocooned together, naked and giggling, we waddled outside. Hunter positioned me in front of him and wrapped his arms around me, curling his hands beneath my boobs. When I leaned back to his chest, I'd found my home.

The fireworks exploding along the beach perfectly matched the fireworks bursting through my heart. I placed my arms over his, pulled him closer to me, and turned to look up into his stunning blue pools. Our eyes met, and my heart skipped a beat as I knew I'd found my treasure, my one and only, my holy grail. "If you'll have me, I offer you my heart. I love you."

His lips brushed mine, just a brief kiss that said so much more—*I want, I trust, I need*. When he pulled back, his eyes glistened as he looked right into my soul. "I love you too, Jane Nichols."

THE END

"If you enjoyed the Rise of Memphis series, would you please consider writing a review about it so other readers can enjoy it too? I only needs to be a couple of sentences from where you bought this book from, or Goodreads. It would mean a lot to me."

Thanks, Kitty k.

Dear Reader,

This is the end of Rise of Memphis, but it's not the end of my writing journey. Sign up to my newsletter and be one of the first to discover my next adventure. http://www.kittykendall.com/newsletter.html

When I took on the challenge of writing the Rise of Memphis series, I wanted to explore the sexual journey of my character, Jane. But what started out as a fun roll in the hay became so much more. Jane, became so real to me that I wanted to take her on an extraordinary journey of self-discovery. This journey was as much about exploring the wonderful world of sex as it was about exploring the highs and lows of being a woman.

Before I became a writer I was a reader, and I grew more and more disappointed with the sex scenes I read. In particular, they were always too perfect, too convenient, and most of all, too serious. I wanted to show that sex doesn't always go to plan. And that it can be loads of fun.

In addition to this, I wanted to present a series where every man was beautifully flawed. Some of the men appear to be Mr. Average but end up being Mr. Holy Hotness on a Stick. And, contrary to that, some appear to be at the top of their game, but scratch that crystal façade and simmering beneath the surface is a man only just holding it together.

Rise of Memphis is a journey to the Holy Grail—love. I hope you find yours, but along the way, I hope there's plenty of joy, adventure, and most of all, incredible sex.

You may not know this, but I write under two pen names. Now that you've discovered my sexy Kitty Kendall books, you may wish to check out my award-winning and best-selling Romantic Suspense and Crime novels that I write under the pen name of Kendall Talbot. These are adrenalin-fueled adventures, filled with sexy characters, exotic locations, and breathless romance.

You can find more information on my website: http://www.Kendalltalbot.com

Thank you for riding the Rise of Memphis wave with me, I couldn't have done it without you.

Cheers, and happy reading!
Kitty Kendall

Kitty Kendall

Kitty K News

Sign up for all the yummy updates at Kitty K News and you'll never miss another Kitty Kendall Book. http://www.kittykendall.com/newsletter.html

Or jump onto the **Cheeky Memphis Facebook Group** because this is where the fun begins. Kitty Kendall needs your help with serious stuff like what shoes her characters should wear and which sexy man should revisit her pages. You can get involved, share your thoughts, invite your friends and meet other people who love the Rise of Memphis series too.

Go to this link to join group.
https://www.facebook.com/groups/CheekyMemphis

ABOUT THE AUTHOR

Kitty Kendall is a bucket list achieving, junk jewelry collecting, hopeless romantic who loves great wine and a good adrenaline rush from time to time. She also collect classy shoes and expensive perfume. But her greatest thrill in life is writing romance and the steamier the better.

Bring It On!

She's travelled extensively, some 37 countries and counting and she's addicted to experiences that make her scream... white water rafting, scuba diving with sharks and hang gliding are just a few. Her stories reflect her sense of adventure and her love affair with her very own hero.

Kitty also writes romantic suspense under the pen name of Kendall Talbot. She's won numerous awards, including Romantic Book of the Year, and several of her books are Amazon bestsellers. Check out www.kendalltalbot.com to find out more.

Read more at www.kittykendall.com

Kitty Kendall

ACKNOWLEDGMENTS

I couldn't have written the Rise of Memphis series without my husband. His willingness to help out with the necessary choreography was commendable. But seriously, I wouldn't be an author without his unwavering support. He entered my heart more than thirty years ago, and I'm crazy lucky to have a man like him at my side.

Writing a book is never a solo effort, and I wouldn't have survived this series without my wonderful editor Lauren at McStellar Editing. Lauren's tough love helped me polish the rough drafts until they were shimmering diamonds.

Along this journey I started a secret Facebook group - Cheeky Memphis, and although I've never met any of the women who joined me there, I want to thank them for making this journey so special. Without their very intimate details and stunning pictures of totally hot men, this Memphis project would've been a very lonely one.

So in no particular order, special thanks goes to:
Brandi Warhank, Dawn Viertlbeck, Revva, Janet Ross, Sarah Frost, Raven Johnson, Vikki Clay, Michelle Harris, Jay Epiha, Ronda Thayer, Sunny Lane, Kathy Allred, Jennifer Kennessey, Tina Whitley, Sam Young, Evelyn Lazenby, Romana Purkiss, Maria S, Nicole Holt Sexton, Nicole Detalon, Vickie, Amanda Petersen, Gayla File, Angela Davisson, Babel of Literaria, Michelle R, Christina Conrad, Barbara Laarhoven, Lala Poara, Debbie Schrum, Emily Maynard and Marita Lightbody. I hope I didn't miss anybody, but if I did I apologise from the bottom of my heart.

I'd also love to acknowledge my writing buddies who are all incredible authors too. For more than a year they've had to listen to me bang on about Memphis, and this journey has been made much more enjoyable knowing that they've been there with me. Special thanks to: Tania Joyce, Noelle Clark, Isabella Hargreaves, Anthea Jones, Matt JX and Claire Austin.

And finally and most importantly I want to thank you—my readers. I wouldn't be living my dream of being an author if you didn't support me. I hope my stories take you on an emotional journey that fills you with joy, makes you laugh, and helps you to believe in true love.

You can write to me any time at kitty@universe.com.au.

Kitty Kendall

BOOKS IN THIS SERIES

Rise of Memphis Box Sets:

Rise of Memphis Touch Me (January, February, March)
Rise of Memphis Tempt Me (April, May, June)
Rise of Memphis Tease Me (July, August, September)
Rise of Memphis Tame Me (October, November, December)

Rise of Memphis Monthly Chronicles

Rise of Memphis January Chronicles
Rise of Memphis February Chronicles
Rise of Memphis March Chronicles
Rise of Memphis April Chronicles
Rise of Memphis May Chronicles
Rise of Memphis June Chronicles
Rise of Memphis July Chronicles
Rise of Memphis August Chronicles
Rise of Memphis September Chronicles
Rise of Memphis October Chronicles
Rise of Memphis November Chronicles

Don't forget to sign up for all the yummy updates at Kitty K News and you'll never miss another Kitty Kendall Book.

http://www.kittykendall.com/newsletter.html

Kitty Kendall

Rise of Memphis Tame Me

Kitty Kendall

Printed in Australia
AUOC02n0707270417
285145AU00001B/1/P

9 780648 027331